SELF

SELF

Yann Martel

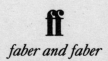

faber and faber

First published in 1996 by Alfred A. Knopf Canada, Toronto
First published in Great Britain in 1996
by Faber and Faber Limited
3 Queen Square London WC1N 3AU
This paperback edition first published in 2003
Printed and bound in England by Bookmarque Ltd, Croydon

The Hungarian passage is from *Bluebeard's Castle* by Béla Bartók.

A CIP record for this book
is available from the British Library

ISBN 0-571-21976-4

4 6 8 10 9 7 5

*Pour leur soutien durant la
création de cette oeuvre, je
tiens à remercier le Conseil
des arts et des lettres du
Québec, pour la bourse;
Valérie Feldman et Eric
Théocharidès, pour leur
hospitalité; et Alison
Wearing, pour tout le reste.*

*For their support during the
writing of this novel, I
would like to thank the Arts
Award Section of the
Canada Council, for the
grant; Harvey Sachs for
laying before me the
splendour of Tuscany; Rolf
Meindl, for the computer
help and the sofa to sleep
on; and Alison Wearing,
for everything else.*

à l'une, survivante
à l'autre, disparue

to one who survived
to another who didn't

CHAPTER ONE

I AWOKE and my mother was there. Her hands descended upon me and she picked me up. It seems I was mildly constipated. She sat me on my potty on the dining-room table and set herself in front of me. She began to coo and urge me on, running her fingers up and down my back.

But I was not receptive. I distinctly remember finding the woman quite tiresome.

She stopped. She placed her elbows on the table and propped her head on her hands. A period of fertile silence ensued; I looked at her and she looked at me. My mood was in suspense. Anger was there, lurking. So was reconciliation. Humour was hovering. Sulking was seeping. It could go any way, nothing was decided.

Suddenly I stood up mightily, like the Colossus of Rhodes, I bent forward a little, and in one go I produced. My mother was delighted. She smiled and exclaimed:

"Gros caca!"   "Big pooh!"

I turned. What a sight! What a smell! It was a magnificent log of excrement, at first poorly formed, like conglomerate rock that hasn't had time to set, and dark brown, nearly black, then resolving itself to a dense texture of a rich chestnut hue, with fascinating convolutions. It started deep in the potty, but after a coil or two it rose up like a hypnotized cobra and came to rest against my calf, where I remember it very, very warm, my first memory of temperature. It ended in a perfect moist peak. I looked at my mother. She was still smiling. I was red in the face and sweaty from my efforts, and I was exultant. Pleasure given, pleasure had, I sensed. I wrapped my arms around her neck.

My other earliest memory is vague, no more than a distant feeling that I can sometimes seize, most often not. Being so dimly remembered, perhaps it came first.

I became aware of a voice inside my head. What is this, I wondered. Who are you, voice? When will you shut up? I remember a feeling of fright. It was only later that I realized that this voice was my own thinking, that this moment of anguish was my first inkling that I was a ceaseless monologue trapped within myself.

Later memories are clearer and more cohesive. For example, I remember a cataclysm in the garden. At the time I thought the sun and the moon were opposite elements, negations of each other. The moon was the sun turned off, like a light-bulb, the moon was the sun sleeping, the dimples on its surface the pores of a great eyelid, the moon was solar charcoal, the pale remains of a daily fire — whatever the case, one excluded the other. I was in the garden at a very late hour. It was summer and the sun was setting. I was watching it, blinking, squinting, burning my eyes, smiling, imagining the heat and the fire, the sizzling of entire neighbourhoods. Then I turned and there it was floating in the sky, grey and malevolent. I ran. My father was the first figure of authority I encountered. I alerted him and dragged him out to the garden. But his adult mind didn't grasp how this apparition threw my understanding of astrophysics topsy-turvy.

"C'est la lune. Et alors?" Je me cachais derrière lui pour me protéger de la radioactivité. "Viens, il est tard. Temps de faire dodo."	"It's the moon. So what?" I was hiding behind him to protect myself from the radioactivity. "Come, it's late. Time for bed."

He took my hand and pulled me indoors. I glanced a last time at the moon. My God, it was a free orb. It moved at random in the universe, like the sun. Surely one day they would clash!

My earliest aesthetic experience revolved around a small, clear plastic bottle of green-apple bubble-bath. To my parents a casually accepted free sample at the supermarket, it was to me a jewel that I discovered while my mother was giving me a bath. I was held in thrall by its endless greenness, its unctuous ooze, its divine smell. It left me dumb with pleasure.

When someone thoughtlessly made use of it a week later and I came upon my disembowelled treasure — I vividly recall the moment: my mother was wiping my bum and I was idly looking at the bathtub — I shrieked and threw the worst tantrum of my toddlerhood.

Other facts of my early life that are held to be important — that I was born in 1963, in Spain, of student parents — I heard only later, through hearsay. For me, memory starts in my own country, in its capital city, to be exact.

Beyond the normal overseeing of parenthood, neither my mother nor my father intruded unnecessarily into my world.

Whether my space was real or imaginary, the bathtub or the Aral Sea, my room or the Amazon jungle, they respected it. I can't imagine having better parents. Sometimes I would turn and see them looking at me and in their gaze I could read total love and commitment, an unwavering devotion to my well-being and happiness. I would delight in this love. There was no cliff I couldn't jump off, no sea I couldn't dive into, no outer space I couldn't hurtle through — where my parents' net wouldn't be there to catch me. They were at the central periphery of my life. They were my loving, authoritarian servants.

At the supermarket I would gambol about happy and care-free, playing with the cereal boxes, shaking the big bottles of mouthwash, looking at all the funny people — as long as I had my mother within sight. But if — the momentous if — if she skipped an aisle unexpectedly while I was still staring at the packaged meat, wondering what the cow looked like now — if she dashed for the fruits while I was still examining the jars of pickles — if, in other words, she became lost to me, that was a very different state of affairs. My body would tense, my stom-ach would feel light and fluttery. Tears would well up in my eyes. I would run about frantically, oblivious of everything and everyone, my whole being concentrated on the search for my mother. When I caught sight of her again, as, thankfully, I always did, the universe would instantly be re-established. Fear, that horrible boa constrictor of an emotion, would vanish with-out a trace. I would feel a hot burst of love, adoration, worship, tenderness, for my sweet mother, with somewhere in there a brief roar of intense hatred for this brush with oblivion she had put me through. My mother, of course, was never aware of the existential fluctuations, the *Sturm und Drang*, within her small fry. She sailed through the supermarket serenely indifferent to my exact location, secure in the knowledge that she'd find me right next to her by the time she got to the check-out. That's where the chocolate bars were.

I cannot recall noticing, as a small child, any difference between my parents that I could ascribe to sex. Though I knew they weren't the same thing twice over, the distinctions did not express themselves in fixed roles. I received affection from both of them, and punishment too, when it came to that. In the early years in Ottawa it was my father who worked outside the home, at the Department of External Affairs, which had an awesome ring to my ears, but my mother was working at home on her Master's thesis in linguistics and philosophy. What my father did during his daylight hours at External was unknown to me, and therefore remote. My mother, on the other hand, wrestled daily with stacks of thick books, in Spanish yet, and she produced endless reams of paper covered with her precise handwriting. I was a witness to her labour. Her thesis was on the Spanish philosopher José Ortega y Gasset. She fetched a hammer once and held it in front of me and told me that the nature of a hammer, its *being* (her word), was defined by its function. That is, a hammer is a hammer because it hammers. This was one of Ortega y Gasset's key insights, she told me, fundamental to his philosophy, and Heidegger had filched it. Pretty obvious to me, I thought, I could have told you that, I thought, but I was nonetheless duly impressed. My mother was clearly involved in deep and difficult matters. I took the hammer and went outside and bashed dents into the edge of our driveway, reinforcing the hammer's identity.

So while my mother sat at home pondering over hammers, perhaps my father sat in his office pondering over screwdrivers.

Anyway, this state, this dichotomy, was temporary; a few years later my mother also joined External Affairs.

In other ways, too, my parents were indistinguishable from each other. Housework was shared, as far as I could tell, but I'm not a reliable witness since I fled at the least sign of domesticity, for fear of being asked to do something. Both my parents were so-so cooks. To be fair, my mother did handle some dishes well, and she displayed more imagination than my father, who overcooked eggs throughout my childhood. But he made delicious tacos and a superb *tortilla de papas*, potato omelette. In later years it was he, I think, who did most of the cooking. In their postings in Mexico and Cuba, they were delighted (and I when I visited) to have a live-in cook.

On the question of punishment: only when I had committed the most heinous of offences was I spanked, and this mildly, more tapping than whacking. I screamed blue murder anyway, because I knew this was the ultimate punishment and therefore called for the ultimate wailing. I believe I was spanked three times in my life. Other than that, my parents never raised a hand to me. At most, when he was exceptionally angry and was chastising me, my father would hold me just above the elbow to ensure that he had my full attention, and sometimes he would squeeze and it would hurt a little. It was rare that my mother got truly angry at me, though when she did, when she narrowed her eyes and fixed me with them and hissed through her clamped jaw, it was a source of real terror. I knew then that in shaving Luna's mother's dog bald with a hair-clipper or in burning down a neighbour's hedgerow I had gone too far, and I would hurt inside and I would do everything to make things better. Mercifully, it was only a few times that I provoked her to such anger.

My parents got along very well. In fact, I have never seen such a harmonious, complementary couple. She was highly articulate. He was a published poet. She had a disciplined mind that could work with great intensity, a mind that was always open to the world. He had lost his father when he was ten and was a rather moody, brittle man, prone to melancholy, yet he had a capacity to marvel at things. She had a naturally optimistic bent and she loved the arts. They nourished her soul and her wisdom. Her emotions were never wrong. He and I discovered writers together — the wonderful Dino Buzzati, for example — and we both had a fondness for golf, a game we hardly ever played. There is a long-ago black and white photo of the two of us on a beach in France: he surrounds me and our four hands are holding a golf club which he is showing me how to swing. The camera catches me just as I am looking at it, a smile on my face, one eye peeking through wind-blown strands of my long hair. It was she who was appointed Canada's ambassador to Cuba. She was more prudent, more apt to find the fruitful, pragmatic compromise. He sometimes had a daring, a willingness to seize the day.

I remember fantasies I had as a child of having to choose between my parents. They were on crosses being tortured and I had to decide which one to let live. Or was I being tortured to force me to choose? If I ever settled on one, I can't remember who it was.

At the last minute my father, by then a translator, editor and desktop publisher, decided to accompany my mother to Mexico City, where she was going for a regional conference of Canadian heads of missions. Not fifteen minutes after leaving Havana the plane was a ball of fire crashing into the Gulf of

Mexico. Such is the intrusion of the tragic, when one becomes aware of the turning wheels of life. But I am getting ahead of myself. I must first deal with carrots and washing machines and many other things.

Though there are notable exceptions, it often happens that we do not remember the first time we did something, or even any one particular time, but remember only the repetition, the idea that we did the thing over and over. This is the case with me and the boiling of carrots. I spent entire afternoons watching carrots boil in water. Our rented house in Ottawa was so arranged that, from the chair on which I stood near the stove, I could turn and see my mother working at her desk (or rather, our rented house in Ottawa was so arranged that, from the chair on which she sat at her desk, my mother could turn and see me staring into my pot). When the carrots were terminally mushy, which I would determine with a long fondue fork, I would call out and she would come to the kitchen. She would empty the pot into the sink, fill it with fresh cold water and set it on the stove again. Then she would get back to work, giving me a peck on the cheek on her way. I was old enough and more than careful enough — there were never any accidents — to be left with the thrilling task of selecting from a large plastic bag the hardy specimens, thick and orange, that I would drop into the water so that the spectacle could start again. During those afternoons my imagination boiled and bubbled like that exuberant water. I explored, made deep connections. It was the transformation from hard to soft that fascinated me, my mother said later. Indeed, from my earliest years the idea of transformation has been central to my life. Naturally so, I suppose, being the child of diplomats.

I changed schools, languages, countries and continents a number of times during my childhood. At each change I had the opportunity to re-create myself, to present a new façade, to bury past errors and misrepresentations. Once, secretly, I boiled the hammer, wondering if its fundamental nature, its *being* (her word), could change. When I started to lose my baby teeth and was told that larger, more durable teeth would grow in their stead, I took this as my first tangible proof of human metamorphosis. I had already gathered evidence on the metamorphosis of day and night, of weather, of the seasons, of food and excrement, even of life and death, to name but a few, but these teeth were something closer to home, something clear and incontrovertible. I envisioned life as a series of metamorphic changes, one after another, to no end.

I abandoned the boiling of carrots when I discovered the washing of laundry. Staring down into the toss and turmoil of clothes being cleaned mechanically is the closest I have come to belonging to a church, and was my introduction to museums. I followed every step of the absolution of laundry, these stations of the cross from filth to salvation, this lineup at the Museum of Modern Art. It would start with my mother fooling the washing machine's safety stop by jamming a coin at the back of the machine's lid — the price of admission to the exhibit, the alms dropped into the alms box. I would hurry to my pew atop the dryer. The laundry was pushed into the machine like so many wicked souls into hell. The powder detergent settled like snow, at places as thick as on a plain, at others as sparse as on an escarpment, my first glimpse at landscape painting. The hot water rose slowly, a gentle immersion into grace — something I felt intimately since this was exactly how I took my baths, sitting shivering cold in the empty tub while the hot water crept up, submerging goose-pimple after goose-pimple, the comfort of warmth all the greater for the misery of cold. The water would stop rising, there would be a moment's pause to collect ourselves, a click, and then high mass would start in earnest. I took an evangelical pleasure in the to-and-fro motion of laundry being sermonized. It was a tempest-tossed sea in which my small ship, my soul, was braving the frothy waves. It was Davy Jones's locker in which I, a spat-out Jonah, frolicked alongside a school of socks. And then it was a painting — abstract expressionism in its purest, most ephemeral form. For entire cycles I would watch this kinder, broader-stroked Jackson Pollock feverishly at work in his studio. Dashes of red succeeded swaths of green. Eruptions of white overwhelmed spots of purple. Five intertwined colours danced together before vanishing to blue. The drama was generous and open, truly ecumenical. When the washing cycle was over, the holy water would retreat through the pores of the washing machine's barrel. I would behold a cavernous sculpture, hell empty. The laundry would begin to spin. I could feel the water seeping away, oozing out of me. Suddenly a torrential tropical storm would whip at me. Was this temptation? And after that another storm! But this one too I would weather. A final click and it would be over. I would call my mother. Shirts, skirts, blouses, underwear, pants, socks and I came out of the machine renewed, remitted of our sins, damp with vitality, shimmering like Christ rising on the third day. And the coin at the back of the lid was mine!

Do children look into mirrors? Do they look at themselves, beyond checking that their unruly hair has that degree of tidiness demanded by a parent? I didn't. Of what interest was a mirror to me? It reflected me, a child — so what? I was not in the least bit self-conscious. The world was far too vast a playground to waste any time looking at part of it reflected, except perhaps to make funny faces, two fingers pulling down the lower eyelids, one pushing up the nose.

Childhood, like wisdom, is an emotion. Feelings are what register deeply of one's early years. What the eye catches, the visual aspects of these feelings, is secondary. So it is that I have no memories of mirrors, no memories of clothes, of skin, of limbs, of body, of my own physical self as a child. As if, paradoxically, I were then nothing but a huge eager eye, an emotional eye, looking out, always looking out, unaware of itself.

It would be impossible to talk of my childhood without mentioning television (religion never played an important role in my life and here, early on, is as good a spot as any to deal with it. I first met the notion of God in a song, a *comptine*, my parents sang to me. It went:

Il était un petit navire	There was once a little ship
Qui n'avait jamais navigué	That had never sailed to sea
Ohé ohé!	Ahoy ahoy!
Il entreprit un long voyage	It set sail on a long trip
Sur la mer Méditerranée	On the Mediterranean Sea
Ohé ohé!	Ahoy ahoy!
Au bout de cinq à six semaines	After five or six long weeks
Les vivres vinrent à manquer	There was no food left at all
Ohé ohé!	Ahoy ahoy!

On tira à la courte paille	They decided to draw straws
Pour savoir qui serait mangé	To see who they would eat
Ohé ohé!	Ahoy ahoy!
Le sort tomba sur le plus jeune	Fate fell upon the youngest mate
C'est donc lui qui sera mangé	It was he that they would eat
Ohé ohé!	Ahoy ahoy!
O Sainte Mère, O ma patronne	Oh Holy Mother, O my patron
Empêche-les de me manger	Stop them from eating me
Ohé ohé!	Ahoy ahoy!

Thus ended the song. When I came to understand it, when I actually listened to it, it was not the cheery chorus of cannibal sailors that took me aback, but the inexplicable and suspended plea at the end. To whom was it addressed? Who was this holy patron? And was the plea answered? Was the young sailor savioured or savoured? Before religion came to mean nothing to me, this is what it meant: a possibility of salvation at a crucial moment. When the course of experience made me see that there is no saviour and no special grace, no remission beyond the human, that pain is to be endured and fades, if it fades, only with time, then God became nothing to me but a dyslexic dog, with neither bark nor bite. I am a natural atheist); indeed, I think it would be impossible to talk of my *generation* without mentioning television.

I met the beast shortly after we moved to Costa Rica. I believe I had just turned five. It was not my parents' set, but one lent to them by the embassy. It was a piece of furniture unto itself: large, heavy, wooden, loud, unavoidable. It took as its lair a full third of the den, a space which had previously been my favourite corner. The first time I saw it, it was awake. I had just strode into the den, unaware of the usurper, and the cur, sensing my presence, turned towards me. I stood frozen, staring at its broad, flat, animated face. I would have run away except that my parents, fresh from installing the thing, were sitting side by side in front of it, passive and unafraid. They looked at me, smiled and said words that were not heard. I took the television to be another sort of four-legged animal. A huge, squat dog with pointy ears and a very long thin tail (it was still my understanding that motion, animation, entailed life. I treated the vacuum cleaner — a distant cousin of the elephant — and the washing machine — a relative of the raccoon — with the greatest respect. My mother's cold and unceremonious manner with them filled me with private offence. Upon her departure I would pet and kiss them and whisper words of appreciation). But though I liked most animals, I warmed to the beast television only with time and misgiving. There was something about its size and behaviour that did not sit well with me. Unlike the washing machine, I felt the television was selfish and uncaring. With only two exceptions — at which times it mesmerized me — it would be years before I felt close to television. I much preferred to rock in the rocking chair, listening to music and day-dreaming. I did this for hours at a stretch, a pet rabbit cradled in my hands.

THE FIRST TIME TELEVISION MESMERIZED ME AS A CHILD:

(1) I can't remember when the idea of love came to me, when I first consciously became aware of this force in human

affairs. Clearly I received love before I started returning it, and I returned it before I knew it had a name. But at what moment these emotions I felt — *oh, there you are! I am happy; if you smile, I'll smile; I want to touch you, I want to be with you, don't let go* — lost their cloak of anonymity and entered the dictionary of my mind, I don't recall. What I do recall is that it was television that formalized my notions of love, that brought together into a unified theory my disparate ideas about it.

It was perhaps a month or two after I first became acquainted with television. To watch it was still a decision that I took with deliberation. "I will watch the television," I would say, still using the article. I would gather up my favourite blanket (a towel, actually), I would move the rocking chair into position and I would slowly pull on the plastic button, which resisted until it jumped out at me with a loud click, always surprising me. Instantly there would be sound, sound travelling faster than light; then, in succession on the glass screen, a point of light, a line of light, a shudder of light, and finally an expanding rectangle of colourless reality. I would sit and rock myself and do what I had said I would do: watch the television, watch human beings deal with other human beings, indoors and outdoors, in a language (Spanish) I had not as yet absorbed. It bored me completely. When I realized that I could change the beast's mind with the help of the difficult wheel-like knob, watching became more interesting, a little, but even so I don't think I ever did it for more than two bored-children hours — that is, ten minutes. Only a full year later, upon discovering the plastic, elastic world of cartoons and having mastered enough Spanish, did I start to watch television regularly.

But at the moment I am talking about, the first time television mesmerized me as a child, when I still watched it out of a sense of technological obligation, one minute was sufficient. Less. I turned the set on, watched for a few seconds, was marked for life, turned it off.

I was alone and in a quiet good mood, receptive to new ideas. The first thing I saw was a fixed image: a simple anatomical drawing of the cross-section of an eye. Next came the fluid images of hundreds of silvery fish swimming as a school. They were like bricks in a magic wall, alternately showing me their long sides, blocking my view, then, with an instant turn, their narrow sides, allowing me to see through them.

I was thunderstruck. Eyes . . . tears . . . saltiness . . . seawater . . . fish.

I walked to the garden and sat under a tree, my senses bloated, my head racing with the thoughts that come from a sudden understanding of things.

The clear liquid in our eyes is seawater and therefore there are fish in our eyes, seawater being the natural medium of fish. Since blue and green are the colours of the richest seawater, blue and green eyes are the fishiest. Dark eyes are somewhat less fecund and albino eyes are nearly fishless, sadly so. But the quantity of fish in an eye means nothing. A single tigerfish can be as beautiful, as powerful, as an entire school of seafaring tuna. That science has never observed ocular fish does nothing to refute my theory; on the contrary, it emphasizes the key hypothesis, which is: love is the food of eye fish and only love will bring them out. So to look closely into someone's eyes with cold, empirical interest is like the rude tap-tap of a finger on an aquarium, which only makes the fish flee. In a similar vein, when I took to looking at myself closely in mirrors during the turmoil of adolescence, the fact that I saw nothing in my eyes, not even the smallest guppy or tadpole, said something about my unhappiness and lack of faith in myself at the time.

This theory has accompanied me all my life, like a small friend perched on my shoulder, like a pocket-sized god. I expose it at length here, but under that tree in the garden, aged five, after that epiphanous moment of television, I only sensed its rudimentary elements. It developed as I gained insights and knowledge. For example, a joke I overheard one day among teenage boys as I was hurrying by — I didn't understand the joke, I was afraid of the boys, but it linked girls with the smell of fish — made me see that the fishiness of love goes beyond the eyes. Over the years the theory became enormously complex, a system, really, with countless ramifications, the sort of scientific arcana likely to be fully understood only by children and Albert Einstein.

I no longer believe in eye fish in *fact*, but still do in metaphor. In the passion of an embrace, when breath, the wind, is at its loudest and skin at its saltiest, I still nearly think that I could stop things and hear, feel, the rolling of the sea. I am still nearly convinced that, when my love and I kiss, we will be blessed with the sight of angelfish and sea-horses rising to the surface of our eyes, these fish being the surest proof of our love. In spite of everything, I still profoundly believe that love is something oceanic.

My time as a rabbit was closely related to that strange condition called sleep. I would lie in bed, looking up at the ceiling, thinking, "This is ridiculous. I am lying here, wide awake, waiting. But what am I waiting for?" I would look to my left and right. "There's no one here except me! There's nothing to do. I should get up."

But I wouldn't. There was something inexpressibly comfortable about this lying in horizontal softness, cosily blanketed, in well-lit darkness. I would continue waiting, passively impatient, for *it* (no antecedent). Then I would casually look down and see that my hand was a furry white paw. "Heavens! I'm asleep," I would realize, and in so doing I would wake up. I remember this nightly transformation in Costa Rica with absolute lucidity. Not the process — the shrinking in size or the stretching of my ears and legs, although, if I close my eyes and concentrate, I can nearly feel the growing of my soft, thick fur — not the process, but the result: a medium-sized rabbit, brown and white except for the tips of my ears, which were black. I would immediately leap out of bed. I would hop to great heights on my powerful hind legs, jump from my bed to the chest and back. I would stand and do one, two, three somersaults in a row. I would dance, pounding the carpeted floor with gleeful mania. There was nothing I couldn't do, for though I was small and thin my body was (and always has been) faithful to me. It did my bidding. Only the fridge frustrated me, when I attempted to open it to get a carrot, and even this was not for lack of strength, but for lack of height. (Reach was also a problem the time I slipped a carrot beneath my mattress before going to bed. I placed it beyond my bunny grasp and subsequently forgot about it. It was discovered three years later, quite green.)

We had pet rabbits in the garden, real permanent ones that my parents had bought to my delight. But I never ventured out to play with them when I myself was a rabbit. Once I did go to the glass doors at the back of the living-room to look out into the garden, and Salt, Pepper, Boot and Butterfly came up to the doors and we stood forepaw to glass to forepaw, staring at each other. But I realized then, looking into their dark eyes, that these rabbits were strangers to me, and children do not seek the company of strangers. I was glad for the glass between us.

My clearest memory of my time as a rabbit is of a gesture I made with my forepaws to scratch my ears. No, not scratch. It was more like a stretching, a stretching of the ears. I would stand them very erect, lower my head and then run my forepaws over them, flattening them against my head, first the right ear, then the left, then both at the same time. It was a quick, round motion which I repeated several times. Afterwards my ears felt alert and tingly. I could twitch and hone them to the smallest, most distant sounds — a curtain rustling in the dining-room, a floorboard cracking arthritically in the living-room, a sudden respiration from my sleeping father, why, even the stars blinking. There's nothing to make you more aware of the roaring pulse of life than minute, nearly inaudible sounds.

I started my formal education in 1968 at Jiminy Cricket Kindergarten. It operated in English, but my parents had no choice. At the time it was the only quality kindergarten in San José.

"Tu seras bilingue. Même trilingue," qu'ils me dirent. "Très canadien."

"You'll be bilingual. Even trilingual," they told me. "Very Canadian."

So it was that, by a mere whim of geography, I went to school in English, played outside in Spanish and told all about it at home in French. Each tongue came naturally to me and each had its natural interlocutors. I no more thought of addressing my parents in English than I did of doing arithmetic in my head in French. English became the language of my exact expression, but it expressed thoughts that somehow have always remained Latin.

The earliest incidence of violence in my life occurred at Jiminy Cricket. A maladjusted boy attacked me for no reason. He pulled my hair and bit me on the neck. I was too young then to be a coward and we clashed in a fierce fight. The teacher separated us and I vaguely remember the two of us hanging in mid-air at the end of her arms, swinging like pendulums. We were put to bed for enforced naps. I peed in my sleep and the teacher called the embassy and my father came to get me.

The boy who attacked me remained not only in the same school as me for the next three years, but in the very same class. We were together the rest of that year at Jiminy Cricket, and in grades 1 and 2 at Abraham Lincoln Academy. But he never got so close to me again. With blond hair that was long and dishevelled one week, crew-cut the next, and staring brown eyes, he was a sullen boy who kept to himself and had no friends. But from the other side of the bars of his imaginary cage he watched me, watched me intently all the time, for three years, especially when I was with Noah. Sometimes our eyes met, but even now I'm not sure I could read those eyes. He would be the first to look down, after a second or two, but only, I know, to look back as soon as I had turned. Perhaps he loved me.

My parents were early feminists and they did not use the word "opposite" when speaking of the sexes. Indeed, why should they be considered opposite? The word is aggressive, defines by negation, says very little. The sexes are complementary, said my parents — a more complicated word which they explained to me by analogy. Male and female were like rain and soil. Except that whereas they were speaking of sex, of impersonal details of biology, I understood them to be speaking of love, elaborating on what I already knew. The universe struck me then as amazingly well engineered. Imagine: somewhere out there, totally separate, of independent origin, was a sexual organ tailored to suit mine, to suit me. I set out to find my complementary sexual organ, my true love.

There is no greater mystery than this, the mystery of cathexis. Why do some people make the fish crowd our eyes, and others leave them utterly fishless? Is love some unique food that will feed only our fish? Or is it whatever food happens to be nearby when our fish get hungry? I have no idea why I fell in love with Noah Rabinovitch. It was too long ago. Memory is sometimes a distant spectator which can name emotions but not convey them, and this is the case here. To be sure, in some way Noah was my complement. When I was alone I was happy and whole, but when we were together the whole was greater. There was an added brightness to things, a greater and deeper perspective. But I could say the same thing, to only a slightly lesser degree, of other people, even of animals and objects. There was more to it than that. Only I don't know what. I think I remember that I liked the way Noah walked. He walked, therefore I loved him.

One day, as my mother arrived at the kindergarten to pick me up, I informed her that I had found my future wife and I proudly pointed to Noah, who was new at Jiminy Cricket.

His father was an Israeli diplomat and they had just arrived in
Costa Rica, mid-year. Noah came up to my mother, extended
his hand and said he was pleased to meet his future mother-
in-law. (Noah was sickeningly polite.) But then he had the effrontery to add that *I* would be *his* wife, and the two of us
started again on the same tiresome argument we had had all
morning, which I thought was settled. For some reason, neither of us wanted to be the wife.

My mother interrupted us by asking me why I thought
Noah would be my wife. There are some circumstances where
one cannot blurt out, "Parce que je l'aime!" "Because I love
him!" "¡Porque le amo!" I was more concrete: Noah had the
sexual organ complementary to mine. Did he, she replied, an
uncontrollable smile running across her face, my first clue that
I had missed something. She took my hand, said goodbye to
Noah in English and we headed for the car. I clearly remember
turning as we were walking off and bleating, with infinite
sadness in my voice, "Bye, Noah," for in a vague way I realized
that I had just lost my husband. Before opening the car door
for me, my mother bent down and gave me an unwanted hug
and a kiss. On the way home she gave me the first facts of my
sexual persona. Things were far more limited than my open
mind had imagined. There were in fact only *two* sexes, not
infinite numbers. And those little bums and little fingers that
I had seen in the various I'll-show-you-mine-if-you-show-me-
yours exercises I had conducted were the complementary
sexual organs in question, all two of them, one little bum for
one little finger. I was amazed. This question of complemen-
tarity referred merely to a vulgar point of *biology*, an anatomical whim? The menu for ocular fish had only two items on
it? And it was decided in advance which they could select,

either little bum or little finger, steak or chicken? What kind of a restaurant is that, Mother? I had indeed noticed only little bums and little fingers so far, but I thought this was simply a reflection of the small size of my sample. (In a similar vein, though most of my coevals at Jiminy Cricket were white, on the basis of the skin colour of a few of them, reinforced by things I had seen on television and in magazines, I was quite confident that there existed people who were black, brown, yellow, red, blue, orange, perhaps even striped.) But no, there were only two, my mother insisted. Even more astonishing, she said that little bums were to be found exclusively in girls and little fingers exclusively in boys. Girls, *by definition*, were females with little bums who could only be wives. Boys, *by definition*, were males with little fingers who could only be husbands. I should remember these permutations for there were no others. No, husbands could not be girls. No, a wife could not marry another wife. No, no, no.

In the time of a brief car ride I became an indubitable boy, I discovered one of my defining characteristics and the universe, up till then myriad, broke into two camps. I was grief-stricken.

"Est-ce que je peux toujours aimer Noah?" je demandai, éclatant en sanglots.

"Can I still love Noah?" I asked, bursting into tears.

"Bien sûr," repondit ma mère doucement, me passant la main dans les cheveux. "Aime-le autant que tu veux. Il est important d'avoir des amis."

"Of course," my mother replied soothingly, running her hand through my hair. "Love him as much as you want. It's important to have friends."

Friends? Oh, Mother. I was given permission to love, yet I could sense — I cannot quite explain how — that oceans were now trapped in aquariums. She must be mistaken, I thought. I kept at her, convinced that there had been a misunderstanding. But I was so immeasurably confused that I could only approach the matter from the small end, this niggling point of biology.

"Female and male? Is that all? Even on other planets?"

"We're only on this planet, love. We're only on planet Earth."

"Why is it called Erth? What does Erth mean?"

"It means 'here' in Greek and Latin."

"And we're only on this planet?" I said, looking out the window, as if the edge of the planet were just beyond the field.

"It's a big place, you'll see."

"There's nobody on any of the stars?"

"Not that we know of."

"And there's nobody on the moon?"

"No."

"Seulement ici?"

"Seulement ici."

"La Taire?"

"La Terre."

"Femelle et mâle?"

"Mâle et femelle."

"Alors elle est femelle ou mâle, cette voiture?"

"Euh . . . façon de parler, elle — non, non. Mâle et femelle s'appliquent seulement aux êtres vivants. Cette voiture est une simple machine. Elle n'a pas de sexe."

"Ahhh."

Un moment de réflexion.

"Alors il est femelle ou mâle, cet arbre?"

"Non. Seulement les êtres vivants — et qui bougent."

"Mais il bouge, l'arbre. Et tous les autres. Regarde."

"Oui, mais c'est le vent ça. Ils doivent bouger d'eux-mêmes. Vivants, et qui bougent d'eux-mêmes."

"Il est quoi, le vent? Femelle ou mâle?"

"Non, non, non. Le vent n'est pas un être vivant."

"Mais il bouge!"

"Just here?"

"Just here."

"Erth?"

"Earth."

"Female and male?"

"Male and female."

"So this car, is it female or male?"

"Uh . . . well we say — no, no. Male and female apply only to living things. This car is just a machine. It has no sex."

"Ohhh."

A pregnant pause.

"So that tree, is it female or male?"

"No. Only things that are alive — and move."

"But it is moving. And all the others, too. Look."

"Yes, but that's the wind. They have to move on their own. Things that are alive, and move on their own."

"What's the wind? Female or male?"

"No, no, no. The wind isn't a living thing."

"But it moves!"

"Oui, je sais. Mais il est invisible. Pour être mâle ou femelle, une chose doit être vivante, bouger d'elle-même, et être visible."

"Yes, I know. But it's invisible. To be male or female, a thing has to be alive, move on its own, and be visible."

"Alors c'est pour ça, les microscopes? Pour voir le sexe des petites choses?"

"So that's what microscopes are for? To find out the sex of small things?"

"Tiens, regarde, une vache."

"Oh look, a cow."

"Elle est femelle ou mâle, cette vache?"

"Is that cow female or male?"

Ma mère regarda. "C'est une vache femelle."

My mother looked. "It's a female cow."

She smiled. She'd got it right, she thought.

Many biology classes later, when I learned that plants do in fact have a sexuality, when I fully understood the terms pistil, stamen and pollen, I discovered with pleasure the slow, charged sexuality of nature. No wonder spring was such a sensuous time. Trees were not hard, irritable things, but discreetly orgasmic beings moaning at a level too deep for our brutish ears. And flowers were quick explosive orgasms, like making love in the shower.

As for Noah Rabinovitch and the strange mutilatory practices of the Jews, it would be a while yet before I understood that his clipped foreskin complemented something other than my own penis.

The next day at recess we hid around the corner and I offered right away, happily, to be his wife.

"Okay," he said, as casually as if I had just offered him a marble rather than my life. "Here, look what I've got," he added, pulling out of his pocket a brand new Coca-Cola yo-yo. "Let's go play with it." And he walked off, his disappointed and disgruntled wife in tow.

My relationship with Noah was nonetheless deeply satisfying. On the outside we appeared and behaved like no more than the best of friends (her word), but on the inside I felt that wonderful, sizzling feeling, the basis of all love: complicity.

Noah disappeared from my life as suddenly as he had appeared. Prime Minister Levi Eshkol died of a heart attack on February 26, 1969. Golda Meir replaced him. In the long domino-chain of changes that this brought about, a distant, painful one was the recall in the summer of 1970, at the end of grade 1, of diplomat Etan Rabinovitch to Jerusalem after barely a year and a half at his new posting.

I spent my last year in Costa Rica a widow. For company I had only the beast television, which I watched avidly, expressing my dislike of it by sitting far away, and the boy who had attacked me, this savage on the periphery of my playground.

Though I was interested in the sex of others, I don't recall as a child being very curious about my own penis. It was the organ with which I urinated, a casual part of my identity, *c'est tout*. By an imperceptible cultural osmosis I gathered that it was a "private" part, but this did not turn it into a source of interest, let alone of shame or embarrassment. It was private in much the same way that a bedroom is: guests are invited to sit and chat in the living-room, and only once they have achieved a sufficient degree of intimacy may they be shown around the house and see the bedroom. At puberty my level of interest would change dramatically and my penis would become the object of dedicated attention, the source of a pleasure so powerful that I might call it extraterrestrial, but even then I never felt that this small member — for that is what it is — was an inspiration for architecture or organization charts or anything else.

I have a black and white photo of me when I was very young, perhaps three. I am outside on a hot sunny day, naked and standing at the top of some wooden steps. I am holding onto my adored, tattered towel. The photographer, my father, is below me and I am looking at him gravely. I am not yet inhibited by modesty — the way I stand then, every square inch of my skin is equally presentable. My sex seems very large for the size of me. Perhaps sexual organs have their own rate of growth, or get started earlier. Yet it's tiny: a scrotum like half a walnut shell and a penis attached to it that is no more than a stubby cylinder of skin. But what really surprises me is the way the two float on the surface of my body. Atop my layer of baby fat, they seem unconnected and unimportant. They are there, but they could be elsewhere, like a large mole — and could seemingly be excised like a large mole by a simple operation should they become malignant. There is no hint of how deeply rooted in me they are, how, in a way, they are half of me, and how the point at which they join my body is a fulcrum.

A short time after that momentous car ride with my mother, I showed her a thick, juicy worm I had captured in the garden.

"Il est femelle ou mâle, ce ver de terre?" "Is this earthworm female or male?"

My mother, a cool woman, a woman who always displayed grace under pressure, hardly squirmed. She carefully gathered up the papers she was working on from beneath my dangling worm, and she looked at it and at me.

"En fait, les deux. Le ver de terre est à la fois mâle et femelle. C'est une exception à la règle."

"Well, as a matter of fact it's both. The worm is both male and female. It's an exception to the rule."

Both male and female! I looked closely at this supreme brown creature as it twisted limply in my fingers. Both! How extraordinary.

"Où sont ses organes sexuels?"

"Where are its sex organs?"

"Je ne suis pas sûre. Ils sont très petits. Tu ne peux pas les voir."

"I'm not sure. They're very small. You can't see them."

"Eh bien, son nom est Jésus-Christ et elle est ma meilleure amie!"

"Well, his name is Jesus Christ and she's my best friend."

"Et aucun des deux ne reste dans la maison. Ils seront plus heureux dans le jardin."

"And neither one of them is staying in the house. They'll be happier in the garden."

I carried away this miracle of the universe. Every time the words occurred to me — "Both male and female!" — I was amazed anew. Surely if God existed — ? — He, She, It must have the wriggly blunt head of a worm. I looked up at the sky. I could see it very well: an enormous, beautiful worm circling the earth, gracefully moving around and through the white clouds. I played with Jesus Christ for a few minutes and then cut them up into very small pieces with a sharp knife, trying to find their sex organs. Both female and male. Incredible.

I am puzzled now by this knack for torture that I had as a child. For long before the beautiful, forsaken worm, I martyred a snail. Our house in Costa Rica had an enclosed garden that teemed with life. One day, while exploring this, my dominion, behind a fringe of leaves, I came upon the largest snail I had ever seen. It was making its way up the wall. I dislodged it with my finger and it tumbled to the ground. I picked it up. Seconds later the discombobulated creature oozed out of its shell, eyes sallying forth to assess the situation. What extraordinary eyes! Translucent white tentacles with ocular black dots at the end, like others I had seen, but never of this magnitude. I was seduced by these eyes. That there could be fish so minuscule as to swim freely in them astounded me. I fetched a pair of scissors. But try as I might, the black dot retreated into the grey-green flesh before I could cut it off and release the seawater. By then the small animal was as fully extended out of its shell as it could be, slowly twisting this way and that, obviously trying to apprehend what was holding it so fixedly. On one of its contortions it came into contact with a blade of the scissors. It held onto it and began to pull itself along the cutting edge, its sticky pad overflowing the sides, its strange harelip mouth leading the way. After a centimetre or two I closed the scissors, catching the creature between the eyes and slicing its head in two. It gave a spastic shudder and retreated into its shell. A liquid started to drip. I tossed the shell; I considered crushing it, but did not. Torturing the soft is one thing; torturing the hard, another.

I burned ants with a magnifying glass. I starved two small turtles to death. I asphyxiated lizards in jars. I exploded spiders with firecrackers. I poured salt on slugs. I attempted to drown frogs and, when they would not drown, I threw them against the wall of a boat-house and watched them float upside down in the water. I killed a huge toad by throwing broken roof tiles at it (the creature never moved, only slumped and ceased to live. I don't mean to anthropomorphize it, but I do wonder what it was thinking, and in what terms. Not anger or bitterness, though a toad's aspect conveys these, but surely that universal emotion of the organic: fear. "I'm going to die, I don't want to die. I'm going to die, I don't want to die. I'm going to die, I don't want to die. I'm —"). I committed these atrocities in solitude, without glee, deliberately. Each cruelty, each final spasm of life, resonated in me like a drop of water falling in a silent cave.

SIX MORNING DELINQUENT ACTS I PARTICIPATED IN:

(1) From the doorstep of a house, took a bottle of freshly delivered milk, carefully removed the cardboard top with the tip of a knife, drank a sip and then urinated in the bottle just enough to bring the level of liquid back to what it had been. Replacing the top, returned the bottle to the doorstep. Seven or eight times, until Eckhardt dropped a bottle and it shattered and we fled in terror.

(2) Put toothpaste in car locks. Numerous times.

(3) Deflated tires. Numerous times.

(4) Poured sugar in a car's gas tank. Once.

(5) Drilled a hole at the base of a magnificent cactus as tall as a house, introduced a firecracker into the hole and lit it, the cactus falling over like a tree, its arms breaking off to reveal strange, sweaty green flesh. Once.

(6) Set a long L-shaped hedgerow on fire. Once.

The emotional nadir of my life as a child came during a walk on a beach in Guatemala. I was seven, perhaps just eight. It

was a desolate Third World beach hugged by low, ugly buildings. To my right was plastic refuse thrown up by the sea. To
my left was plastic refuse thrown down by humanity. A heavy,
grey sky. Not a single being within sight. I could have been
drowning, no one to save me. I walked along, already in a
fragile mood. Up ahead, an indeterminate object lay on the
beach. It slowly materialized. It was a large sea turtle, over a
metre long, lying on its back, dead — oh, very dead. Its head
hung back, the leathery neck exposed, the sharp lipless
mouth open, the black eyes staring. Who would do this to
such a beautiful creature? Who would deliberately overturn it
to let it die thus slowly? For no purpose, for this was no soup
in the making. While these questions dragged me down, I
heard a yelp behind me. I turned. A small three-legged dog
was running up to me. Its left foreleg was gone, the stump
messy and gnarled. The animal yelped at me but carefully
made a circle around me, sniffing the turtle only, secure in the
knowledge that the dead can give no blows, no kicks. There
was a sinking in me, a collapsing such as I had never felt
before. It was at this moment, long before I learned the
words, that I first felt it, blowing through me like a frigid
prairie gust: nothingness, nullity, vacuity, the void — life,
consciousness, as being something as superfluous as a television left on in an empty room. I felt that if I made a wiping
motion in front of my eyes, a swath of black would appear in
the air, and in my hand the torn, bunched-up surface of
reality, the wrinkled picture of a maimed dog sniffing a dead
turtle. I couldn't take my eyes off the turtle's belly. What
struck me was not its apparent hardness, or its colour (banana
black and yellow) or the patterns (curious, softly delineated
rectangles that I would recognize years later in the Inca stone

walls of Peru), but its slight inward curve. I felt very strongly that this curve fitted exactly the curve of the earth. In my mind I could see the round earth, and on this round earth a bump of a turtle hugging it. And it was good, it was the order of things. This inversion here, baby curve facing away from mother curve, facing the great emptiness of the universe, was a barbarity.

But was there not an element of necessity to this killing? This was the question that cracked through the wall of my happiness, through my security. What I had here, I sensed, was nihilism, the deliberate wrecking of being to assert being in the face of non-being. To insult, otherwise not to exist. To strike, even if in vain, at this sterile abundance of stupid life.

The final thought emerged: "This turtle — good thing it was overturned before my arrival, for I couldn't have managed it on my own." I backed away and returned to our hotel, the dog following me a little way before vanishing. Two days later I cried for hours in bed before falling asleep. And again some months later.

We moved to Paris. We were staying in a hotel before moving into our repainted apartment, but on the second day a French painter and his Canadian wife came to see us. Philippe and Sharon were friends of friends paying us a courtesy visit, but they and my parents hit it off so instantly and famously that spontaneously, sincerely, they invited us to stay with them, an invitation my parents accepted with delight.

Two days later, in the early evening, the doorbell rang and it was a man. He was the very portrait of misery: tense, tired, embarrassed, clearly distraught. Not in French but in halting

English, which Philippe understood only a little, he introduced himself: a friend of mutual German acquaintances.
They had given him Philippe's name and address in Paris. The
man held up the paper on which the information was written.
Stammering, with the difficulty of one not used to asking for
help, he asked for help, which Philippe, without hesitation,
extended. He invited the man in. He offered him a seat and a
glass of wine and the man began to explain himself. It came
out that he was Czech, a lawyer, that his brother had just been
killed in circumstances that I did not understand, that he and
his family had fled Czechoslovakia in catastrophe, leaving behind their belongings, their lives, everything, that they were
now lost and confused, that — that they were now lost and
confused, he said once again. And sat there, lost and confused.
And shaking.

Everything that could be done on the outside to try to
make the inside happy was done. While Philippe, my father
and the Czech, Pavel, went to get his wife and his daughter,
who were waiting at a café, the table was set, food was prepared, the corks from red wine bottles were drawn and bed-
sheets were brought out.

I suppose that in reality she entered the house exhausted
and unhappy, sticking close to her mother, dressed in a
slightly dirty white dress with embroidery of bright red and
purple, her hair tied in a fraying French braid. But to me she
was an apparition of sudden, extravagant beauty. I neither saw
nor heard Eva's contrite apologies and thank-yous in her ap-
proximate French, or Pavel's echoes of the same in his English
or Sharon and Philippe's assurances that neither apologies nor
thank-yous were necessary. I only paid attention to Marisa,
who looked about and sensed the warmth. I don't know if I

was part of that warmth, but she looked at me, then away and around, then back at me, and smiled. My chest tightened.

She gave off sunshine. She had thick, crinkly blonde hair, skin that was honey-coloured, very dark eyes and a face so clear and open that years later, when Tito and I were hiking in the Himalayas and there was a change of wind and suddenly, in an explosion of clarity that cut my breath short, we beheld the mountain Nanga Parbat in its massive, microscopically accurate entirety, the first word, the only word, that came to my lips was her long-forgotten name. She was my age, eight, and she spoke, as far as I could tell, no language known to humanity beyond the Esperanto of our first names. We looked at each other, mutually surprised at the gibberish the other was speaking. But she smiled again.

After a quick clean-up, all of us, the French, the Canadians and the Czechs, sat down to eat. The Czechs ate hungrily; I, who was beside Marisa, hardly at all.

Pavel and Eva were beginning to relax and they and my parents and Philippe and Sharon started on one of those endless conversations that adults specialize in. I don't recall any of this blah-blah-blah-blah on art, politics and life. How could I, when Marisa was next to me? After she had finished stuffing into her mouth all the food her body could possibly take, she sat back. She watched her parents for a few seconds, then shot me a side glance that transfixed me. We began — in spite of not sharing a common tongue — to communicate, although I'm not sure what. She whispered to me in her sweet East European Chinese and I whispered back in a French that I thought painfully clear and boring, but she seemed happy enough, for she replied right away each time, hardly letting me finish. The only word she spoke that I understood, the most powerful word in her language, was my name, which she said four or five times, each time dazing me for a few seconds.

Though we were the ones whispering and the adults the ones talking, quite energetically sometimes, to my ears it was the reverse: their intercourse was a distant muttering, near silence, while Marisa's unintelligibility came through loud and clear.

A strangled cry from Pavel abruptly ended our intimacy. His face was congested, he was biting one of his index fingers and he was staring at the table. His eyes were watery. Marisa's face lost its good cheer. In a voice several notes higher than normal, she asked a question of her father. There followed a brief exchange of Czech between father, mother and daughter. Marisa seemed on the verge of tears. I felt I had lost her.

This display of adult emotion was taken to signal that it was time we children went to bed. Then fate took one of those turns that change a life for ever. Philippe and Sharon's house, while generous in its open spaces, was not especially large, and accommodating six adults and two children was a challenge. It was decided expeditiously that Marisa and I would sleep in the same bed.

Just like that, with the casualness of an afterthought — thanks perhaps to the wine — passion was thrust into my life.

I was ready long before her. In a minute flat, teeth and hair were brushed, clothes were etc., and I lay in bed, eagerly patient. Meanwhile, she was bathed and dried. I don't remember what I was thinking, but most probably, like adults about to make love, I was deeply content with the here and now, and not going much beyond the rapid and circular thoughts that constitute anticipation.

Looking serious and composed, she appeared at the doorstep of the bedroom, a beauty in a white nightgown at the centre of an explosion of frizz. From the foot of the bed she crawled on all fours, like a lion, to her assigned spot, and she entered the den of our sheets next to an excited, expectant gazelle — me. Her hair overflowed her pillow. We were good-nighted and kissed by the crowd of parents. Normally I couldn't fall asleep without this ceremony, but that night I wanted it to go as fast as a baton passing in a relay sprint. Instead, it lasted like a scene in a Noh drama.

"To ale byly tri dlouhé dny, vid milácku. Ale uz to bude v porádku. Nový zacátek v nové zemi. Budes mít nové kamarády. Tak se na nás usmej. No vidís, ze to jde. Vzdyt vís, jak moc te mámc rádi. Moc a moc. Zítra pujdeme na australskou ambasádu a uvidíme, jak brzy budeme moci jet za tetou Vavou do Melbourne. Konecne uvidís opravdové klokany, to bude neco úplne jiného nez v zoologické v Praze. To se ti bude líbit, vid? Tak ted uz spinkej milácku, dobrou noc. Uz

"Dors bien, chéri."
"Oui, oui."
"Demain nous irons voir la cathédrale Notre-Dame."
"Oui, oui."
"Ne dérange pas Marisa."

tady más dokonce kamaráda.
Je príma, vid? Zítra se
pujdeme podívat na
Eifelovku, kdyz to vyjde.
Treba by mohl jít s námi, co
ríkás? Tak dobrou."

What did that mean, *ne dérange pas Marisa*, don't bother Marisa? I narrowed my eyes. If my parents had died that second I would have been delighted.

Finally, with the clicking of a light-switch and the snapping of a latch, they left.

I could smell her. She smelt wonderful, and I took this not as an artifice — some soap, some shampoo — but as a natural emanation. The fragrance of beauty. It is amazing how smells can pull one back into the past. I think that if I smelled that shampoo again today I could practically materialize Marisa in front of me.

We lay side by side, pyjamaed from head to toe, looking up at the ceiling, the darkness made limpid by the moonlight coming in from the window, and she quiet, and me, me? *me!* — thrilled to my core. And quiet too, just soaking in the thrill, deliciously swept away, deliciously passive. To be this close to Marisa, within inches of certain adventurous strands of her hair — I asked for nothing more. If we had fallen asleep at that moment, I would still have remembered that night for ever.

She rustled a little, adjusting her nightgown. She turned to me and spoke.

"Ich bin nicht müde.   "I'm not sleepy. Are you?"
Und du?"

German? Not that I spoke a word of the language, but in Costa Rica, two houses down from us, I had had a friend, Eckhardt, whose parents were German immigrants.

I replied in the language which, by virtue of being my third and last, was the most foreign to me and therefore, surely, the closest to Czech.

"Ocho años. Casi ocho y medio."

"Eight years old. Nearly eight and a half."

"Hier gefällt es mir überhaupt nicht."

"I don't like it here at all."

"Tengo calor. Pero estoy bien. Estoy contento."

"I'm a little hot. But I'm fine. I'm happy."

"Ich will zurück nach Prag. Die Leute hier sind schrecklich."

"I want to go back to Prague. The people here are nasty."

"¿Te gustan los helados?"

"Do you like ice-cream?"

"Mit meiner Tante Vavou wahrscheinlich. Aber die Känguruhs interessieren mich gar nicht. Ich will zu meinen Freunden."

"With my Aunt Vava, probably. But I don't care about kangaroos. I want my friends."

"Tienen buenos helados aquí. Berthillon. Tomamos helado ayer. Vainilla con miel y nueces; mi favorito."

"They have good ice-cream here. Berthillon. We had some yesterday. Honey vanilla with nuts is my favourite."

"Ich bin ja gar nicht froh. Und der arme Onkel Tomas."

"I'm not happy. And poor Uncle Tomas."

"¿A lo mejor tomamos mañana?"

"Maybe we could have some tomorrow?"

I said this nervously, amazed at my boldness. I would ask my father to get her a double, one scoop of honey vanilla with nuts and another of white chocolate. She was on her side with her head propped up. A few strands of hair fell across her face. She tossed them back.

"Ach, die Hitze. Es ist hier viel zu warm. Wir können mal unsere Schlafanzüge ausziehen."

"Oh, it's so hot underneath all these blankets. Let's take our pyjamas off."

She sat up and to my amazement began to gather up her nightgown in her hands, and then pulled it off over her head. Her hair cascaded down.

"Mir geht's jetzt besser. Zieh doch den Schlafanzug aus."

"That's better. Take yours off."

Her hands reached for my pyjama top. I sat up and she helped me take it off. We remained sitting for a few moments, looking at each other. I suppose she had a chest very much like mine: flat, with two pale round nipples. Except that hers was a touch golden. She smiled.

We lay down and she turned me around so that I had my back to her. Her arm came up and around me. She held me plainly and openly, our bodies tightly fitted to each other, our skins touching, hers very warm, my head resting in her soft, rebellious hair. My eyes were open, but I was more aware of smell and touch than of vision. I felt dizzy.

"Kehr dich mal um."

"Turn around."

Her hands made her meaning clear. I turned slowly, ever so slowly, like the planet Earth turning towards daylight. When she spoke, when she breathed, I could feel it against my face. We continued to whisper sweet Hispano-Teutonic nothings.

At a pause, she closed her eyes, covered three inches of space and kissed me on the lips.

It has only happened to me twice in my life: I could hardly see her for the fish in my eyes. At that moment I wanted time to stop, I wanted the night never to end, I wanted the sun to be gutted.

"Gracias, Marisa."   "Thank you, Marisa."

I was so blissfully happy, so wide-eyed and glowing with it, that I fell asleep. I awoke in the morning with the conviction that love is an insomnia that wakes us from the sleep of life. I had been asleep before, but never again. I vowed to be awake like this for the rest of my life, a full awakeness, a clear one-litre glass bottle with one litre of water in it.

My mother entered and right away I asked the question.

"Est-ce qu'ils vont rester   "Are they going to stay
à Paris?"   in Paris?"

"Non, ils veulent s'établir   "No, they want to settle
en Australie."   in Australia."

The answer echoed in my head. *Non, ils veulent s'établir en Australie. Non, ils veulent s'établir en Australie. Non, non, non.* I was at the end of the bed, mostly dressed. She was bringing me a clean shirt.

Will I be understood when I say that sometimes numbness can hurt? That you don't want to feel because what you feel will be pain, so you try not to feel, and just sit there, immobile, numb, in pain?

That day, we, the three nations, visited Notre-Dame, a big, cold place except when Marisa and I stood on the hot air vents. I stuck close to her. She made me feel much the way the cathedral did: draughts of warmth amidst draughts of cold. I kept thinking, "She's here — but not for long, she's here — but not for long, she's here — but not for long."

We returned to the hotel for one night, and then moved into our new apartment. I saw Marisa many times after that, but never in the same circumstances. She was becoming happy, reconciling herself with fate, thinking of Australia, already speaking her first words of English — "boat", "bed", "dictionary". The last time I saw her, for the good-byes, she came up to me and publicly kissed me on the left cheek, on the right cheek, on the left cheek, and then, once, on the lips. I felt my life was over.

She was a new teacher at my new school, the English School of Paris. It was my first day. A boy sitting at the back was making things difficult for her. He was being very insolent. At a climax of tension between him and her, she lost control and slapped the first boy within reach — which happened to be me. Did I make a comment? A wisecrack? Something that would have been a specious excuse? If I did, any memory of it was instantly erased by this full slap in the face. I did not cry — pride — only stared down, red in the face. But as soon as I got off the school bus and was greeted by my parents, hours later, I burst into great, choking tears. My schoolmates surrounded us and in their shrill voices, one over the other, they recounted what had happened. In truth, the teacher had not really meant to slap me, and even before the school principal received an irate and flushed visit the next morning from two young Canadian diplomats, who meant to get to the bottom of why their much-loved little boy was being physically abused — something never, *ever* done by them, they emphasized — and unjustly abused on top of it, even before this, she received a visit from the young woman (with her boyfriend), who, immediately after the class, had gone to the bathroom to cry and had spent a sleepless night and whose eyes were still red and who was obviously remorseful about the incident. The rest of the year she was extra nice to me, and I received a final mark of 94, though I can't even remember what the subject was. This slap was one of my few direct contacts with violence during my early childhood. The others came through art.

I would like to move quickly through this episode. It is a mistake from my childhood, regret for which still nags me. What I would give to undo it! I see it as one of the forks in the river of my early life, one of those moments that begin the tracing of a pattern. The details annoy me and bore me, I have gone over them so often, but still I must relate them. What comes through loud and clear to me is the fact that I learned nothing from Marisa.

Ten years old, same school, same class, a little shorter than I, a smile like — no metaphors, quickly: I was in love with Mary Ann. I would set eyes on her — and what a difference one person can make! I would look at all the other people in my life — my parents, my classmates, my teachers, strangers in the street — and nothing would happen, so many bottles moving along in a bottle factory. But I could never get enough of looking at Mary Ann. There was something about her that was beyond my understanding. I would gaze at her in circles, from her hair to her forehead to her eyes to her nose to her smile to her whole face and then back again to the details, circle after circle. Mary Ann and I were friends. We played together all the time, and on the bus I sat beside her, or near her, regularly. And she came to my home at least once. It's engraved in my memory.

Kelly was there, Mary Ann's younger sister. We were playing submarine in the modular furniture of my bedroom.

Kelly, who was running the engines and operating the missile silos, was below, at the desk, while above her on the bed, out of sight, lay Mary Ann and I, commanders of the sub. We talked, we whispered, we gave orders, we laughed, we looked into each other's eyes — it was there in the air, to be had. I only needed to lean forward and do it. Instead I fell back as if exhausted, and gave Kelly her final order, "Surface," and the spell was broken.

One day I will be old and if you push me, if you prod me, I'll spill this trivial incident of a ten-year-old boy who failed to kiss a ten-year-old girl. I will be bitter about it.

It was after the submarine, on the bus on the way back from school. Mary Ann was sitting with Diane in the seat in front of me. They had placed their coats over their heads and were whispering secrets to each other. But I could hear them. Through the cleft between their seats, I could hear them. Mary Ann asked Diane whom she liked, what boy, and there was giggling and some answer and I didn't care. Then Diane asked Mary Ann whom she liked, what boy, and immediately, without a pause, there was an answer, some Paul, some Henry, that I so little wanted to hear that I momentarily went deaf. I sat back in my seat and looked out the window and managed not to cry until I was in the bathroom at home.

That summer I spent two weeks in Canada with my paternal grandmother. She lived in a small village on the St. Lawrence and I spent most of my time fishing off a pier. It amused the city boy I was to be doing that, to be capturing wild fish from the wild, wild seaway — thirty-five kilometres wide at the level of my grandmother's village — and it meant that I could be alone, for she never came with me; alone with the wind, the seaway and the sun. But something had to be done with my catch. It was a fish called the loach, whose taste my grandmother did not like. The garden, she said. So it was that for two early summer weeks I fished alone every day off a pier and returned to my grandmother's small house to fertilize her garden with fresh fish. I dug small trenches and into these I laid my loaches, one by one, head touching tail, quickly burying them before they could flip-flop out of position. Some nonetheless swam up to the surface of the garden and I had to dig a deeper trench and step on the soil over them to make it compact. I wouldn't have tolerated this nonsense except that television and the rest of my upbringing had taught me the many ways in which a man or a woman can be killed, but not a loach. As I buried the fish, I said to myself over and over, to the point of stupefaction, "There is no love, there is no love, there is no love, there is no love." With a vengeance, in the cool, dark soil, I meant to bury the fish in my eyes.

I was staying at Jonathan's. It was a house with a garden, so it must have been somewhere outside of Paris. We found a condom. It was soft and yellow and it smelled disgusting. Jonathan's sister, Louise, was coming. He hid the condom. She was wearing her bathing-suit and sunglasses. Without saying a word to us, with only a look of exasperation, she lay on the deck chair. Jonathan looked at me and then at her significantly. *It came from her.* I stared at her, awed. We both stared. She turned to us. "Get lost," she hissed. We left.

"She had a fight with her boyfriend," said Jonathan. He was lucky to have a sister. He was spying on her all the time. We went upstairs and from the back window we looked down on her, hoping she would do something, don't know what. She lay very still, mostly brown (it was high summer) except for two circles and a triangle of blue bikini. We looked for a long time, off and on, and she never seemed to move. Then, when I was looking but not Jonathan, I saw two shiny rivers of tears appear from under her sunglasses and trickle down her cheeks, and I didn't want to look any more. I felt a sudden tightness in my throat. I thought of Mary Ann. Jonathan was taking down his BB gun to show it to me. We'll shoot things, he said. I got a pigeon yesterday, he said. But I didn't want to look at his BB gun or shoot anything. I proposed television.

This pain, the pain of unrequited love, occurred at such regular intervals during my childhood and adolescence that I don't care to write about it. It was a terrible and continuous pain and there was no deflecting it, only bearing it. When my parents prepared spaghetti, I always noticed the one noodle left behind in the strainer, forsaken, forgotten, while its companions lay intertwined in each others' arms, hot and steaming, in the large bowl at the centre of the table. When love was pain, I felt like that noodle. I never ate pasta without beforehand going to the strainer in the sink. I would look upon this bereft noodle, curled upon itself in search of comfort, and I would bring it love by eating it tenderly.

I do not want to discuss the subject of unrequited love. If love is the sea, then let us journey inland for a while.

THE SECOND TIME TELEVISION MESMERIZED ME AS A CHILD:

(2) I knew something forbidden was coming because the television screen had a little white rectangle in the bottom right-hand corner, a signal at the time that the program was

"for adults only". In the absence of my parents and my baby-sitter — they out for the evening, she in another room reading — I hesitated only a little. I turned the volume down to make the immorality of my act quieter. A picture emerged from darkness.

An empty arena.

People walking in.

Lights coming on.

At first I hardly paid any attention, for it was the white rectangle itself that gripped me. I stared at it much as Eve must have stared at the apple. Then the movie started in earnest. It was set in a future where there were no longer any wars, since countries no longer existed, only multinationals, and where global frustrations were contained within the arena of a violent team game played on roller-skates and motorcycles on a circular track. The camera caught it all: the blows and the pain, the accidents and the bodies. We lingered on the dazed, sweaty face of a dying player, then zoomed to blood-thirsty spectators throwing themselves against the plastic barrier shouting for more, more, more. I watched in shock. I noticed anew the white rectangle. I thought of plunging forward and clicking the television off, but I did not. I kept watching. I remember this movie for the way my emotions teeter-tottered between recoil and attraction in a shifting balance. I could feel how fascination was pushing back the bounds of horror.

ON THE CURRENCY OF THE WORDS "NIGGER" AND "FUCK":

My school in Paris was attended mostly by children of diplomats and foreign business executives. Consequently, there was a large contingent of dark blacks, middle blacks, pale blacks, dark browns, milk-chocolate browns, pale browns, yellows and olives among the freckled whites, the English transparent veiny whites, the Australian tanned whites and the just plain boring whites. We even had a No Colour, an albino, and an Irish cripple. I was fascinated by the colour of a fat girl named Gora. She was Indian or Trinidadian. Her skin was a shimmering soft brown that seemed to have depth. I could imagine dipping a finger into her skin and seeing it disappear into her brownness. At home I used to take milk and carefully add chocolate powder to it, trying to get precisely the colour of Gora's skin but never managing it because there is a quality of yellow-reddishness that Nestlé's just doesn't have. "Nigger" was the only racist slur I, we, knew at my school and we were very fair in our use of it; anybody who wasn't black was exposed to it. Our most consistent nigger was Beatrice's brother, a British pasty white by the name of Anthony. He was a touch mentally retarded, and we called him nigger with such regularity that we practically forgot his real name. Then one day Mr. Templey overheard Tristan calling him that and he got hell for it. It was then that I first heard about Martin Luther King, the American Deep South and the Civil Rights Movement. Nigger fell out of fashion and we called Anthony a moron instead. Another reason racism didn't stick was that it was limiting and impractical. Gora was snooty and it was with delight that I told her once that she was shit-coloured, but Tony, the Nigerian ambassador's son, was great. He was really funny and he had sticks of firecrackers that blew up like dynamite. He was also a leader. His words and his actions carried weight.

We wondered how the word "fuck" was spelled. Was it *fuk* or *fuke* or *fuck*. I don't think any of us really knew what it meant, the biological or emotional details. The word was an explosive mix of the mysterious, the forbidden and the obscene. It was a word we revelled in. It was a power word. To roll a "Fuck off" or a "It's a fucking nice day" off the tongue was the mark of someone to be reckoned with. Only vandalism and thievery had a greater cachet. It was also a word that I don't recall using against or with or about girls. Whereas vulgarity among boys was fun, among girls it generally felt ugly and unnecessarily abrasive. Girls managed to be mean and nasty — Beatrice, for instance — without being rude, an elegant feat. "Fuck" was a boy's word.

Jonathan, Ali and I took to exploring the garages and sheds of the school. It was like exploring a far planet of the galaxy. We came across a Solex. Solexes are antique marvels of French engineering. They are motorized bicycles — painted black, always — with fat little engines incongruously perched over their front wheels. We unscrewed the gas cap and poured sawdust into the tank. We explored this particular garage for several days running. It was large and full of mechanical things. On our last time there we found a moped, which delighted us since a moped's tank is much bigger than a Solex's. We were about to fill this tank chock-full with sawdust when, from behind a lawn-mowing tractor, in a moment of heart-stopping horror, one of the school's French workers appeared. He had been hiding, waiting for us. He was a hairy, thick-wristed, muscular man. Instantly we were running away, scared out of our wits. He lumbered after us. But he knew us, we saw him every day, so it was crazy trying to escape him even if we were faster. Jonathan and I stopped and stood against the wall. We were quaking with fear. He had enormous brown hands with skin that looked like hide. He came up to us and wagged his index finger, a finger that with one tap would have crushed our little Anglophone skulls.

"C'est méchant, faire ça, c'est pas gentil," dit-il, sans crier, tout simplement. "It's mean to do that, it's not nice," he said, not shouting it, just stating it.

Then he turned around and walked away. That was it. And it did the trick. Jonathan and I looked at each other, amazed. It *was* not nice, it was *méchant*. When we saw Ali, who was waiting for us beyond, we resented him, as if he had been unfairly spared the worst beating of his life.

When I saw the worker the next day I went to him and apologized. He smiled and ran his hand over the back of my head and neck. It felt rough and very warm.

It was at ski camp during Christmas. After a day of skiing we had gone swimming. We were in the showers, all of us weary to our bones and lingering under the steaming hot water. Jean-Luc, our group leader, turned to me and without a word started washing and rubbing my back. Perhaps he was motivated by more than genial camaraderie, I don't know; he was always nice to me. I felt no little pride that it was *I* who was the privileged recipient of his attention and not someone else. I knew everyone was watching us, envious. And it felt good, this vigorous back massage, very good — there was that simple pleasure, too. The curious happened: first one boy, then another, then all of us. In no time we were a circle of boys washing and rubbing each others' backs. Though we never talked about it, this shower was one of the high points of our skiing holiday. It resulted in a raucousness of laughter that I remember to this day. High-pitched squeals of mirth. Faces contorted with guffawing.

We were leaving Paris for Ottawa after a stay of nearly four years. As I climbed the steps of the plane and turned and looked at the people on the open terrace of the airport, I didn't know that it was not only Europe that was waving its hand good-bye to me, but my childhood. I was twelve years old.

It is difficult to describe the metamorphosis that begins at puberty. There are so many different strands. At first, puberty was a physical phenomenon for me. It was a new hairiness, an awkward physical growth, a skin disease, the discovery of a secret pleasure. Only dimly did I realize that it was also a mental phenomenon. I barely noticed that a new universe slipped itself in front of my eyes. One where the most paralysing anxiety could run alongside the greatest elation. One where the idea of choice, real, personal choice, was introduced. One where knowledge and confusion increased exponentially. One where notions such as success and failure, will and sloth, appearance and reality, freedom and responsibility, the public and the private, the moral and the immoral, the mental and the physical, replaced the simpler guiding notion of fun. At the centre of these changes was a new ache, that of sexual need, and a new loneliness — deep, bottomless it seemed, pure torture. Puberty for me was a path unmarked by signposts or sudden illuminations. I thought I was the same as always, absolutely the same, until I realized that I no longer enjoyed playing with toys quite so much, or being with my parents all the time.

I wonder, for example, when I took my last shower with my father. When was that precise last time that we alternated being beneath the showerhead? That we passed each other the soap and the shampoo? That we stepped out together and dried ourselves? All without thinking about it. The progression from nudity to nakedness was slow and imperceptible — but there must have been that last shower, that border that would not be crossed again.

The direction of my gaze changed. Questions no longer sprung from me like arrows from a bow — Why is the sky blue? Who wrote the Bible? Why do elephants have long noses? There were mysteries on the inside, too. I began to look into mirrors. At first I would busy myself with the unavoidable externals: the clogged pores of my nose, the pustules on my forehead, the curls and waves of my hair. Then I would truly look at myself; that is, I would look at my eyes, those repositories of the soul. Behind those little black holes — who? So much flux. Was it like this for everyone?

I discovered my body. Till then my mental and physical selves had been in such harmony that I had never considered them separately, or as separable. The two were as integrated as they are in Rodin's *The Thinker* or in Roger Bannister and John Landy's Miracle Mile. But now my mind's vessel began to show signs of waywardness, to reveal that it could deliver unexpected pains and pleasures of its own making. The result was a more complicated, multifaceted "I", with more mouths to feed, more needs to tend to.

Solitude became a pleasure. There are certain moments of adolescence that are beyond the grasp of words. You are quiet, you are looking at a field, say, or a row of books in a library, when suddenly things appear sharp and precise, and there is a tinkle. That's not the right word. What I mean is, because of your youth and overarching vitality you have tricked life into overlooking you, and you have crept up on it from behind and you are near its heart and you can hear its heartbeat. It's not a roaring throb you hear but something very quiet, a gentle quiver to the field, to the row of books, something so quiet that it is more visual than aural, the merest shimmer. This heartbeat brings no words to your mind, but you feel an expansion; doors open in your head onto immense empty rooms and your mind exclaims, "Heavens, this place is bigger than I realized!" So while the furniture is the same as the moment before, the house of your mind has suddenly expanded fourfold. This is what I mean by tinkle, by shimmer, by heartbeat: a vague awareness during adolescence that vitality is outstripping comprehension.

I monitored the growth of my body hair. These tokens of maturity first appeared on my lower legs, anklets of manhood on a child's body. It seemed that the hormones triggering this growth had to battle gravity, for it was only after these dark shoots had crept some distance up my legs that they appeared on my pubis. Then they sprouted on my chest, three, four hairs in the centre of my sternum. Next, the benign blond hairs that I had in my armpits were supplanted. Only after this did my cheeks join in. Lastly, the hormonal elixir touched the top of my head. Throughout my childhood my hair had been thick but easy enough to manage. I have memories of my father working me over with a comb, with tugs that eventually overcame knots, one "Ow!" for every jerk. The jerks weren't really painful; it was just another way to bug my father. But with puberty, by slow degrees, my hair began to curl and wave and kink. It became an unruly mess.

I took pleasure in my developing hirsuteness. Hairiness was beautiful, it would suit me. The hair on my chest delighted me the most. I wanted my chest to be thick with hair, so thick that I had to comb it. I remember an ad I saw in comic books, next to the mail-order sea-horses, for a soap that was claimed to promote hair growth. I dreamed of sending for it, and never did only because I didn't know how to pay for it through the mail and I was afraid my parents would catch me. In time my chest did grow hairy, though it never achieved the thickness I yearned for. But my stomach, at least, gave me satisfaction.

Starting at age fourteen, I began to shave. It was more pre-emptive than necessary; the hair growth on my face has never been spectacular. Not for me the flowing beard of Charles Darwin or Karl Marx, or the magnificent moustache of the mad Friedrich Nietzsche. My upper lip and my cheeks produced many trees but never a forest, and I needed to change my axe only every few months. But I enjoyed shaving — this manly ritual of splashing warm water on the face, lathering the shaving cream to a frothy white sea and then scraping it off in short, clean strokes with a gingerly held razor. It was a form of recollection, and had a soothing effect on me. I shaved one to four times a week, depending on my mood.

Acne. The word belongs to adolescence. Like the anxiety of virginity, it is something most adults hardly remember.

I remember.

Acne was the lowest circle of hell that I visited during my adolescence. Large, flaky pustules that were at first no more than external curiosities — a little mould on the surface of a fresh cheese — persisted, and then multiplied like hydras till they invaded me on the inside, like gangrene in the body of a young soldier, like bubonic plague in a sunny town. The horror of acne was what it did to my image of myself. It was a rot of ugliness that attacked a boy who had till then thought himself beautiful.

The disease seemed to have favourite areas. My cheeks were nearly always spared, my forehead not. The rot seemed to prefer my right temple over my left. My nose suffered. My chin. The edge of my upper lip. The area below my jawline was a real battlefield. To add further humiliation, my skin was terribly oily, with a glowing film. Throughout my adolescence, two, three times a day, I cleaned, rubbed, scrubbed my face with a pumiceous, highly abrasive soap product. Away oil, away dead skin, away acne! I would pat my face dry with a towel. For a brief hour or so, until my skin began to ooze oil again, my face would feel dry, expressive, presentable. This cleanser — the version marketed for adults is for washing motor oil and the like from one's hands — is an excellent product, and I would recommend it to anyone who wishes to erase his or her face, as I wished.

Dermatologists — when I finally allowed my condition to be acknowledged and discussed — were consulted and I religiously applied their expensive creams and swallowed their expensive pills, to no effect. I treated myself. Clogged pores were quickly dispatched, their corks of blackness squeezed out. Large yellow pimples I relished, for they were easy to remedy; with my fingers wrapped in toilet paper for a better grip, I would nudge and squeeze each offender until it broke with that minute tearing sound of exploding pus. Pus, clear liquid and blood would be wiped away; all that was left was a tiny crater, a little red around the rim, nothing more. Soon it would disappear (not soon enough!) But not all my pimples were this easy. Many were red, not yellow, their lava of putrefaction not yet ready to erupt. They would simmer on my face, angry, lumpy, disfiguring. I would squeeze them anyway, hoping to accelerate the volcanic process, which would only make them angrier and redder.

It was not uncommon that this disease reduced me to tears. I informed myself about *acne vulgaris*, but talk of hormonal imbalances and dietary co-factors did nothing to appease me. The humiliation and ugliness were too great to be explained away by biology.

But there was splendour, too. At a time when many of my classmates were losing interest in their studies, I awoke to them. I was lucky to have several good teachers at my high school, who kindled my intellectual interests. Because I had a good geography teacher, I became interested in geography. The same with Latin, history, biology and mathematics. I began to read voraciously. I blossomed in the regimental order of organized education. In slots of forty-five minutes, without effort, I consumed centuries of accumulated knowledge in the sciences and the humanities. Mesopotamia struggled to fertility, the Roman Empire grew and shone, the Dark Ages blew the candle out, the Middle Ages flickered, the Renaissance blazed, the Industrial Revolution roared, the world fought twice, the Germans killed six million Jews, the United Nations was set up, the moon was trodden upon, and onwards, onwards — it was all there in my notes. Artesian wells, plate tectonics, Caesar's invasion of tripartite Gaul, the Treaty of Westminster, Krebs' cycle, Vasco da Gama, quadratic equations, the Domesday Book, Huckleberry Finn, Edward the Confessor, Tycho Brahe, the neolithic period — none hid their secrets from me.

These were the years of two seasons: summer and the sacred September to June school year. Everything fitted into this cycle.

Jesus Christ carefully had himself born and crucified during the holidays. Queen Victoria chose another such day for her birthday. Surely Alexander the Great stampeded across Asia on weekends only. Nothing disturbed the grand march of the school year — or only the occasional dental or medical appointment, when I would stare with incomprehension from the taxi at all the people in the streets. What were they doing out like this? How could they stand the loitering? I would hurry back to dissecting frogs and Shakespeare, back to doctors Banting and Zhivago. I saw my life as a straight, upwards staircase, with education as my handrail. After the usual academic landings — B.A, M.A, Ph.D; Toronto, Oxford, Harvard — I would start my climb for the ultimate landing: the prime-ministership of Canada.

I wasn't settled on which constituency I would represent — my sentimental favourite was Jack London's Yukon, but it was so far away; I liked the word "Algoma" and it was Pearson's old riding — but my address was certain: 24 Sussex Drive, Ottawa. While waiting to move in, I honed my political skills by reading anything relevant, usually biographies and autobiographies, but also Hansard, parliamentary committee reports, Royal Commission reports and the like.

Question Period, which I attended as often as I could, was the highlight of my apprenticeship. I revelled in this theatre of power, this heady mix of principle and posture. I never sat in the Public Gallery, at one end of the House of Commons above the Speaker and the parliamentary reporters; the view was not very good and it was noisy with groups coming in and out. Instead I obtained passes from my Member of Parliament, borrowed a tie and jacket from my father and sat in one of the members' galleries, which are on the sides of the House — one side reserved for the governing party, the other shared among

Her Majesty's Loyal Opposition and the other parties. Since the MP for my constituency was Progressive Conservative, I always sat above the Liberal government benches, facing the Conservative opposition. I was therefore more familiar with the performances of those without power than those with it. An arrogance of Prime Minister Trudeau's I would witness only from the back of his head, but the convulsions of indignation, the shouts, the pounding of desks, the gibes, heckles and taunts that were barely within the bounds of parliamentary decorum (and sometimes not) that it provoked I would get full front. I loved these men without power, whether official opposition, New Democrat or Social Credit. I was as fast as the Speaker himself in identifying So-and-so standing up for attention as "The Honourable Member for Winnipeg North Centre", or Esquimalt-Saanich-The-Islands or Missisquoi-Brome.

Of these hours perched in the Members' Gallery during Question Period, what struck me most forcefully about the opposition — which had legitimacy but no power, or only the power of words — what has stayed with me to this day is that no matter the pitch of emotion in the House, the din of howling, the cries of fury and resentment, the shaking of fists — and sometimes it was no pretence, sometimes the smugness of men of long-standing power is enough to leave one bereft of articulate expression; once I saw a book flying through the air, hurled by a red-faced member overcongested with his impotence — no matter the decibels or the state of near insurrection, except for the words of the one member who had the official attention of the House, this overflow would all go down in Hansard as:

Some hon. members: Oh! Oh!

These shorthand compressions of emotion jumped out at me whenever I came upon them. They conjured up in my mind all the rage and hurt of disenfranchised men. I modelled myself after these members of the opposition. Their rage became mine. Everything would be different, I vowed, when I got to power.

So you see, when you are a good student and a future prime minister, you can be happy at times despite your acne and your adolescent gawkiness.

TEN WHO SEIZED MY IMAGINATION:

(1) Sir Edmund Hillary, to name only one of the many mountaineers who awed me with their devotion to the beautifully useless, despite the price in fingers, toes, eyesight, even lives — a New Zealand beekeeper who was the first man to reach the summit of etc.

(2) Neil Armstrong, who etc.

(3) The Second World War and her brood of heroes and villains, all there in black and white photos and colour movies to fascinate every boy of my etc.

(4) John Dillinger, dashing gangster of my fancy, who despite sensing his doom and breaking into a run from the woman in red who had accompanied him, betrayed him, was gunned down coming out of a movie house by agents of the etc.

(5) J.F.K., who lived in my mind the day he was etc.

(6) Linus Pauling, the only man to win two whole Nobel etc.

(7) Bobby Fischer, victor of Reykjavik, who though awkward, inarticulate and of uncertain intelligence, nonetheless had a wizardry about him that etc.

(8) Yukio Mishima, who terminated his life in a most spectacular way (*seppuku*, the traditional samurai suicide of self-disembowelment), after taking over an army base with his

own private army and addressing the soldiers about the decay of Japan, having finished that very morning his last etc.

(9) Sacco and Vanzetti, who, despite world-wide appeals for clemency, were etc.

(10) Miguel Hidalgo, whose impassioned call in 1810 for Mexican independence is considered the starting-point of his country's struggle to break away from Spain. This call has become known at *El Grito* — The Shout — and Hidalgo is always portrayed in paintings and sculptures with a clenched fist, fiery eyes and his mouth wide open. It is this vision that struck me — that strikes me still — that of a man at the centre of his country, far away from any sea, who has had enough, more than enough, and who tosses his head back and lets out a shout so long and so loud that it rolls across every plain and down every valley of his country, and in all the towns and villages people hear this strange cry and turn their heads to listen to it. Miguel Hidalgo was arrested by the authorities and summarily etc.

There is another strand, intertwining with the physical change strand, the acne strand, the prime minister strand. Perhaps it started earlier, but I wasn't aware of it. For me, it started on my first day of school in North America.

I'm not sure whether it was more the fashion of the time, the mid-seventies, or my parents' personal liking, but at that age I had rather long hair, nearly down to my shoulders. Had I been a trailblazer I could have flaunted a ponytail. I didn't think anything of my long hair; nor did my classmates in France. I recall no more than occasionally being mistaken from behind for a girl by Parisian shopkeepers.

But in North America, I discovered quickly and brutally, girls could have their hair short or long, though most had it long, but boys, boys I say, could only have it short. The first day of school, within the first minutes, just as I sat down, the class clown came up to me and asked me if I was a boy or a girl. I said flatly that I was a boy, but my response didn't register, or even matter, since he was not really asking a question so much as making a comment which elicited the desired chuckles and snickers from the class. The teacher called us to order. As the boy turned away, he spat out a word. "Faggot!" At recess I heard it again, and another, "Fag." When I learned the North American meaning of the epithets, I was dumbfounded by the hostility behind them.

If a friend of mine in Paris had confessed that he was in love with a Simon or a Peter, I would have compared notes with him on my love for Mary Ann. Gender in matters of love struck me as of no greater consequence than flavours in ice-cream. I imagine the absence of religion in my upbringing was one factor that had allowed this belief to survive. Perhaps, too, I had a natural openness in the matter. At any rate, it was completely unwittingly that I had disregarded this fundamental polarity of North American society.

In the years that followed I began to get my hair cut shorter and shorter. I didn't do it in one dramatic operation, which might have instantly salvaged my emerging manhood in the eyes of others, because I was too young and self-conscious to be so daring and — isn't life a series of difficult choices? — because my unmanly long hair helped hide my acne. Despite the social cost, without hesitation, I chose homosexuality over acne.

From that first day of school onwards, fear and misery were a routine part of my existence. With them came a feeling of confusion. It was not over this bigoted division of desire;

that was easy enough to deal with. With a monstrous coldness I could have thought, "The Nazis didn't like Jews, the KKK don't like blacks, North Americans don't like homosexuals," and that would have been the end of it. A socio-political observation and a consequent adjustment in dress and deportment. A tidy act of conformism. What prevented me from fitting in so nicely was that none of the symbols or attributes of this loathsome bent seemed original. They all derived from a single source. Long hair, gentleness, an eye for beauty, a longing for boys — these were plainly terms that described *girls*. So except for the fact that they were female, girls looked and behaved *far* more homosexual than I. Yet they were not condemned for it, seemingly, while I was. He — Jim — would taunt me, shove me, terrify me over my long hair and putative desire for boys — "You faggot! You faggot!" he would hiss — while next to me sat one who had long hair and would soon desire a boy. She — Sonya — would always come to my rescue, hurling shrieks and taunts at Jim.

I sought guidance where I could. At one point I turned to the French language, which gave me the gender of all things. But to no satisfaction. I would readily agree that trucks and murders were masculine while bicycles and life were feminine. But how odd that a breast was masculine. And it made little sense that garbage was feminine while perfume was masculine — and no sense at all that television, which I would have deemed repellently masculine, was in fact feminine. When I walked the corridors of Parliament Hill, passing the portraits of my future predecessors, I would say to myself, "*C'est le parlement*, masculine. Power, it's *le pouvoir*." I would return home to *la maison*, feminine where, as likely as not, I would go to my room, *la chambre*, where I would settle to read *un livre* masculine, until supper. During the masculine meal, feminine food would be eaten. After my hard, productive masculine day, I would rest during the feminine night. At one time, for a few days, I even took an affected aversion to being in the kitchen, *la cuisine*. As I entered it I would put on a disdainful expression and say to myself,

"Les femmes font la cuisine ici, mais pour moi, une cuisine, c'est un endroit où Robert Kennedy se fait tuer."

"Women cook here, but a kitchen, to me, is a place where Robert Kennedy gets killed."

But this is nonsense. I write it to be truthful to the moment, but it is nonsense. Not far from my house in Ottawa there was a large field, a vast, rolling expanse of grass. Often I would go there alone and lie down, angel-like. I would look up at the male yellow sun and the male blue sky. I would turn and smell and feel the female green grass. Then I would roll over and over and over down the incline till I was dizzy, mixing up the colours and the genders. I felt neither masculinity nor femininity, I only felt desire, I only felt humid with life. Sometimes — no, more often than that — often, I would crawl to the edge of the field, not like a soldier at war but because I liked the feel of the grass rubbing against my body, and I would lie on my side and masturbate onto the bushes, delighting in the shooting arc of my sperm and the way it splattered against the dark green leaves and dripped heavily while I wiped myself ineffectively with soft green shoots.

A word about Jim. Adults are so confident in the authority of the law and the power of its enforcers that they tend to forget that criminal jurisprudence does not apply to children. Such legal niceties as "libel", "theft", "assault and battery" are no comfort to a thirteen-year-old boy scared witless of another thirteen-year-old boy.

I doubt I can fully convey the degree of fear that Jim inspired in me. No one made my heart stop and then beat at triple speed, no one made my blood freeze, the way he did. I avoided him at all costs. If that meant eating lunch in hiding, if that meant running home — running, I say — right after school, so be it. I realize now that one shocking punch would have tilted the balance of power, but I was a physical coward. It wasn't anything reasonable that made me so afraid, fear of a broken tooth or a bleeding nose. It was fear of confrontation itself that paralysed me.

Sonya told me that girls could be cruel too, and she looked at me meaningfully. As an example, after I had prodded her one time, she confessed that once she and some friends had been in the school bathroom when a girl from a younger grade had come in to pee. They noticed that in her cubicle she had let her skirt drop to her feet instead of lifting it around her waist, something, apparently, that only little girls did, not mature girls like them. So they started laughing about it and mocking the girl, and knocking on her cubicle door. The girl wouldn't come out. They stayed the whole lunch hour, until a minute before class. Cruel indeed, I thought. Poor little girl. Surely the last time in her life she ever dropped her skirt to her feet. But another voice in me was saying, "Where are the animal noises? Where's the water thrown into the cubicle? Where's the spitting? Where's the attempt to get at her skirt and rip it to shreds? *Where is the assault on the person?*" I told Sonya that once a boy was yawning and another boy who was passing by, for fun, spat into his etc.; that once a group of boys were attempting, for fun, to stuff a boy into a locker and had nearly managed it except for his left foot and gave up only because they were afraid his hysterical shrieks might attract the attention of etc.; that once a boy was standing in the school corridor and another boy who was passing by, for fun, kneed him in the groin and continued walking without a break, laughing at the fluid grace of his gesture while the other bent over in pain and loudly burst into etc.; that once a boy came back to his locker to find that another boy had poured urine into it through the etc.; that once a boy didn't eat lunch for an entire week because every day another boy terrorized him into giving him his lunch bag, which he would go through, eating the brownies, throwing out the rest, until he tired of this fun and etc. I told these and other stories to Sonya, pretending that they had all taken place in the third person. She frowned.

I never saw a boy strike a girl. An unspoken rule against it. Certainly not any rule of not picking on one weaker than oneself; that was the norm among boys. Perhaps it was a logical consequence of desire — one doesn't beat what one wants. Not at that age, anyway.

Once at the McDonald's near the school, at an unhappy moment of tension, I stood in front of the washrooms with Sonya, sweet Sonya. MEN said one door, WOMEN said the other. I thought, "No, no, this isn't right. It shouldn't be this way, not MEN, not WOMEN. It should be FRIENDS and ENEMIES. That should be the natural division of things, one that would better reflect reality. That way Sonya and I could go together through one door, and the others through the other."

Let us return to the sea. Though for girls it seemed considerably less than a thrill, and certainly never an aesthetic or transcendental experience, I was always fascinated by the female menstrual cycle. I don't recall when I first learned of its elements. I think they entered my mind in odd, disconnected bits and it was only after I had acquired a fair knowledge that I suddenly realized the beauty of this monthly blood-letting. It struck me that there was nothing in the human drama so patently fertile as this ability to bleed vitally. I saw it in vivid contrasts of colour. Red from white, red from black, red from brown. That the menses of women who lived together, of the same generation or not, in the same bedroom or not, two or a boarding-schoolful, should become synchronized, like musicians who strike up the Jupiter symphony once they have finished tuning their instruments, was a source of deep wonder to me. I felt there was a latent unity among women, a unity for which I could find no equivalent among boys, try as I might. We were orphans among sisters. A girl could fight and be nasty, mock and degrade, pour forth pure venom from her mouth, cut herself off from everyone — yet still be connected by that melody of blood. Whereas if I cut myself off, I was truly alone. With nothing to tie me to the rest of life except my stubborn stupid metronome of a heart. The controlled randomness of the cycle — that periods could vary in length, in flow, could stop, even, depending on a myriad of factors; that ovaries worked together yet idiosyncratically, one ovulating three times in a row while the other remained idle — reminded me of the physics I was learning: the Big Bang Theory, Newton's laws, the Theory of Relativity, the Heisenberg Uncertainty Principle. Science teachers explained these as referring to the vast cosmos beyond, as if they could so easily disguise what was plain to me: the principles of the female cycle were those of the universe. The cosmos was out there, and next to me. Sadly, I was beyond this universe, outside it, in the vacuum of vacuums, at most able to contribute a few white comets of sperm.

Sonya's cycle became an affair between the two of us. We went through the entire female hygiene section of a drugstore once, the only time in my life that I can remember looking at commercial products labelled in English without understanding what they were for. When she had cramps and wanted to go home to bed right after school, I would go with her and lie beside her until her father came home. I thought that if only I could understand the menstrual cycle, this slow, balancing ballet of hormones, this one mystery, I would understand everything. My curiosity became a starvation. I asked question after question of Sonya. In the calm, thoughtful way that was hers, she tried to oblige me with answers. Menstrual cramps in particular baffled me. I knew of cramps from swimming, in the calves, but there, in the lower abdomen — I could not comprehend it. In my body that area was a dull crossroads of organs: legs joined trunk, my intestines sat in the bowl of my pelvis, the bladder filled and emptied and on the edge hung my scrotum and penis. About as unknowable as a suburb. Certainly not the temperamental cornucopia of independent personality that Sonya lived with. I would ask her to describe her cramps to me. Her hands on her belly, looking up at the ceiling, her eyebrows knit, sometimes suffering from a touch of fever, she would try. "Well, it's like...um...a pulling. Or a tearing. It tears. It's like a . . . um . . . a cramp. It's a cramp." We always came back to that word, precisely accurate to her, utterly meaningless to me. I could only observe, making sure that the wet hand-towel on her forehead was fresh.

She once showed me a tampon she had just pulled out of herself. From its white string it dangled in the air between us, like a mouse held by its tail. Her face bore an expression of total disgust. I looked on quietly at this compact cylinder bright with blood. I brought my nose to it. Sonya's expression went up another notch of disgust. A smell of iron! I was amazed. I had no idea. The earth itself. Pure Promethean rust. I stuck my tongue out, but Sonya gasped and pulled the tampon away. She turned and tossed it into the toilet bowl and flushed, and I watched it disappear in the vortex of water.

I took to sports and exercise at puberty in tandem with my discovery of masturbation. If my body could deliver such pleasure, it was worth cultivating. Over the years, in addition to the simple activity of walking, I have practised swimming, judo, cycling, squash, tennis, running, cross-country skiing, climbing, hiking and canoeing. But the exertion that gave me the greatest satisfaction during my teen years was weight training. Even before I saw my first weight room, I used to lock the door to my bedroom and place two volumes of encyclopedia on my back and strain my fourteen-year-old body to five push-ups. When I saw the muscle room at the YMCA I knew instantly that these machines would assure me a body much better than Britannica could. I eyed with envy the men who were in this room. They had such smooth, bulging muscles. I watched their power pushes and their power grunts. In the showers I spied on their beautiful bodies.

I began to venture into weight rooms, at first waiting till a machine was free, absolutely free, before daring to use it. If a man happened to come up unexpectedly, I would finish quickly and scurry away. He would move the weight pin from the one or two lead bricks I managed to push to the twenty or thirty he could handle.

But I persisted and my confidence increased. I learned the proper ritual, never failed to do my twelve to fifteen minutes of stationary bicycle, did the number of repetitions that would build muscles of a spongy bulk, always exhaling on the exertion. I became familiar with weight-room etiquette, with my rights and responsibilities. There was never a machine that I didn't carefully wipe with my towel after I had finished with it.

My ambition was large: I wanted a body, and especially a chest, like the ones I saw in the showers. I worked all round, devoting particular attention to my pectorals, deltoids and abdominals. The result was a chest that pleased me — not large, but well proportioned and nicely shaped. Only my legs seemed irretrievably thin, however much I exerted my quadriceps and calves.

I never saw girls in the weight rooms that I frequented, and rarely women, but this didn't surprise me. It was only boys who had to create their bodies through strenuous efforts. Girls, it seemed, acquired theirs naturally. Only later, at university, would I see women pushing weights.

I must say that I have never regretted these hours of slow sweaty exertion. I forgot my acne and my other woes and I looked down on a body that felt to me lean and nimble, strong and supple. There's a tightness of frame, a lightness of foot, that you feel when you are fit — it's wonderful. Every pound I lifted, mile I ran, hour I skied, lap I swam, every limit of my physical capacity I pushed, I felt that I was reaching for life, that it was all expanding not just my lungs or this or that muscle, but my very vitality. A feeling much less powerful

than, but still akin to, what I felt when I gushed sperm into
tissue paper.

My discovery of the sin of onanism was fortuitous. I was alone
in my room, a volume from a series on sexuality in my lap, my
penis in my hand. The volume was the fourth and last in a series and was intended "For Late Adolescents". I suppose the
authors strove to be didactic and clinical. Nothing doing. My
imagination turned the book into racy erotica. Every significant word — penis, erection, vagina, breasts, penetration —
danced in my mind like an obscene stripper. My favourite
cross-sectional diagram was of The Man and The Woman
doing it. They were reduced to their relevant essential parts,
the rest being mere outline, and I loved the snug fit of those
parts; not only were the vagina and uterus in cross-section,
but the penis and testicles also, so the connection between the
testes and the ovaries was direct, clear and leakproof, something that pleased the plumber in me. I also gazed at length at
the cross-section of The Erect Penis, magnificent in its size
and intent. My favourite frontal diagram was of the female internal parts, that unmistakable triangle of uterus with flourish
of fallopian tubes and ovaries, a soothing shape I still see in
vases with wilting flowers, or beasts and their horns. When I
read of the *Voyager* space probe, which would drift off into
the infinity of space after exploring Jupiter and Saturn and
which bore a plaque for the possible perusal of alien eyes, I
thought that, in addition to the greetings in a hundred and
fifty languages, including whale language, and the various scientific data, NASA should have added this anatomical Golden
Mean, perhaps a little simplified, to say, "We are the people of
this shape."

I am straying from my point. At the age of which I am speaking, I went through this volume with wide open eyes and a beating heart and not a thought about the befriending of space aliens. I mention words and various diagrams that jumped out at me; these were only a prelude. What opened my eyes the widest, made my heart beat the hardest, were the photos. Black and white, headless, artless, bodies that could only be called ordinary — these photos couldn't have been more clinical had they been of corpses in a morgue. Still, the nudity of these boys and girls, men and women, excited me deeply. To this day I remember the Adult Woman; I only wished I could see her face. I was sorry there wasn't a single shot of an erect penis, adolescent or adult. I longed to see this pure expression of male desire, still couldn't quite believe that such an extraordinary thing could be.

My pleasure at this stage was visual. Occasionally I brought my penis into the show, pressing its softness against a picture that I particularly liked, but usually it was a simple by-stander, no more. If, of late, I had involved it more in my enjoyment of the book, it was only because its new, slow growth of dark hairs made it more interesting to me. There was still no real connection between it and the pictures.

But one day my hand happened to start a to-and-fro motion with my foreskin. I don't know where the idea for this came from. I was not searching for anything, and I had certainly not received any advice. It was a common act of genius.

The motion was distinctly pleasurable. I continued it, somewhat increasing the speed. Rapidly I had a taut erection, a new state of affairs. But I didn't stop to consider it. A strange physical tension, a compelling ache, drew me on. "This is quite something," I thought, breathlessly, not knowing what I was doing, where it would lead.

I lay back on the bed. I half-closed my eyes. "Oh, this is *really* quite something."

Faster still.

Then, in a spasm of physical tension, a response both fresh and ancestral was triggered by my body for the first time. A sort of convulsive exaltation overcame me, a rapture that pulsed through me in five waves, each one cresting in an explosive white gush from my penis.

When it was over, I stared, drop-jawed and astounded. The stuff was all over my hand, my shirt, the book, my face, my hair, the wall behind me. It had a smell, a colour, a stickiness like nothing I had ever seen.

I had *no idea* such pleasure was possible. My God, how could it be a secret?

For a fraction of a second I wondered if this was normal. Quickly the thought vanished. If this was abnormal, then I was joyfully bound for the nether depths of abnormality. I looked again at the sperm-splattered book. Its authors suddenly became great, winking jokesters, going on so seriously about human reproduction. I laughed. So this was part of it. What a truly wondrous thing! Positively unearthly. A revelation. No wonder the earth was overpopulated.

I cleaned up meticulously, though I could do nothing about the wrinkled spots on the page where the sperm had had time to seep in. I put the book back in exactly, precisely the position I had found it. I went to take a shower. This matter would have to be researched further, investigated, pursued. Why, right now, in the shower.

Upon my discovery of masturbation the universe once again split into two. There was the human and there was the ecstatic. The task was simple: to accommodate the two. All my life I have sought to do this. Mostly I have failed.

I met Sonya at a time when I was still hugging the walls of the school corridors, hoping to be invisible. Classes were just over and I was nervously on my way to being happy away from school. My hand was reaching for the bar of the double metal doors, for freedom, when I heard a breathless question behind my back.

"You speak French, don't you?"

She was a girl in my grade but in a different class. She had short brown hair and brown eyes and a very slight down moustache. She was a little out of breath. She must have been running to find me.

"Yes, I do."

She smiled and diverted her eyes. "Gem le frawnsay. Say la ploo bel long doo monde."

Amidst the Anglophone intolerance that reigned in the capital of my country during the years I lived there, where those who spoke two languages were despised by those who spoke only one (and poorly at that), she was the only person my age I met who saw French as an oral alchemy, able to gild instantly the most ordinary, leaden communication. That I spoke the language fluently turned me in her eyes into a magician of the highest order. Upon her request, commenting on the weather, I would say, "Le temps est très froid," and through this alternative way of saying things I would transform the reality of the nasty cold weather and she would warm up to it. Her own French, beyond her simple declaration of love for it, was atrocious, mired as it was in a quagmire of tortured syntax, criminal grammar and non-Gallic vocabulary. But I am thankful Sonya didn't have better teachers or more practice, for if she had she might have been less enamoured of the language and we might never have met.

"Oui, c'est vrai, elle est   "Yes, it's a beautiful
belle," je répondis.   language," I replied.

I don't recall what else we said that day, but we must have said more for I left the school happier than I had been in weeks and months, knowing her name and knowing she was my friend.

One of the happiest moments of my adolescence was the first time Sonya called me. I had called her earlier but she wasn't home. I nervously left a message with her father, who didn't seem pleased at the notion of a boy calling his daughter. I was convinced she wouldn't call me back. When the phone rang a little later in the evening and my mother said, "It's for you," my heart jumped. "Hi, it's Sonya," came a voice from the receiver. I barricaded myself in my room and we talked for two hours.

We went on long walks, weekend peregrinations through Ottawa, often to Parliament Hill, where we would examine the statues, or look over the river from behind the Parliamentary Library, or try, as we did once, to get into the Langevin Building, where Prime Minister Trudeau had his offices; or along the Rideau Canal and then Sussex Drive, past the War Museum and the Royal Mint, into that windswept, wide-open space just after the curve in the road, where one catches from a height the dazzling sweep of the Ottawa River, and beyond, past the Department of External Affairs, past City Hall, to reach 24 Sussex Drive, where we would peer between the metal fence-posts, trying to see the house, hoping to see movement in spite of the vegetation; or in Rockliffe, neighbourhood of the rich and diplomatic; or on the grounds of Rideau Hall, official residence of the governor-general, which grounds were at the time still open to the public; or to various museums, the one I remember best being the Museum of Science and Technology, especially the room built at a 30-degree angle from the horizontal with the furniture all out of proportion — the point being to jar our notions of perspective — where Sonya and I laughed and laughed and laughed. And all the while, during all this walking, we talked.

After she was gone I went on these same walks on my own, but I had not realized how much of their pleasure lay not in the historical sights or in the exposition of a great future political career, but in the company. I missed Sonya terribly. The statue of D'Arcy McGee, one of the few Canadian politicians to suffer the apotheosis of assassination, now left me indifferent. I wandered through Laurier House, home of Sir Wilfrid Laurier and William Lyon Mackenzie King, without looking at a single photo. Though I did not catch it at the time, this was my first hint that I was not suited for public affairs, that my interest in politics would never extend beyond a constituency of one.

Sonya's mother had died when she was little. Her father, a tall, balding, bearded man who worked for the Ministry of Agriculture, was strange and Catholic, Catholic and strange. He had promised his only daughter five thousand dollars if she never kissed before getting married. As older teenagers we might have laughed at this lucrative interdict and disregarded it, or our hormones might have overwhelmed us; in either case, we might have done something and then lied about it, but as obedient young teenagers she took it seriously and therefore so did I. We shared our every thought, we held hands in secret, when we lay in bed we lay very close to each other, feeling each other's heat — but kissing was out of the question. And since the touching of lips and the greeting of tongues are the doorway to the house of passion, we sat meekly on the threshold.

I felt no frustration over this since I still did not make the connection between the human and the ecstatic. They ran parallel. I loved Sonya, as she loved me, and it came out in our words and in our closeness — and then at home I indulged in my secret pleasure. Only once she was gone did I start to dream of linking one with the other.

Things came to an abrupt end. An unexpected offer of a promotion for her father, but not here, far away, and right now — an alacritous response in the affirmative — and suddenly Sonya was moving to British Columbia. School had just ended and we had thought we had the summer. The last time we saw each other in private, we cried openly in each other's arms. She kissed me on the side of the mouth, coming perilously close to giving up five thousand dollars and her lease on a wisp of cloud. We made plans for the future, desperate definite plans. Then she was gone.

I cried in my room. I became snappy and aggressive with my parents and isolated myself from them. I wandered about the house, the neighbourhood, the city, but found nothing to make me happy.

Salvation, if it can be called that, came through an eating disorder of sorts. It was in early August. The weather complemented my mood: it was hot and heavy and I was bored and listless. I had embarked upon one of my regular exploratory forages through the house, hoping to discover something new, something forbidden, something exciting. My parents, having moved so often in their lives, didn't tend to accumulate things, and my expeditions usually yielded nothing either new or exciting. But this time I was richly rewarded. In a cluttered corner of the basement, in three stacks, I came upon forty or so old *Playboy* magazines. Catching sight of these magazines made my heart stop. I had never gone through one, but I knew well enough what *Playboy* was about. My father had been a reader in the late sixties, when the magazine seemed to be in the spirit of the times, a time of great music and stormy politics, sunshine and Vietnam. The magazine was full of polemical articles on this or that, interviews with the likes of Fidel Castro, Barry Goldwater, the leader of the American Nazi Party (interviewed, deliberately, by a black reporter), opinions by U.S. senators, profiles of various personalities, short stories by incredible writers — Nabokov, Updike, Böll — round tables on various subjects, photo essays, and of course pictures of young women whose nudity seemed to symbolize the Age of Aquarius. A few years later, when times changed and *Playboy*'s claims to be at the forefront of sexual liberation and other good things appeared dubious and it began to acquire an unsavoury reputation, my father stopped reading the magazine. But he had never thrown out his old copies, and so they lay dormant until they exploded into my life. For this was exactly the impact they had on me — an explosion. As I reached for the closest one, feeling like Ali Baba as he entered the den of the forty thieves, Sonya faded from my memory. By the time I caught sight of the first picture, with a thrill that whistled through my mind, she was forgotten. These pictures, these magazines, would be my companions.

Thus was I introduced to that poisonous Western concept: the beautiful female body. Thus did I start my ingestion of naked paper women. I was always in mortal fear of being found out by my parents, so it was a secret, paranoid activity, performed with my ears cocked for the least signal of their unexpected early return from work. In direct contrast to the headless, colourless bodies from the volume on sexuality, which gave my imagination the minimum fuel with which it could fly, the pictures in *Playboy* sent me sky high. These disrobed young women displayed a beauty that was truly incredible to me, yet there they were, smiling, laughing, prancing, looking pensive, speaking of themselves and their families, of where they lived and what they did, of their favourite books, singers and movies. That these monthly beauties were from the American sixties, from an era that seemed so colourful and momentous, gave them an added degree of attraction. I ogled not only their breasts, but their hippyish ways and dress, their lingo, their politics. Masturbating while looking at these young women was far and away the most powerful, sensuous experience of my adolescence. I remember how one time, after a particularly intense moment of gratification, I came up from the basement and stumbled outside. I was in a daze. I lay on the grass, looking up at the sky. It began to rain, at first gently, then with the unfurling waves of a storm. I didn't move, but stayed there till I was soaked through and through and my teeth were chattering.

My desire went in cycles. Sometimes I would spread out several magazines and masturbate compulsively, as much as three times in a row. Like a sultan going through his harem, I would flip through the *Playboys* searching for just the right smile, just the right breast, to push me over the edge. As I got to know my Playmates I became pickier, flipped longer. At other times I felt bloated with overconsumption; it came with a feeling in my stomach, a pit of solitude. Then I masturbated to a single picture, or none at all, using only my imagination.

In this erratic hunger for paper women — I want many! I want none — I might have perceived the real poverty of my diet, an intimation of what it was doing to me, but the pleasure was too great. It's the way I see myself then: I binged on paper women, stuffing my mouth, then I vomited them out violently. Can you see a boy on his knees over a toilet bowl, a finger down his throat, vomiting pictures of naked women? That's me. A boy suffering from pictorio-sexual bulimia. Although, in truth, that's not the way it went. At the time, I ate. It was so good, so amazingly good. It's now that I vomit. Now, when I see pornography, I am instantly seized by nausea. It's beyond my control. My stomach flips and my mouth waters unpleasantly.

I was busy (there was school, there was exercise, I read books and saw movies, I watched plenty of television — no longer an enemy but the companion of my lonely hours — there were my furtive minutes of ecstasy, there were all the moments of anguish, idleness and discovery that make up adolescence), but I would say that my busyness took none of my time, for the one thing that truly consumed me was emotions — and my consistent approach was to shy away from the greatest source of these emotions.

In the lineup at the school cafeteria, Carolyn once got close to me and pressed one of her breasts against my arm in a way that penetrated even a shyness as obtuse as mine. I feigned not to notice, then masturbated about it at home. Some time later, when I first saw her holding hands with Graham, I felt all the pain of dashed love. When they languorously kissed by their lockers for minutes on end, eyes closed, heads gently moving, I pretended to be busy at my locker but in fact stood there in cold misery. She was so pretty, Carolyn, as pretty as a Playmate. I knew well enough the pleasure she could give as a picture, but what I wanted was the pleasure she could give in person, her soft lips pressed to my lips, her glossy paper body pressed to my body.

If you'd asked me then what love was, I would have replied in terms of a deep, upsetting beauty-hunger, with at its centre, the tang of it, lust; and I would have said that love was my favourite emotion, though I was far less familiar with it than I was with desolation and frustration.

In 1979, at the age of sixteen, I entered Mount Athos School, an all-boys boarding school. This unexpected turn of events came about because the powers that be had decided that there was a need for more women ambassadors, and so my mother had been plucked from relative juniority and appointed Canada's representative to Cuba. My father, who by then was sick of the civil service and gladly accepted a golden handshake, was going to run from Havana his Ediciones Sin Fronteras/Editions Sans Frontières, which would specialize in the two-way translation of Quebec and Latin American poetry, an affair of little profit but great love. But the rub was that there was no secondary school for foreigners in Castro's republic. Thus, with funding from the Department of External Affairs, the un-Canadian option of boarding school presented itself.

My parents were heart-broken at the idea of being separated from their son, but I jumped at the idea. *Boarding* school! It set my imagination on fire. What an adventure it would be!

I passed the stone and iron gates of Mount Athos on a sunny September afternoon. I had a trunk and two suitcases, I had a name tag in bright red letters tirelessly sewn onto my every item of clothing by the ambassador-designate to Cuba, I had three new blazers, a smart new trench-coat and a fine selection of my father's ties, I had bright hopes and great expectations.

The vista that offered itself as we drove up the long, curving driveway was promising: expanses of green lawns and playing fields bordered by great leafy trees, a well-integrated assortment of grey-stone and red-brick buildings, some old, some new, a number of neat gravel paths, a chapel with stained-glass windows, and one large stone cross in the centre of the grounds; and the village we had just come through was one of the prettiest I had seen in central Ontario.

My room, my new home, was a perfectly symmetrical arrangement of two cupboards with drawers, two beds, two desks and two wrought-iron windows with a third-floor view, from atop a hill (the said Mount Athos), of a rolling apple orchard and, in the distance, Lake Ontario. I was assigned the right half of the room. This parcel of territory delighted me. I tested the bed. In my hand I had a thick manila envelope containing all sorts of information on the school, omen of further promise.

I felt my life was beginning.

I don't have fond memories of my two years at Mount Athos. As a school it was good enough. We learned our calculus and biology well, that sort of thing. But what I mainly remember is the climate of disrespect that pervaded the institution, a disrespect that often descended into emotional savagery. Just about the only delicacy I can trace to my Mount Athos days is the fact that when I pass through a door I hold it open for anyone coming through behind me.

TWO REASONS WHY I HATE MOUNT ATHOS SCHOOL:

(1) I asked Gordon, the returning boy who was showing me around, what my roommate was like. "Croydon?" he said. "Oh — he's nice." But in saying this he looked away. I should have taken note. Instead I rolled this odd name around in my mouth, taking a liking to it, already considering it that of my best friend.

Gordon's reply contained another sign of things to come: the propensity of boys and masters at Mount Athos to call the boys by their last names. For Croydon was a surname, and Croydon was Croydon, not John. The intimate first name disappeared, was reserved for only the best, closest friends. To others one became an impersonal last name, like a brand name, a turtle with a word painted on its shell, a wall with a single window too high to look into.

As I was sitting on my bed, reading the information in the envelope, two boys came in carrying a trunk.

"Are you Croydon?" I asked the first, a smile on my face. He had a sharply featured face and sandy hair.

"No, he is," he said with a smirk, jerking his head towards the other, who laughed. They dropped the trunk and left.

A minute later, the first boy, the one I had spoken to, returned. He opened the trunk and started unpacking it. He didn't say a word or even throw me a glance.

He was Croydon.

He didn't want a roommate. He had asked for one of the few single rooms in Baxter House. He didn't get it. He got a double room and me.

One day we were in our room, each at our desk, back to back, studying for a math test. From the corridor, not loud but coming through, we could hear Kleinhenz and another boy arguing. I suppose Kleinhenz *was* a little pompous and disdainful. The argument was not acrimonious or even personal — I found out later that it was about the merits of different systems of education, and that Kleinhenz was quite satisfied about the excellence of his native German *Gymnasiums* — but it was enough for Croydon to grab the garbage can, walk out, throw the garbage can at Kleinhenz's head and start punching him in the face. Thus would Croydon make him pay for his accent, with the personality it suggested! Kleinhenz put up as good a fight as he could — he brought up his fists in the classical stance of boxers and danced about — but though he was taller and had a greater reach, he was fifteen years old to Croydon's seventeen, and even if things had been otherwise equal he lacked Croydon's hard edge of nastiness. With every punch that met its target, my roommate took increasing pleasure in the contest. It ended when Kleinhenz unexpectedly turned and fled down the corridor. My image of him will always be of the multicoloured mask of abuse he wore for days afterwards: the greenish-blue rings around his eyes, the red welts on his cheekbones, the purple cuts on his lips.

Like the other boys, including the one with whom Kleinhenz had been having the argument, I did nothing but watch the fight, mesmerized by its violence. Not the first time, and certainly not the last, that I would display moral deadness at Mount Athos.

That was Croydon. Not a rogue element at Mount Athos, but a rogue in his element.

(2) I remember McAlister. There were three classes of boys at Mount Athos. There were the elites: the top athletes, the best students, those with a certain charisma, those with famous last names — these could do no wrong. The institution coddled them, humoured them. Beneath these elites floated a slightly oppressed but complacently content middle class, the average element in contrast to which the elites could shine, the spectators who did the clapping and cheering. Lastly, there was a class that was lower and marginal (though it paid exactly the same astronomical tuition fees). These were the "zeros", the nobodies of Mount Athos, those who were unable to fit in for whatever reason — a curious physical appearance, a social awkwardness, an ineptness of one sort or another.

I was a zero. My acne and messy hair advertised it, my petulance confirmed it, my French name sealed it. Only my good marks and the cachet of Madam Ambassador My Mother placed me in its upper echelons.

But McAlister of the stupid face and the cheap blue suit — he was the zero of zeros. He suffered unremittingly. His ego must have been shattered so many times that I can't imagine he ever managed to put it back together again, like all the king's horses and all the king's men with Humpty Dumpty. That's how I see McAlister: a boy with broken eggshells in his head.

They used to whip him viciously with wet towels; he stopped taking showers after sports, waited till evening, when he hoped the showers would be clear. They dumped fresh garbage into his bed. They shit on his books and notes. They threw buckets of cold water on him in bed at night when he was asleep, something that was done to me several times. Once he ordered himself a pizza and it was taken from his very hands as soon as it was delivered; he later found the anchovies on his pillow.

I never saw such an unhappy boy as McAlister, poor Andrew McAlister. May his sufferings be memorialized here.

ONE REASON WHY I LOVE MOUNT ATHOS SCHOOL:

(1) On a class trip to Toronto we saw an exhibit at the Art Gallery of Ontario called "Turner and the Sublime". I have never forgotten it. We had a guide and we heard the usual art history blather, but I paid no attention to it, for these paintings spoke to me directly. The show consisted of oil paintings and a small number of watercolours. Though I can't recall any one work in particular, I vividly remember the effect of the whole. I looked upon mountains and gorges, lakes and ruins, meadows and streams, each landscape tinged with such colour, infused with such light, that I indeed felt a sense of the sublime, a sense that has never left me, that has given me my one rough axiom of aesthetics. These vast canvases, probably smaller in reality than the imprint they left on my memory, made me feel powerfully, durably, that beauty has meaning, that beauty *is* meaning.

FOUR MORE REASONS WHY I HATE MOUNT ATHOS SCHOOL:

(3) There was the institution of "gitching", which consisted in holding down a boy, reaching behind to grab his underwear and pulling it until it ripped. Alas for the boy who had quality underwear that did not rip easily. This action was

prefaced by the long shout "Giiiiiiiiiiiiiiiitch!", which would make the intended victim turn in terror, and was perpetrated to a barking chorus of "Gitch! Gitch! Gitch!" Funny to all except the younger or weaker boy who was the target of this gang attack. It went around the school, with chortles of laughter, I tell you, when it was discovered that McAlister, that shadow against the wall, no longer wore underwear.

(4) There was huge, fat Wilford, who, on a lark, threw me to the ground and sat on me. I can still remember the compression of my chest, the horrifying sensation of my organs being squeezed and pushed about. I struggled to keep breathing. But boys and masters — this was in the dining-hall during lunch hour — seemed to find the sight of a mouse of a boy squashed under an elephant of a boy very amusing, right out of a cartoon, perhaps. I remember that when he got off me and I could sit up, my face very congested, my thoughts confused, feeling faint, the only sound I heard, other than my heart pounding in my ears, was laughter.

(5) There was the night when the light was suddenly turned on in Karol's and my third-floor room — this was in second year; I had changed houses and roommates — and I awoke to recognize Croydon and his gang standing around my bed, all of them wearing pillowcases over their heads with eye-holes ripped in them, in the manner of the Ku Klux Klan. If I had had three seconds' warning, I would have seriously considered jumping out the window, trusting the lawn below and my ability to grab tree branches to cushion the blow. But they were hunting for Preston, thank God, and they were just checking to see if he was hiding in our room.

Preston was nowhere to be found. He spent that night, as he had others, hiding beyond the football field, behind trees, two suitcases in his hands jammed with his schoolbooks, class notes, clothes and other valuables, ready to skulk away should the gang start roaming the school grounds. Which they didn't. They merely sacked his room, upturning the furniture and destroying anything he had left. He forgot his calculus notes in his room and had to use Karol's to study for the final exam. But the theft and destruction of material objects, that was routine at Mount Athos, banal, not even worth going into. We were a community, a tightly knit brotherhood — so why should we be allowed to lock the doors to our rooms? Of what spirit of distrust, of suspicion, would this speak? Such was the noble philosophy of the institution, whose masters walked around to the jingle-jangle of the keys with which they made secure their apartments, houses, offices and cars.

(6) Indignities were dished out by masters, too. I recall one who, when asked in class what "pusillanimous" meant — the word was in a book we were reading — looked around, landed his eyes upon me, and said, "Here, this is an example of pusillanimity." The class, though still no wiser as to what the word meant, burst into laughter.

ANOTHER REASON WHY I LOVE MOUNT ATHOS SCHOOL:

(2) The setting. Such a constant, daily beauty — I was there two autumns, two winters, two springs; I have mentioned the expanses of green grass and the great oak trees and the stately old buildings and even Lake Ontario, but I forgot to describe the shimmering jewel of a little river that coursed through the area — such a beauty would have a durable echo in even the most brutish mind. And the school was a small, self-contained community; within it, away from the forces of disrespect, took place unforgettable moments of friendship. I

remember the midnight munchies with Karol — making toast and peanut butter, scrambling to pull the battery out of the smoke detector when a burnt toast set it off. I remember the two of us walking to the river on a green spring day of such clarity I can't tell you. We slipped into its calm waters and swam downstream with it, just two heads moving along the surface, insects skimming by, the swaying trees filtering the sun, fish dimpling the surface of the water. It was magic, pure magic. We could have swum like that to the Pacific. I remember a bunch of us playing "brick" in the pool, the brick in question being made of rubber and fitting perfectly into the pool's excess-water trough, thus giving us our ball and our goal. I remember jogging down to the lake in the dead of winter and discovering the accumulations of snow and ice along its shore and scrambling over them to get dangerously close to the open water, to death, and staying there for an hour, thinking about my parents, turning to see Holt-Royd, a boy two grades below me whom I knew only slightly, standing just behind me. "I thought you were maybe going to jump in," he said. With calm and simplicity, we talked.

It is memories such as these that explain the legions of Old Boys who, to their dying day, donate money to the institution, with the McAlisters and Prestons at the forefront of these nostalgics, as if pain and humiliation were the seeds, and time the water, of the plant Amnesia.

ANOTHER REASON WHY I HATE MOUNT ATHOS SCHOOL:

(7) When disrespect is a climate and a system, it becomes contagious.

I remember standing about and watching as a group of boys gitched and did I don't know what else to Preston, who

struggled like a fish out of water. I watched with a degree of satisfaction, because Preston really was a jerk. I felt the same when his room was wrecked yet again.

The real reason why I hate Mount Athos School is that I was the one who put the anchovies on McAlister's pillow.

"Ante todo, el viento y el ruido. Aquel día el mar estaba como un espejo sin nada de viento. Yo estaba remando. Oí algo como un grito, un grito de niña, no más, y al darme la vuelta ví un inmenso chorro de llamas viniendo hacia mí. Cayó del cielo azul como un volcán. Vino un viento para dejar sordo, apabullante, como el último suspiro de Dios. Tenía el color de una naranja. Aquello me echó del barco, el ruido tanto como el soplo. Pensaba morir de calor pero me salvó el agua. Nadé hacia la barca, temblando de miedo. La vela estaba en pedazos. Un trozo de algo se estaba quemando, clavado en la popa. Segundos después vinieron las olas. Enormes olas de agua ardiente. Era el

"First there was the wind and the noise. That day the sea was as flat as a mirror and without a whisper of wind. I was rowing. I heard what I thought was a scream, a little girl's scream, no more, and I turned to see an enormous flaming streak of colour coming towards me. It fell down from the blue sky like a volcano. There was a deafening, roaring wind, like God's last breath. It was orange. I was blown clear off my boat, as much by the noise as by the wind. I thought I would die of heat, but I was saved by the water. I swam back to my boat, shivering with fright. My sail was in tatters. A piece of burning matter was lodged in the stern. Then, within seconds, came

infierno. La barca estaba en llamas. Una ola apagaba el fuego y la otra lo volvía a encender. Yo gritaba y gritaba y gritaba. Me tiraba al agua para salvarme y después me salvaba otra vez subiendo a la barca. Apenas si podía respirar. No podía ver más allá de las llamas. Ya le digo, era el infierno. El infierno. No, no me acuerdo de donde venían las llamas cuando el avión estaba en el cielo. Era un humo grís oscuro, con hebras negras. Olía a petróleo y a gazolina. Y la madera de la barca que se quemaba. No, no pienso que ha sobrevivido nadie. Nada más que cosas flotando en el agua. Me gustaría irme ya, por favor."

the waves. Huge waves of burning water. I was in hell! My boat was on fire, one wave putting out the flames, the next setting everything on fire again. I screamed and screamed and screamed, one moment saving myself by throwing myself overboard, the next saving myself again by clawing my way back aboard. I could not breathe, I could not see beyond the flames. I was in hell, I tell you, in hell! No, I don't recall where the flames came from when the plane was in the air. The smoke was deep grey, with wisps of black. The smell was of gas and oil. And the burning wood of my boat. No, I don't think there were any survivors. Only things that floated in the water. I would like to go now, please."

My parents' death was witnessed only by an old man and the sea. I was told that when the old man could no longer answer questions, he fell to his knees and shut himself in prayer.

Padre nuestro que estás en el cielo, santificado sea tu

Our Father, who art in Heaven, hallowed be thy

nombre. Venga a nosotros tu   name. Thy Kingdom come,
reino, hágase tu voluntad en   thy will be done on earth . . .
la tierra . . .

It so happened that we were studying *The Old Man and the Sea* at that very moment. I reread the book not long ago at the Saskatoon Public Library. My reaction was a blend of blankness and upheaval, for my memory had mixed the work of art with my parents' death. I can't see a plane crashing into the sea. The noise, the colours, the burning, the scattering of bodies and luggage — it's beyond my imagination. But I can see a large fish tethered to the side of a skiff. I can see it being attacked by sharks and other fish until nothing is left. I can see Old Man Santiago climbing up the beach, carrying his burnt mast like a cross, still cursed, still *salao*. Sometimes I have to scold my memory and remind it that my parents did not drown, their bodies found by a fisherman, but died in a plane crash, their bodies found by no one.

It was near the end of September. My second year. I had left them three weeks before, having spent the summer in Havana. The headmaster's secretary interrupted our geography class to say that he wanted to see me. As we headed for the administration block, the secretary said nothing to me except when we walked through the courtyard, at which point we could briefly feel the day.

"Such lovely weather, isn't it? Still so warm," she said.

"Yes, yes," I replied eagerly, paying attention to the weather for a moment.

She knew; I guess she wasn't supposed to say anything but wanted to say something.

The weather was cloudless for Nativity; if not, the Wise Men wouldn't have found their way. Though it is not recorded by Matthew, Mark, Luke or John, I am convinced that Christ on the cross must have considered the weather during his agony — the heat of the day, the desire for a breeze, the passing of the clouds. Everything during his hours of agony must have been constant — his pain, the mockery of the soldiers, his Father's neglect — except for the weather. And so in talking of the weather, this topic of conversation as familiar to our speech as air is to our lungs, we talk of everything, for the weather, having witnessed every joy, every tragedy, is a mirror to all our emotions. In alluding to the Indian summer, this secretary was saying to me, "I'm sorry for you, you poor, poor boy."

I was surprised to find my aunt, my mother's only sister, with the headmaster. I knew her only slightly; she was a Christmas acquaintance. She had driven from Montreal. There was also a man I didn't know. My aunt was the person who informed me of my parents' death, in French, in the presence of Anglophones who probably didn't understand what she said but knew what she was saying. I don't recall her exact words. Later that day I also heard of their death over the radio. The man was from External Affairs. I was told that my life would not change, that part of my parents' pensions would go to me, that they both had good life insurance plans; in short, that the material aspects of their love would continue. In time I would receive various official papers attesting to this, and regular dollops of money. I would meet on three or four occasions with this man from External, who was in charge of my case. As for emotion, I was a spectator at its theatre. I sat there taking it calmly, nearly indifferently. My aunt was quite broken with pain. The official and the headmaster spoke gently. All of them expected me to burst into tears. But I strove to show them that I could handle it, that I wouldn't cry because I was an adult. The only thing that moved me, I recall, was that for the first time ever the headmaster was calling me by my first name. I suddenly felt deep gratitude and affection for the man — surely a minor case of the Stockholm syndrome.

I was asked whether I wished to return to Montreal with my aunt after the funeral. The reasons why I might want this, and the length of time they had in mind, were left unstated. No, I said. The year had just begun, I was in a new house with a new roommate — not the Boston Strangler this time, but Karol, my best friend — there were classes to be attended, assignments to be done, pieces of toast to be burned at midnight — I had a routine, I did not want it disturbed. My life, as they said, would not change. But I would go to Montreal for a few days. I walked back to my room to pack my suitcase.

My parents didn't have a religious bone in their bodies so there was no church service. But there was a ceremony at a funeral home in Ottawa. Since my father had been an only child, the family consisted of precisely three people — actually, two and an in-law: me, my aunt and her husband. Still, there were so many people — friends who were colleagues, colleagues who were friends, friends who were friends, acquaintances, former neighbours, writers, poets, editors, official representatives from External Affairs, including the Secretary of State himself, representatives from the Government of Cuba, a slew of Spanish-speaking ambassadors — there were so many people that slowly the street became clogged with parked cars, and then with people, so much so that it became impossible to drive through and someone called the police. The police looked around, asked what the crowd was for, took note of the Secretary and closed the street, with a police car parked across its entrance. I remember the policewoman who listlessly waved her arm at cars so that they would not turn into the street.

Everyone had loved my parents. They were the perfect friends, bosses, colleagues, subalterns, contacts. An ambassador from Latin America who looked like a warty toad with hornrimmed glasses went on at such lengths about my mother's perfections, ending with the one that was clearly closest to his heart, that she was beautiful — "pero liiiiiinda!" — that I got the impression he would have ascended instantly to toad-heaven had my mother kissed him. A secretary told me that my father had been the best, most considerate boss she had had in thirty-two years at External Affairs, and that she had heard my mother was even nicer. A Cuban somebody, with three aides to help him, handed me a letter. It was a handwritten condolence from Fidel Castro saying that his loss was double, for "he perdido a una amiga que representaba a un país amigo" — I have lost a friend who was the representative of a friendly country.

It pleased me, these great numbers of people, these tributes personal and official. So much grief expressed by others seemed to lighten my grief. As if it were measurable in kilos, and all these people took a little load until I was left with only a few grams. I avoided looking at the two caskets. The worst thing about them was that I knew they were empty.

In many ways I denied my parents' death. When one is an adult, one's parents' deaths are usually a slow, waning process, first one, then the other, and these are a painful reminder of one's own mortality. They are death echoing death. But I was still fully imbued with that quite stupid, invincible thing called youth. My parents' sudden, foreign deaths struck me not as the tolling of a bell, but as another stage in my ever-expanding, metamorphic life.

A further mitigating factor in my callous resilience was my environment. Grief and tears were incongruous at Mount Athos because the place in no way reflected my loss. There was little difference between Mount Athos the boarding school and Mount Athos the orphanage. In fact, the orphanage turned out to be a better place. Suddenly, previously indifferent masters began smiling at me and taking interest in my studies. Suddenly, my enemies and bullies began holding themselves at bay. I became untouchable. That year at Mount Athos was my best.

I remember Thanksgiving, for example. My aunt's clumsy attentions had been unbearable and I didn't want to return to Montreal so soon. I decided, quite happily, to spend the long weekend at empty Mount Athos with Karol and Michael, who lived too far away for the trip home to be worthwhile.

But no, that wouldn't do for a boy who had lost his parents so recently, thought the school. And so, because of me, the three of us were put in charge of Mr. Broughton's house, hardly two kilometres from the school, while he was away with his family. He had animals — donkeys, sheep, goats, chickens, a cat named Shakespeare — which we had to feed. It was in giving the donkeys straw that I discovered that straw and hay are not synonymous. I liked the way the chickens pecked at their grain, in motions that were so quick, robotic and precise. We went for long walks along the shores of Lake Ontario. Mr. Broughton's stone house was crammed with that careful clutter of material objects that only sedentaries can accumulate, that breathes life into a home even when there is no one there. Mr. Broughton had several prints by the Canadian artist David Blackwood, haunting scenes of the hard, sometimes terrible life of Newfoundland fishermen and their families, engravings that were scratched out in fine lines of black and white with only the occasional, vivid use of colour — red for a house burning down, for example. One night we carefully unhooked the Blackwoods from the walls, brought them to our bedroom, lit up the room with candles and stared into them until we were practically hypnotized, feeling that we were the ones who were shipwrecked and lost, starving to death on a lifeboat, or running up a hill to our burning house. Shakespeare stayed docilely in my arms the whole time. I had a wonderful four days at Mr. Broughton's house that Thanksgiving, every moment intense and memorable.

And anyway, what was I supposed to do? Cry in front of other boys? Cry in the arms of masters who had only recently acknowledged my existence? Was I thus to strain my new untouchability?

When I thought of the tragedy that had struck me, I would think, "They died together. This strikes me as very important. It gives their lives a completeness, an unshattered wholeness, with no messy debris. And they died quickly, which means painlessly. And they led happy, successful lives. I'll never see them again, but I'll remember them and talk to them in my head. That's nearly as good."

I burst into tears under the head of a hot, noisy shower a number of times, but mostly I relegated my grief to the dark basement of my consciousness, there to swim about and have the effects that Freudians will delight in surmising.

As Trinity term started, the last term, I realized that I was nearing the end of the assembly-line of education. This dawning of freedom felt more oppressive than liberating, but I dealt with things quickly. I dismissed the hundred million things that a soon-to-be 18-year-old boy could do with his life and decided to continue with my formal education. After poring over university calendars in much the same way I had pored over boarding-school brochures, I made my choice of three Ontario universities and carefully filled out the computer-friendly standard applications. My freedom securely restricted, I felt better.

You don't get much mail when you're a single child with no parents. Every day I saw boys with fat letters in their hands or, worse still, parcels under their arms. I stopped checking my mailbox. Why open it when all I would see would be an empty universe, when all I would hear would be a great sucking empty sound? The person in charge of the mailroom was an amiable, chatty woman by the name of Mrs. Saunders. Every week she had a boy assigned to her who helped her sort through the mail at lunch-time and place it in the mailboxes. When my turn came up, I asked to be excused from the duty.

It was the sensitive issue of mail that sparked an incident that I wouldn't mention if it weren't that it was on that day, in the evening, while masturbating in the shower, that I first noticed that my erection was smaller.

A letter from my aunt, short and not very interesting, really, but precious nonetheless, had been found by the groundskeeper in a bush, postmarked three weeks earlier and already opened.

I found Mrs. Saunders and asked her what boy had been working for her that week.

"Three weeks ago? Let me see . . . that was Arthur."

"Who's Arthur?"

"Arthur Fenton."

Fenton?

A word about Fenton: he was an odious little twit. In the protracted armistice that was declared about my person after my parents' death, he was the one breach. I hated him viscerally, as he did me. I believe our relationship truly embodied the cliché "personality clash". Immature, affected, arrogant, spoiled — no one liked him. He should have been a real zero, a Christian in Croydon's Roman circus. But Fenton was untouchable too: his parents were filthy and famously rich. (They visited the school once, chauffeured Rolls-Royce and all. Their little Arthur trotted along on one side, the endowment-seeking headmaster on the other. Looking at Papa Fenton, at his expensive suit that made his flabby paunch and weak shoulders look smart and sharp, at his silk tie-knot so crisp and impeccable, loudspeaker of his power, I suddenly understood the Pol Pot urge to be expeditious, the quick-fix joy of red terrorism, the Joseph Stalin adrenalin rush. Ah, to have had a Kalashnikov and to have mowed them down!) Fenton would have had to set Bill, the headmaster's basset hound, on fire before the headmaster would have cleared his throat at him.

But I didn't care. I wasn't afraid of him — he was no Croydon, I was stronger than him — and this was it. I was going to rip his eyelids off, I was going to tear his ears off, I was going to break every bone in his body with a hammer, I was going to — I left the mailroom, my face red, my head throbbing.

Imagine this play:

DRAMATIS PERSONAE:

INSANE RAGE, *a seventeen-year-old boy*

ANNOYING IMMATURITY, *a seventeen-year-old boy*
MINOR CHARACTER, *a seventeen-year-old boy*

SCENE: *a staircase*

(Minor Character *is to one side of the stage.* Annoying Immaturity *is coming down the staircase. When he is at a small landing,* Insane Rage, *holding a letter in his hands, appears on stage, and sees* Annoying. *He bounds up the stairs, stands squarely in front of him and blocks his way. The exchanges between the two are in tense, angry voices, but with no shouting.*)

INSANE RAGE (*showing envelope, glaring at* Annoying): What's this? Why did you take it and open it?

ANNOYING IMMATURITY: I'll take full responsibility for it.

INSANE: I want to know why you took it.

ANNOYING: I'll take full responsibility for it.

INSANE (*placing his hand on* Annoying's *chest and slowly pushing him against the wall*): Don't *ever* do it again.

ANNOYING: Just watch it or I'll punch you across the room!

INSANE: Yeah, right.

(Insane *steps down to the stage floor.* Annoying *follows him.*)

ANNOYING: Rage, you're an asshole!

(Annoying Immaturity *punches* Insane Rage *in the face and turns to leave.* Insane *takes hold of him and brings him to the ground, though* Insane *remains standing.* Insane *looks at* Annoying *but does nothing.* Annoying *gets to his feet.* Insane *looks at him but does nothing.*)

MINOR CHARACTER (*interposing himself*): You guys should cut it out.

(*Exeunt omnes.*)

CURTAIN

I couldn't hit him. For all my fury, against all my expectations, I could not hit him. Placing my hand on his chest and pushing him against the wall, which was only a foot or so behind him, was as far as I could go. I stepped down the stairs — moved away from him — because I was so confused. Even when he punched me in the face — and to be struck in the face is to be struck in the soul; it's an attack not against a provincial stomach or leg, but against your very capital — even then I could not hit him. I thought, "I can hit him now, I have the right." But all I could do was bring him down to the ground. Not throw him down, not push him down — bring him down, with the guiding help of my arms. Once on the ground I noticed that his head was near a radiator and I thought, "If I hit him in the face with my knee, his head will strike the radiator." But I could not. As he was getting up I thought, "I can easily kick him now." But I could not. When he was standing I thought, "I can hit him now, he's standing, it's fair play." But I could not. Then it was over.

I went to sit in the chapel alone. I was both dazed and elated. *I couldn't hit him.* What an amazing discovery! How incredibly unexpected! Suddenly I no longer resented Fenton. I thought of him carefully, went over my worst moments with him, encounters that had left me seething, that had launched me on sessions where I tortured him elaborately. I glided over these moments without feeling even a ripple of annoyance.

In the days that followed I was careful to avoid him, but within a week he no longer perturbed me in the least. I said goodbye to him on the last day of school.

That night after our confrontation, just before lights-out, I took a shower and indulged in my secret pleasure. That's when I noticed it. I was certain that the motion of my hand had greater amplitude before. But then the thought slipped my mind — my orgasm was such that I thought I would faint. My legs wobbled and only by leaning against the shower wall was I able to stay on my feet. By the time I had recovered, my penis was losing its stiffness and I was ready for bed.

Graduation day came, at last and so soon. I watched all the parents. I walked about the whole school to have a last look at everything. I *was* sick of the place. A slippage in my marks right at the end of the school year reflected this. I nearly failed physics. And I did not participate in the usual festivities of a high-school graduation.

But after Mount Athos, what? For all its flaws, for all the misery, it was the only organized home I had. I sat quietly in my room, bare now. I took in the washrooms: the long row of sinks, the toilet cubicles, the showers down whose drain so much water, soap and sperm had flowed. I looked at the classrooms, the gyms old and new, the various playing-fields, the decrepit pool, the squash courts, the dining-hall, the chapel. I stood near the stone cross and took it all in. Memory is a glue: it attaches you to everything, even to what you don't like.

My choice of university, ironically, had come down to the one closest to Mount Athos, half an hour away, but where the fewest of its new Old Boys were heading: small, congenial Ellis University. So my September was certain, and I was looking forward to it. But on that graduation day it gave me little comfort. The intervening summer opened up at my feet like a chasm. What to do with it reminded me of the question of what to do with my life.

I stepped into my aunt's car and saw Mount Athos School disappear in the rear window.

I felt totally ill-prepared for life.

My aunt lived in a Portuguese neighbourhood of Montreal, with Portuguese restaurants, stores and travel agencies. A few days after arriving, I happened to stop and look at one such agency. It was much like every other one I had seen: it looked run down and cluttered, the back wall was a kitsch stucco composition meant to convey the spirit of Portugal, the furniture and promotional posters seemed to date from the sixties, and the three people at the desks had that overworked appearance the underemployed sometimes have. In the window was displayed a large, colourful map of Portugal, with photos and drawings of attractions linked by black lines to their geographical locations.

What I think decided me was the rectangularity of Portugal. I like rectangular countries, where human will imposes itself on topography. I imagine that if I had been looking at a map of Spain, France or Australia, I would have spent the summer in Montreal. As it was, not needing to work, not wanting to stay with my aunt, without any notion of "finding" myself but simply because of pleasing geometry, a week later I was on a TAP flight to Lisbon.

At first I hated it. Travelling; and alone. In every new town there was a pit of anxiety in my stomach until I found a place to stay, especially if the day was ending (that is, as soon as it was past noon). The idea of arriving in a strange town at night terrified me. It happened once, in Tomar. I walked tensely and quickly, as if I were breaking curfew. After some searching I found what looked like a cheap hotel. I thought that from the desperate expression on my face the manager would charge me a king's ransom, but he surprised me with a reasonable price, and the room was fine. I discovered shortly that the corridor went fully around it, a square corridor around a square room, and that all the room's windows gave on to it; the stuffiness was hot and permanent. But it was shelter. I was safe at last.

In time I became more adept at handling the inevitable practical details of travelling. The pleasures of the day began to push back the anxieties of the night. Portugal is a magnificent little country, the north especially. I have nothing but fond memories of it. As on subsequent trips to other countries, I brought back a rich, redolent knowledge of the place, a masala mix of sights, sounds and tastes, literature, history and politics, personal and public experiences, that I would slowly forget, though talking of it now, it comes back to me — the strange Pessoa, the Alfama, Coimbra, Nazaré, Henry the Navigator, Sagres, Camoens — like a savoury aftertaste. Travelling alone is like an extended daydream. You catch the sights, you watch the people, you admire the scenery, all the while inventing your own company and your own scenarios, on your own time and at your own pace. It's the only way to travel, if you can stand the regular loneliness, which often I couldn't. But thank God there were the easy friendships of fellow travellers, friendships that lasted an hour or three days, a meal or a train ride, that were a gold-mine of travel lore and useful information, that always started with "Where are you from?" and ended, when you felt like turning left, not right, with a simple, honest "Bye."

Then she was looking at me with an intent, open expression. There were no words, but the situation was all the clearer for it. Inexplicably our heads moved towards each other and our mouths collided. Lips adjusted themselves in a somewhat graceless way, tongues sallied forth and touched, then she pulled away and I ran to catch my bus.

Contact had been made. It was my first kiss. Between two buses . . . a walk . . . a small, deserted public garden . . . a girl who smiled at me from a second-floor window . . . who came down . . . a conversation more smiles and charades than words . . . then. . . .

Extraordinary. Like a meteorite.

The smaller my erect penis, the more intense my pleasure. Every morning my chest was itchy. When I scratched it, hairs cascaded onto the bed-sheet.

In Batalha there is a magnificent Dominican abbey founded in 1388 by King João I to commemorate his victory over the Spanish at the Battle of Aljubarrota, which secured Portugal's independence. Nearly in its shadow, I got a room. I had entered a restaurant to ask for directions and the girl at the counter had asked me if I was looking for a room. We crossed the street to a two-storey whitewashed building. The room she showed me was on the second floor at the very end of a corridor and, though it was small and didn't have a view of the abbey, its proportions were pleasing and it was neat and clean and nicely furnished. I also seemed to have the building to myself. I was spared the discomfort of bargaining, for right away her price was good.

I stayed in that room for three weeks, longer than I stayed anywhere else in Portugal.

The room was soothing in its monastic simplicity. It was rectangular, like the country. The door and the window faced each other on the narrow sides of the rectangle, the door dead centre, the window a little to the left. There were precisely four salient features to the room: to the left as one entered, a narrow metal-frame bed with a bearably lumpy mattress that did not shelter a colony of bedbugs; farther along, in the corner, a sink single-minded in its supply of very cold water, from which one could look out the window as one washed; facing the sink, on the opposite side of the room, a creaky cupboard with a speck-led mirror whose ripples distorted one's reflection; and lastly, facing the bed and diagonally opposite the sink, a drawerless table with a plain chair. The walls were of such an austerity that I can't even remember what they looked like. The stone floor was cold except for the small faded patch of carpet, which I moved around depending on where and what I was doing.

I loved this bare room. I would have been perfectly content to live there for the rest of my life.

I spent a good part of my days in quiet domesticity, divid-ing my hours between the bed, on which I read, slept and masturbated; the desk, on which I wrote in my diary (the only time I kept a travel diary. I would throw it out within the year — can't keep track of every moment); the sink, in which I brushed my teeth and splashed water on my face; and the cup-board, on whose shelves I carefully arranged the too many clothes I had brought and in front of whose mirror I stood naked and gazed. My only expeditions beyond my room were to use the toilet; to relish the very little hot water that the shower mustered every morning; to eat; and to visit the abbey, which I did every day. I spent my afternoons in its beautiful cloister, walking around the arcade or sitting under one of the arches, alternately reading my book (Camoens' *Lusiads*) or resting my eyes on the quadrangle with its neatly wild assortment of flowers, shrubs and small trees. Bumblebees buzzed about in the golden light with the serenity of monks. The hours passed, marked out by the shifting lines of shadow — free-floating, intangible clock hands that changed the nature of the cloister with each silent tick.

If I had to think back in terms of *symptoms*, if that's the right word, as if it were an illness, four stand out in my mind:

(1) The creeping up of my voice.

(2) A slight ache in my hips. Walking around the cloister and stretching made it better.

(3) The clearing up of my acne. It got very bad, worse than it had ever been — I got a headache from all the pustules on my forehead, and my throat looked like a turkey's — and then, in a day or two, it vanished completely. Acne, that cursed disease, and its attendant oiliness, disappeared from my life while I was in Portugal, leaving me with a normal, satiny skin. I remember looking in the mirror and gliding my fingers over my new face. Hell was over, hell was over. I could finally look people in the eye. I could finally smile. I was doubly a new person.

(4) A passion for sweet potatoes. Funny how the great transformations of life come with dietary quirks. The restaurant across the street was a small place of no pretence, with a staff of two: the girl who had showed me my room, who acted

as waitress and bartender; and her father, who was the cook. Sometimes I saw the mother, but I believe she worked elsewhere. On the menu was whatever the father found at the market that day and felt like cooking. I quickly fell into the habit of having my meals there, and the three of us developed a friendship of smiles and sign language. I peppered my gesticulations with Spanish. When he found out that I was Canadian, the father decided to have a try at what he thought was North American cuisine.

It was an evening or two after this, as a mere garnish — only for the colour, really — that the sweet potato came. It lay there in a corner of my plate, soft and orange, beside the neat slabs of pork with their dark sauce and the white mounds of mashed potatoes. Had it not been for the friendly, expectant attentions of the two, I might even have left the sweet potato untouched. I had eaten the vegetable before, but I couldn't remember when, and I assumed this was because I hadn't liked it — and wouldn't like it now. But not at all. As soon as I tasted a tiny helping, I burst forth with a loud, spontaneous and wide-eyed "Hmmmmmmmm!" In an instant the sweet potato on my plate had vanished. I had *never* tasted anything so good in my life. I still think of this explosion of savour in my mouth as the apogee in the career of my taste-buds. I complimented the father effusively, emphasizing his deft treatment of the sweet potato. I asked for more the next day, for lunch. I spent the evening dwelling on this darling potato, its bright orange, its creamy texture, its divine taste. I regretted not having asked for it for breakfast. The noontime tolling of the cathedral bell the following day had me salivating like Pavlov's dogs. I asked to have it again for dinner, in greater quantity, please. And then for breakfast.

I ate Batalha out of sweet potatoes. No hors-d'oeuvres, no entrées, no side dishes, no sauces, no desserts — for close to two weeks they were all I had. The locals thought I was bonkers, of course. But I was a foreigner and therefore bemusedly indulged. Some of the most significant, enduring myths — and problems — of this late twentieth century are the misconceptions people have of foreigners and their countries. In this case, I contributed significantly to the misrepresentation of my country. In the minds of Messiao Do Campo and his daughter, Gabriele, Canada and the sweet potato will be for ever linked.

Cela s'est terminé au cours d'une nuit. Je me suis réveillée soudainement. Je ne sais pas pourquoi ni à quoi je rêvais. Je me suis dressée. Tout était confus. Je ne me rappelais de rien, ni de mon nom ni de mon âge ni où j'étais. L'amnésie totale. Je savais que je pensais en français, ça au moins, c'était sûr. Mon identité était liée à la langue française. Et je savais aussi que j'étais une femme. Francophone et femme, c'était le coeur de mon identité. Je me suis souvenue du reste, les accessoires de mon identité, seulement après un bon moment d'hésitation. Ce

It was over the course of a night that things came to completion. I awoke suddenly. I don't know what I was dreaming, why I should have awakened. I sat up. I was confused. I couldn't remember anything — my name, my age, where I was — complete amnesia. I knew that I was thinking in English, that much I knew right away. My identity was tied to the English language. And I knew that I was a woman, that also. English-speaking and a woman. That was the core of my being. The rest, the ornaments of identity, came several seconds later, after

dont je me rappelle le plus clairement de cet état de confusion, c'est le sentiment qui m'est venu après, que tout allait bien. J'ai regardé la chambre autour de moi. Un sentiment de quiétude m'envahit, profond, si profond, à en perdre conscience. J'étais en train de me rendormir. Je me suis allongée sur le côté, j'ai tiré le drap jusqu'à ma joue, et je suis retournée dans les bras de Morphée, le sourire aux lèvres. Tout allait bien, tout allait bien.

some mental groping. What I remember most clearly of this confusion is the feeling that came upon me afterwards, the feeling that everything was all right. I looked about the dark room. A deep sense of peace sifted through me, so deep that it felt like a dissolution. I was falling asleep again. I lay on my side, brought the sheet up to my cheek and returned, smiling, into the arms of Morpheus. Everything was all right, everything was all right.

This happened on a special night. I got up in the morning, stood naked in front of the mirror looking at myself and thought, "I'm a Canadian, a woman — and a voter."

It was my birthday. I was now eighteen years old. A full citizen.

LAST MEMORIES OF PORTUGAL:

(1) Fatima. On May 13, 1917, three children, shepherds, claimed to see the Virgin Mary. She would come back to speak to them the next month on the same day, she told them. They returned to the spot on the appointed day. She appeared again, spoke to them and told them to come again the following month. This went on for four more months. On October 13, the day of her last apparition, the children were accompanied

by seventy thousand people, who witnessed a "miraculous solar phenomenon". A Marian cult became established. Fatima is a major Catholic pilgrimage site, like Lourdes, like Saint James of Compostela. In its essential part, at the centre of the circles of stores selling religious kitsch, Fatima is an unappealing white basilica on the edge of the largest expanse of asphalt I have ever seen. This vast carpet lies unmarked by lines, arrows or directions of any sort. It glistens in the sun, pure and charcoal-black. I found it strikingly beautiful (and if I were a modern artist of means, I would use asphalt as my medium, exploiting its rich blackness, its beguiling friction, its interplay with the sun. Imagine in a rolling plain of Saskatchewan a splendid circle of asphalt. Not a blight of civilization, not nihilism, but the dot of an exclamation point, the other part of which, the upright stroke, would be whoever is standing on the dot — you). The shape is concave, so that there is a rise to the salvation of the white basilica. Into this enormous bowl of asphalt come those who are wanting in a Catholic way. They walk, they shuffle, they hobble, they wheel themselves, they crawl. I saw one aged woman crawl towards the basilica from the very lip of the bowl at the other end, a distance of a good three hundred metres, with two distressed-looking children — her grandchildren, I presume — on her back and the rest of her family walking along beside her. With her gloves and knee-pads she looked like a mountain climber, which, in a way, is what she was — a Catholic mountain climber scaling a summit that my atheist senses couldn't even perceive. As she inched along, she begged and prayed aloud. When she collapsed, which she did at regular intervals, the children toppled over and burst into hysterics and the family fell to their knees in prayer. After a few minutes' rest, declining all offers of help, turning down all requests to desist, she carried on.

Below the basilica, to the left, is a small chapel, the supposed site of the Virgin Mary's apparition. The chapel has a crematorium of sorts into which the devout throw life-size wax effigies of those parts of their loved ones that are a source of suffering. What you see is a gleaming mountain of yellowish body parts of all sizes, all ages, sharply delineated, down to details of wrinkles and hairs, slowly melting and, in melting, moving. A head tumbles and melds at the neck with a leg to form a freakish creature, until the leg buckles. A young boy's chest has three ears. A knee bends to smell a footed hand. Breasts lactate to oblivion. Two male heads are approaching, perhaps for a kiss, until one is crushed by the stamp of a foot. An entire baby lands face down with a loud plop and vanishes in moments, except for his small bum with its cleft, which floats for the longest time. A serious head stands upright and alone and seems to say, "What is happening here will not happen to me," until fate forces itself upon it and it weeps to death. Everything turns to river.

Facing this scene is a discordant choir of true believers, most of them dressed in black, most of them women, who wail, supplicate, cry, pray, harangue, whisper, whimper, sing and move their lips as they continually toss in fresh body parts. Meanwhile, the overseers of the place, the priests, mill about with expressions of comatose impassivity. The last thing I remember before I pulled myself away was a kneeling woman who produced a minuscule ear from her corset, whispered into it and then tossed it into the crematorium, bursting into loud sobs as she did so. Had her baby died of an ear infection? It was Fellini in hell.

(2) Jack, a friendly Californian I met at the Coimbra Youth Hostel and spent three days with. He was a few years older than I, twenty or twenty-one, and bright and shy. He was studying violin and composition somewhere very famous in California, Berkeley or Stanford or something. That's what he wanted to be, that's what he was: a composer. We talked about music. At the train station — he was heading south to Lisbon to fly back home, I north to Porto — he was more bashful than usual. Goodbyes sometimes compress emotions until they burst out in uncontrolled ways, like juice from a squashed orange: Jack hugged me and then made an awkward, halted attempt to kiss me.

(3) Lisbon again, before my return home. I hated arriving in Portugal, I hated leaving it. In the meantime nearly three months had passed. Travelling is like an acceleration: it's hard to stop, you don't want to stop. Change becomes a habit and habits are hard to change. I walked about, exploring the ordinary neighbourhoods of an old European capital. I bought new clothes, figuring that they would be cheaper in Portugal than in Canada. I tanned myself lobster-red on the endless beach across the Tagus. I got a new passport, which turned out to be an easy matter thanks to a not-too-punctilious, locally engaged consular officer, all smiles and befuddlement ("They made a mistake. Do I look like a man to you?" Thank God for my androgynous name. Would that my hair would grow faster). As I climbed the metal gangway of the TAP plane, I turned for a last look at the Portuguese blue sky and I thought, "I'll be back, though not here, somewhere else. China? India? South America?"

Roetown's Ellis University is one of the smallest universities in Canada, with fewer than 2,500 full-time students when I started. At the time, its reputation was somewhat lacklustre. "Easy to get into," was said of the place. "C+ is all you need." It was known for welcoming the huddled masses of poor, mediocre high-school graduates, those who hadn't made the grade of the more illustrious, career-track universities. It was precisely this lack of elitism that attracted me to Ellis. After Mount Athos, I was ready for the Open Air University of Albania. But easy as it was to get into the place, it wasn't easy to get out — with a piece of paper, at any rate — as I would find out through personal experience. Ellis turned out to be a first-rate liberal arts university.

It was arranged on the college system, with three of the colleges on the modern main campus a few miles out of town, and the other two in Roetown itself, two separate mini-campuses in an old (by Canadian standards — 1850) central Ontarian town of sixty thousand.

It was on the doorstep, so to speak, of one of these downtown colleges that I presented myself, tanned and Portuguese-swept, in the fall of 1981. I had chosen Strathcona-Milne (S-M to everyone) because it was the smallest of Ellis's colleges and seemed the most informal and alternative (and perhaps the closest to a family that I could find), which turned out to mean that it was a tossed salad of lit-crit types, theatre types, poet types, budding artist types, earth-lover types, gays and lesbians, and would-be revolutionaries of one colour or another, with a light vinaigrette of marijuana and late nights. The place was a haven of tolerance, exploration and intellectual obfuscation. I loved it.

The college was a mix of constructions ranging from the main building, a stately nineteenth-century mansion that housed the small library, the dining-hall and various offices and classrooms, to five or six 1920s houses that retained the cosy feel of homes despite being converted into classrooms and professors' offices, to a few modernish buildings, mainly residences, including an insignificant, squat yellow thing, a sad tribute to 1950s architecture, that turned out to be my residence — but no matter. Whether I was amidst the flights of concrete of the main campus, in the quaint, oldish, bourgeois constructs of S-M, in the wordless mediocrity of my room, or somewhere in between — on the shuttle bus looking out at the Wade River, for example — I was happy to be here. The constraints of Mount Athos were gone. I was free to be myself, to be what I wanted. I believe this was a common feeling among us zeros, this exhilaration at discovering that we could now be somebodies.

And let me not forget Roetown, to which I hadn't given a thought when I applied to Ellis. It was an unexpected gem, a diamond I stumbled upon on my way to higher learning. With trees, lots of trees, houses built *around* trees, not over their uprooted stumps; and rolling hills for the sake of vistas; and a river which opened up to a beautiful lake while still within the confines of the town; and clear, broad streets; and gabled stone and wood houses, and red-brick factories — architectures varied in purpose and style but always pleasing to the eye, and without the cosmetic fakery of too much money; and weather — crazy to celebrate a town for its weather, but weather that fully participated in the life of the town, like a prominent citizen, like a councillor with visions of civic grandeur, sometimes so savage and cold that you only wanted to peer out at it from the warm side of windows, sometimes so crisp and clear that you felt the landscape was made of glass, sometimes so hot, green and humid, so Babylonian, that you wanted to be naked

— weather in which, for every degree Celsius, there was a light, a colour, a wind, a cloud, a scent, an emotion.

Roetown, of mixed economy, neither boom nor bust, just ordinary times — that is, hard — had a slightly run-down aspect, I suppose. But in a pleasing way, like a man you love who has buttoned his coat up wrong.

I decided to major in anthropology. I enrolled in the department's first-year course and in a second-year introduction to archaeology that was open to first-years.

Psychology's appeal was immediate. Of course I was interested in the workings of the mind.

English literature (The modern period and its roots: Browning, Hopkins, Dickens, Hardy, Conrad, Joyce, Lawrence, Yeats, Pound, Eliot) was a natural choice also.

For my fifth and last course, I hesitated. I went to several introductory lectures during intro week. It came down to philosophy, history or political studies. Curiously, for one who thought herself so political, I struck the politics course from my list first. I listened to the professor attentively, I leafed through the heavy textbook at the Ellis bookstore — but it didn't grab me. Not the macro approach, not the word "system". I preferred staying with the individual.

It was the memory of my mother's hammer that brought me to philosophy (Introduction to: Plato, Aristotle, Descartes, Locke, Berkeley, Hume, Kant, J.S. Mill, Nietzsche).

All these courses, except for the archaeology course, had the same number, nearly proverbial, the starting-point of all knowledge, it seemed: 101.

Residence fees included a complete meal plan — three meals a day for six days and a Sunday brunch, every week.

Ancillary fees covered a pass to use not only the Ellis shuttle bus but the entire Roetown bus system, and open access to the excellent sports centre.

My room was one of the largest in the Yellow Squat Thing Building. One window, one door, one closet, one chest of drawers, one desk and chair, one bed — it was nearly Portuguese. There was a sweet housekeeper, Mrs. Pokrovski, who changed our sheets once a week.

I had pocket money to spare (but remember where it came from. Every movie ticket, every little extravagance, was a reminder of this blood money).

Roetown had a thriving cultural scene, animated not only by the university but by the citizens of the town. Between the two, there was always something happening — a lecture on American cultural imperialism or an American movie at the Imperial, modern dance at Artspace or a minor-league hockey game, Reverend Ken and the Lost Followers or Handel's *Messiah*, Peter Handke or Noël Coward, a Take Back the Night march or a Walking Tour of Historical Roetown, etc. or etc. I say "or"; in most cases I tried to make it "and".

That was the setting, those were the courses, those were the distractions — my student life could begin. I threw myself into it. It was like that of most students, I suppose, only in some ways more active, in some ways more isolated. I usually got up fairly early, by student standards at any rate, and rarely missed breakfast. I never missed lectures or seminars, even morning ones after late nights, for I was a serious student, which didn't mean that I was a good student (I wasn't; I was an intelligent not-good student) or that I started my essays any earlier than the night before they were due, but meant that what I considered, I considered seriously. I quickly became involved in student politics: I was elected first-year representative to the S-M student cabinet and in second year I was elected to the university senate. I joined the swim team and the cross-country ski team, though I was neither a fast swimmer nor a fast skier; I was a slow, graceful swimmer and a slow, graceless skier. I joined more for the fun of being part of a team, and the satisfaction of being fit (the one enduring legacy of my university years is probably my discovery of the most pleasurable part of exercise: the deep breath. To be swimming length after length, non-stop, sometimes not even counting how many, only aware of the incantation of my breathing and the splashing rhythm of motion, was a kinetic form of meditation). And I had many friends. They were mostly friends of circumstance, true — I haven't kept up with many of them — but the circumstances were good.

Despite this activity, I often felt lonely, more so as time went by. My life was a busy kind of solitude, much motion with little emotion. Elena played a major part in this feeling, but there was more: the beginning of a certain *mal-de-vivre*. Hardly had my university career started than it began to go awry. "Existential crisis" would be the name of the syndrome, but I will not dwell on it. Angst is not much of a peg to hang things on. We all go through it, we all cope with it, or try, so why talk about it? I say this though I think my case was bad enough, a befuddlement such that no degree of reasonableness could assuage it; or no more than whispering reassurances would calm a freshly captured, terrified monkey. I saw a documentary at Ellis once in which scientists — I believe that's what they were called — played the recorded sounds of a fire burning and then of river water rising to a caged monkey, to test its instinctive fear of both. The recordings started very low, barely audible (but already the monkey was looking alarmed), and ended at full volume. It struck me as fairly self-evident that turning down options like being burned to a crisp or having only water to breathe didn't require much more than a slug's intellect let alone the nimble wits of a monkey. Indeed, when the sounds were at their loudest — a roaring forest fire, a roaring torrent of water — I have never seen such an incarnation of pure fear. It was not the cowering in a corner, the trembling paralysis, the rapid panting, the sudden release of urine and excrement — it was the look on the animal's face, its silent, open mouth, the rolling of its eyes. When my academic career was derailed, when my nebulous but ambitious future dissolved, when I clutched for any sense of meaning in my life, I thought of this monkey. But it doesn't make for interesting reading, I'll be the first to admit it.

I quickly lost interest in anthropology. I found pre-Columbian New Mexican pueblos magic in my imagination but dull in reality. Their study was like a reverse form of undertaking, where the bliss of death is shattered by a reanimation leading to a paltry, diminished life. Civilizations were reduced to monographs with precise drawings of floor plans and cross-sections of pits indicating where each artifact, each pot shard, each bone was found, with dry academic paragraphs surmising the tribe, the linguistic grouping, the level of artistic achievement. Like saying "My grandmother — she was an extraordinary woman," and pointing for proof to a tattered dress and shoes of a long-ago style. I suppose these tatters are better than nothing, but they were not for me. (Though later, in Turkey, in Mexico, in Peru, I would stand in the troglodyte churches of Cappadocia, climb the pyramid of Uxmal, run along the lines of Nazca, and I would feel the magic again.)

I became interested in philosophy. In fact, were it not for the study of wisdom I doubt I would have lasted more than a year at university. I found philosophy genuinely stimulating. I still remember the trepidation I felt upon entering Plato's *Republic*. Even more astonishing to me was Descartes's radical doubt and Berkeley's *esse est percipi*. I readily admit that Plato's *Republic* is hopelessly hierarchical and undemocratic, that Descartes's starting-point of we-are-perhaps-but-puppets-in-the-hands-of-a-mean-puppeteer is the very definition of paranoia, and that closing one's eyes and refusing to perceive has never saved anyone from an oncoming truck — but it was not the products of these ruminations that struck me so much as the process. I was taken by the careful, open think-through of things that characterizes the philosophical method. It was both simple and very difficult. I rose to the challenge. I too would be reasonable, I said to myself.

It was several months before I had my first period. The exalted view I held of the menstrual cycle dimmed considerably the morning I awoke in bloody sheets after a night disturbed by fever, headache and nausea — I thought I was coming down with the flu. My reaction was horror and shock. I jumped out of bed. There was blood on the sheets, on the mattress, it was trickling down my legs, now there were several drops on the carpet. And the pain — this was serious, I felt awful, down there and in my head. So this was what Sonya was talking about! This ache, like having a rubber band wrapped around your testicles. I could nearly vomit for it.

I knew that it was coming, that it had to come, but to me it was like death: the oldest story in the world, yet still a surprise. You will tell me, "Oh, that's nothing. You were eighteen. An adult. Intelligent and resilient. Imagine having it when you're *twelve*. A child. I remember I was at my friend Stephanie's . . ." and you will tell me your story. Perhaps. No doubt. Thank you. But that's no help to me. I whispered to myself whatever a person can come up with to make the unbelievable believable: that it was normal, that I should be proud for I was now a woman, that it was only once a month and all I needed was (and I reviewed all the pharmacies I had visited with Sonya), and things like that. But at the same time I was thinking, "This messiness, this filth, this stench, this pain — once every month! THIS IS UNFAIR, COSMICALLY UNFAIR! No, no, no, no, no, no, no, no, no, no, no, NO! I want out. I want to be sterile. To hell with reproduction. I want to be reincarnated as a mule, the last of my line."

I tried to get my act together. I believe I was whimpering. I opened the door to my room, bloodied sheets in hand, off to attempt cleaning them in the sink — and who should be in the hallway at that moment but Mrs. Pokrovski. Who always greeted us with a smile. Who treated us as her own children, perhaps missing hers, but without judgement or intrusion. Who had the warmest hands I have ever touched.

She turned. I didn't move. That day was not the day for clean sheets.

"Is something wrong, dear?"

Some words you can only say looking away into mid-air, and you're conscious of every hollow syllable. "I—just—got—my—period—and—I—made—a—mess." I could feel my face going red. The awareness only increased the rush of blood. I was this close to bursting into tears.

"Oh, that's no problem." She came up to me. "Here, give them to me." I let her take the bedding, though I hardly unclenched my hands. I was mortified at the thought that she might see the blood, which I had buried at the centre of the ball of sheets. "Come along, I'll give you some clean ones."

I was wearing my bathrobe and in my underwear I had stuffed about sixty-five tissues, but still I walked gingerly, as if I were the last brick securing the Aswan Dam.

She unlocked the closet. It had a full-size door but it wasn't a walk-in, though the shelves were cut away just enough to allow someone to step in and close the door. Which is exactly what I felt like doing. There was something about that closet, so cosy, so orderly, that I found comforting. One shelf was stacked with perfectly folded bed-sheets and pillowcases; another was the domain of toilet-paper rolls; a third sheltered cleaning products, each for a precise purpose; and on the floor lived a sturdy vacuum cleaner with its long nostril and attendant parts. From a clothes hook at the back of the door hung Mrs. Pokrovski's street coat. And lastly — what drew my attention most — there was a shelf of odds and ends.

A bottle of Aspirin.

Alka-Seltzer.

A thermometer.

Batteries (AA and 9-volt).

Two boxes of Bic pens, blue and black.

Disposable razors, blue and pink.

A can of shaving cream.

Needles, threads and other notions.

Laundry detergent in small sandwich bags.

Bars of Ivory soap.

Snickers chocolate bars.

Lined writing paper, for notes and for letters.

Envelopes.

Stamps.

A bottle of White-Out.

Scotch tape.

A stapler.

A box of paperclips.

A big box of tampons.

A big box of sanitary napkins.

Everything in a perfect little order. It was like looking at a city from high above, with its buildings and streets.

None of it for sale. All for giving.

She gave me two sheets and one sanitary napkin, which she neatly laid on the sheets. I looked at it blankly.

"Um, thank you very much, Mrs. Pokrovski. Um, how much do I owe you?"

"Oh, don't be silly." With a smile.

She closed and locked the closet.

On her part-time salary as a housekeeper she stocked things to handle student emergencies. Or so-called emergencies. For example, this immature eighteen-year-old who was overwhelmed by her first period.

Except for a quick trip to the drugstore, I spent the rest of that day in bed.

When I got tired of feeling that I was wearing diapers, and wet and mobile ones at that, and my mind had worked itself up to confronting the logistics of menses, I took to using tampons.

That Christmas I went around the house and had everyone sign a big card for Mrs. Pokrovski.

I imagine this is atypical, but in time I came to enjoy my periods. No singing and dancing about them — but quiet satisfaction, yes. It's not that I felt linked to my body because of this blood. I didn't. Sex linked me to my body; exercise; extremes of temperature; hunger; sun in my face. My menstrual cycle had the opposite effect. I felt it happened *to* me, not with me. It emphasized to me how foreign and separate my body and I could be.

But what it did make me feel was linked to other people. Every month this non-arrival of future humanity reminded me that I was part of a *species*, of something larger than just myself, whether I liked it or not. It was as if I lived in complete isolation in the country, never seeing a soul, except once every twenty-eight days, when on the road not far from my house a bus full of noisy people roared by. My period was like that bus — baffling, interesting, annoying, marvellous.

When a friend pointed out to me that the lunar and menstrual cycles are of the same length, I thought it was astronomy's gift to flaky women. Then I remembered the charismatic role the moon plays in ocean tides; how the earth is round, but its waters are oval. Now when I see a full moon I imagine that it too has tides that ripple across its surface. I can nearly see them. They are red.

Back on earth, the tantrums of this small wilful being called the uterus can be a real burden. The bloody mess I produced on a night bus in Turkey — I still can't believe I didn't wake up — comes to mind as a perfect example of this, the unmitigated hassle of it, the maddening exasperation (and of course my backpack, with its salvation of tampons, clothes and towel, was deep within the bowels of the bus, and I was wearing pale-coloured pants). Mercifully, my cramps were never so bad that I couldn't go about my normal day (though I certainly didn't forget about them; my uterus made damn sure of that), and my cycle was as regular as Kant on his walks in Königsberg, and my flow manageable and of predictable duration — but I had friends who were nearly incapacitated by their periods. Cramps that made them wince. A touch of fever. A day or two at home in bed. A seemingly endless blood flow. This preluded by PMS so bad they circled at least one day a month when they would "disconnect from reality". This is an arduous feminine normality. It would push anyone to worship the goddess Anaprox. But even in these cases, I feel that the burden remains a meaningful burden. It's like a large suitcase you have to carry on a long trip. You hate it, it slows you down, but at the end of the trip you open it and it's full of things, some of which glitter. Or imagine hearing a sound only through its echo, how you would turn your head, searching for its source. Or imagine having a small oboe within you that once a month begins to play, but only a few notes, never giving you the full melody. Oh, I don't know, something like that.

(Another reason I came to like my periods was that I grew tired of *dis*liking them. I was pulling a tampon out, glancing at it to check how much I had been bleeding, about to toss it into watery oblivion, when this distaste wearied me. I decided to make my periods beautiful. "This dull ache, it's a sign of good health." I looked at the red tampon again. "My system works. *I* work. Good." My cycle was like the German language. When you travel you meet Germans, countless Germans; the Americans export their culture but not their tourists; the Germans, the contrary. In the depths of West Sepik, Papua New Guinea, you will meet Germans. Behind their backs — and sometimes not — in a conversation among non-Germanophones, will come the almost universal conviction that "German is an ugly language," as harsh as sandpaper and mostly barked (the usual winner in this Miss Universe beauty pageant of the languages, tears streaking down her face for joy, waving her white handkerchief at her adoring fans, is Italian). Well, I heard this dumb drivel once too often. With a will, I decided the opposite. With its words as long as novellas, its syntax like a medieval cathedral and its grammar like Einstein's science, German became my favourite foreign language. In Montreal I took a series of Goethe Institute courses and for years my bedside book was Heinrich Heine. Every night I read a few pearly pages. I've also read some Nietzsche in the original, stuff of incendiary lightness and wit.)

I met Elena on my first day at Ellis. She was American, one of a number who came to study in Canada because university was cheaper here than in the States. We were both at Strathcona-Milne. I can't remember who introduced us. My memory starts when I am already in front of her. The weather was warm and she was wearing a new dress, a light summery thing. She was standing barefoot in the grass of the Quad, the communal area between the college townhouses, feeling the fabric and appraising the pattern and lifting the dress and letting it fall. I noticed her tanned legs with their few shiny blonde hairs. She looked right at me. "Hi, I'm Elena," she said. The words went straight to my heart. She was not very tall, her voice was slightly raspy, she often wore her sandy blonde hair in French braids and she was a true beauty. She was very young — I don't think she was eighteen yet — but she had an intelligent self-possession, I might even say a dignity, that made her seem much older. We fell into easy conversation. We were friends right away. And right away I was in love with her. I spent the better part of two years studying wisdom while my heart thumped with pain. To maximize my misery, I used to go swimming with her, beholding a body that I could love only in dreams, and I stayed in Roetown with her the summer after my first year. I took a summer course in ancient philosophy (Parmenides and the Eleatics, Heraclitus, Empedocles, Plato, Aristotle) while Elena took one on medieval romance (she did her major essay on courtly love. It was a painful irony: she told me all about the subject while I, her courtly lover, listened attentively).

She lived at S-M in a townhouse with five other students, a heterogeneous group thrown together by the college office. One of her housemates was a Hong Kong Chinese named George. He always wore a cap. For some reason — a free act of generosity — he took it upon himself to be my romantic manager. Over the course of two years I spent hundreds, perhaps thousands of hours with Elena; we saw movies, plays and lectures together, we went on long walks, we took a few weekend trips to Toronto, yet I don't think she ever realized that I loved her, and how much it consumed me. (It's true that I hid my love well, followed a practised pattern.) Within two weeks, however, George was greeting me at the door of their townhouse with "Hi. You are looking very nice. That dress suits you. Elena will like it," in his clipped, smiley, Hong Kong Chinese English voice, and at the end of visits, when I was feeling hurt and lonely and hungry, he would walk out with me and encourage me, or try to, with "Don't give up. Give her time." He was sweet.

But Elena was soon in love with Jonathan, who was nice, I had to admit, who was a struggling actor, who was older, who played the saxophone. My love was something useless.

It poisoned my life. Once, late at night, leaving the college library, I was so overcome with misery that I stamped the ground and the words "I am *so* unhappy!" burst out of me. They were said in such a strange voice, with so little restraint or modulation, that I was astonished. I stood still. For the duration of a few seconds expressing the emotion seemed to deal with it. The pain was out of me, floating in the air, catching onto the branches, infiltrating the bark of trees, seeping into the grass. But then I thought of Elena — saw her, felt her — and the pain rushed back in.

There is no pain so hard to imagine when you're free of it, yet so real, so overwhelming, when it afflicts you, as that of unrequited love. It's simply unbearable. Elena's person, Elena's bed, Elena's room, Elena's house, Elena's street, Elena's park — all were charged with a meaning that nothing else had. Anywhere but near her was nowhere. All reality beside her was a thin surface hiding a vacuum, a hollowness. Hollow tree. Hollow cat. Hollow me. I was sick with love, truly sick with it.

I was in her room one day. This was in second year, and she was living in a large, ramshackle house with other students. A week or so before, she and Jonathan had painted her room a lovely cerulean blue. The furniture was typically student: there was none. Only a futon. The hardwood floor was seat, cupboard and bookshelf all in one, and Elena's lap was her table. There were clothes and books strewn about. I noticed *One Hundred Years of Solitude*, another of the heavy ironies that jumped out at me. She had just woken up from a nap, her hair a dishevelled mess, and she was in a dreamy mood. Our talk was mostly silence. I couldn't take my eyes off her bed. The rumpled sheets exuded such intimacy. Oh, to crawl over and lie in them! (To kiss her, to *sleep* with her — that was well-nigh inconceivable.) But I could not lie in her bed. She probably wouldn't have objected, she would have laughed, but she would have thought me strange. So I just sat there on the floor, a few feet away from her, burning in hell, my eyes congested with fish, while we talked about nothing in particular. She thought *One Hundred Years* was amazing.

Towards the end of my second year I came to the conclusion that in all my life — I was nineteen at the time — I had had only two original ideas (discounting my early theory on love). I don't know why I was thinking in those terms, perhaps it was the study of philosophy, but that was the conclusion: only two. Every other idea I had had was a hand-me-down from someone or somewhere. Except for these two ideas, my mind was a mishmash the flavour of pap.

My first original idea was an insight into the nature of questions. Any utterance will fall into one of two categories: either it's a statement or it's a question. There is nothing else. There are myriad kinds of statements, but declarative or imperative, simple or complex, understood or nonsensical, they all share one feature: they stand on their own. For example, the statement "Elena sleeps with Jonathan" is magnificently autarkic. It just doesn't give a damn about anything else. Questions, on the other hand, do not stand on their own. By their very nature, they imply the existence of something else: namely, answers. Questions are tango dancers in search of partners. My insight was that a question is a question only if it has an answer. By which I don't mean that this answer must be known, merely that it must be known to exist. For example, the proof to Fermat's Last Theorem, that there are no non-zero numbers x, y and z such that $x^n + y^n = z^n$ in which n is greater than 2, is an enigma that has baffled mathematicians for over 350 years. Yet it still remains a valid question, a tango dancer (if lonely), because a definitive answer exists at least in theory. It doesn't matter whether the answer is two hundred pages of mathematical arcana or the simple statement "There is no proof to Fermat's Last Theorem" — either way question and answer could dance to Django Reinhardt.

But there are questions, or so-called questions, that will remain for ever on the edge of the dance floor, against the wall. They may look like questions, they may sound like questions, one can go about them as one might with real questions — but they are not real questions for they have no answers. This is where my insight was useful, for if there was a way of picking out false questions, then one would be spared the useless effort of searching for the impossible: the answer to a non-question.

A question is a question only if there is something outside it, separate, that can function as an answer. A pseudo-question, on the other hand, gobbles up all possible answers by becoming a bigger and bigger pseudo-question, until at last it has swallowed up the entire universe and there is nothing outside it that can act as an answer. Sometimes the very same words will be both a question and a pseudo-question, depending on the context. If a doctor asks, "Why did Georgie die?" referring to seven-year-old Georgie, the doctor is asking a valid question to which "infantile leukemia" is a valid final answer.

But let's say Georgie's mother is asking the same question. "Why did Georgie die?" Listen to her tone of voice. Is she really asking a question? Is "infantile leukemia" what she's looking for? It isn't. If you gave her that answer, she would ask,

"Why is there infantile leukemia?" Would she want to hear detailed explanations of the malfunctioning of bone marrow? Of course not. Every possible answer you could give her she would swallow up in a greater question, each one more bloated than the last: "Why is there pain?" "Why is there existence?" "Why is there God?" "Why is there anything?" Are these questions? Can one tango successfully with them? No. Georgie's mother's questions are really statements in disguise. In asking "Why did Georgie die?" she is saying, "I cannot accept this loss." In asking "Why is there pain?" she is saying, "It hurts so much." The statements behind pseudo-questions are usually of fear, pain or bewilderment.

We sometimes spend a lot of time searching for answers that can't exist. Better to realize how we feel and proceed from there, no false questions asked.

This was my first original idea. I owed it to no one but myself.

My second original idea was to fall in love with Elena. It came from within me, like a deep swell. I saw her in ways that no one else did, loved her in ways that no one else did. My emotion was — sadly for me, for the pain it gave me — original to me.

Those were my two original ideas. Huff and puff like the big bad wolf and blow a chill wind through me: at age nineteen they were the only two things that would have remained standing in me. A point about questions and love for a girl.

The problem was, these two ideas cancelled each other out. My first idea told me to decide how I felt, and only then ask questions. My second idea told me exactly how I felt, but led me to such questions as "Why doesn't she love me?" Which, I am the first to admit, is a question that cannot bear an answer. It is plainly a pseudo-question, yet one that I tried to answer for weeks and months.

Amidst the bustle of my student life, things started to go wrong. It wasn't only Elena — there were other muttering questions at the back of my mind (that existential monkey I mentioned earlier. It seems so melodramatic to say this, so undergraduate, but I could find no meaning to my life, no purpose, no direction). I began finding academic success increasingly difficult. My choice of courses for second year was a disaster to my spirits. I became the great defender of relativism in moral philosophy (Hobbes, Pascal, Cudworth, Locke, Price, Hume, J.S. Mill, Sidgwick, G.E. Moore, Rawls). There was a rakish appeal in wiping away every notion of inherent goodness, in tearing down every signpost at the fork between good and evil. I remember lively discussions about the hypothetical innocuousness of throwing babies into bonfires. Worse still, irony of ironies, was a course on existential philosophy. Nietzsche, Kierkegaard, Camus, Sartre, Merleau-Ponty, Heidegger — I thought for sure that they would speak to me, but they did not. As for nineteenth-century philosophy (Fichte, Hegel, William James, J.S. Mill, Marx, Nietzsche, C.S. Peirce, Schopenhauer), I sat through it in a dumb, uncomprehending stupor. One of the most depressing things I suffered at this time was the breakdown of my ability to read. I had essays to produce, thinkers' thoughts to digest and chronicle, but I became incapable of reading these thinkers, let alone writing about them. I spent hour after dismal hour in the S-M library staring at the same paragraph of Sartre or Hegel. Even the ability to read literature nearly abandoned me. I limped through a course on early twentieth-century authors (Conrad, Ford, Forster, Lawrence, Gide, Mann, First World War poets), my interest aroused only by the grim poems of Sassoon, Owen, Rosenberg, Blok and Graves. My marks in second year were a mix of charitable passes and miserable failures. I thought of dropping out (but where would I go?)

I went to swim practice morning and evening, three hours a day, every day, seeking solace in the amnesia of the body. I wasted hours on *New York Times* crossword puzzles. I went on endless walks.

I resigned from the university senate, not halfway through my two-year term, and renounced my prime-ministerial ambitions ("I choose not to run," said Calvin Coolidge. "If nominated, I will not run; if elected, I will not serve," said William Tecumseh Sherman). Politics is not for the tortured at heart. Once you're tortured, you're no longer good at it, you're on your way out. The responsible exercise of power requires a dull-headed certainty about things, a limited linear quality called "vision". To knock on strangers' doors and canvass, to stand up and make partisan speeches, to set priorities and make decisions — in short, to peddle conviction in a daily way — you need vision. I had, have, none.

In the winter of my second year, I wrote a play. I had had an idea and I had drawn an awkward but detailed sketch of the set and stage. In considering these two things, the wordy idea in my head and the plotless sketch, I felt impelled to write the thing out, to people that stage. The result was dreadful, a truly awful one-act play. About a young woman who falls in love with a door, who commits suicide when that door, her Romeo, is unhinged and tossed out to sea by an arrogantly well-meaning friend. I showed the play to three older people whose opinions I respected. From two, my heart-wrenching drama elicited bursts of laughter. They thought it was a parody on tragedies. "I hope this isn't autobiographical," remarked one. I was profoundly mortified, though I chuckled along. My third reader, a writer-in-residence at Ellis from Scotland, sent me a tactful note in which he complimented me on some of the writing and said my play was "an intellectually sensed melodrama". The critical edge in that phrase was sufficiently ambiguous for me to feel a guarded sense of satisfaction. It helped me recover from my first two readers and I was able to destroy all four copies of the play with passable equanimity. But there had been pleasure in its making, that's what I retained. Before and after I was restless; but during, my mind was focused. One sign of how taken I was by the work of creation was the importance the play had in my mind. My room could burn down, the college, the whole city — I would be all right so long as I saved my pen-scrawled sheets of paper. The play, while I worked on it, was my most precious possession in the world.

After this first effort, heeding the well-known adage, I tried to limit myself to what I knew best, which was very little. My first finished story was about an event that had taken place at a lecture in my first-year psychology course. We — meaning three hundred students — were waiting for the lecture to begin. There was a heavy noise in the air, each component no more than a quiet exchange or a rustle or a cough, but adding up to a dissonant yet strangely uniform mass of sound, seemingly weighing hundreds of kilos. Into this heaviness were thrown a few grams of music. A student had detached himself from the group, sat down at the upright piano and begun to play. The piano was always there, a piece of furniture, a carcass. At the first note, silence blew over us like a wind. The air was clear except for those notes. He played for a minute or two what I could only describe as something limpid and in a higher range. Then he stopped, there was a ripple of applause, the professor happened to appear at that moment, and before the weight of noise could return the lecture started. At the next lecture he played again, but with less success. We were expecting him. There was silence, and therefore tension, as he stepped up to the piano. He delivered his notes with less confidence. At the lecture after that, he did not play. I watched him. He looked towards the piano, surely thought of trying again, but remained in his seat. It had worked best when it was spontaneous.

I wrote the story as an interior monologue in three parts, one for each lecture. The thoughts ranged in emotion from whim and insouciance to arrogance and vanity to defeat. It began with the words "I will play" and ended with "I will listen." It was of no great interest, and hardly had I finished it than I read it over, thought "Hmmm" and tore it up. But I remember thinking that I had captured the modulation of emotions nicely.

The majority of my plays and stories were aborted after a few pages. In my head, airborne, my ideas were full of grace and power, like a soaring albatross. When they landed on the page — quite aside from the fact that they seemed to have the commensurate awkwardness of a big bird on foot — I could no longer enjoy their company. For what was written was over. I had to move on. I might have to endure thoughts of Elena, might have to suffer my loneliness until I could think of another fiction. This is as close as I can come to an explanation of why I started to write: not for the sake of writing, but for the sake of company.

I decided to spend the summer between my second and third year in Greece, for an airfare equivalent in actuarial terms to one of my parents' fingers. I'd heard the country was cheap and beautiful, and Elena wasn't going to be in Roetown. She was heading home. Things were going so-so with Jonathan and she was confused as to what she was doing at university. She wasn't sure she would return to Ellis. We said goodbye on the street. We hugged — the first and only time I felt her breasts against mine — and I kissed her on both cheeks, the way the French and aspiring lovers do. She gave me her mother's address. (It used to jump out at me when I flipped through my address book. Now it's an overgrown tombstone at the back of a garden.)

I was better prepared for Greece than I had been for Portugal. I read up on the country, I bought a good practical guidebook, my backpack weighed in at six kilos, I felt I was better at assessing situations, at bargaining; in short, the prospect of sunset was less terrifying. Still, like the last time, I left Canada feeling depressed, lonely and nervous. I knew no one, no one knew me, where was I going? why was I doing this? — round and round.

Blue and white are the colours of Greece, blue of sea, white of marble, set in an air that has a certain glow. It was in the midst of these simple elements, three days after landing in Athens, that I rediscovered the pleasure of travelling. The temple of Poseidon at Cape Sounion, a bus ride of a few hours down the Attic peninsula from the capital, is Greece in its purest, most archetypal form: a solitary Doric temple on a rocky promontory overlooking a vastness of sparkling blue. I spent the whole day there in an ecstatic reverie. Everything would be fine, everything would be fine.

During my time in Greece I was a chameleon who favoured blue and white (and black, the black of the billions of olives that fell from trees and peppered the hilly, arid ground). In the presence of these colours I was still and happy. By which I mean that I was content to do nothing except listen to the pulse, the rustle, the roll, of time flowing by, which felt not like a tick-tock marking something coming to an end but, on the contrary, like something increasing all the time, all the seconds adding up to a whole.

I travelled in a leisurely way, seeing the major sights because it would be crazy to be blind to them, but also getting lost by going to places not usually visited by tourists. I read poems by Cavafy and novels by Kazantzakis.

It is one of the ironies of travel in the late twentieth century that, unless you make special efforts or are lucky, if you go to England you will meet Australians, if you go to Egypt you will meet Germans, if you go to Greece you will meet Swedes and so on. In my case, while seeing the glory of Greece, while smelling it, while eating it, while treading upon it, I met America.

Upon arriving in Pilos, in the south-western Peloponnese, I went for a walk about the hills outside the town. It was more of a village, really; the division between settlement and wilderness was uncertain. Early that morning I had split up in Kalamata with a Canadian drummer and a Dutch architect who were returning to Athens. We had visited Mistra and Sparta together and we had shared lively conversations and a lot of laughter. I was feeling a little left out in Pilos. I spent hours walking among beehives and down countless sheep paths that led nowhere.

In the evening I was very tired and I decided to eat at my little hotel. The place was run by a family, and their restaurant was more an extension of their kitchen than a proper dining establishment. The menu had x items of which x–1 were unavailable. I discovered later, from Ruth, that the determinant of this sole offering was either the family's whim or, if they were in a good mood that day, the result of a rough poll conducted in the morning among the guests, a consultation in which democracy might triumph. On the days when the family's whim was at work, guests were offered menus so they could see in print what they were — and were not — going to eat. On democratic days, menus were dispensed with — since guests already knew what they were having — except for new guests, who had to go through the exercise of being rebuked on every item except one. My first evening, it turned out, was one of family whim.

All this to say the following: that I was handed the menu, that the first item I struck from my mental list was the moussaka — I had had enough of moussakas with fatty, granular ground lamb that dripped with oil — but that I ended up ordering moussaka.

A woman at a table next to mine, clearly a tourist, smiled at me during the menu elimination process. When the man had left with the preordained order, she said, "It's not bad, actually. They eat it themselves."

"Good — then if we die, we shall all die together."

She chuckled. "Are you American?" she asked.

"No, a neighbour."

"Ah." A pause. "Buenos días, cómo está usted?"

I looked at her. I was going through a quick series of anti-American thoughts.

She smiled. "I'm joking. I have a daughter who's studying in British Columbia."

I laughed. Damn my presumption, damn it.

Up till that moment I had been tired, so tired that I could have fallen asleep then and there. But suddenly I felt recharged. Soon, from being at neighbouring tables, we were neighbours at one table. Her name was Ruth and she was from Philadelphia. She was in her forties and she was alone; there was no husband or family that was late for dinner. Till a week before, she had been with a friend. They had taken the boat from Bari, in Italy, to Corfu and had worked their way south. Her friend had returned to the U.S. from Athens — commitments, attachments, obligations — but Ruth's ticket was open. For the first time in her life, she had decided to travel on her own, "like a student", as she put it. She had commitments, attachments and obligations too, but they could "feed themselves, clean themselves and drive themselves on their own for once," she said, laughing (though she did miss and worry about her nine-year-old son, Danny. He came up regularly).

I don't remember when I started learning all the things about Ruth's life. We travelled together for a little over two months, and I'm good at remembering details but not chronology. That first evening she was still a stranger to me (how strange to say that — Ruth a stranger to me. Quickly I couldn't recall for the life of me what she was like as a stranger. First impressions are such strange things). We had both liked Corinth — New, Old and Ancient — but she had seen nothing else of the Peloponnese after that, since she had taken a bus from the isthmus clear across the peninsula to Pilos, thus committing her, she felt, to visiting everything in between. Her resolve needed that. (We'd get as far as the Turko-Iranian border.)

The moussaka came and went hardly noticed, and when it was time for bed we agreed to have breakfast together in the morning.

We spent the next days in Pilos together. We walked and talked and played backgammon on my small magnetic set. It came naturally. In our regular settings, Ruth and I would never have got to know each other the way we did in Greece. Our differences would have kept us apart. But here it was precisely these differences that made us interesting to each other, although Ruth was more of a novelty to me than I was to her; the daughter who was at Simon Fraser University, Tuesday, was a year older than I and she had another daughter, Sandra, who was two years younger. Her stepson, Graham, was Tuesday's age. They, with Danny, were "good kids all," she said. She used the word "kids". I was hardly the first twenty-year-old she had known.

I, on the other hand, realized with amazement that I had never truly spoken with an adult woman before, never got beyond outer facts and functional interactions, never simply and profoundly chatted. Whom I had been speaking with for twenty years I don't know, but it seems it wasn't mature women. This is what drew me to Ruth. Next to her I felt so new, shiny and stupid. I felt like a piece of plastic to her worn leather. She was forty-six years old and she looked it. She was twice divorced and she had three children and one stepson. Her first husband, whom she had married when she was nineteen, was a gynaecologist-obstetrician who loved money and was an asshole (that's all I ever learned about him. Clearly "asshole" fully conveyed his essence and there was nothing more to be said. Words can be so wonderfully apt sometimes). He was the distant father of her two daughters. Her second husband had been her best friend's husband, but one day the best friend had been swimming with her young son, Graham, and they had been caught in a riptide and swept out to sea. The friend had spent all her energy pushing her son to safety, which she had succeeded in doing — Graham managed to struggle to the beach — but she had no strength left for herself and she drowned. In mourning her friend Ruth had got close to the husband and eventually she had married him, more from a feeling of responsibility for Graham than from any romantic inclination. He wasn't a bad man, he meant well, but he had trouble with being alive and he was an alcoholic. She divorced him, taking with her his belated gift, baby Danny. In the quiet eddies of this turmoil, sensing that she would have to earn money on her own one day, she took a course to become a computer programmer. She worked for a company that did contracts, a job of no significance or interest to her, which had nothing to do with who she was, except that it allowed her to pull in money, at the cost of eight of her daylight hours five days a week.

All this was etched not on her face, for forty-six is not very old, but in her manners. She exuded an experience of life, a road long travelled, that made me want to listen to her. I hated my youthfulness, which came out in too many words, too many opinions, too many emotions. I wanted her calmness, the simplicity of her approach to things. Once, later on, we had a fight. That is — more accurately — I was upset at her. It was in Marmaris, in Turkey. I can't remember why, what over.

I was fulminating and sulking at the same time. It ended when she came over, touched me lightly on the forearm — three tips of fingers touching three dots of skin — and said, "I'm sorry." Then she went to bed. I was instantly disarmed. She had said her two and a half words plainly and definitively. They fully expressed what she felt and had to say. I reflected on the way I would have apologized ten times over, with emotional sloppiness and needless gesticulations. I went over to her and apologized for having been upset at her, trying to match her sincerity and economy of words.

But this was not the way Ruth saw it. She couldn't believe she was forty-six. She felt life had happened to her, with no direction. She had strong insecurities. For example, she kept a diary, had since she was in her early twenties, but she never showed it to me because she thought she'd never learned to write properly in high school. Whereas I! She envied me. She even found me a little intimidating at first, she told me. She thought I was so smart, so daring. Such energy, so much enthusiasm. And I had travelled so much. And what a tragedy to have lost my parents like that.

Typically, this is the way things went. Imagine this play:

DRAMATIS PERSONAE:

    YOUTH

    AGE

    FUNNY-LOOKING CLOUD

SCENE: *a hot, sunny beach in the south-western Peloponnese*
(The curtain rises. Youth *and* Age *are lying on the beach, facing the sea and the sun.)*

YOUTH: *(rattles on at a hundred miles an hour while* Age *listens.)*

(Funny-looking Cloud *enters stage right.)*

AGE (*pointing*): Isn't that a funny-looking cloud?
YOUTH (*looks, smiles*): Yes, it is.
(*They both look at the* Funny-looking Cloud *until it
    floats off stage left. A long pause.*)
YOUTH: (*rattles on at a hundred miles an hour while* Age
    listens.)
    CURTAIN

The natural thing to do after visiting Pilos is to visit Methoni
and Koroni, the two other towns at the end of the Messinian
peninsula, the westernmost of the three fingers that form the
south of the Peloponnese. It was equally natural that Ruth and
I should do this together. We were both happy to have a travel
companion.

In Methoni we got a room together to save money. It was a
large room with bright whitewashed walls and plain furniture
that was so arbitrarily scattered about that it seemed planned.
The cupboard stood three feet from the wall. The two beds, in
opposite corners of the room, also stood some distance from
the walls, but crooked, with an un-Greek blindness to align-
ment and symmetry. Similarly with the table. It was all to make
sweeping the floor and changing the beds easy, I suppose, but
in the way it made each piece of furniture stand out, alone
within its own space, the effect was to make the room feel like a
stage. When I opened the shutters, there was such a flood of
light it felt as if the sun star itself had entered the room. The
window was surrounded by leafy, invasive vines with heavy
white flowers that gave off an exquisite fragrance. I don't think
I'd ever seen such a pleasant room, so bright, bright, bright.

Methoni is prettier than Pilos, and Ruth and I walked all
day. There were the ruins of a castle, and dunes and paths

besides. By late afternoon we were tired and returned to our room. Someone suggested foot massages.

It was doing that, pressing my thumbs into the soles of Ruth's warm feet, that I first felt it. It came on with the suddenness of an idea.

Desire. I wanted to be close to Ruth not only in words, but in deed.

I stood up. I felt a touch dizzy. There was *so* much light in the room — it felt like a liquid, and I was floating in it. I looked down to my naked feet. The tiles were cool. I looked towards the window, out into the world. But at that moment nothing out there interested me.

Ruth was still lying on the bed. I sat next to her. I wasn't nervous. Rather, I was incredibly alert. Though I was just sitting, doing nothing, it felt as if a lot was happening. My concentration was very busy.

Our gazes met. An attempt to remember a line by T.S. Eliot flitted through my mind, a thought of no relevance, just me shying away from my desire again, just me trying to reach for something while not looking at it. I bent down and we kissed. I am amazed now that I was so bold, that I, virgin inexperience, should not have waited for her, experience, to make the move. Ruth told me later that she never would have dared.

Between one kiss and the next Ruth said quietly, "I was wondering...," as she played with my hair, which by now was long and was falling in her face.

I wanted to kiss for ever. There was nothing preliminary about it to me. Till then my lips had been instruments of speech, no more, except for smiling. But this was much better than words, infinitely better. Ruth once joked about my fondness for kissing ("but I love it," she said, bright-eyed, and gave me only a quick kiss because we were in a place that was possibly public). It's true that when I kissed her I tended to linger. There was so much to do — to the left and right, up and down and dead ahead. There was the flat smoothness of her incisors, the roundness and pointiness of her upper canines, the ruggedness of her bicuspids. If gods kissed the earth, wouldn't they linger on the mountains? And then there was her tongue, that busy, solitary hermit, that funny indivisible organ bursting with personality. I loved kissing Ruth. She would sometimes turn away and laugh and say, "I feel like *such* a teenager!" Then we'd kiss some more.

I eased myself beside her. I pressed myself against her, one of her legs between mine, trying to feel as much of her body against mine as possible. I felt as if I were drunk. I didn't think I had ever felt so intensely while doing so little.

"I can't believe we're doing this," she said, smiling, short of breath.

"It's nice, *very* nice," I replied, burying my face in her neck.

"I've been masturbating the last couple of nights thinking about you," she whispered.

"Really?" I looked up. I loved it that she had used that word.

"In fact, when you suggested that we get a room together my first thought was *Oh no, where am I going to masturbate?*"

We laughed. How extraordinary that the same thought hadn't occurred to me. I masturbated every night before falling asleep, and always in bed. Yet the inconvenience of having Ruth in the same room had never crossed my mind. We kissed again.

Finally to break with Elena. To desire someone else.

"Have you slept with other women?"

"No. Once, long ago, probably before you were born — God I feel old."

"Yes?" I nudged.

"This friend and I kissed and fooled around a bit. But that was it."

We fell silent.

My drunkenness got a keen edge. I was feeling incredibly horny. I was holding on tightly to her leg and rubbing myself against her. I was wet right through.

She smiled, a knowing smile, and turned to face me, propping herself up on an elbow. She cleared the hair from my face and gently drifted her fingers down from my forehead, kissing me in their wake. She ran her hand over my body, lingering over my breasts and pressing between my legs.

She suddenly got up. "Too much light," she said. She closed the shutters and pulled the curtains. The penumbra of intimacy. She checked the door, and stood looking at me. I was on my knees on the bed. I was nervously, deliciously tense.

She came close to me again and, while we kissed, hands began to act of their own accord. Hers slowly unbuttoned my shirt, undid my bra, held and caressed my breasts. Mine wavered in the air, accommodated the removing of clothes and then settled on her shoulders. I stood on the bed, my pants and underwear were assisted off — and I was completely naked. Ruth gently took one of my breasts into her mouth. She glided her hands over my back, from bump of shoulder-blade to curve of bum.

I did not so much help her remove her clothes as trail my hands behind the task as it was done. As soon as she had removed her pants and underwear — I can see it still: she bent over, steadying herself with a hand on my hip, first one leg, then the other, then standing straight — I touched her between the legs. Her light brown hairs were silky, softer than mine, and she was wet, wet at the first touch. What an incredible feeling, a sameness that is someone else. She caught her breath.

She pushed me onto the bed. We lay body against body, skin slightly cool at first, soon very warm. We spoke little; our sentences were short and practical — secondary language. Mostly we spoke with our hands. A communication that even had the structure of a conversation: she spoke with her hands, and my body listened without interruption, then my hands replied on her body.

Such a lovely form, the feminine form — so soft, so open, so receiving. Ruth had small breasts, smaller than mine, with nipples that had fed two girls and a boy. Her euphemistic tummy, which had produced three babies, twenty-seven months' hard work, had a little bulge, which she hated, which I loved. I always placed my hand on it, as one would on a globe, which is exactly what I thought her belly was like — a slight curve that traced a history and a geography. A globe representing the planet Tuesday (I was young and eager: I wanted to put *everything* into words. My metaphors — which I worked on hard — made Ruth roll her eyes. "A planet! Oh, what next? College students!" she said, and laughed, and kissed me. Always a kiss). My body was fit only for plain adjectives: young, slender, nimble. I liked it plenty, don't mean to say the contrary, it has always been faithful to me — I had nice breasts, not large but pleasing in their shape, and though my legs were a little thin, I was well proportioned — but it was barren ground for rich metaphors. I hungered for a sexual history.

Ruth ended up speaking the most that first time. With her hands, I mean (later she would speak to me with her mouth, oh me oh my). I lay on my back, she on her side, right next to me, her legs tucked against my bum under my legs. Her fingers roamed, eventually drifting to the gravitational centre of my desire.

When I came, I squeezed my legs together and pressed my hands onto her hand, to keep her there, on me, in me. It was amazing and perfectly ineffable. That floaty feeling.

I felt giddy with life, overflowing with it. If I had taken hold of a light-bulb at that moment, it would have lit.

"Good?" said Ruth.

I broke out laughing. For once I didn't try to put things into words. I turned and kissed her and kissed her breasts and glided my hand down. She was so wet, so so wet. As I rested my head on her chest, and her hand, whose fingers smelled of me, distractedly played with my hair, I titillated that wetness. As her breathing grew more urgent, I held onto her more tightly. When her body tensed and she burst with inner pleasure, I closed my eyes. In the dark I could see fish darting about.

I remember that first time with Ruth, in that liquidly dark white stage of a room in Greece, as a moment of perfect felicity.

After Methoni, Koroni. After Koroni, Kalamata. After Kalamata, Mistra and Sparta ("Is this it? Is this *really* it?" said Ruth in disbelief, looking at a stump of rock nearly overgrown with grass, typical of the few remains of great, ancient, masculine Sparta. "Yes, but don't worry," I replied. "You'll like Mistra. The Byzantines were wonderful"). Then down the Mani. Then over to Monemvasia. At every step Ruth enjoyed further pushing the openness of her airplane ticket. I don't recall any discussions as to *whether* we should proceed, only as to where. Ruth called Philadelphia regularly to touch base with Tuesday, Sandra and Danny (Graham was staying with his father, in Baton Rouge). The three kids would share the phones in the house. Tuesday, the woman in charge, home for the summer from Simon Fraser, told her mom that Danny repeated word for word what she told him to whoever cared to listen; so that when Ruth said, "We're in, uh, Rhodes, like the Colossus, and we're leaving tomorrow, uh, by boat for a place called Marmalade, or something like that, in, uh, Turkey. Oh! It's called Marmaris," Danny would tell everyone, "Mom's in, uh, Rhodes, like the Colossus, and she's leaving tomorrow, uh, by boat for a place called Marmalade, or something like that, in, uh, Turkey. Oh! It's called Marmaris." He repeated the words aloud even when he was alone, Tuesday said, "like a mantra," until she called again and gave him a new one. "He doesn't even know where Turkey is or what the Colossus of Rhodes was," she added. There was a little spite in her voice, Ruth said. I guess they were right in wondering what their mom was up to, whose two-week-or-so trip was into its second month, with no end in sight. All hell broke loose at the mention of *Turkey!*, which they always pronounced as if it were written with an exclamation point, land of would-be Pope-killers and the Midnight Express ("But I'm neither the Pope nor a drug dealer and the Turks are actually very nice, nicer than the Greeks, in fact, and I just got you a beautiful carpet," said Ruth; "but Mom's neither the Pope nor a drug dealer and the Turks are actually very nice, nicer than the Greeks, in fact, and she just got Tuesday a beautiful carpet," said Danny said Tuesday said Ruth to me). Still, she, we, travelled. The phone calls to Philadelphia got longer the longer we were in Turkey, and Ruth carried around a carefully wrapped kernel of maternal guilt about Danny, but still we travelled.

We heard that the Greek islands were overrun that summer with tourists, mainly British, so we decided to step around them and go to Crete. We backtracked from Monemvasia to the ramshackle port city of Gytheion — where, in a tiny open-air cinema, projected against a bed sheet to the loud clatter of the projector, we watched what must be the worst American B-movie in history, a piece of such outrageous but deadly serious badness, *The Sudsy Massacre*, starring blonde nobodies, that it stayed with me for years, exactly like great art — and from Gytheion we caught a ferry to Crete.

We walked through towns, we rented mopeds and sputtered into remote mountain villages (one during its annual festival), we caught vistas that were vast, rich and green, we lay on deserted beaches (one so inaccessible that we stripped and swam naked), we hiked through the Samaria Gorge, we visited museums and archaeological sites, we caught noisy, crowded buses, we had Ruth's camera fixed in Heracleon, and every night, every day, we made love and slept together in cheap hotels.

Everyone assumed that Ruth was my mother, and we let it go since it made things easier. But it became a running joke between us that each time this happened Ruth muttered under her breath, "I-am-not-your-mother."

We landed upon Crete's left end. When we reached its right end, we needed a new destination.

It was I who suggested Turkey!, so close and so enormous, and surely with fewer tourists. We hesitated — the country *did* have a bad reputation at the time — but we decided to go for it. After a night in Rhodes, we embarked on a nutshell of a boat for Marmaris, reassuring ourselves that if things got bad, Ruth's credit card would be our magic carpet out of the place.

We were nervous at customs — we'd both seen that movie — but it was the Turkish passengers who had all their luggage opened and thoroughly searched, while we were waved through with big smiles. Our passports received such thunderous stamps as to cripple them for life. Mister Hairy-Armed Official was so gleeful in delivering the blows that I thought *he* was one who should have been checked for drugs.

We crossed a threshold and advanced a few steps. The sunshine was warm against my face. I noticed a young man who was trying to catch my eye.

Which I let be caught.

"Are you looking for room?" he asked, with a smile that was neither menace nor malice, just friendly.

"Yes," I said, my first word in Turkey.

Ah, what a country! Strange how a place so big, such a maelstrom of history, can yet fit into my heart.

The room we were shown was clean and rustic, with bright bed-covers and carpets, in a four-hundred-year-old family home with a doorframe only five feet high, and very cheap.

When we were alone we sat on one of the beds. "This is nice," said Ruth.

"Yes," I said, again.

We had an unpleasant encounter a few days after arriving. We were on a quiet, deserted beach when some American soldiers appeared. When they realized that we spoke English, and one of us was American to boot, they came over to talk to us. Friendliness is a good quality, but it should be accompanied by other qualities. Otherwise it is like gift-wrapping an empty box. These boys — I say boys though they were all older than I — were posted at a NATO base in Turkey and were "R'n'R-ing" for a few days. They hated Turkey. Nothin' to do, nothin' to see, miss my girl, miss my wife, miss my football games — they had thick necks, and brains that wouldn't have overflowed a thimble. One in particular stuck in my craw. Perhaps he thought I was feeling left out. To reassure me that I was no orphan, that really I too was part of the Great American Family, he told me that there was no difference between Americans and Canadians. He was from Michigan, was his evidence. Same language, same TV, same culture, same everything. He wore mirror aviator glasses so I couldn't see his eyes, he imposed his scrawny white chest on me as if it were a work of Michelangelo, his tone of voice made it clear that he was speaking the plain universal truth and — as if that weren't enough to whip my internal rage to a froth — I could think of little to refute his border-erasing arguments. I pointed out that both Australians and New Zealanders spoke English, yet they were from different countries. Yeah, but New Zee, as he called it, could have been a part of Australia if it had wanted to, like Tasmania. Or like Hawaii with the U.S. They just used the ocean as an excuse to have their own country. Or look at Austria and Germany, he persisted, a bulldozer of reassurance. I was posted in the south of Germany, was his evidence. There's no real difference between the two. Or no more than there is between the north and south of Germany. Austria could perfectly well be a part of Deutschland. Really. Same language, same culture, same country, that's what I say, he said.

I was at a loss for words. I searched among the icons of the Canadian *Gestalt* — maple syrup, beavers, niceness, the Queen, no guns — for an essential difference, an originality, something to War-of-1812 about. But the only irrefutable difference I could come up with was that I *wanted* to be different. I looked at my hegemonic comforter and I thought,

Je ne veux pas être comme	I don't want to be like
toi, je ne veux pas être comme	you, I don't want to be like
toi, je ne veux pas être comme	you, I don't want to be like
toi, je ne veux pas être comme	you, I don't want to be like
toi, je ne veux pas être comme	you, I don't want to be like
toi, je ne veux pas être comme	you, I don't want to be like
toi.	you.

I deflected things by asking him what he did in the army.

The air force, he corrected me. He was a mechanic for military jets.

They eventually left. With their Frisbees, footballs, ghettoblasters and beers, which they offered but no thank you.

"They're not very nervous about being in Turkey, are they?" said Ruth.

"No."

She patted my thigh. "I could tell you were upset by that mechanic."

"I'm not American."

"Of *course* you're not. Nor am I your mother. Canadians are very different from Americans in lots of small, important ways. I'd *never* mistake you for an American."

I grinned. "You liar! You thought I was American when we met."

"Oh. Right."

We laughed.

A pause. A search for fundamental differences.

"Do you think we can take our tops off?" she asked.

"I don't know," I replied, looking around. "I don't think we should."

"I guess you're right." She looked out at the water. "Let's go back to our room," she said brightly, with that twinkle in her eye.

"Okay."

As we walked back she said, "And of course you're different. You can't be American, you don't have an American passport. And you speak French in Quebec." Which, for as long as I knew her, she pronounced Kweebec.

They were the only Americans we met in Turkey.

We stayed in all kinds of cheap hotels and pensions during our stay in Turkey: some that were unique, like the troglodyte lodgings of Cappadocia; some rustic; some functional and forgettable; and some that were filthy, with dirty sheets and heavy smells. In this last category, I'll never forget one that had a wall so mildewed and rotten that I could put my hand on it and push it in several inches, presumably startling our neighbours, if we had any. When I let go, the wall slowly sprang back. Would that Buster Keaton had been in the next room, we would've had a merry time. Ruth was the arbiter of hotel rooms, since I was game for anything. I was very much a student of the the-more-I-rough-it-the-more-I-am-alive school of travel. If a hotel room didn't kill me, it made me better. Ruth walked out of many a room saying, "This one kills me." But the woman was surprising and resilient, and she developed a tolerance for grunge that came to equal mine. By the end of our trip we would peek into rooms that were dungeons of degradation, sties that would have made swine blanch, and Ruth would emit a flat, unironic "Great" and drop her pack on the bed. It helped that we were running low on money. Necessity is the mother of tolerance.

We bought double sheets in Kuşadasi. I carried one and Ruth the other. Every night we brought them together. This, and a shower with only a few degrees Celsius of warm water, made us happy.

We became minor experts in Turkish carpets, and damn good bargainers, able to ingest gallons of sweet tea and resist all kinds of smiles and ploys to make us buy what we didn't want. One carpet that Ruth bought had an impossibly intricate gold and green pattern. When I saw it in Philadelphia, a tide rippled through my mind, a watery carpet of fleeting images and wordless feelings. I bought a kilim, the sole decoration in my bare student rooms, a magic carpet in the way it spoke to me of Ruth.

"The seeds of all things have a moist nature," I said to Ruth, in Miletus.

She looked up from her bag and squinted. "What's that?" she said. She was sitting on a great lion, at one time surely proud and menacing, but now old, worn and half-buried in sand.

"Greek philosophy started here. A guy named Thales. He said the source of everything was water."

She looked around. "Well, he's right."

Miletus, once a port of such prosperity that it could afford philosophy, is now a desert, the river Meander having silted up and pushed back the sea. It's a dry, dry place. Ruth brought out a Coke. She was incorrigibly American.

"He also said, 'All things are full of gods.'" Just as I said this, Ruth pulled the tab on the can. There was an explosion of spray. "You see. Excess, compressed gods."

She laughed. "Want some?"

As usual, I looked offended and then drank half of it.

We were alone; Ruth slipped her hand into mine. We walked about, pulling each other this way and that for no reason except the pleasure of knowing that the other was there. We kissed against a column. The seeds of all things. . . . I wished we'd been back in our room.

After Ephesus, on the Aegean coast, we made the decision to head east. We rested in Pamukkale's white travertines, basins that thousands of years of flowing mineral water had created, all pure white in colour and overflowing with hot, calcium-rich water. Ruth piled mud onto her head.

The land pulled us along. Pamukkale wasn't far from Cappadocia, wonder of wonders, refuge of the early Christians, who dug habitations into the friable rock, a lunar landscape like nowhere else on earth. And there was Konya in between, city of the whirling dervishes. And beyond, just beyond, was Nemrut Dagi, a sanctuary atop a mountain, with huge stone heads. From there it was an obvious step to Dogubayazit, site of the Kurdish castle of Ishak Pasa (and Little and Big Ararat besides).

In Dogubayazit we took a taxi to the border. We peeped into the Islamic Republic of Iran. I would have gone if the border hadn't been closed because of the Iran–Iraq war. Ruth looked at me. "Right," she said. "Sure. We'll go tomorrow. Just hop back into town to exchange our bikinis for one-pieces, and we'll be all set to do Iran," which she pronounced "I ran", first person singular. In Dogubayazit at the same time as us, filling up the best hotel in town with his team, was James Irwin, an American astronaut who had walked on the moon (and presumably found it full of God) and was now unsuccessfully looking for Noah's ark on Mount Ararat. "Let's find the crackpot," said Ruth. But Mr. Irwin was hard at work on the mountain.

We returned westward along the Black Sea coast until Samsun, where we headed inland towards Ankara. I regretted that we had not seen Urfa and Harran, in ancient Mesopotamia, near the Syrian border, and that we would miss the entire Mediterranean coast, but it's always like that with the two vectors that rule our lives: space is truly infinite, we have ample proof of that, but it flies in the face of all experience to say the same of time.

The only story I wrote in Turkey came to me in Ankara. Ankara is partly a planned city; Atatürk plucked it out of provincial obscurity in 1923 so that the capital of his European nation would be firmly in Asia. It is a modern, bustling city. But it does have its own memory, its own history. After visiting the ninth-century citadel, Ruth and I went walking in the old city, along the narrow, twisting, hilly streets with their low, sometimes vividly coloured houses. It had rained earlier, but the sun was out now. There was a refreshing coolness to the air. Puddles were mirrors. We walked with no destination in mind, for the simple pleasure of the activity, a voluntary lostness. We turned left or right beckoned by a potted plant or a shade of blue wall. Children played in the streets. Some who weren't too frenzied over their fun stopped and looked at us in silence. Others, between the catch and throw of a ball, called at us in their shrill voices. "Hello to you too," one of us would reply, which as often as not triggered a cacophonous chorus of shouting and giggling in return, one voice more high-pitched than the next, a sound that is internationally familiar to the human species. One little girl, no more than three years old, got so caught up in the commotion that our appearance caused that she went gaga. She trembled, she stared, she dripped saliva — she looked as if she were about to explode. Instead, she arched back, closed her eyes and put out a shriek that was so loud and piercing it would have shattered crystal. "Aren't you a little screamer?" said Ruth, bending down and making her eyes big. Momentarily I saw her in a different light. She knew children intimately, intimately three times over. I so rarely saw her in that way, even when she was talking of her Philadelphia brood. The screamer's mother came out and swept the little diva into her arms. She and Ruth exchanged looks and smiles, women of different languages but mothers in common.

Others watched us too, but silently. Old, ill-shaven men who followed us with their eyes, perhaps nodding if theirs caught ours.

The street was too narrow for traffic. We came upon a woman sitting on a carpet beneath the open window of what was clearly her own dwelling. Beside her lay a sleeping baby. She was sewing. She took no more notice of us than a glance's worth.

We walked past her.

At a turn we beheld the same thing, only double. Two old women on carpets opposite each other, one with a baby quietly prattling and playing with a piece of cloth. Old they were, these women, with bright, multilayered clothes and few teeth. They were in animated conversation. At the sight of us they waved and smiled and spoke to us. I smiled back and pointed ahead, meaning that we were on a walk and ahead was where we were heading. At exactly the same time they both fell silent and looked where I was pointing, as if I were indicating something amiss, a cement truck coming their way, perhaps. They looked back at us, and both repeated my hand gesture, probably not knowing what they meant by it, only that it might please the foreigners. One held up an empty glass. An offer of tea. We sat down and had tea and another of those conversations we'd had with women throughout Turkey, where many words are spoken, none is understood and much is communicated. Ruth pointed at the baby and said, "Is this your grandson?" and instantly the baby was propelled onto her lap and then mine. "Doctor Livingstone, I presume?" I said to the gurgling child.

When it came time to go, after many emphatic thank-you-very-much's, *Teşekkür ederim* in Turkish, we got up, gingerly walked on what few inches were left of the street between the two women's carpets and proceeded.

But again, only this time triple, quadruple, quintuple. To our left and right whenever we came to a cross street. Women, babies and carpets. Ruth and I looked at each other. "I feel like we're *trespassing*," she said. It was exactly that. We felt we had moved imperceptibly from the public sphere of the street to the private sphere of the house. In this feeling lay the genesis of my story.

It was about a man walking along Atatürk Bulvari, Ankara's aorta, broad, tree-lined and busy. But our man is busy himself and has no time for its distractions. He is thinking about an important business deal. He turns off Atatürk Bulvari onto a quieter street; let us say it is an artery. Our man is thinking hard. He is not paying attention to his surroundings. What is important to him at that moment is what is inside his head.

The honk of a car, the shout of a hawker, something disturbs him. Without a thought he turns off again, this time onto an arteriole. There are no distractions now. No cars, no people. He can walk in peace and concentrate fully. His eyes are open, but they see nothing. Only his feet are aware of the change in things. Our man has not yet come to a decision when he wakes up to the fact that he has stopped walking and is looking at a small table with a pair of glasses on it. What is this, he asks himself, still distracted. He would like to continue walking and thinking, but his feet no longer know where to turn. He realizes that next to the small table there is a large canopied bed, unmade. He notices drops of blood on the sheets. He looks at them, astounded. He spins around. He's in a bedroom. In a capillary, let us say. The room is described in detail for it is elaborately furnished. Our man is in a near-panic. "What am I doing here? How did I get here?" he asks himself. He quickly walks out of the room. He finds himself in a library, then a living-room. He continues on to a dining-room. Then into a kitchen. He opens a door and runs down a corridor. There are several doors; one leads to a bathroom, another to a bedroom, another to a closet. At the end of the corridor, a staircase. He bounds up it. But it continues: living rooms, bedrooms, bathrooms, kitchens, pantries, libraries, dining-rooms, closets, corridors — never a door that leads out, never a window through which he can climb out. An infinite domestic honeycomb. The story ends to the sound of the man's screams, his despair equal to that of a woman who goes shopping and then discovers that she cannot find her way home, but must roam the busy, noisy streets for ever.

Where do men feel ill at ease? In airplane cockpits, bus depots, construction sites, dance halls, elevators, forest paths, gas

stations, hotels, interesting little alleys, junkyards, kiosks, lexi-
cographers' offices, mountain meadows, newspaper rooms,
Oxford, parking lots, queer bars, restaurants, South America,
taxis, underpasses, volleyball courts, waiting-rooms, xylo-
phone schools, yak-petting zoos, zouave recruitment offices,
auction halls, big stores, cockfight pits, deserted subway plat-
forms, effigy burnings, Freemason halls, government offices,
hospitals, intelligence bureaux, Jesuit seminaries, Knights of
Malta meetings, lepers' colonies, movie-houses, necktie parties, opium dens, Plato's cave, quarantine stations, resplendent
bordellos, sunny pink beaches, truckstop diners, utopian islands, villas, war zones, Xmas parties, youth hangouts, ziggu-
rats, army headquarters, ballparks, churches, da Vinci's studio,
essay-writing workshops, filibuster-planning sessions, gener-
als' beds, hobbyists' conventions, International Socialists' col-
lectives, junkies' flophouses, klezmer bands, libraries, the
moon, night-time, oil rigs of the North Sea, penitentiaries,
quiet places, rainbows' ends, slaughterhouses, theatres, un-
American activities committees, voting booths, wreath-laying
ceremonies, xenophobic demonstrations, yachts, or in zero-
hour countdown rooms? No. In all these places, a man will
never be told that he is not welcome because he is a man.

At times it was difficult travelling in Turkey. There were
hassles. Because they took place under the sun of an exotic climate they often became *adventures*, something not only easier
to take, but even sought after. By that bizarre paradox of
travel, the worst journey — the endless bus trip, the mattress
with the million creepy-crawlies, the hotel with the soft, rotten walls — becomes the best, most fondly remembered one.
But when I look back now, some of these hassles were unac-
ceptable. They had one common link: men. Men who openly

stared up and down at us. Men who cracked smiles at the sight of us and turned to their friends, pointing us out with a nod of the head. Men who brushed themselves against us to pass us in streets that were not busy. Men who brushed themselves against us to pass us in streets that were not busy *and* who ran their hands over our breasts. The young man who ran up to me from behind in a dark street of Ankara, pinched my ass and vanished just as quickly. The one in Istanbul, too. Men who clicked at us. Boys who clicked at us. Men who felt they had the right to ooze their unctuous, unwanted attentions upon us regardless of our words, opinions or indifference. Men who decided they knew what we wanted, what destination, what product, what service, what price, before we had even opened our mouths. The bus driver who, seeing that I was asleep on the last row of seats, stopped his bus on the side of the highway, came back and kissed me, so that I woke up to this stranger looming over me and pushed him away angrily, calling out to Ruth, while he walked back smiling and laughing, proud of himself. The man who exposed himself to me at a roadside stop, grinning and playing with himself.

We brushed it all off. We were tough, we became tough. By the time we caught the train from Istanbul to Athens, we were veterans of combat travel. Though we washed every day, we felt as though we hadn't bathed in months. We were not tanned — we were weathered. Our lungs, our minds, had that weary ache of time spent in the great outdoors. We were wary, cunning, skeptical, argumentative, dismissive. No Johnnie Turk was going to fuck around with us. If we'd stayed longer, we would have developed plate armour that clanked as we walked.

But we were not Sherman tanks. We were two women wearing conservative cotton clothes travelling in a big, male country. It wore us down. More than we realized. Some doors became very important to us in Turkey: the doors to our hotel rooms. When we closed and locked them, it was not to secure Ruth's camera, but to secure our shelter. Shelter meant a place to be together — and away.

Which is not to say that we didn't meet Turkish men who were nice. We did. Lots. Who were nice; proper; civil; friendly. But this approach — some good Turks, some bad Turks — is all wrong. My point is neither demographic nor democratic because it was not primarily individuals that struck me, so much as an attitude. And an attitude can slosh around like the sea, rising in one man, ebbing in another, surging forth anew in a third — all beyond the accounting of numbers.

I'd say the seas were high and rough in Turkey. Ruth and I sailed through without a problem, but I wonder about my Turkish sisters. Moving through the public spheres of Turkey as we did, we met Turkish women not a tenth as often as we met men, and nearly always when they were without men — at the market or on buses or on carpets in small streets in Ankara. They spoke to us, they smiled, they sat beside us, they touched us, we spoke in sign language and nodded heads; with them we could relax, let our guard down. They were happy, I guess — happiness is such an incredibly hardy plant — but I believe it was happiness within strict confines, like plants that grow in pots.

We met a woman who worked at a bank in Ankara, not as a clerk but a little higher up, and we had supper with her. Meral told us that she would never become a manager at her bank, never, because she was a woman. "Things were better sixty years ago, under Atatürk," she said. "He gave us the right to vote. He believed in women."

This is what I was approaching, trying to digest, in my story about a man caught in a honeycomb house.

I showed it to Ruth.

"I *loved* being a housewife," she said. "I hate working. Who needs it? My husbands were the only problem I had when I was a housewife. You should have seen Tuesday when she was a little girl. She was such a clowny goof. Danny's best friends are Hispanics and they're teaching him Spanish. He spices up his English with it. It's the funniest thing. My son gets excited about something and suddenly he bursts out, 'Yo soy Pancho Villa!' and he's swaggering up and down the room with an imaginary sombrero and pistols. It cracks me up. With Jerry, we had a nice house with a garden and I had my own car. God, I'd be a housewife anytime. Just give me a good man."

She meant her words to do no more than describe her own experience. It's just my opinion, just mine — that's what her tone of voice said.

But it was a voice that carried weight with me. The inexperience of my fiction seemed to dash itself against the finality of her experience. My story felt stiff and simplistic, the baroque element terribly arty, the whole thing a flimsy nothing. The one conclusion I drew was that I was young. I had fuelled my story with an indignation that was swaggering, like Danny's Pancho Villa. In areas where I had not yet felt my way — men, motherhood, work — I had projected a great scaffolding of ideas.

I kept my sense of wonder at these women in Ankara who domesticated the streets, I kept my indignation at the status of men in Turkey, but I threw out the story. I was hurt and frustrated. Not at Ruth. In a general way. I remember that as I methodically tore my story into square shreds I wondered why things had to be both so simple and so complicated. I vowed that I would never have children. Not me, no sirree. And no man would ever have control over me.

Ruth said, "Let's go for rice pudding," and that was the end of it. They make excellent rice pudding in Turkey, creamy and with lots of cinnamon. That was always the exit from our problems: the senses. Rice pudding or a caress of her hands on my breasts, an aubergine dish or me pushing Ruth onto a bed.

We met him on one of those endless bus trips Ruth and I endured. Perhaps it was between Kayseri and Malatya. A gleaming black snake of a road that meandered across the undulating green and treeless plains of Eastern Anatolia. One bus, no traffic. A farmer, I guess he was. A man of the land, wed to the black earth. He got on seemingly from nowhere and got off in a place not much different. In between the two, we met, our parallel lives touched. He looked to be in his late twenties and he had the rugged, very masculine good looks characteristic of handsome Turkish men: clean, classical features, perfect white teeth, clear eyes, a thick black moustache and a body packed with muscles and hair. His arms and torso strained at the clothes he wore and his forearms were so hairy I could barely see his skin. Hair burst out from the top of his shirt like flames from the window of a burning house.

I don't remember how the three of us got to speaking. I suppose the usual: eyes becoming aware of each other because of his looking, nods and smiles, his first tentative word. He had fewer English words at his disposal than he had fingers, words that he must have learned in schooldays long past. Yet he was so eager and determined to communicate with us that it was nearly a miracle of Jesus: he transformed his drops of

English into decanters of rich meaning. He pronounced my country's name with such solemn, serious emphasis — Kah-nah-dah — that I did what I hadn't done in a long time: I considered it from the outside, as if for the first time. What a curious name it is, sounding so much like a nonsense word, the babble of a child, with the giant C and the three syllables like three dance steps.

We communicated in broad emotions, something like waving at someone from a distance. He smiled and tilted his head a lot. When he was touched, which was often, he slapped both his hands against his chest, which made a booming sound. He was a sweet man, as decent as a nineteenth-century novel. We lavishly praised his country. This nearly brought tears to his eyes. I said, "Atatürk!" and shook my fist, signifying "Great leader!" He slap-boomed his chest and exclaimed, "Atatürk!", signifying I'm not sure what, but it was positive. In fact, "Atatürk!" "Atatürk!" were the last words we exchanged as we shook hands before he got off, as if we were members of an Atatürk revivalist society.

When he was no more than a dot on the horizon and we could no longer see his waving, we sat back.

"Wasn't he a nice man," said Ruth.

"Yes," I replied dreamily. I dwelt on his niceness, his integrity. It took some long minutes before my ambiguous thoughts resolved themselves into focus. He was a sweet man — and one I lusted after. This thought, the popping of the word "lust" into my head, shocked me. A man! Him! To sleep with him! What a thought! I closed the curtains of my eyes and approached my object of desire. Everything that had never turned me on before did so now. Weight, hair, smell. I took his shirt off and imagined his hairy, muscular chest.

Imagined running my hands over it. Pressing my naked chest against it, so slight and hairless in comparison. It was this, his warm, hairy bulk, that excited me. His head so massive and hirsute, so deep brown and rugged, as he took one of my breasts in his mouth. His hands, powerful, rough and gentle, grazing over my body, lingering over my clitoris. He stood fully naked in front of me, his erection standing out. I couldn't imagine him penetrating me, not in reality or in fantasy. But my hands ran over his thighs. I could see holding it. Sucking it.

If I could have masturbated at that moment, I would have. But I had to contain myself and make do with fantasy as the bus drove onwards across Anatolia.

We made the decision to catch the Istanbul–Athens train when we were in Ankara. From that moment on we were conscious that our trip, our odyssey, was coming to an end. Each practicality made this clear — the train reservations, the plane reservations, the thrift so that we wouldn't have to cash another travellers' cheque in Turkey.

We visited Istanbul distractedly. After a two-week trip that had lasted nearly three months, having resolved to close her open ticket at last, Ruth was now dying to see her children. We spent hours in the Great Bazaar, where she bought all kinds of gifts big and small, some for her friends, but most for Tuesday, Graham, Sandra and Danny — one gift for every day she was away, it seemed. I bought Ruth a beautiful silver brooch with an amber inlay. She was chipper, having suddenly realized how much she missed home and how soon she would be there. While I wasn't averse to returning to Roetown, it would hardly be a homecoming.

At my initiative, we went on long walks through Istanbul. I wanted to get as much travel out of our time together as possible. But in many ways Ruth had already left. In bed we were more bed-mates than lovers. She was not deliberately pulling away — she emphatically invited me to Philadelphia for Christmas — but it was becoming increasingly clear, though not openly, that we were from vastly different worlds and that only the suspension of travel, that abnormal fold of time and space, had permitted the romance to bloom. It was a romance that could not travel beyond travel. The change, that inner change that alters the way reality is perceived, was mutual; it was only that I lagged a little behind Ruth. I don't mean it to sound so dramatic, but beyond her I had no one. The whole trip had been one breathless rapture, every minute a pleasure and an adventure. Now I had to catch my breath.

The train ride to Athens was long, sunny and melancholy. I was thankful the Greek landscape was so beautiful. Every mile absorbed a tear, so that I was able to smile at the airport.

We spent our last day together wandering in the Plaka. In a deliberate last moment of romance, in the shelter of a doorway in the shadow of the Parthenon, we kissed the way lovers do. At the airport it was sad but sober. Ruth wavered between elation and memory, between *I'll see my children soon* and *Oh! the times we had.* I nodded. I had achieved a balance. The mind shushing the heart.

The greenness of her eyes struck me for some reason at that moment. She turned, found her American passport and presented it with a smile to the man in uniform; she hauled her heavy carry-on pack onto her shoulder; she walked a few paces into the duty-free zone; turned; we waved to each other, eye to eye; she walked off.

I took a single room that night. Alone in bed I burst into tears.

It was near the end of August. I spent a few days in Greece, such easy travelling after Turkey. I slept in dorms, I walked around Athens, I returned to the Temple of Poseidon at Cape Sounion, and then I flew back to Kah-nah-dah.

It was surprisingly pleasant to be back in Roetown. School had not yet started and there were few students around. I had several days of peace. I had expected to be quite depressed, but to a new scenery, a new mood. I would see Ruth at Christmas, and I had her phone number, could always call her if I felt low — so why feel low? This, and solitary walks in warm, sunny Roetown, and thoughts of the coming year's courses, and Elena's absence, all kept my spirits up. She wasn't returning to Ellis. There was a letter for me at Strathcona-Milne from her. She said that she didn't know why she was studying what she was studying so she had decided to stop. She would work for a while and then see what she wanted to do.

Before the summer, a group of friends and I had arranged to rent a house in downtown Roetown. It was the last house on its street, tucked away just beyond the top of a hill. The street, after a sharp turn, ended in a parking lot. It served a factory which was next to us, quite a bit lower down, where the land levelled out. It was a cookie, breakfast cereal and porridge factory. I seem to recall that sometimes in the fall and spring the air carried the fragrance of roasted oats, but I believe that's a fabricated, wishful souvenir.

In front of the house was the municipal jail, complete with barbed wire atop the walls and a whirling camera. From my desk I would spend the year glancing at that wall, wondering whether I might see a criminal suddenly pop up, ease his way beneath the wires, fall to the ground and break for freedom. But there was never such a break — or it took place while I had my head down, trapped in the prison of the inept novel I had started.

I was the first to move in. The place was an empty mess and I spent several hours at odd times in haphazard, frenzied cleaning. For a while I slept on an old mattress I found, stained by past people's incontinence, menstruation and love-making. This didn't disgust me. The stains were dry, ancient history. It was the mattress's lack of comfort that pushed me to buy a white, virgin futon. I took two small rooms on the second floor: one, facing the street, as my office; another, even smaller, as my bedroom.

I went on long walks. I was amazed at how inconspicuous I was; by Turkish standards I was invisible. This played a good part in my high spirits. It was refreshing and liberating to walk down a street unnoticed, left alone with my day-dreams; to speak and be understood right away; to look around and feel a part of things. This is my street, my park, my house, my country. These are my people, my wide acres.

My roommates trickled in. We were not close friends, but the house didn't require that of us — it was spacious enough to accommodate distance — and the routine of organized education kept us busy. But, just in case, we built those good fences that make good neighbours that Robert Frost so deplored. We divided the fridge into five parts (five chunks of variously aged cheddar cheese, five separate litres of homotwopercentskim milk, five etc.) and we divided the cupboards in five parts (five packages of pasta, five cans of tuna, five etc.). I believe the only victuals we shared were salt and pepper. In the bathroom there were five bars of soap and a profusion of hair products (but

divisible by five). We shared the toilet paper. In our relations
with each other, things were also generally divided by five. Five
sets of joys and pains behind five closed doors. I say "generally"
because there was a living-room, a common area, and we did
lie about and talk and listen to music and watch Sarah's clunky
TV together; and over the course of the year we did form a few
duets of intimacies. There was open friction only over the
matter of dishes. Someone else's dirty plate or two in the sink
was exasperation enough to cause a huge pile-up of dirty
dishes.

There was Daniel, exceptionally bright, always getting
A+'s in his history papers and later pulling off a major international scholarship, but emotionally fragile, the sort of fragility
that would eventually require the glue of lithium to hold him
together; Karen, cheery and independent, who in the course
of the two years I knew her blossomed from a nice, small-
town hick into an actor who amazed me with her Ophelia;
Martha, despondent, withdrawn and witty, who spent most
of her time at her boyfriend's place; and Sarah, with whom I
was the closest, beautiful, bright, easygoing and funny, and
just about as lost and confused as I was, who half-way through
the year eased herself out of the world of academia into the
world of waitressing; and Spanakopita, who, despite his great
name and great looks (brown and orange, and fat), was a surly
cat who never reciprocated my affections.

The only thing the five of us had in common, I realize now,
was lostness and confusion, in varying degrees — Karen, who
seemed to have a natural ability to be happy, the least, while we
others slip-slided along whatever scale measures happiness,
sometimes joyful, often miserable. This was, perhaps, a normal
lostness, typical of our age — maybe even salutary. I certainly

didn't envy the dead certainty in things that some commerce students displayed, being in a rush to graduate and set themselves up at age twenty-three the way they would be living at age sixty-three. But it was not easy to take, not in my case at least. Better remembered or imagined than lived through. I believe it was this lostness that prevented us from getting closer to each other. We were each jealously possessive of our wilderness.

The school year, the cafeteria-style getting of wisdom, started. I decided to take only three courses, two less than a full meal. I became a part-time nibbler of philosophy of religion, early modern philosophy (Descartes, Spinoza, Leibniz, Locke, Berkeley, Hume, Kant) and English literature, in this case the American Renaissance (de Tocqueville, Emerson, Thoreau, Melville, Hawthorne, Poe, Whitman). With the extra time I had, I started the frustrating, blissful task of writing a novel, and I enjoyed the pleasures of idleness.

Many people envied my travels. "Turkey! Wow! I spent the summer in boring (pick one: Belleville, London, Ottawa, Burlington, Oshawa, Mississauga) doing nothing/working as a (pick one: lifeguard, house-painter, waitress, library worker, filing clerk, gas-pump attendant)." Though it's true that I'd rather spend the summer in Turkey than in Belleville, nonetheless I thought, "Kill your parents. Wire their car's ignition directly to the gas tank so it blows up and they become charred, crusty and black on the outside, but red and liquid on the inside. Like solidifying lava. Like my parents before the salt water and the sharks. Then collect the money and run."

One important difference between my roommates and me was that they were all attached. Daniel had Isabella, Karen had James, Martha had Lawrence, and Sarah had a few. But I was firmly unenvious of these romantic relationships. Martha's Lawrence was a pretentious twerp. Once or twice I saw Karen transform herself into a whining, cloying kitten when James wasn't doing what she wanted, something mortifying to watch, but which he revelled in, playing it for all it was worth. And I was struck by something Sarah said to me once: that she had never been without a boyfriend since the age of twelve. She had broken up that summer with a boyfriend of a few years and she was clearly unhappy and out of balance over it. I wondered if she was capable of being alone and happy at the same time. At night, lying on my futon in my tiny bedroom, I could occasionally hear love-making — Daniel and Isabella's to my left, very quiet, hardly more than an intense sigh or two, or Sarah and whoever's to my right, slightly raunchier. It only made me happy that I was independent and unfettered. A few thoughts of Ruth, a little ecstatic masturbation, many thoughts about my novel — and I would fall soundly asleep, free the next morning to be free.

I painted my office entirely in white — the walls, the floor, the window frame, the door, my small desk, my chair. It felt like the inside of a cloud, especially when I looked out my window upon the world. It was from inside this cumulus that I set myself the task of being a small goddess.

I wanted a corporeal novel, full of foul smells and crude sensations. Three months of Greco-Turkish toilets lingered in my nose from the time when I was discovering my own body, the full pleasures it could give, the fair amidst the foul. There was also a fart; it too was one of those quiz-puzzle links between fact and fiction that academics so love to explore. I was in a toilet on the main campus, peeing — an innocent pee —

when along came the urge to fart. So be it. A discreet breaking
of wind, no more. My stomach was still adjusting to the change
of diet from Turkey to Canada. But it boomed like a cannon
going off, the sort of sound that has so much ego as to demand
the applause of echo. "What was that!?" came a voice beyond
my stall, alarmed. A second or two of silence passed, during
which I am sure my stall's door was pointed out. I heard several
repressed giggles. I was annoyed. In Turkey, Ruth and I talked
of our shits as a matter of course. They were not mere fecal
matter; they were communiqués, they were précis. Which is
why we looked at them before washing them down the hole
with the pitcher of water — so that we could read them and be
told about ourselves. Colour, consistency, quantity, smell — so
many chapters in an autobiography. In Turkey, after this
atomic flatulence, I would have gone to Ruth and said, "Ruth,
I just farted like a cannon going off, the sort of sound that has
so much ego as to demand the applause of echo." "Really!" she
would have replied, paying me her full attention, placing a
hand on her belly. "But I feel fine. I haven't farted in hours. Did
you shit too? What was it like? How do you feel? Have you
been burping? Didn't we eat the same thing this afternoon?"
And we would have talked about it for several minutes. But in
Canada it was a source of embarrassment. This observation
juxtaposed itself upon another, from a minute before: when I
entered the washroom, as the euphemism goes, it struck me
that the first smell my nose identified was neither piss nor shit
but hairspray. Three girls, three Christmas trees, were touching themselves up in front of the mirror, each the sole actor
and spectator of her vanity. "This place is supposed to smell
bad, not chemical," I thought. "It *ought* to smell like shit." I
vowed that my novel would brim with shit.

I also wanted to address this matter of God. In quiet moments I had sometimes noticed how, having dismissed God, we — you and I — were left not with the plenitude of life, as I expected, since a false being cannot take space, but a vacuum, a sucking emptiness. Could this false being be occupying a necessary space, one that demanded filling? It wasn't often that I felt this, usually when I was thinking of my parents, but at such times life seemed little more than a meaningless shuffle over a short distance for a brief time. It lacked the spirit that would have turned each step into a dance step, with its proper measure, rhythm and grace. I had no real regrets over this — my life seemed a greater challenge for its spiritual orphanhood — but occasionally I could intuit how much grander the march of life would be if God *were*. At such moments the truth or falsity of God's being seemed irrelevant. It was a fiction of such magnitude, why not believe it? What was gained by a truth that left one with an empty feeling? I could get by without God in the illusory infinity of my daily hours, but if I were in a plane about to crash, would I not miss Him? Would I not create Him? And if I survived, would I want to dismiss Him a second time? I wanted to approach religious spirituality in my novel not with the intent of proving anything, but simply to see what it would be like to have faith, regardless of proof.

My novel, to which I gave the working title *Crazy Jane*, was a first-person religious allegory set in 1939 in a small Portuguese village some days away from Fatima. To suit my needs I gave the country high, savage mountains. There were a number of characters, but the three protagonists were Corto, a shepherd to whom I gave a club-foot; a magnificent wooden Christ on the Cross, the pride of the village, by the sixteenth-century Portuguese master João Ribéra do Nova ("Renaissance in its anatomically precise depiction of the suffering body of Christ, a great bulk of tortured wood it is, nailed to a cross and *hanging* — see the tension in His hands! see the contorted stretch of His magnificent chest! — yet truly divine in the grace of His expression"); and the narrator, whom we would meet on the first page, as she is sitting in the middle of the main street of the village, calmly looking out of the novel, so to speak, waiting for us: Corto's dog, a friendly, loquacious, religiously devout mongrel. The bulk of the novel would be narrated by this dog. She would greet us ("Hello!" would be the first word of my first novel), would shit in the middle of the street ("Ohjustonemorepiece! Ahhhhhhhhh such rapture. Amen!") and then she would take us aside to introduce us to the village and its denizens, pissing here and there to demarcate the territory of our fiction. A dog both scatological and religious ("I've always felt that I belonged to a religious order. To have my days marked by the call of prayer, from the early morning adoration of matins, fresh and scintillating like the dew, to the gentle, weary exaltation of complines, as comforting as sleep, would be my *summum bonum*") struck me as the balance between body and spirit that I was seeking.

The story would turn on a pilgrimage that the villagers undertake to have their Christ on the Cross blessed by the Archbishop of Fatima. With food and water, and taking turns carrying the cross, they would set off, with Corto's dog in tag to bring us words. The going would be easy. Time for talking and laughing and praying and tea at sunset. But the pilgrims would get lost in the high, savage mountains. There would be terrible snowstorms. They would run out of food and firewood. Out of desperation, and each time throwing themselves onto their knees supplicating God for forgiveness, they would start to eat those villagers who had died of hunger and exposure, roasting them — and keeping themselves warm in the process — by burning the Christ on the Cross, first the cross ("They gently brought down Our Saviour from His cross") but then Christ as well. But they would run out of bodies, as they would of Body. As a last act, mad with hunger and the desire to continue living, they would eat the dog, Corto himself doing the killing ("weeping like Abraham"). But this would not mean the loss of our narrator. She would have her head smashed with a rock and she would be skewered and roasted over Christ's burning head, but still we would hear her. Only when she was dismembered and shared among the twelve remaining survivors would we hear her differently: at that moment her voice would split into the twelve voices of the survivors. The novel would end with these voices. The dog's last word, at the bottom of a page, would be that all-embracing word "and" ("For what is it to give up one's life when Christ is so close? He has turned His head. He is looking at me. He smiles! Oh! There is so much light! Take me and"); the next pages of the book would fold out and there would be twelve parallel paragraphs, each different but each starting with that enigmatic word "I", thus: "I was given part of the dog's right leg and though I cannot say that it tasted good, it nonetheless sustained me and I could feel a little strength return to my weary body and I wished that the leg had had more meat on it if . . ." or "I was not so lucky and I received the dog's bony head, the brains of which had been lost in its killing and the eyes melted away in its roasting, to my famished regret, and I had to content myself with its crispy ears, its rubbery lips and cheeks and its unexpectedly palatable but small tongue, but I should add that though I derived little carnal pleasure from this feast, it gave me sustenance of another kind, for to hold this small, very warm sphere in my hands reminded me of the time when I was little and I slipped away from helping Mother and I went inside the empty church and played with the chalice, much the size of this skull, balancing it on my open hand, throwing it in the air and catching it, knowing that if I broke it there would be hell to pay, but I didn't break it, and this memory brought me comfort and strength, enough to ...," each voice going on to relate the same story in a different way, like some books of the New Testament: how the next morning, with the strength that eating the dog had given them, the group would manage to struggle and stumble the last few dozen miles down the mountain to reach Fatima, where, in thanks for the reprieve, they would assemble in the basilica and sing the praises of God, their faith unshaken, João Ribéra do Nova's Christ on the Cross now sculptured in that loveliest but most difficult of materials, air. After a few more words on how each had fared since the tragedy, the twelve voices would close with a common word: "Goodbye."

My idea in splintering the dog's voice into twelve was to introduce democracy to voice. In the absence of faith, of one Voice, what I could do was celebrate voices, first a small one, then twelve, then more, depending on the vagaries of love and childbirth. A hymn to polyphony was my idea.

The walls of my office became covered with index cards. These cards were the various puzzle pieces of my novel — twists of plot; stylistic reminders; bits of dialogue; descriptive dashes; words that struck me, around which I would construct a long sentence, perhaps even a scene ("mendicant look"); themes that should not be forgotten; insights that needed elaboration or proper context; and so on. I neatly bordered each card with a different colour — blue, brown, green, black or nothing, white — depending on its importance to my story. At first there were just a few jottings stuck in front of my desk, little helpmates to creativity. In time these cards proliferated and became my novel, all it was, all it would be.

This geographical Talmud grew upwards till it was nearly touching the ceiling and downwards right to the floor. At midheight flowed a river, the blue cards, with actual sentences and paragraphs from the novel; it started at the light switch to the left of the door with a card bearing the word "Hello!" and ran from there right around my office, like a panorama, until it opened onto the Sea of the Twelve Goodbyes at the doorframe. Above and below the blue cards were the brown ones, directions that were essential in giving an episode its meaning — the banks of the river — and just beyond these the green ones — the fields of good but general ideas. Farther on lay the black cards of less certain value — less arable, I might say — though occasionally I took one down and recopied it and gave it a new colour. Finally, on the very edges of my novel, were the plain index cards, as white as snowcaps. Ideas that had fizzled, aborted characters, deleted incidents — it was only out of fearful hoarding that I didn't destroy these jottings. Unsure of what I was doing, I was unsure of the value of my words.

The only interruption in my vista was the window, one landscape breaking in on another. I tended to gaze at this second landscape when I was in search of inspiration and resolve.

I placed my desk and chair in the centre of my office, clear of any wall, so that I could glide over the topography with ease. Which is what I did week after week, month after month, for hours at a time. With my eyes I would hover . . . hover . . .

hover — and then swoop down and catch an index card. I would transport it to my desk and work on it, spilling over onto another card, or two, or three, despite my efforts to make my handwriting microscopic. In some places on the wall where I found myself with much to say but little space, the land became hilly and the river broke into rapids and waterfalls.

I should have taken photographs of my office when my walls were in full bloom. The Artist and Her Studio: A Novel in Twelve Kodachromes.

The truth was, I had no idea how to write a novel. I was a Doctor Frankenstein who had accumulated an impressive collection of body parts, and I even knew how they would go together, what parts went where, but the secret of life still eluded me. At regular intervals I sensed that an essential act of conception had not taken place, but I don't recall much misery or anxiety over the matter. I was a happy spectator of my own device. I talked out loud, waved my hands, acted out scenes and when a brilliant new idea struck me — such as a lovely scene in an empty church of a dog watching a girl playing with a chalice — I captured it like a passing butterfly and cheerfully pinned it to the wall.

My novel was a dream — and it had the value of a dream. It was a form of rehearsal.

As planned over the course of three or four phone calls (each time a shock at hearing her voice, which triggered a tumble of memories), I spent Christmas and New Year's in Philadelphia with Ruth and her family. I met the famous Tuesday, Sandra and Danny (but not Graham). Of each I had formed a precise mental picture, having transformed Ruth's descriptions into photographs. But Ruth's testimony proved to be as accurate in describing her small tribe as the shape of clouds would be in describing a landscape. Her children neither looked nor behaved anything close to what I had expected. Colour of hair, expression, height, weight, dress, tone of voice — I had created pure fictions. Having heard strictly the maternal angle of things, I had imagined them child-like. Having only heard of them second-hand, I had made them passive, spirits that would disappear as soon as we weren't talking about them, as they had for me in Turkey. But Tuesday and Sandra certainly weren't children, and Danny wasn't passive. In that house — which wasn't actually in Philadelphia, but in a suburb — there were unmistakably four live human beings. Tuesday was a year older and a year ahead of me, an economics/sociology major seemingly untouched by the existential monkey. Sandra was in grade 12, friendly but restless and testy at times. Danny was a ten-year-old American kid, graceless, loud and whiny; on several occasions I wanted to kill him. And I was the "friend" their mother had met in Greece and travelled with in "Turkey!"

The dynamics were a little odd. It was with Tuesday that I should have had the most in common. We talked about Ellis and Simon Fraser universities, about our different majors, about Roetown and Burnaby, about movies — we traded in all the aspects that made up our common student culture. Yet it was clear that it was with her mother that I truly connected. Before Tuesday's eyes the twenty-odd years, that chasm that separated Ruth and me, would vanish, and her mother would appear to her as a stranger. It would be during the telling of an anecdote. We would become animated, we would laugh, we would interrupt each other either to refute a little jab with humorous indignation, set the record straight, or the contrary, to exaggerate a point for dramatic effect. The sheets were so dirty they were as rigid as plywood! The ice-cream was like chewing gum, you just couldn't finish it, you had to spit it out! The bus trip lasted forty-eight hours! Cost forty-eight cents! That we knew each other very, very well, our foibles, our strengths, our sore spots, our funny-bones, was evident. Suddenly Tuesday *was* a child, and Ruth and I would set the agenda of conversation, direct it, apt to shoo the child away if she became too obstreperous a spectator. Then she would comment apropos, with a touch of sarcasm, usually, as miffed adults are prone to do, and Ruth would reply and landscapes would indefinably shift, currents would change, winds would turn — an earthquake just beyond the range of the senses — and Ruth would become a stranger to me; she would play that role, source of joy and exasperation, through which she by and large defined herself. I would think, "She could be my mother too. She is double my age and some," and I would notice her wrinkles, her mature hands, her manners, the chasm between us.

There was Christmas and the litter of bright gift-wrap paper — Ruth gave me a book on how to work one's way around the world, from *vendang*ing in France to teaching English in Czechoslovakia to kibbutzing in Israel to modelling in Japan to sheep-shearing in Australia; I gave her Kazantzakis's *Zorba the Greek*— and there was the great dinner with the hullabaloo of its communal cooking — I made the mashed potatoes, extra-garlicky — and there were a few visits to Philadelphia between Christmas and New Year's. My tourist preparation for Philadelphia was to read a lengthy essay by Octavio Paz on Duchamp's *The Bride Stripped Bare by Her Bachelors, Even*. I saw the *Bride* at the Museum of Art, with her chocolate grinder and the cracks in her glass, accidental but oh so appropriate, and I might even have got a sense of the Bachelors, of their intents, but for Tuesday, who wanted to get going, I could tell. I take for ever in museums. Her mother used to get impatient with me too. We saw a movie in a cinema the size of a shoebox in a mall the size of a city, with parking lots that had horizons (but the movie was unexpectedly good and funny, *Splash* by Ron Howard, and I laughed my head off). We played games, canasta among adults, Monopoly with Danny, who won every time, wouldn't you know, even when I had hotels on Atlantic, Ventnor and Marvin Gardens, Pacific, North Carolina and Pennsylvania, Park Place and Boardwalk *and* I controlled all four railways. Ruth told me that Danny didn't like losing.

All the while I was feeling that some dial within me, having nothing to do with the year reaching its end, was rolling towards 999, about to turn over.

My room was directly opposite Ruth's. This might have been meaningful, but it was just where the guest bedroom was. It was a small room whose bare beige walls felt slightly oppressive, as the only window was so high up one needed a stepladder to look out. I shared this bottom of a well with the sewing machine. I mention this because I find these machines intriguing, and I remember Ruth's clearly. At night, after I had clicked off the bedside lamp, light would seep in from the window and dilute the darkness enough that I could make out the sewing machine. I would consider it. What a curious, unmistakable outline. A mechanical woodpecker. I had read that sewing machines were highly intricate pieces of engineering that had required great ingenuity in their development. I imagined that the Singer who had made millions was the semi-worthless grandson of the humble, hardworking inventor whose device would free nineteenth-century middle-class women from household drudgery and enslave nine-teenth-century working-class people in factories, but I have no idea, I'm just saying that. Then, after other, less determined thoughts in which I was uncertain what words to match with what emotions, I would fall soundly asleep. Having no home of my own, I always sleep well in other people's homes.

For several days after my arrival Ruth and I communicated through glances and slight smiles at moments when they would go unnoticed by the others. The few times we were alone together our glances were steadier, but our talk was still vague. If these glances could have spoken, I'm not sure what they would have expressed. Longing? Lust? Anticipation? Farewell? Finally, late one night when everyone was safely asleep, our two doors quietly opened at the same time, like two eyes, and we stood in our doorframes and looked at each other. I was wearing a T-shirt, Ruth a nightgown. I can't really say what happened then. There was desire — if she had beckoned me, I would have gone; when I retreated backwards into my room it was partly in the hope of drawing her in — and there were memories of ache and release and salty skin and there was resistance — I am forty-seven, a mother, I have a family, it cannot be; I am twenty, a student, I am a foreigner, it cannot be — but amidst that complex swirl there was still something else, a surprise, a small but harbinger emotion that whispered in me: ambivalence. At that moment I could see Ruth whole, not as a Turkish lover or as a Philadelphia mother, but whole. And I did not want.

We looked at each other for a minute or so. We spoke not a word. In part it was out of fear that the least syllable would awaken Tuesday. But what was there to say anyway? After our eyes greeted each other, they floated for some seconds before we returned to our gaze of old, eye to eye, smile to smile, memory to memory. Then, with serene, goodbye smiles, we backed into our rooms and into our roles, she to her wide heterosexual bed, I to my uncertain single bed. It was over. We must let things pass. I slipped into the sheets. I felt a flash of regret, a sudden push towards tears. What have you done? What have you thrown away? Go to her now. Crawl up, curl up. Offer your breasts. Bring out your right hand and let it glide down naturally. Kiss. No. Stop. I fell back in bed. My eyes on the sewing machine, I sifted through my confusion.

My dial had turned over. I was at 001.

When Ruth drove me to the bus station on a cold sunny day in the new year, we kissed on the lips softly and said farewell with a sense of peace. I will always remember Ruth with great tenderness, and I wish her and her family nothing but happiness and good fortune. Graham, whom I never met — that poor ten-year-old boy who struggled to shore with the high-pitched words "Go, Graham, go!" ringing in his ears, while his mother sank — has haunted my imagination for years.

I slept once more with a woman — she came on to me and I went along on the spur of the moment — but it's nothing worth the telling; all I remember is a yawning sense of boredom. Ruth and Elena retained their aura of carnal allure, but in the museum part of my memory, where they elicited smiles and a glow of fondness rather than a move of my hand to between my legs.

I'm not sure why, as a woman, I began to desire men. After a moment of surprise it became a matter of feeling — and I acted upon that feeling, without reflection. It's an odd thing to question desire.

On the outside my life didn't change much. I worked a little harder at my studies, pinpricked by the possibility of rustication. I read *Moby-Dick* in sixteen hours, put my exhausted B-range thoughts in a C-range essay and got a D for it because it had been due before Christmas (but my first-term enthusiasm for Emerson, Thoreau and Hawthorne saved me from failing). Philosophy of religion I enjoyed, though with ups and downs. Berkeley and Hume helped me survive early modern. But even when my studies interested me intellectually, I had difficulty sticking to them. Somehow they always missed the point. My need was elsewhere.

I pursued work on my mural, which continued to give me satisfaction with only fits of torment. My walls were now so thick with index cards that I'm certain they insulated me from the surrounding world more than Proust's cork walls did. I was no closer to producing a viable piece of fiction, but this was an observation I never cared to make, though I did spend more time gazing out my window.

In my first year, timid virgins used to hang around my room for hours on end, willing neither to leave nor to make a move on me, which was for the good since I was not at all inclined to sleep with a boy then, though I did enjoy their company, distractions from Elena that they were. The bolder, older ones, who made clearer their intent, I sent packing with outbursts of laughter and witty retorts, which, repeated a few times, put an end to their persistence. I suppose I acquired a reputation as hard to get.

Now I wished that some of them would come back, would think of walking up the street where the municipal jail was to pay me a visit. Unfortunately most of my friends were female, and those who weren't were irrevocably gay. I once asked Joe if he had ever slept with a woman.

"Yuck! What a revolting thought."

"What about a pig, Joe? Ever fucked a pig?"

"No. But I tried to sodomize a Norwegian elkhound once. At camp in the shower-room. At the first yelp I let it go. It was terrible being a virgin."

My lack of romantic involvement began to frustrate me. Independence — from what? Freedom — for what? What stupidity. To be on intimate terms with someone struck me as the only meaningful source of happiness. The mawkish, gluco-romantic aspects of my roommates' relationships no longer repelled me. My way of going about it would be different, that was all. More like Joe's and his boyfriend Egon's, free of predetermined roles.

Never having desired men before, I went about finding out what exactly I found desirable in them. It was all very strange, this. I had gone through a process of induction where I had reached the general — men — without any reference to the particular. I began to look for the particular. I became vividly aware of male physique and symmetry, of manner, smile, walk, hair. I scrutinized my memories, examining the men in them in a new light. I started paying attention to men's glances, those pestering glances that men give to women. I considered each one, if only for a fraction of a second, to see what it had to offer.

In most circumstances my imagination nourished my

vision, acted as a close counsellor to its testimony. But in this case my fancy was nearly empty and needed stoking before it could be fired up. The only advice it could give my eyes concerned a Turkish farmer met once on a bus, a body strong and hairy yet pliant, with a handsome head and a full erection rising from hair, something vague in outline but precise in its effect on me. This one ember glowed vermilion in my mind.

I was at the library on the main campus, nestled in a comfortable chair, an open but idle book on my lap. I noticed a student, ill-shaven and dishevelled, who was looking at books in the stacks. He had small gold-rimmed glasses and was wearing an array of clothes that seemed to have come to him by storm rather than by intent. It was a little past two in the afternoon and my day had started over six hours ago; he looked as if he had got up a minute ago, and awakened forty-five seconds later. He was rocking back and forth on his feet, eyeing the book titles. From his expression, it looked as if the books were all shouting at him. He was slim and handsome, his sandy blond hair a mess. Perhaps sensing my gaze, he turned his head a quarter and gave me a smile. I smiled back. In nearly a whisper he said, "It's easier in a church. Only one book."

I replied, "You should try a swimming-pool. No books at all."

He chuckled and turned back to his search. After a few minutes he picked off three books. As he left: "Bye." With another smile.

I realized how far I had gone when the thought of kissing him, and being kissed in return, was not only conceivable but acutely desirable. To kiss *him* — no man in the abstract, but specifically, particularly, *him*. To see *him* naked, and wanting me and plainly showing me his lust. My heart began to pound. I brought my legs together.

Thus did my imagination take possession of men.

One of the signs of spring in Roetown — or one that I was quick to pick out, sooner than the buds in the trees — was the appearance of posters and leaflets announcing "Canadian Images". Those brightly emblazoned words, usually with a loop of celluloid making out the year, told me that soon the cold of winter would end.

Canadian Images was a one-week outbreak of cinematic culture that took over every available venue at the university and in town. It came and went like a springtime shower. For the duration of a week the clouds were made of celluloid and, to the furious clickety-click of projectors, they pelted the town with movies.

Every year I bought a program and went through it carefully, trying to guess on the basis of words what the images would be like. It was a process of elimination that was sometimes easy, sometimes difficult. The end result would be a large piece of paper with a tight schedule on it, a feat of diplomacy that reconciled the imperatives of interest, transportation and hunger. Festival pass in hand, excusing myself from school and even from writing and swimming, I would disappear. Though the days were getting longer and brighter at that time of year, for me there would be darkness at noon — on some days, in fact, from 10 a.m. to 10 p.m. Hungry, tired, eyes sore, dying to pee, I would sit and take in every conceivable kind of movie. The only criterion for being shown at Canadian Images was that a movie be Canadian. It mattered not a jot what it was about or how long it was. What flickered on

the screen went from the staidly documentary to the weirdly
arty, from the realistic to the surrealistic, from one minute to
feature length, everything and anything that was made in the
Canadian shadow of America. There were in fact few feature-
length movies, such orchestral productions being beyond the
capacity of most Canadian filmmakers. Those that were
shown were usually awful — pale, cash-strapped imitations of
American formulas. The majority of the fare was short-length
and medium-length movies — solos and chamber pieces, one
might say — fuelled by originality and passion rather than
dollars. And bound for limbo. For besides a festival or two
there was nowhere else they would be screened.

Which was a true pity. At Canadian Images I saw obscure
feats of creativity that have radiated in my memory ever since.

A man leaned over and whispered to me, "This is my
movie coming up."

It was called *Snowflakes*. There was no plot, no narrative,
no music. The man beside me had taken hundreds of close-up
shots of snowflakes and strung them together. Three or four
flashed by every second. How he had managed to magnify his
starlets without them melting under the heat of the attention,
I don't know. But he had done it, there it was, in a sequence:
five hundred mugshots of snowflakes. Each one pure, sharp
and delicate, yet powerful enough to break up light so that
pinpoints of spectral colour sparkled here and there. Every
crystal was the same size and had six points, but at that the
similarities ended. The configurative variations — in the
barbs, in the flying buttresses, in the concentric hexagons —
were all perfectly geometric and seemingly endless. I wondered about that, endless. Is it true that snowflakes are unique
individuals, with none like any other? After three minutes,

when it was over, I asked the production team beside me if this was so.

"I don't know," he replied. "There were too many."

He was still looking at the screen, now blank. He was clearly enthralled by his own work. There was applause — not quite enough to make a ripple, but a few good sonorous drops, I'd say. He didn't seem to notice. I found this touching. He was the only spectator he needed. He had done something, found it beautiful, was happy. A perfectly circumscribed creative act. As the lights were going down for the next movie, he got up to go. I leaned forward and said, "That was very good. I enjoyed it."

"Oh. Thank you."

He stood for a second.

"I'm working on sand now," he revealed. And then he was madly running up the steps before it got dark. I would like to say that he had a good daytime job, that he was a dentist, but I don't know.

Another jewel under ten minutes was *A Study into the Damage Done to Dictionaries by Firearms*. It was shot in black and white, with that excruciating visual sharpness that the absence of colour seems to confer upon objects. A string piece, gentle and introspective, played very quietly throughout. It wasn't overlaid — every crack and thunder of firearm silenced it — yet it always came back, as quiet as a whisper, and with a similar magnetic insistence.

The movie was what its title promised. On a pedestal in a field, *The Shorter Oxford Dictionary of the English Language* stood like a soldier at attention. A man dressed in a lab coat holding a shotgun in his hands stepped into our view and blasted the lexicon from a distance of about four feet. The noise was a fierce, compressed roar, an angry lion given only a second to express itself. The book, a good ten pounds, sailed through the air and crashed to the ground. A flutter of paper butterflies danced about. The blast was shown again, only this time in slow motion, that cinematic elixir of life that allows a second to live for twenty. Everything was clear: the shotgun's rebound, the tensing of the man's face and the involuntary closing of his eyes, the blurry vomit emerging from the gun's mouth and reaching for the dictionary, the crash of the pellets and the pulverizing of the front cover, the jolting departure of the book along a horizontal line, the explosion of paper, the heavy, awkward crash to the ground, which would break bones in a human. And always that string piece coming back.

In the following minutes we witnessed similar executions with a variety of shotguns, handguns and rifles. Each firearm looked more fearsome than the last. The final weapon was a piece of machinery that seemed driven more by electronics than by gunpowder, with a curious chamber, a telescopic sight and the daintiest trigger you could imagine. It made only a restrained *tuc* sound when fired.

The movie concluded with close-up shots of the wounded dictionaries, each laid out on a white table next to the firearm with which it had been shot. The mutilations were varied. Some dictionaries were faceless corpses lying supine. Others had had their backs blown out and lay awkwardly on their sides. A small number appeared only moderately disfigured, but had massive internal injuries. The last dictionary, the one hit by the gun with the innocent-looking trigger, was little more than a devastated front cover with bits of pages clinging to it. The rest of the body, what was found of it, was nearly a powder.

The string piece was by Schubert, said the credits. The movie ended with a dedication: *In Memoriam Marie-France Desmeules*.

It was at Canadian Images that I met Tom. Tom of the gratifying ten days. I arrived for a showing of three medium-length movies at the Tecumseh amphitheatre, Ellis's largest venue, just as the lights were dimming. It was on the festival's third day, I believe. I don't recall the time of day; my mind had already habituated itself to a timeless Arctic-winter darkness. I quickly scanned the amphitheatre for a seat. There was a good attendance. I saw a waving hand. It was Joe; there was a free seat beside him. By the time I got to the seat it was pitch-black, and it was Joe's extended hand that guided me to it.

"Hello, sweetie," whispered Joe.

"Hello, dearie. Thanks for the seat."

It was the way we always greeted each other.

"Hello, darling."

Oh. It was Egon.

"Hello, Egon. I didn't see you."

"My sad fate," he replied.

"Hi," came yet another whispered voice, this one unknown.

"Hi," I replied into the darkness.

The movie started. A scream of a little comedy. A young man is looking down at another young man lying in bed. "Frank," he says, waking the young man, "there was a dirty plate in the sink. I've had it. I'm leaving you."

"What?" says Frank. He props himself up and in a dead-pan voice, looking straight at us, launches forth on the unpredictability of human relationships. The rings of Saturn, the disposal of toenail clippings, the continual pregnancies of male sea-horses, the dimples that reduce the drag on golf balls, the importance of good posture, Buster Keaton's dentition and the history of doughnuts in North America are all pertinently mentioned.

Between Frank and his fastidious boyfriend and the next movie, there was a lighted pause of a few minutes. I met Egon's neighbour, the unheralded greeter, Tom. He stretched his hand out and we shook hands. He was from Halifax and was billeted with Egon and his roommate. He went to Dalhousie and worked for an alternative movie-house which, thanks to the partial sponsorship of a local travel agency, had — but the lights went out, and it's strange how darkness inhibits speech, as if spoken words had colour.

A movie went by, less successful than the previous one since I've clean forgotten it, and I found out that his alternative movie-house had sent him over to check out this year's crop of Canadian movies. He was to see as many as he could and make a selection that the Halifax Slocum-Pocum Movie-Shmovie House would show (I asked about the name. Joshua Slocum was the first man to sail around the world solo, in his thirty-seven-foot boat, the *Spray*, in the 1890s; he was from Nova Scotia). Tom had a schedule that was even more crowded than mine. I asked him if he had seen *A Study into* — but the lights were dimming and bossy Joe was shushing us.

"The one about the dictionaries?" asked Tom at the lifting of darkness.

"Yes."

"I loved it. I've already written to the filmmaker. We're showing it for sure."

Joe and Egon hadn't seen it so we had to explain. They played hard-to-please, though Egon said that he liked Schubert.

Joe, who was tone-deaf and was irked by knowledge and appreciation of music, retorted, "Well, I prefer Webster to Oxford. I can't help it. I adore modernity. I'm sorry." And he looked at Egon and away. If looks could be hooks, Joe's would have been big and sharp, with a fat, juicy worm on it with its thumbs to its temples, waving its fingers and chanting, "Come and get me, na-na-a-na-na." Egon opened his eyes wide and swallowed hook, line and sinker. "Now, now, Jo-Jo, just because you're as musical as a can of tuna doesn't mean you have to take it out on Oxford," he said — and they were off, out of nowhere, Joe-Blow-Usage against Egon-Blow-Historical-Principles, with a few jabs thrown at poor Schubert for good measure, and it was my turn to shush them for the next movie.

Which I barely watched. My mind was elsewhere. I was thinking about Tom. Vague, titillating thoughts.

When it was over the four of us got up.

"I think we've had our fill of celluloid today," said Egon.

"Yes," agreed Joe.

After the merest fraction of an uncertain pause, felt only by me, perhaps, they were gone, just goosey-goosey happy to be with each other, not giving a fuck about dictionaries, only Egon turning and saying, "You've got a key, right, Tom?" Tom nodded, and got a smile and a wave back, and the two of us were left standing there.

"What movie are you seeing next?" I asked, my answer to his answer already prepared — "Oh, so am I" — even if it had to be the documentary on the P.E.I. potato again.

"Uh" — he unfolded his program — "I was thinking of seeing *The Wars*."

"Oh, so was I." Which was true. It was one of the much-trumpeted features at the festival, with director Phillips and author Findley in attendance. It was playing downtown. A bus ride away.

"Oh, good."

Without a further word, just like that, we started walking together, our strides matching perfectly.

We talked, went about that curious, demanding task of meeting someone new and trying to extrapolate a personality from a few points of words. He was very organized, he said, had to be. At the end of every day he sat down and wrote to the filmmakers and distributors whose movies he wanted for the Slocum-Pocum. I saw his stack of letters, sometimes ten a night; on the portable he had brought he banged them out flawlessly on Slocum-Pocum letterhead (Joshua on his sloop, his hand on the rudder, but it's a projector and his sail is a screen. "You can't make it out, but it's supposed to be *Citizen Kane* on the sail," said Tom). The paper was heavy bond, and stiff ("corporate gift"), and it gave the envelopes a thick, spongy quality. The maker of *Snowflakes* would be thrilled to receive such an envelope. Tom hadn't seen the movie, but he took my word that it was worth it. I volunteered to be the stamp-licker.

After *The Wars* (so-so), Tom was seeing a movie I had made the mistake of saying I had seen on the first day. For me to see it again two days later would have strained the credibility of casualness, so we said goodbye. I added that I would probably bump into him again the next day since we were both such avid cinephiles.

"That would be great," he said (which I immediately weighed. Not *Yeah*, not *Maybe*, but *That would be great*. Great).

He was a little shorter than I, an inch or so. He had wiry black hair, bright dark eyes and a smile that appeared and vanished quickly. He was a touch pudgy, but in a pleasant way;

his belly looked as if it were the centre of something, the proper context for a navel, rather than an excess. His limbs were well connected and well oiled, by which I mean that he moved in a perfectly unselfconscious way, something I have never managed. He was older, twenty-two, in fourth year, politics, loved Bergman, Buñuel and Cocteau, and I felt butterflies in my stomach when I thought about him in a certain way.

It was he who saw me first the next day. Around two o'clock, coming out of an abysmal feature with Donald Sutherland. Surely only financial desperation could have induced that great artist to play a Mountie, complete with red and black get-up and horse. Stupid script, clunky dialogue, cardboard characters, insulting stereotypes, false emotions, unconvincing action, fake-looking sets, shiny foreheads, syrupy music — there was only the pleasure of seeing and hearing Donald Sutherland. I was mulling over the badness of the movie, the hows and the whys, when a voice, *his* voice, called me. I turned. Two smiles, his, there and gone in a moment, and mine, lasting a little longer. Immediately we had so much to talk about. He had arrived late, which was why I hadn't seen him. We proceeded to tear the movie apart with ferocious glee. With our two minds working on it we discovered even more outrageous flaws. The horsemanship! The footwear! The cutlery! Why, it was the shoddiest movie in history! Worse even than *The Sudsy Massacre*, which I told Tom about.

"But of course," he said, "I must have it for the Slocum-Pocum."

"What!"

"Well, sure. Donald Sutherland's from Nova Scotia."

Ah yes. Later, Tom sent me the Slocum-Pocum Movie Shmovie Monthly Shmonthly program. The blurb went:

"Come and see Donald Sutherland's Worst Movie! A great actor in a horrible Canadian production. Nothing is good about this movie except Nova Scotia's native son. See the stark solitude of genius. See it cope with dross. A must-see!"

Our schedules matched effortlessly. We often had similar views on movies. When we didn't, that was even better: we went at it like two dogs that want the same bone. Tom had an exceptional argumentative streak, a match to mine, I'd say. We celebrated the rubber chicken in *The Discreet Charm of the Bourgeoisie* and had merry tussles over *La Grande Illusion, Last Tango in Paris*, Kubrick, *The Tin Drum*, Otto Preminger.

On a warm Friday evening we gave up on movies. There was a Claude Jutras retrospective, but we'd both already seen *Mon Oncle Antoine*. Instead, we had dinner at Egon's place (which reminds me that I brought over a cast-iron frying pan that I never got back). There was Egon and his roommate Terry (straight) and Joe and Tom and me. Egon made a delicious pizza of fried aubergines, red peppers and ripe goat's cheese, I concocted an authentic Caesar salad, Tom brought three bottles of California red wine, Joe baked a marvellous pecan-caramel pie, and the whole resulting mess of dishes was dreamily cleaned up by everyone thanks to Terry's marijuana. It was a great evening. I have never been a gregarious person and I usually dread planned time-slots of geniality, but that evening was genuinely genial.

We talked about painting. Joe was a painter, a very good one at that. When he spoke of his paintings, it was usually with a prickly, defensive arrogance, with arias of meaningless mumbo-jumbo. But that evening we were mellow and receptive and stoned; we turned the sofa to face one of his best paintings — a richly coloured acrylic portrait of an ear and Joe for once got his words plain, simple and right. The tones of the painting were flesh, ochre, burnt almond and black. At the centre of the ear, deep within it, was the tiniest drawing of an empty chair, a symbol of expectancy, said Joe; an empty chair is an "expectant chair, a nostalgic chair."

Towards two in the morning, we were all falling asleep on the sofa. I struggled to my feet and announced my departure. I could hardly keep my eyes open. Tom offered to walk me home. With sleepy alacrity I said yes. I'm not sure what I was thinking, but I was thinking.

As we walked towards my place through the quiet, deserted streets of Roetown, we got our second wind. The air was pleasantly cool. We stopped and looked at a few churches.

When we started the climb up the hill beyond which I lived, my heart began to beat hard. What now? I was terribly nervous.

We reached my house.

I could see light in the living-room. Someone was still up. I felt unbearably self-conscious. What to do with the space between us? Where to lay my eyes? I pointed out to Tom the oatmeal factory and the jail with its whirling camera — of no great interest in the middle of the night except when silence is the enemy.

While we were bent on the fascinating subject of dandelions, of which the small front lawn had five or six, I managed to pop the question.

"Do you" — why am I scuffing the sidewalk with the side of my shoe? — "want to come in" — will you look at him! — "for a cup of tea?"

"I'd love to."

Good, a reprieve. We could now shut up and talk normally. We climbed the cement steps.

There was not only light in the living-room, but music, a British folk rock band that was Sarah's record. *"Everything But the Girl,"* said Tom, to which I replied, "That's right." But there was no one. Sarah had an antique stereo system, the sort with a tall central pin and a plastic arm so that several records could be played in a row. It was cheap but faithful. Dogged, in fact; sometimes it started up on its own. That night for example. The evil-tempered Spanakopita was square on the sofa. Martin, Sarah's latest and fondest, was not fond of cats, so when he spent the night the cat got the boot from Sarah's room, which usually brought on a three-act drama of meowing, sofa-scratching and guerrilla-warfare shitting (having learned from first-hand experience, I always kept my rooms closed off). Clearly, we had trespassed upon Act Two. Spanakopita was methodically kneading and clawing the sofa.

But my first thought was "Isn't this nice," and I smiled. Isn't it nice to come in at two in the morning to the dim charm of a red-shaded forty-watt light-bulb and the charming din of music and no one around? Though to Tom's perky "Oh, a cat" I was quick to respond that I wouldn't touch the fuming feline if I were he.

I clearly remember that "Isn't this nice." It was a little emotion that spoke its words and then flooded me. I believe it was at that moment that I emphatically decided that I wanted to sleep with Tom. It made me happy to see us remove our shoes and pad about in our socks.

We went to the kitchen and performed the simple, pleasing ritual of making tea. With a full pot and two big mugs, we headed for the living-room. Spanakopita hadn't budged, still had that dead-ahead stare of a cat machinating evil deeds, so we set ourselves up on the floor. I had my back against the sofa. We were fresh and ready to go for hours yet.

As the stereo played Side A of *Everything But the Girl* over and over, we talked about this and that, nothing and everything, life in the future, life in the past. The subject of parents came up, and my lack thereof, which brought on a silence from Tom, which I interrupted by saying that it was all right and what did his parents do, which was schoolteacher father and Halifax Humane Society president mother. At that precise moment, at the mention of the Halifax Humane Society, Spanakopita dropped down from the sofa and silently stalked off. Act Three was upon us. I said to myself that if I had forgotten to close the door to my bedroom and that cat shit on my pillow again, it would be the Roetown Humane Society for it the very next morning.

Tom got up to refill the pot. When he came back, he set it on the floor next to me and sat on the sofa, his leg comfortably against my shoulder.

"Here, I'll give you a massage," he said, swinging his leg over me so that he was sitting directly behind me.

I could feel his hands gathering my hair, fingers brushing my neck. I raised my arms and held my hair against my head with my hands, leaving my neck and shoulders exposed to his touch.

It was with an audible sigh of pleasure that I took to his pressing, probing, circling fingers as they plied the crucifix of my shoulders and spine. I straightened up and he brought himself closer. I rested my arms on his knees. He worked east and west as far as the beginning of my arms, north a little beyond my hairline, south until it tickled, and round and round on my trapeziums, those muscles that seem to hold the world together. It was so relaxing that I felt the four points of my compass distending, a deeply enjoyable form of quartering. All the while, I was aware that it was Tom's fingers that were playing along my shoulders. Each time they crossed over one of the straps of my bra, I wondered what he thought.

After a long while, the cooling off of all tea, he stopped and his hands rested against the back of my neck. Two of his fingers lazily scratched me. I flopped my arms around Tom's legs.

"I'm exhausted," he said. He rested his head on mine, chin to crown. As I played with the balance of that weight, I had an image of a Third World girl carrying a jar of water.

Suddenly my heart, rushing ahead of me, anticipating me, began to beat very hard, in just the right rhythm to make my whole body shake, like that gentle breeze that brought down a big suspension bridge in the U.S. I shifted to break the rhythm.

"You can spend the night here, if you want," I said quietly, in a tone of voice that I hoped was like a suitcase, of neutral appearance and changeable contents depending on the destination.

"That would be nice," he said, and kissed the top of my head. Which I felt like an echo.

I was equally divided between shock and thrill.

"Let's go to bed," I said, taking his hand in mine, though I didn't exactly look at him.

I had the presence of mind — which otherwise was rapidly dissolving — to unplug the stereo system. We tiptoed up the stairs, I ahead of him. The landing was Spanakopita-free and the door to my room closed.

I opened it, we entered, I locked it behind us. The click-clack of the mechanism signified to me *This is it, this is it.*

I turned, we smiled, he came up to me and kissed me on the mouth.

He's a man. This is homosexuality. I'm a homosexual. This was what had flashed through my mind downstairs when Tom had kissed the top of my head, and what began racing through my mind as soon as our lips touched. I was against the wall and Tom was against me, not hard but unmistakably, one hand on my left shoulder, the other on the wall. The slight scratch of his skin, the feel of his body against mine, his way of kissing so different from Ruth's, the rhythm faster, the probing a little furious: *He's a man. This is homosexuality. I'm a homosexual.* Which is crazy, I know. We were doing the perfectly heterosexually normal, the banal even, but it came, over and over, *he's a man, this is homosexuality, I'm a homosexual,* though this sense of committing the forbidden forbade nothing, only both my legs were trembling and I needed air. I broke off the kissing and moved away a little, though I kept both my hands on his shoulders.

"You're nervous," said Tom.

"I've" — pause — "This" — pause — "is my first time." A lapse in saying it, but right away in my mind: "But it's all right."

I came close to him again and kissed him, my tongue going out.

He ran his hands over my body. I placed my hands against his chest, his unequivocally male chest.

He unbuttoned and eased off my blouse. I removed my bra.

He took his shirt off. There were swirls of black hair. *He's a man. This....*

We embraced again, warm skin to warm skin. My nipples were erect and aware of every brush against his chest. His hairs were soft. One of his legs was pressed between mine. I could feel my wetness, could feel that peculiar nag for attention from down there. Would that my heart would stop beating so hard. Would that he would go down on me. He lowered his head to my breasts. He alternately caressed them with his hands, slightly cool, then with his mouth, a jump in temperature.

I brought a hand down to between his legs and squeezed. It felt hard. Tom pulled away and began to undo his pants. He brought them down with his underwear in one motion and kicked them off. In two motions, his thumbs like hooks, he got rid of his socks.

I could not take my eyes off what I was looking at. Beneath a small, neat patch of dark, bushy hair stood an erect penis. My breathing was shallow and intense. I mechanically brought my hand out. Surrounded it. Squeezed. Pulled to and fro. It was so warm! Nearly hot. I could no longer stay on my feet. If it wasn't the bed, it would be the floor I collapsed on.

I quickly removed the rest of my clothes, yanked the top sheet aside and dropped onto the bed. He lay beside me.

We rolled about in each other's arms, pressing our bodies together, caressing, kissing. I was aware of every touch of his burning erection. I took hold of it again and propped myself up to look at it. I pulled the soft skin back and forth gently, exposing and covering the head.

"I don't have any condoms," he whispered.

"Oh. Nor do I."

My fertility? It was the last thing on my mind. The notion that I might get *pregnant* seemed unreal. I couldn't even imagine it. Anyway, to stick this thing into me seemed a crazy idea:

it was definitely too big to fit comfortably, however wet and craving for attention I was down there, and the pleasure from the proposition seemed dubious. A finger, a tongue — that was all I needed.

I was thinking of taking it in my mouth. The very idea sent shivers down my body. In my mouth. His cock. Oh!

I stopped thinking about it when Tom glided his hand to right where I wanted it. Oh good! I lay back and closed my eyes. I let go of his penis, but slid right up to him so that I could feel it against me.

I can't say he was outstandingly adept at what he was doing — a little too fast, too hard, not enough beating around the bush, so to speak — but in its very imperfection lay the perfection of the moment. It was a *male* hand, that's what turned me on.

He stopped. I opened my eyes, alarmed. He couldn't stop now. Not at this point of ache.

"I'll just go in a little. I promise I won't come."

"Okay." This held promise too.

He moved between my legs. He leaned down. I could feel his hard bluntness pushing at me — too low — there — there — that was the right spot, I thought — AH! But it hurts!

It's not like breaking a bone, but to hurt, to tear, where I usually had my most exquisite pleasure made me jump as if I'd been jolted by a power line.

"It hurts!" I whispered urgently.

"Sorry. I won't go so deep."

He played with his inch or so of leeway, backing off when I began to push him away with my arms.

He eventually withdrew.

"I'm sorry," I said. I wondered if he might be upset.

"Oh, don't worry. I didn't mean to hurt you. Man, I'm tired."

He laughed and flopped down beside me.

I wanted to do something for him so I thought again of taking him in my mouth. I moved down and took hold of it with my right hand. Up and down I went, lightly. I'd forgotten about that funny line underneath the penis that looks like the seam along which it's been sewn shut. When I squeezed, a clear bead pearled up from the slit.

I opened my mouth and took him in. At first I tasted me; then not much beyond a faint sour taste. I went about sucking. I liked it, the lewdness aroused me, but it was tempered by difficulty. My teeth were in the way, my lips were soon aching and sometimes I gagged.

Tom's penis began to go limp. I was disappointed. I looked up at him.

"Tell me what I should do."

"It's all right. Here, come here." His voice was friendly and undisappointed, his hands reaching for me. I slid up beside him. "Do you hear the birds?" he added.

The window above the futon revealed the paling blue of a dying night, with here and there a chirp bringing on the morning. We knelt at the window, which I opened farther. A cool breeze blew against us. The day was developing rapidly, yet with indescribable subtlety. I couldn't remember when I had last seen a day break, with its hazy brightness and its increasingly vivid palette of colours. It's an image that has stayed with me: Tom and I kneeling naked on my futon with our elbows on the windowsill, numb with exhaustion, looking out at the new day. He ran a gently scratching hand over my back. We talked of dressing and going out for a walk and an early breakfast, but our resolve didn't go beyond words. Instead he glanced at my breasts and brought his mouth to them.

We flopped down onto the bed, covered ourselves and fell into a few hours of fitful sleep. He held me from behind. Even when we were not touching I was aware of his presence. Glad of it, but incapable of sleeping for it.

In the morning, or rather, later in the morning, we took a shower together, which I liked very much. We kissed until the water turned cold. It felt strange to get dressed, to see Tom disappear behind piece after piece of clothing. And then, our accoutrements of normality back on, to step out of my room as if nothing out of the ordinary had taken place. The dressed Tom felt like someone else now. I wondered what Sarah would say.

But there was no one home except for Karen, who rushed up from her basement room and grabbed breakfast on her way to rehearsal. She may have thought that Tom had arrived a few minutes earlier. She may have thought nothing at all.

We had a coffee and then went to Morrie's for a greasy-spoon breakfast. And then to movies, the last day of Canadian Images.

Tom and I spent the next week together. In Roetown and in Toronto, which he didn't get to see very often. On one of those days — I can remember the bed, the room, the circumstances, but not the date — I lost my virginity, my anatomical virginity, an event which I would qualify as an uncomfortable act of physiology, more than a little painful — less so than the first try, thanks to a stinking lubricated condom and a coordination of effort, but certainly no source of pleasure. There was blood, too, more than I expected, and even some the next day;

it was like having a mini-period. Right after, while Tom lay in dreamy repose, I took a shower, blood trickling down my thighs. I remember thinking, "So there we go. I'm twenty and no longer a virgin," and shrugging to no one but myself.

My pounding heart being the scribbler of my memories, I remember more clearly meeting Tom, I remember more clearly my first night with him and my last, I remember more clearly walking along Bloor Street with him, holding hands.

At least the room was memorable. We were staying in a dive of a hotel just off Spadina Avenue. It was shabby, sordid and exciting. It didn't smell, not at all, not one molecule of odour, but in view of the colour and feel of the carpets, the state and style of the furniture, this was suspicious. It was a room that *ought* to have smelled.

We stayed in that room for five nights and five lazy mornings. I masturbated Tom several times; I took him in my mouth three or four times in the shower, to slightly improved effect, though he never came; I had my first orgasms with a man thanks to a system I instituted in a few hurried words, whereby a touch downward on his forearm meant a little harder, a touch upward a little gentler; we scratched and massaged each other methodically; we spoke volumes and laughed gales; we kissed; and we did it twice more, on the last night and again the next morning.

After my first experience of intercourse, I was inclined to give it a rest, especially the next day and the day after that and onwards, may the subject simply not arise, thank you, but *it*, Tom's *it*, arose all the time, to our mutual pleasure, and eventually, while I was playing Horowitz on Tom's forearm — fortissimo! . . . piano . . . piano . . . fortissimo! — he brought up the subject of what we could do with *it*, and finally, in an advanced state of lascivious dissolution, I thought, *Oh hell, let's try it again. How pain and blood can transmute into pleasure, I can't see. It's a pity you don't ejaculate through those nice fingers of yours, but let us deal with that drooling dick before it goes mad with misery. In it goes.* Only this time it didn't hurt. No pleasure, still, but no tearing either, no nerves jolting, none of the edgy is-it-nearly-over self-consciousness. A relaxing of the body and the mind. Just a guy pumping in and out of me, bizarrely. I settled down, moving my legs to get more comfortable. I took in the tawdry room, I day-dreamed a little, I listened to Tom, I ran my hands over his moving bum. This time, when he made his strange, dying noises in my ear, I smiled. I could possibly get into this, if it makes him so happy. Hadn't done anything for me, not really, not like the magic finger-work, not like if he went down on me, which he hadn't yet but I must mention it to him, it would be oh! — but in a way this slippery contact *had* done something for me. Something close and intense, that generated heat. And attachment.

I kissed him and I hugged him with my arms and legs as he lay heavy and still on top of me. We fell asleep. In the morning, it happened again.

Then he left. Telling me at the station, while we were waiting for his bus to the airport, that, ahem, he didn't mean to hide it from me, ahem, he liked me a lot, but, ahem, he had a girlfriend in Halifax. Not that things were always peachy with her, but, ahem, she was, she existed.

Oh, that's all right, I said, rushing to his defence, nearly mentioning Ruth, but she wasn't, she didn't exist, not any more, so I repeated, that's all right. The open invitations to stay with each other in faraway Halifax and faraway Roetown were understood to mean "just as friends". Whoever mentioned the word "relationship" anyway? That's all right. He smiled, and when the bus was there he kissed me goodbye on the mouth. And my pounding heart engraved *that* in my memory, his straight, bee-line kiss for my mouth, lips puckered.

On the bus back to Roetown I remembered how he had reacted when I had shown him my office, my inner sanctum, my novel. A "Huh" and a look around that bordered on the uninterested. Not one step forward to look more closely at the index cards so that I would have to say, *No, no, no* and shoo him away in mock horror. And he was a little pompous, taking his Slocum-Pocum self very seriously. And he had never gone down on me, the selfish boor. And who would want to spend a summer in Halifax? Might as well spend it in Belleville.

When I saw Sarah in the kitchen she smiled slyly and said, "We thought you'd never come back."

"I'm back."

"And?"

"And what?"

"Well, how was it? Did you have a good time?"

"It was fine. Interesting exhibit at the Royal Ontario Museum."

Sarah's Martin was another man who took himself very seriously, this time as a hero of the Catholic working class. She told me once that she was *completely* in love with him. I can see the shake of her head to emphasize the *completely*, her black silky hair echoing the movement. She would eventually have a child by him, since he didn't care for contraception. We in the house didn't care for Martin. As for Tom, I told myself that I was certainly not in love with him, neither *completely* nor even a bit. He had only been a week-long frolic. Must get back to my novel.

A while after, on a late night, I told Sarah about Tom's girl-ahem-friend. She was very nice, said sympathetic words. Thank you, Sarah.

I had a few more affairs before I met Roger (or rather, met him anew). By "a few more" I mean three. But nothing worth going into. How it came about, what we did — in each case my heart pounded, but after, in the collapse of fulfilled lust (mostly his), my mind would perk up again, like a parrot when the cloth is thrown off its cage, and it would say to me, "Who is this guy? Do you know him? Do you *care* to know him? Why is there silence now? Forget it, I say, forget it," and memory would dutifully wipe the slate. What strikes me now is not how much I've forgotten, but how little I care to remember. They were pleasures of an instant, like fireworks. Beyond the lust there was no enchantment, nothing to talk about, nothing to share.

There is only one image, one urge, that I naturally remember: I'm beneath this really big swimmer guy, as dumb as an ox but with a swimmer's chest covered in blond hair, and it's hot and we're both glistening with sweat and he's so big that I feel quite alone beneath this gorgeous chest, his straight arms like two Corinthian columns, and I'm hanging on to him feeling like a sloth hanging from its Amazonian branch, only with considerably less peace since this swimmer guy is grunting and thrusting in and out of me, right through me, actually, and it's vigorous and fantastic and getting better every second and I'm thinking, "I could really, *really* get into this, oh yes."

I was determined to have intimacy again. At night each of Sarah's whimpers seemed to echo in my room, reverberations of my loneliness.

Summer and the end of the university year came. Students dispersed to home towns. I decided not to travel. I couldn't imagine that I would have the same luck as last time, and my novel gave me the perfect excuse: I would stay in Roetown and finish it. Sarah and I were the only ones to remain in the house. The other rooms we managed to sublet.

I had known Roger since the first week of first year. Everyone at Strathcona-Milne knew Roger. He was the previous Master of the College and was still very much involved in its affairs. It had been during his mastership that the university considered closing the two downtown colleges and centralizing everything on the main campus. This had provoked the closest thing to armed insurrection in the history of Ellis University. There were meetings, marches, petitions, sit-ins. Barricades were erected around S-M's main building and for a while they were manned day and night. This was meant to be symbolic, but unfortunately for the university administrators the theatre crowd at Ellis was centred at S-M, and they took to building these barricades with revolutionary fervour. They looked like the real thing. You had to get within a few feet of the barbed wire to realize that it was knitting yarn. Students dressed in rag tag pseudo-military uniforms kept vigil and shouted, "Hark! Who goes there? What is your business here?" at the approach of anyone associated with The Enemy, pointing their wooden rifles at the poor enemy's chest. Enemies who were sufficiently vile would be escorted by two "soldiers" who made it their business to be as hilariously obnoxious as possible.

The one who had done the master-minding, the demanding, the refusing, the urging, in defence of the downtown colleges was Roger. When the university backed down, a cartoon
came out in *The Gadfly*, the student paper, with Roger riding
in a chariot dressed as a triumphant Caesar and the university
president following behind him in chains. All this had taken
place two years before my arrival at Ellis, but its energizing effect on the downtown colleges had been long-lasting. It had
even become folklore: during my first year there was a play at
Artspace that celebrated the events. The actor who played
Roger was made up to look like Che Guevara.

When my year met Roger he had resumed being an ordinary professor of English literature, specializing in Joseph
Conrad, but he was one of those people you seemed to see all
the time — standing talking to someone, walking in and out
of this or that building, having a coffee in the dining-room,
playing go in the college pub, and so on. Everyone knew
Roger.

Yet, curiously, hardly anyone really knew him, among students at any rate. When I got close to him, I discovered that
this putative revolutionary, stormer of the Bastille, trumpeter
at the walls of Jericho, guerrilla in the jungles of Bolivia, was
in fact an old-fashioned aesthete who cared not a jot for any
kind of politics. I don't mean anything pejorative by that —
old-fashioned — only that it came as a surprise. It shouldn't
have since, when I got to remembering our conversations, I
realized that they had always been about art. My first memory
of Roger is of overhearing him talking to someone about *Nostromo*, which I hadn't read at the time. My first conversation
with him was about *The Secret Agent*; my hesitant quibbling
about it was interrupted by his final, "No. It's a perfect novel. I

can't think of a single flaw in it. A drama in which the central, motor event is never described, a presence that is an absence, like a stone that provokes ripples but is long gone, an entire construction with at its centre nothing — I've never seen anything like it." The first step that led to a common bed was when I came upon him in a deserted café, musing over a paragraph of *Almayer's Folly*. And the last time I saw him I was thinking how Kurtz's Intended couldn't have known Kurtz very well if she believed Marlow's lie.

For that was the beginning, the middle and the end of Roger: Joseph Conrad, né Josef Teodor Konrad Korzeniowski, 1857–1924. That was the one strand that twined through his whole existence, from age twelve to forty-nine, for longer than he had known his ex-wife or his kids. Only his parents could claim greater longevity. Roger was one of those lucky people who had found that he could make a living doing what he enjoyed. The author of his boyhood adventure stories in Indiana became the subject of his doctoral study at Oxford became his passport to a life in academia. Roger loved Conrad in ways that changed as he changed. So when he was young he sailed the sea in his armchair with *The Nigger of the 'Narcissus'*, with *Typhoon*, with *Tales of Unrest*, with *Victory*. Then he matured into *Lord Jim*, which in time he found strained and a little tiresome to teach, and into *The Secret Agent*. When I knew him, it was around the key insight of *Heart of Darkness* — too well known, too little understood — and around the monument that is *Nostromo* and around Conrad himself that his thoughts tended to collect. If there were politics and revolution in Roger's life, they were only those he witnessed in *Nostromo* and *Under Western Eyes*. He derived his untested dislike of disorder from Conrad's overtested dislike. Just as humour is absent in

Conrad, Roger rarely sought to see things in a humorous way, which is not to say that he was heavy, dour or cheerless, only that laughter was not an exit he favoured. He felt it was a weak catharsis. Roger was serious in a positive sense, as serious as life is serious. He was the first intellectual I met who had little use for irony.

As for the October Revolution that saved the downtown colleges, Roger simply said, "It happened. They wanted to close them down, some people disagreed, I happened to be master of S-M. I just followed along at the head of the parade."

This is what intrigued me in Roger, that Conrad was The Word, The Book and The Way, though he would never say that. Roger taught other writers — the rest who delivered this century — and there was more to him than the books he had read. But being obdurately incapable of believing in God, I am interested in secular religions. Roger apprehended life through Conrad. Conrad was his idealized double. The choice of prophet was arbitrary — it could have been Kafka or Bach or Matisse or anarcho-syndicalism or Zionism or animal rights or baseball, all depending on what a twelve-year-old boy was doing one day — but it is this very arbitrariness that interests me, that we *choose* what thing, what god, to believe in and, thus limited, open ourselves up to the world.

When Roger and I walked the streets of Roetown, we turned a corner as if we were sailing around a bend in a tropical river. We might surprise a leopard lapping at the water's edge, a jewel in a green setting. Or the sight and sound of savages dancing to the beat of tomtoms around an unrestrained Kurtz. Or a calm citizen, of impassive expression, just as fearsome. Roger made me see that Roetown was not a quiet little Canadian backwater, but a Malay Archipelago, a Congo

River, where madness, breakdown and explosion were always possible.

I don't think of Roger very often now, but he influenced me more than I realized. One of the few times that Tito hurt me was when he said that sometimes I had a tendency towards conservatism. I stood accused of the very thing I had accused Roger of, and was deeply upset. On the positive side, it was while I was with Roger that I wrote my first published story, the one about dentures, and that notions of art and meaning came together for me in a roughly coherent way. And we had great sex — I owe that to Roger too, moments of blazing carnality.

It was a coincidental yen for pecan pie that brought us together. That summer I had set myself to a rigorous work schedule: up at eight every day, and three pages of fiction before I could leave the house. Which was nonsense. I did get up at eight, but the three pages were always put off to the next day; for now I would prepare, work on the mural, fine-tune things. I suffered the creative paralysis that is the horror and torment of creators, but is of no interest to other people, who simply work and then enjoy life. I suppose I could have just started the bloody thing, just sat down and launched forth:

Hello! How are you? It is my great pleasure to meet you and to be your Christian guide to this novel. I am a sixth-generation mongrel, this is my village, Corto is my master and Christ is my Lord. We are in Portugal, a human unit of geography which I gather you will find illuminating. One thousand nine hundred and thirty-nine years have passed since He took upon Himself the burden of our sins. It is morning. As you can see, this is the main street of the village. The church is behind you, to your left. We will visit it, be assured. There is something oh so special in it, the inspiration of my life. But wait! Don't go! There is plenty of time yet, I assure you. Let your anticipation grow, let it torment you. The pleasure of satisfying it will be all the greater, your spirit will soar all the higher. Speaking of anticipation, I have been so excited at the prospect of meeting you, quite beside myself, really, that I haven't had the peace of mind yet for my first shit of the day. So let me celebrate the time and place of our meeting with this small monument. Ahhhhhhhhhhhhhhhhhhhhhhhhhhhhhhh hhhhhhhhhhhhhhhh. Ooooooooooooooooooooooooooo ooooooooooh. Ahhhhhhh. Ohjustonemorepiece! Ah hhhhhhhh such rapture. Amen! Here, I'll show you the village. Mark out our territory, so to speak. And you must meet the villagers. They are good, hard-working Catholics. When you have met them, after the awkward small talk, after the smiles and handshakes that you are so fond of, we will go to the church and I will leave you there in silence for twenty minutes or so. Then I will yelp you out of your praying and we will begin on the drama. The where, the how, the why. For it all starts with the priest. With the priest, and with the holy town of Fatima, which is beyond those high, savage mountains that you see to the west. You know about Fatima, of course? You don't! Well, we must start with Fatima then. In the year of Our Lord 1917 — ah, here comes the barber. Barber. Barber, I say! Come meet our reader.

But I couldn't. As soon as I got close to starting anything, I was beset by questions and hesitations. What I was about to do was so important, so significant, that it always required further consideration. My spontaneity would fizzle. I would put off my oeuvre another day. Tomorrow at eight-thirty I would start, for sure. Meanwhile, in joyful anticipation of this, I would go for a walk and then read.

On just such a day, in mid-June, I think it was, in the early afternoon, I suddenly had the urge for the sweet crunch of pecan pie. There was a dessert café a short walk away, a quiet, pleasant place that served dozens of kinds of tea.

Roger was there. There was no one else — just him with a book, and the lazily busy waitress. Up till then I'd say he was an acquaintance. We greeted each other when we crossed paths, and we had had conversations here and there, a few one on one, but mostly in groups. He knew a few facts about me — my parents and Cuba, my former involvement in student politics, my philosophy major with interest in English lit — and I knew a few facts about him. I liked him, the way students can like their teachers, though I had never taken a course with him.

To the tintinnabulation of doorbells, I entered the café. He looked up and we said hello.

"What are you still doing here?" he asked.

"I'm spending the summer in Roetown."

"I was tricked by the department into teaching a summer course on D.H. Lawrence. *Sons and Lovers, Women in Love, The Rainbow, Kangaroo* — I can barely stand it."

I smiled. I didn't want to tell him why I was staying the summer.

"Please join me," he added.

I ordered a slice of pecan pie and a pear-vanilla herbal tea.

"Have you read this?" he asked, holding up *Almayer's Folly*.

"Yes."

"Well, in my old age, this first novel is growing in my estimation. There's this part here...."

He showed me a short paragraph. There was a matter of punctuation he admired, a particularly apt use of semicolons. We talked about punctuation.

A close relationship starts when barriers begin to fall. The first that fell for me was age, the intimidating notion that Roger was over double my age. I had turned twenty-one only a few days before; he was forty-nine. Ruth was also much older than I, but with her it had been different. Right from the start, it hadn't seemed to matter. Was it the foreign environment? That we were both women? Simply the way our personalities mixed? I don't know — probably a mix of the three. With Roger, at first, I felt at every moment, in every exchange, the difference in years. It was a clear measure of our respective experience of life, of our maturity and wisdom. I had talked to him before with perfect confidence, but suddenly I was feeling tongue-tied and incoherent. I kept saying things and thinking right after, "Why did I say that?"

Age was erased with words. The more we talked that day, and in the ensuing days when we seemed to keep bumping into each other, the more I felt we were reaching a sort of equality, an easy osmosis of personalities. This had much to do with something I mentioned before: his lack of a penchant for irony. Roger took me seriously — and so I took myself seriously.

Quite early on, when we were still just friends, with no idea — at least on my part — that we were becoming anything else, I confessed to him that I was working on a novel. I hate the fact that I used that tone of voice, but that's the way it came out, a confession. If *I* had been listening to myself, I would have rolled my eyes. But Roger said, "Really?", there was a pause and then he asked, "What's it about?" I explained the broad outlines, the angle of narration, the splintering of Voice into voices, the theme of the strong sustaining belief, the relationship between ideals and their material symbols, but I cautioned him, protected myself, by saying that I was quite stuck, that I wasn't so much working on a novel as wanting to work on one.

After a moment of reflection, he said, "I've never written a creative word in my life. Anything I've done has hung on the creativity of others. I've been a spectator of books, of my wife's pregnancies, of my children growing up. Mind you, I have no regrets. I'm good at being a spectator. I demand a lot. But still, I'm a glorified traffic cop: I wave my hands at people in their big, powerful engines — this way! that way! — and they roar by while I stay still." And he smiled at me, with a what-can-you-do shrug.

I showed him my office the next day. He looked closely, stretched to his tiptoes, bent down, sailed from source to lake. I hoped he didn't notice the index cards about shit.

"Looks amazing. But you're stuck, you say."

"Completely. It's in my head and on these walls and nowhere else. Certainly not on a page."

"Well, it makes for a terrific sculpture."

"Yeah." A neutral yeah.

He looked at me. "There's no point in being stuck. It gets you nowhere. If you're really stuck, maybe you should destroy all this and start all over."

A simple, bold idea that had never occurred to me.

It was not then, not even in the next week, but it was not very long after. It was surprisingly easy. Outside the house there was a metal barrel that striking workers at the oatmeal factory had used as a fireplace during the winter. One moment my cards seemed as eternal as the Ganges, the next they were on fire in the barrel, along with much of the paint from the walls. The sun was so strong that day that I couldn't see any flames, only index cards that convulsed as they turned black and vanished, giving off wisps of smoke. I was happy. I was free to start again.

When Roger came to my place the first time, Sarah was there and I said, "Sarah, you know Professor Memling, don't you?"

"Hi, Sarah," said Professor Memling.

"Hi, Roger," said Sarah.

I felt a pang of jealousy, a silly pang of jealousy.

The click, the erotic click that flooded my system with adrenalin, took place in his office late one hot evening. After one of his rare laughs we were standing close to each other, a deliberate, unacknowledged closeness, a sort of open secret. I was smiling for no reason. Our eyes met and fled, met and fled. A hand of his was floating in the air, hovering near my shoulder. It landed. He kissed me. I brought my arms up around him.

Now that things were in the open, they could flow — and flow they did, did they ever. Within minutes of starting our kissing I had backed him down onto his small sofa, knelt between his legs, unzipped his pants and flopped out his tumescent penis. Roger had a handsome dick, straight, large but not too large, with a rich, warm complexion — and perpetually at attention in my presence. I sucked till it gushed. It was hot and slimy and tasted strange. Not the sort of thing I would buy at the supermarket in its ice-cream version, but in the state of sexual animation I was in, a thrill to have erupt in my mouth — his dick *pulsated.*

We often did it in his office. It was a turn-on, not a necessity; his house wasn't far. There was something deliciously salacious about doing it in a place that was so functional and public. Roger had his seminars in his office. It was big enough to accommodate nine students — seven on chairs, two on the sofa — and a professor in his comfortable swivel chair. That year I took his fourth-year Conrad course and I made a point of always sitting on the sofa, that very sofa on which later in the day I would lie naked, with Roger looming over me or kneeling with his head between my legs. During class he would display perfect equanimity, considering my questions and interventions with the same deliberation as he did those of other students. He would be egalitarian even in his eye contact, his asides, his peaks of enthusiasm. But at night he would complain to me about the discomfort of unwanted erections.

Roger lived on a street above and behind S-M, a bumpy strip of asphalt with no sidewalks that the city had laid atop a drumlin decades ago and forgotten since. In the quiet of this municipal amnesia the trees became enormous, the houses settled and nothing new happened except for the progressive fracturing of the road. One oak tree, dead set on reclaiming lost territory, had burst through the asphalt with so many rooty kneecaps that the road looked like the folds of an accordion. When I manoeuvred my way down the street on my bike I always thought of that line in Albee's *Zoo Story*: "Sometimes a person has to go a very long distance out of his way to come back a short distance correctly."

Roger's peach clapboard house was tucked away between two larger houses that were closer to the street, down a cracked cement path, behind a massive bush. It looked more like a cottage, what with its veranda, the large windows and everything made of wood. It was a dream of a sunlit lair. I loved it the moment I laid eyes on it. It was small — Jeremy and Leah, Roger's children, still had to sleep in the same room when they came for a visit — the floors were hardwood, the furniture was all renovated antique, it was a mess of books and papers, and everything creaked: the floors, the bed, the tables and chairs, in a wind or storm the whole house, *everything*. You had to remain still to understand someone on the phone or to hear the television properly. The groans and cries of tortured wood make up the soundtrack of my memories of the place. That, and the groans and cries of two beings gluttonously fucking.

The garden was as untended as the house. Years earlier, before Jeremy and Leah were born, Roger and his wife, Penny, had been to Mexico, to the forest where the monarch butterfly breeds. They had been there when the monarchs were coming out of their cocoons. "Millions of them," said Roger. "Every leaf in fact a butterfly. Black and orange all around you. It was like being in a cool fire." He showed me photos, but unfortunately they were black and white, not black and orange. When he read that his green lawn was a monoculture inimical to the monarch, Roger ripped up his backyard and spent a summer orchestrating wilderness. He transplanted goldenrod, dandelions, asters, Queen Anne's lace, thistles, bloodroot, may apples, hepatica, anemones, campanulas and whatever else he could find in country fields. When he saw his first monarch, solitary and tentative, he exulted. This was long ago. Wilderness had since found its own maestro and its own repertoire. Every summer Roger scythed clear a spot here or there. On a blanket, surrounded by the rustle and *bzzzzz bzzzzz bzzzzz* of nature, we did it there too.

Roger had had a vasectomy — "I want my pleasure to be without consequence," he said (I should have taken note) — so we never had to worry about that, were free to do it when and where we wanted. It's strange how there are *classes* of memories, memories that relate to the same person yet do not mix. On the one hand I remember a profound Conrad scholar who influenced me in many ways, whose encounter had intellectual ramifications for me, and on the other, quite distinctly, I remember a tenured satyr and his potent, sterile dick. Facing these two personae I felt I was the same. Naked or dressed, I was me. But he — clothes made all the difference. Clothes, or their absence, changed the man.

On the sofa, on the desk, on the floor, against the wall; in the living-room, in the shower, in the corridor, in front of mirrors, in the kitchen, on the bed (more sponge than mattress, that); in the garden; once late at night in the S-M sauna (he blanched and nearly fainted. I had to drag him out and let him rest for forty minutes); in a movie theatre he worked a hand down to my juice button and imposed an almighty one on me while I had to stay perfectly still and quiet, torture it was; once in Little Lake Cemetery, but disturbed; once a blow job minutes before class, the taste in my mouth throughout and the wonder, the worry, about my breath; slowly; quickly; our eyes closed; our eyes open — there must be some trace chemical exuded by the skin, some combustible pheromone we gave off. Roger once said he wished I were three inches tall — that way he could put me in his mouth and lick me all over. He licked me all over anyway, with the determination of a dog. One of my indelible memories is of the two of us on his bed. Top sheet and blanket have vanished. I am on my back; Roger is on his knees. With one hand he is playing with his erection, with the other he is holding onto the ankle of my right foot. He has my toes in his mouth — nibbling them, licking them, playing them like a harmonica. Sometimes the whole front of my foot disappears into his mouth, with tooth-marks later to show how far he went. My foot is drenched with saliva. Roger is devouring me with his eyes as I mastur-bate while looking at him. He has an expression out of *The Cabinet of Doctor Caligari* and is making the noises of a fam-ished cannibal. I am about to come, but I hold myself back. It is a feeling both frozen and melting. Then the room goes dark, not because of an eclipse but because I am letting myself go and narrowing my eyes. At that moment, with a gurgly groan and a sharp bite on my foot, sperm shoots through the air over me. I see it like a shooting star.

It mattered not a bit if I was menstruating. On the con-trary: it excited Roger, the idea of it, and afterwards to have at the base of his flagging erection a circle of clotted blood, and on the sheet streaks of blood neatly delimited by the diverging lines of my inner thighs, looking, amidst the vastness of the sheet, like the work of a fevered minimalist painter.

Mostly he went on top. I liked it that way; I could feel and watch and touch. We did it from behind, too. At first I was a bit reluctant. He would see . . . I would be exposing my . . . I think it's the area where one's sense of privacy fades last. But Roger had an anal fixation. Far from pretending it wasn't there, the first thing he did the first time was purr, "Nice ass-hole," and stick in a lubricated finger. After a moment of shock I found it quite pleasant. When he penetrated me I felt a double sense of fullness, something approximating capacity.

I arched back farther, my shyness gone. A few times he out-right sodomized me with his greased-up dick, but I took less to that. When my sphincter was intent on closing and he was coming, it hurt; and when I was relaxed and open, it felt as if I were shitting and I found I was not participating, but waiting. Although, at the same time, the sheer indecency of what we were doing turned me on.

When I was especially excited, I had an orgasm while Roger moved in and out of me. It always happened when he was on top and it seemed to come from nowhere. Usually, though, I came before or after his gush, to the fiddling of his fingers or the slobbering of his mouth — these were the *real* volcano champagne bottle pops.

After periods of all-out repeated carnality I was sometimes so sore I could hardly walk.

That's such a long-ago feeling, to fuck so much I hurt.

I spent the summer reading Conrad and fucking. Roger gave me a key to his place. This time, whenever Sarah said, "We thought you'd never come back," I laughed. When the academic year started again we had to be discreet, but I still spent a great deal of time at his house (though far fewer nights, a sore point). Only when his children visited did I stay away completely. Leah was my age, Jeremy older — the awkwardness would have been worse than with Tuesday. Better that I not exist in their eyes. Or in the eyes of others. Though surely many faculty and students knew, in public we behaved like near strangers and we never did social things together, even if we were both going.

It was in Roger's house, in his absence, that I wrote my dentures story. I found the place propitious for creativity —

something about the wood, the books, the quiet and the knowledge that my time was limited, that in a few hours, in a few minutes, he would appear and my writing would stop. The desk in his office being far too cluttered, I wrote the story on a small writing-desk in the living-room. It was slanted and the top lifted, much like a school desk's, but it was far more elegant: it had an inset leather writing surface and lion's-paw feet. Inside the desk I found old letters and odd papers and a small hardcover edition of *Les Fables de La Fontaine*. The book was about four inches by three and was falling apart. I secured the covers with tape and I decided that I would memorize one fable a day until I had finished my story. I got to the fifteenth fable of the third section, which means that I wrote my story in fifty-six sessions, varying in length from a few hours to a full day, with two more sessions to type it up on Roger's computer. I was careful not to repeat the mistake I had made with my novel; I did not overplan. I jotted down new ideas in a notepad that I carried with me, I had a sheet next to my draft on which I wrote reminders of an immediate nature; otherwise, I composed the story straight from my head.

I found that the more I wrote, the more I had to say, one idea leading to another. It turned out to be quite a long story, a little over forty pages. This was in part the result of research, which gave me hard facts around which I could weave my intent. I am in debt to a woman at the consumer relations office of a major American denture cleaner and adhesive company, who sent me reams of information, a complete historical synthesis worthy of Encyclopedia Britannica. I read more than I cared for or needed to on George Washington's wooden teeth, Victorian ivory dentures, the development of polymer plastics after the Second World War, the manufacturing process for dentures and artificial teeth and the proper care of your dentures. Facts, figures, insights, anecdotes — this woman in Michigan produced them all for me, with every letter bearing the motto We Help You Keep Your Smile above a gleaming set of teeth.

With this story I clearly remember the moment of conception. It had to do with Roger's vasectomy. Roger liked it sometimes when I played with his erection from behind, that is, when I held it from between his legs. One day in mid-September, a Saturday or Sunday, I was indulging him in just such a way. We were lying on our sides on his bed, I was behind him and lower down, my arm running between his legs, and my head was resting on his side, watching what my hand was doing. Already a little semen had oozed out and my to-and-fro motion had frothed it up. He ejaculated. It always surprised me how this production — the heavy breathing, the gurgling and groaning from deep down, the tortured expression, the tensing and trembling of his body — resulted in only a few dashes, maybe three millilitres. While he lay there, recuperating from his pleasure, I looked at the blobs on the bedsheet. At that moment, thinking about how this laughably minute quantity of goo could be so powerful, though not in this particular case, the words "toothless ejaculation" came together in my mind.

The final product had nothing to do with vasectomies or ejaculations, but that was its origin.

My story was about a young woman who has no teeth, and the relationship between her and her dentures and a much older, healthy-toothed former prime minister who becomes her lover. I had a picture in my head of a beautiful, toothless young woman in bed with her ageing lover, the two of them naked and lying together like spoons, she the inner spoon, both looking at a glass of water with her teeth in it. I divided the story into chapters, sixteen in all, each with its own title. This allowed me to vary the narrative voice. Some chapters were descriptive and omnisciently narrated, focusing on an event — the cleaning of her teeth, for example, with the fizzing of the cleaning tablets and her careful brushing. Others were carried out in an 'I' voice, either his or hers. Still others were nearly pure dialogue. At the heart of the story I had a simple tension: the love affair must remain secret because the young woman's lover is very famous and much older, and this secrecy increasingly bothers her. She feels powerless — hence the symbol of the dentures.

It was a perfect story, by which I humbly mean that everything was fully intended, every ambiguity precisely circumscribed. I was happy with the result.

I dared to bid for the world's attention. I selected a well-known literary review in the United States — since I felt that to be published down there was the *real* thing — and mailed off my story. The celerity and curtness with which it was turned down — within *eight days* of my dropping the envelope in the mailbox, I received a one-paragraph, rubber-stamp-dated "Dear Writer" form letter — made me feel that I had shot a flimsy old arrow over the border into the American jungle, and that within a second a bullet had whizzed by my head in riposte. Such was the rush of the editors to expel my story from the U.S. that they did not even properly stamp the self-addressed envelope I had dutifully included. Since it is impossible to buy American stamps in Canada, I had paper clipped to my envelope an International Postal Coupon which could be exchanged at any post office for the appropriate postage.

The editors did not sweat over such niceties: it was the coupon itself, a most unstamplike green piece of paper, that acted as the passport home for my story, clumsily taped in the corner where I expected the Stars and Stripes or an American bald eagle. I tried other American reviews, from the big and famous to the small but esteemed. None matched the speedy abruptness of the first, which I came to regret. As months passed by and I heard nothing about my darling story, I realized that it was better to suffer a lynching than an interminable stay on death row. Long after my story was not only published in Canada but *anthologized*, I received in Montreal a scuffed, rerouted, world-weary postcard from Mississippi kindly informing me that, with great regrets, they could not accept my story but that I should try them again.

I had better luck in my home country, eventually. A literary review in British Columbia gave me the nod. A form letter with filled-in blanks, much like a birth certificate, informed me that I was born, with a handwritten P.S. elaborating on the matter. There was the pleasure of galleys and, upon publication, a little money. I now had the bare minimal qualifications to call myself a writer. I didn't tell anyone at Ellis — not even Roger, though I sent him a copy of the review from Montreal — but in my head it was the big news around town. When the story was reprinted in an annual collection called "Best Canadian Short Stories", a real book put out by a real publisher, I felt that well-documented satisfaction that the writer may die but she will live on, if only in one story in an anthology.

I thought of dedicating the story to "R.M." — the tribute even made it to the galleys — but by then I had left Roetown and Roger was over. I felt no resentment towards him, but I saw no reason to flatter him, even in so minor a way. I struck the dedication out.

To get my three-year Bachelor's degree I needed to take two philosophy courses (I chose philosophy of language, and philosophy and the sciences), but I also opted for Roger's Conrad course. So the activities of a summer — Conrad and fucking — were prolonged for a whole year. What with my private creative efforts and the necessities of sleeping and eating and a little swimming, it was a busy year.

It ended in the same weather and the same state of seeming depopulation as it had started in: a studentless Roetown in the hot humidity of summer. Yet again he had been "tricked" into teaching a summer course. I knew he wouldn't be back before nine in the evening at the earliest. I stopped up the bathtub and the bathroom sink, plugged the excess-water drains and turned the hot-water taps on. Roger had great water pressure; his taps were gushers. As the carpet in the corridor was turning a darker shade of red, I wrote FUCK YOU on his bed with his shaving cream. Downstairs, as I was finishing choosing which of his books I would steal — as many as I could carry, including the small *Fables de La Fontaine* — his staircase was becoming part of a fountain, with a rippling effect that was very pretty. I left just ahead of the water. You may think that, having confessed to these immaturities, I feel apologetic. Quite the opposite. I was too young to have the daring to burn his house down; that's my sole regret. A fire is the only suitable punishment for a man with a cold, selfish heart. The worst he came back to was a house flooded with Congo water, with bloated floors that did not creak, for once, as he splish-splashed across them and up the staircase. I am sure he did not seize upon the small detail that this cold water had once been hot.

I will not go so far as to say he was a fraud. But to live with such a discrepancy between intellect and physical passion indicates a lack of integrity. I was supposed to be a secret not only to others but to Roger himself. I couldn't be seen by family, professors and students; most important, I couldn't be seen by Joseph Conrad. I was something neatly and conveniently bowdlerized from Roger's mind. To him I was no more than terrific sex. The passion suffused no further than his loins, certainly not to his heart — which is what he wanted to hide, this chasm between cold indifference and wild abandon, this lack of communication between what he felt and what he did. Surely Conrad would not have approved, he who detailed the twists that humanity can put itself through while he was securely moored to his Jessie. When Roger dressed he made himself presentable not only to the world but to himself. He put on a garb of civility and introspection that was exquisitely tailored to reflect the folly of the human condition as lived in trading-posts and on ships in the distant Malay Archipelago — but not in Roetown. In Roetown, everything would be orderly and on his terms. Thus we fucked on his schedule, at his absolute convenience. He had not only no interest in visiting, say, South America, the very thought of which sent my mind into dream-mode overdrive, but no interest in deviating one inch from his chosen path. If Roger had been out buying milk and I had been on the other side of the street and I had told him that, if he didn't cross over, things would be finished between us, he would have shouted, "No, I'm going to buy milk," and he would have continued.

Meanwhile, not realizing that I was as replaceable as a litre of two percent, I invested myself in him. I never felt I was compromising because it was always a pleasure to be with him. Being the undisciplined student that I was, I always had free time for him. It was only when I understood what little magnetic draw I had on him — none — that I saw it all as a compromise, saw how there was never any balance, only a master and his pet, a dot with a circle around it. The sex we had was amazing, I can't deny that. The memories of it still crackle in my mind like a dry wood fire. But in barely a moment I went from "When next?" to "Never again." Between the last time of carefree carnality and my near-destruction of his house there passed no more than a few days and one conversation, which started when I turned to Roger in bed, when we were reading, after, and I asked, for the first time, "Roger, what are we? I mean, you and me, what are we? What is our relationship?" It was a conversation he would rather not have had. Words, with their precise meanings, even if hedged and taken back, would trap him. They did. When I silently turned back to my book and stared at the page, two feelings swirled in me: surprise and confirmation. My mind was busy going over events, reassessing exchanges, understanding things.

After that I couldn't do it any more. His dick was the same, but something in me had changed. He was a vulgar man — how can you fuck vulgarity?

I was not in love with him, I must make that clear. Despite what romance novels claim, love, like any living thing, settles where it feels it has a future. I never thought Roger and I had a future. I never envisaged settling in Roetown with him in some permanent domestic arrangement. There were too many differences, not so much in ourselves as in our lives. He was fifty, I was twenty-two, he was established, I was not; and so on. So our pleasures were of the moment. My mistake was to believe that he had faith in that moment. He didn't. His vasectomy, that little scar on his scrotum, reflected not only the output of his penis, but that of his heart. If I were not there, if I drowned in the river Wade, he'd find himself another fresh young cunt. I doubt she'd get the key to his house, though.

I left Roetown in a single motion, a single breath. I walked from Roger's place to mine, loaded with books, pausing only to throw his key into the Wade (did he think I kept it? Did he have his locks changed, fearing my return?) I packed my things, dashed off some goodbye letters, made a few phone calls, said goodbye to Sarah, forfeited my part of the rent for the rest of the summer, donated my futon to a future resident of the house, sold my desk and chair to Martin for a song, left some old clothes to fend for themselves, loaded up a taxi like a mule — but he wouldn't take my bike, so I cycled to the bus station while the car rode empty — and departed for Montreal.

It's only when you're young, or living near a volcano, that you can uproot in under three hours. I arrived at my aunt's house in Montreal not in catastrophe, only unexpectedly, and quite tired. And I didn't stop there. By the time I finally allowed myself to catch my breath and think, I was in Mexico, the cheapest exotic destination I had found at short notice.

(Some may wonder at the short treatment I give my only living relative. My childless aunt — and she exuded childlessness, like her husband — was a conventional woman. Her life had flowed like cement: it had been changeable only when it was fresh, for once it had set, she had set. Life to her was a mould, not a moult. I remember coming down one morning to find her ironing some of my clothes. She had been ironing her dog's winter coats, she told me, and thought she'd use the occasion to smooth out these few items of mine. Beside two tartan dog coats (it was a Scottish terrier) lay a carefully folded blouse or two, a skirt, a pair of pants and a man's shirt. She had laid them in two piles: the blouses and skirt in one, the pants and the shirt in the other. When she had finished with a last blouse, I thanked her, pointedly stacked her two piles into one and carried my clothes away. This was as close as we came to broaching the personal matter of sex. Our smiles were the glue that held up our masks: behind hers was an older woman who was shocked and scandalized; behind mine a young woman who was quite happy with who she was. Her husband, a retired engineer, mostly kept himself busy in another part of the house.)

At the Cancún airport the question "What in the world am I doing here?" struck me hard. I thought of scurrying back to Roetown to try to patch things up with Roger, but I steadied myself. I spent two and a half months in the land of the Maya. I met Françoise, a French woman, and together we explored every Mayan site we heard of or read about, which, considering the paucity of public transportation and the remoteness of many of the smaller, less-known ruins, involved a lot of walking, some insistent waving at the occasional passing truck, car or mule, and the odd night in the open air in our sleeping bags. Once we got a ride on the back of a truck with farm workers being driven to the fields. Our presence elicited smiles and shy laughter from these friendly, unassuming men. I idealize them when I say this, but I felt they lived simple, whole lives. They were grounded, their toes like roots, and when they lifted their hands above their heads with their hoes, they touched the blue sky. I envied this.

My most lingering memory of Mayan civilization is of an isolated site whose name I forget, just a few ruins struggling to survive in the jungle. Françoise and I had the site to ourselves. Atop a small hill lay the remains of a square temple. The hazards of decay had resulted in the caving in of all four walls of the ground floor, with only the corners holding things up, and the entire collapse of the second floor except for one expanse of wall. The result was a structure that looked remarkably like a huge chair, a chair for the gods. I thought of Joe's painting. In that setting, though, alone on a hill looking up at the sky, surrounded by a strangling jungle, this chair, empty for centuries, struck me as a symbol not of expectancy but of death. In the other Mayan sites we visited, I could never quite imagine the people who had once hurried in and out and about. But looking at this ruin, transformed into something new, unintended and outsized, I felt in a forceful way the ceaseless passage of time and the silence of those it leaves behind.

We saw a barbarity in a village north of Mérida. With a few hours to kill before catching the bus back to town, we had the good fortune, we thought, of coming upon a *fiesta taurina*, a bullfighting festival. Françoise and I were excited. This was the perfect complement to the austere silence of ruins. We talked animatedly to the people around us. *Oh no, our Spanish isn't that good, but thank you. . . . One month. . . . To Mérida and then to Quintana Roo. . . . Oh beautiful, we love it.* The word Kah-nah-dah spread around us. My country always fared better than Françoise's. A poorly played trumpet split the air.

In fact this *fiesta taurina* was neither a festival— it was a single event starting shortly after we arrived, as the sun was setting — nor a bullfight, since there was neither matador nor *toro bravo*. Here in this makeshift plaza de toros there was no fearsome beast with killer horns that circled the arena furiously, only a bewildered domestic bull, a grass-eating bovine with a camel-like hump of fat on its neck that trotted in, basset-hound ears flopping, and then stood still, surprised at the number of people and the level of noise. It peered about with its moist black eyes, which I imagined short-sighted. It dipped its head, probably searching for grass. As for the putative bullfighter, there was not one but many to confront the single animal, and they were not dressed as matadors but as women. These mustachioed cow-badgerers wore exaggerated makeup, long dresses, hips of stuffed clothes and huge balloon tits that constantly moved about, to the unending hilarity of the mostly male audience. They pushed the bull, they kicked it, they pulled its tail, they spat in its eyes — everything and anything to get it to charge. But it merely bellowed and shook and jumped a little — the limits of its fighting abilities — and so the spectacle was transformed from a bullfight to a rodeo: if it wouldn't charge, then who could stay the longest on it? When it became obvious that the beast had no more bronco in it than it had *toro*, "How many" became the question of the day. The bull staggered as three, then four, then five men clambered onto it. As a sixth made the attempt it collapsed, to an uproar of laughter. A knife flashed and a man in drag stabbed the animal in the neck. Red blood oozed to the rhythm of a pounding heart. *This* would get it going. *Olé, olé, olé*, cried the people. Indeed. The ruminant bellowed and shook as it never had before. It even managed a few arrested charges, which produced quite a hoopla. Dresses swirled. A sword appeared. The brute would be put to death like the real thing, with the plunge of a blade between its shoulders, right to its heart. *Olé, olé, olé.* White handkerchiefs waving. Except that there was this bothersome hump of fat exactly where the sword should go. No matter, he would try it anyway; he placed himself in front of the bull, adopting the pose of a matador, and charged. But all he managed to do, the prick, was to get his sword stuck in the hump. The bull shrieked. Wild-eyed and slobbering, it hurled itself against a truck that formed that part of the arena wall, hoping to push the vehicle aside and get away, while men and boys kicked at it and laughed joyously. Which is when we stood up and left.

I felt the chill of horror — really, a drop of several degrees Celsius within my chest. We burst into tears of rage and hurt in a deserted street. A woman in a doorway noticed us and looked concerned. We turned away and headed for the bus stop.

At odd moments during my trip I started work on a new story. My life lacked any structure, any pattern, seemed to lurch from one heartbeat to the next. But this would steady it. I remember working on the story on a small, wobbly table facing a whitewashed wall in a hotel room in pleasant Mérida. Paper, pen, some ideas — and me, alone, again.

I could have continued travelling, but September had rolled around and my mind still worked like a student's: September was the month when order and discipline started, even though I had given up on doing an honours year at Ellis.

I returned to Montreal and, for no reason stronger than it was where my plane landed, I decided to stay there. I found myself a cosy dive of an apartment in the Plateau Mont-Royal, furnished it with cheap odds and ends that I bought on

Ontario Street, kitchen stuff that I got at a Jewish store up the street, and a thin, hard futon that I purchased on St-Denis street and carried home on my back. It was the first time I was living on my own and, cheerless though I suppose the place was, I was delighted with it. It was *my* place; the quaint gas stove lit up only for me, the bath filled up with hot water only for me, the mail in the box was only for me.

My neighbours were a typically Canadian mixed lot. An old Polish woman, pale, wrinkled and bent over, who spoke neither French nor English, lived across from me. She was an alcoholic and touched with senility. In my bathroom I could sometimes hear her mutter and talk to herself. I brought up her shopping cart whenever I came upon her at the bottom of the stairs. I always wondered how long she had been waiting there for someone to pass by. At regular, infrequent intervals, a middle-aged man, her son, came to visit her. He was shy or surly, I'm not sure which; the odd times I happened to encounter him in the vomit-green corridors he never acknowledged me, not even with a glance. My one-time "Hello" went without response. He was a plumber.

I got the few facts about them from the caretaker, a voluble Haitian taxi driver who was always getting into minor traffic accidents.

Directly above me lived an Indian or Sri Lankan couple with a baby. Down the corridor, across, lived a young, Anglophone gay couple; we established good neighbourly relations, the stuff of greetings and small talk. A young man from somewhere in the Caribbean, Anglophone too, a short-order cook, lived around the corner.

And there were others, whom I related to with nods. A man with a handlebar moustache. A serious, middle-aged

Portuguese woman who always seemed in a rush. A retired couple, Greek, I think, with a husband who was fussing about something or other every time I saw them. A few nondescripts in their twenties and thirties.

Around us, the Plateau; that is, a neighbourhood where the store signs were in French but where inside one might hear Greek, Portuguese, Yiddish, Spanish, Arabic and others, in addition to French, and where the Volapük was often a functional, beaten-up English flavoured with myriad accents. The mix seemed easy between the variously integrated ethnic groups, the Anglophone university students, the hipsters, cool people and wannabees, and the Francophone Quebeckers. Or so it seemed to me. I could identify with up to three of those groups, which made me not so much a hybrid as a chameleon. Depending on the speaker I could change my persona, though unfortunately my Quebec accent has never been very good for having lived in France as a child, so sometimes, far from fitting in, I stood out all the more. On occasion, when I made the *faux pas* of addressing a nationalist Québécois in English and was replied to in French, which would bring out my French French, I went from being *une maudite anglaise* to being *une maudite française*. In chit-chatting in Spanish, as I did a few times at a nearby *dépanneur*, I delighted the older generation but affronted the younger, who probably thought I was questioning their ability to speak French. Such are the pains and pleasures of living close to borders.

One corollary of my slow-burning existential crisis (which I have mentioned only in passing — that monkey, remember) was the evaporation of any particular career path. It would have made me perfectly happy to devote myself to a body of knowledge, to have apprenticed myself to ethnomusicology,

say, or comparative literature, or science history, or Rome and
Greece — anything but dentistry. Over the next few years I
became a periodic, compulsive reader of university calendars,
those Yellow Pages of civilization, taken in by their neatly
numbered, highly synthesized pills of knowledge. "Classical
History 205: International relations in the Greek world *c.*
500–146 B.C.", "Cultural Studies 260: The making of the
modern body", "Economics 361: An economic history of the
industrial revolution", "History 472: A social history of medicine", "Mathematics 225: Introduction to geometry", "Sociol-
ogy 230: Self and society" — each one seemed more interesting
than the one before. I would attend the University of Toronto
and graduate as an anthropologist. No, McGill, as a Russian
literature specialist. Cambridge, soused in the Greeks. Or perhaps I would start philosophy all over again, but at Oxford this
time, and all the way to a D.Phil on Hobbes. No. Mathematics
at Canterbury, in New Zealand. Or playwrighting at Tufts.
But these interests never lasted longer than a day or two. On
my good days, I felt this scattered approach was extensive,
nearly Renaissance; on my bad days, superficial. In real terms,
the result was that I never went to school again and I never
learned how to do anything.

I was left with writing — not the first item on my list, but
the very last. The only thing that had never failed me.

The story I had started in Mexico and finished in Montreal was a brief fictional biography of a crown prince of Norway. Upon his parents' death in a plane crash, he is seized by a
sort of vertigo of agony. As painful as the death of his parents
is, he sees with horrible clarity how much more painful the
death of his children would be. He vows never to have any.
But a king must have an heir. He decides that if he is to have

any, he will have many, thus diminishing the emotional weight of each one, he hopes. The king goes on to have children, via artificial insemination, with the women of Norway. Over the course of his reign he becomes father to some nine thousand children, strangers all, since such numbers make any degree of intimacy impossible. Then one day he is told that one of his sons has died in a horseback-riding accident. As planned, he feels no pain, and he is horrified.

In structure the story was similar to my dentures story, with brief chapters, each with its own title. It was published in a Prairie literary review.

I began work on a novel. Over the course of several months I collected snippets from Shakespeare, Dante, Plato, Aristotle, Goethe, Swift, Cicero, Lucretius, Horace, Dostoevsky, Galsworthy, Virgil, Chaucer, Gogol, Ovid, Byron, Aristophanes, Sallust, Gibbons, Epicurus, Aeschylus, Caesar, Euripedes, Owen, Erasmus, Seneca, Boccaccio, Petrarch, Pindar, Bacon, Aquinas, Pirandello, Turgenev, Aesop, Zeno (of Elea), Thales, Anaximenes, Anaximander, Descartes, Proust, Blok, Milton, Hamsun, Heine, Henry James, Pushkin, Madox Ford, London, Emerson, Thoreau, Pascal, Herodotus, Tzara, Ball, Hulsenbeck, Schwitters, Gurney, Mann, Hawthorne, Hardy, Conrad, Spencer, the Bible, Hesse, Camoens, Sassoon, Ibsen, Tolstoy, Melville, Schopenhauer, Dickens, Chesterton, Quiller-Couch, Artaud, Kafka, Locke, Berkeley, Hume, Shelley, Leibniz, Saint Augustine, Hobbes, Nietzsche, Abelard, Hopkins and Averrhoës, all of them dead and most in the public domain. I deliberately sought out phrases and sentences that were unremarkable. Not the royalties of literature — "Is this a dagger that I see", "Call me Ishmael", "Longtemps je me suis couché de bonne heure . . ." — but the humble journeywords, the J. Alfred Prufrocks that support but never star. These snippets — sometimes so commonplace that two authors penned them (plagiarism!), other times unique but nonetheless trite — I would crazy-quilt into a novel that would appear as smooth and uniform as a wool blanket.

The story I meant to tell was simple and domestic. In the summer of 1914, a woman's adult son is very ill and she takes him to a seaside cottage to care for him. He dies. "Today, a few minutes ago, my John died." She goes over his illness, his last weeks, and from there she moves backwards, year by year. The adult son becomes a sullen, rebellious adolescent, a difficult child, an eager toddler, a beautiful baby. The novel would end with his birth. "Today, my little John was born."

I was moved by an anger against history. I meant to integrate the universal into the personal and then let it die, that is, wipe the slate clean. Thus it is only the mother's words that are original, entirely my own. All my snippets went into the son — into his thoughts, his words, what he does, what he sees, what he eats. I was discovering the Dadaist writers at the time and much of what I read, especially Tzara and Ball, struck a chord. There's no Dada in my novel — other than the Schwitters-like construction of the son — but something of its turbulent despair animated me in its writing. Now I wonder why I went to such laborious lengths to integrate a pattern that no one would see.

I worked on the novel consistently. There was no paralysis here. Day by day it appeared on the page.

At last I come to Tito, Tito Imilac. Before I even spoke of the boiling of carrots, of the comforting liturgy of laundry, of the food of eye fish, I wanted to rush ahead and get to Tito.

I met him in a restaurant. I was waitressing. It was my first time, my first shift, my *last* shift, I resolved.

I had bumped into Daniela, Danny for short. She had studied at Ellis too, same year, same college, but we weren't close friends then. I think it was that we had never properly met. Busy as we were with the illusory concerns of our student lives, we had never had a devoted minute to see how well we got along. It had to wait till that chance encounter on St-Laurent, to that curious psychological happening, akin to an explosion, whereby one recognizes a face in a crowd. "Danny!" I nearly shouted. She looked surprised, and smiled back. Talk ensued, that important minute, and when we parted company, I to my German lesson, she to work, the piece of paper I held in my hand with her telephone number was not a token of politeness but something warm and precious, instantly memorized, a seven-digit poem. Danny was the first real friend I made in Montreal, the sort of friendship where a separation of time and space is merely a pause in an ongoing conversation.

She worked at a posh greasy spoon that served sumptuous breakfast specials and fancy-shmancy burgers with *haute couture* fries. The burgers were open-faced and had proper names — the California, with avocado and alfalfa sprouts, the Romanov, with a red wine and mushroom sauce, and so on. Atop each serving of fries, which came with a choice of ketchup, mayonnaise or a four-pepper sauce, was a tiny flag of Belgium, which the overwrought waitresses planted with a febrility equal to that of the American soldiers raising the flag at Iwo Jima. The place was blessed with plenty of light and a *je ne sais quoi* to the decor that made people want to linger and then come back. It was a great place to eat, hell to work in. The owner, Alain, was a genial roly-poly guy who knew he

had a good business going and knew how to keep it hum-
ming. He was easygoing and considerate with his waitresses.

One mid-morning in winter Danny called me and said
they were in a pinch and why didn't I give waitressing a try, instead of staying cooped up all day writing. I said, me? *Waitressing?* But the closest I've come to that is serving myself from the
fridge.

No matter, Danny said. You'll make a great waitress.

And so, on a lark — telling myself that my parents' blood
money wouldn't last for ever, delighted to have a firm reason
to leave my apartment and my novel, wearing a black skirt
that was Danny's and a white shirt that was Alain's, totally
stressed out — there I was in a busy restaurant, asking customers to repeat themselves, writing everything down in long-
hand, getting everything wrong, serving things from the
wrong side, and I asked this one customer — casually dressed,
English-speaking — how he wanted his chickenburger —
sorry, his Louisiana — done. He looked up at me as I looked
down at him, ballpoint to pad. He smiled. A nice smile, I noticed mechanically, angst nipping at my heels. "Blue," he said.

"Thank you. Yuck," I replied, as I hurried to deliver the piece
of paper and fill somebody's empty glass. I think he was waving
to get my attention as I turned away, but I told myself that I'd get
back to him in a minute. It's amazing how difficult it is to be not
a *good* waitress — heavens, my aspirations were never that high
— but merely a competent one. What with the man who wants
you to check what oil the fries are fried in, the kid who wants
honey on his hamburger, the lady who wants her Romanov
without a patty ("It's just *so* fattening" — and then she orders
the chocolate cake), the two guys who are more interested in
looking than in ordering, the high-powered-full-of-himself

exec who wants his bill pronto, the couple who are tapping their fingers waiting to order and when you're at their table they hesitate and change their minds after you've written it down, the guy who wanted it *without* tomatoes, not with extra tomatoes, it's a chaotic activity, full of hurt, anger, anxiety and rudeness, like war.

My first impression, as Danny leisurely served the few coffee-sipping, newspaper-reading customers while showing me around and telling me what was where and how to make cappuccinos, was favourable. What a great, easy way to earn money, I thought.

Then the minute hand jumped only a few millimetres and it was noon and suddenly, in the blink of an eye, there were a hundred working burghers all clamouring for burgers. Where was Danny, I asked myself in an increasingly panicky voice. But she was off doing her own insane running around. She had no seasoned waitress's wand that would slow down time or make these people go away. It was me against Them. I thought I would burst into tears.

Next time I was in the kitchen, as I was planting Belgian flags, the man in white said to me, "Hey, yo, Mary-Lou, what's this? The guy wants his Louisiana *raw*?"

I looked at the order. "Tell me, do they eat chicken raw in Italy, Luigi?" I asked.

"No, we eat it cooked. My name ain't Luigi."

"Mine ain't Mary-Lou. And *of course* the guy wants his chickenburger cooked, *but with a beer on the side.*"

"Oh." He peered at the order again. "You're supposed to put alcohol on the other side."

"To err is Canadian, to forgive is Italian," I said, as I went about balancing two Canadians and two Romas on my arms.

As I came out, my future true love and I made eye contact across the restaurant and we both smiled. I noticed again, this time less mechanically, that he had a nice smile. When I was by his table, I said, "Sorry about that."

"Not at all. *I'm* sorry. It was a silly joke."

I tried to have another look at him as I served other tables, but our eyes met every time.

When I brought him his Louisiana, I said, "Fresh out of the kiln." He laughed.

After that, not much. The unfailing shyness of humankind. Looks and smiles. A lingering coffee. A mathematically precise 15 per cent tip. A slow, hesitating but irrevocable exit amidst the bustle.

But all was not lost. I asked Danny about him. "The guy with the crazy hair? I've seen him before. He's pretty regular. He doesn't usually come for lunch, though. Usually he comes in the late afternoon, early evening. Did he order a Louisiana?"

"Yes."

"With hot mustard on the side?"

"No."

"Oh. I think he's the one who always asks for hot mustard."

Which quirk engraved itself in my memory.

Alain asked me how I felt. At that moment I felt 99 per cent frazzled, 1 per cent exhilarated. "Fine," I said, dismissing nearly two hours of blitzkrieg with the wave of a hand.

"Good. You were lucky. It was a fairly quiet lunch hour today. Government people had the day off."

I looked at him. "You're joking."

"No. You should have seen it yesterday. It was crazy."

My level of frazzlement went up to 99.5 per cent. Had it not been for Tito, my waitressing career would have ended that minute. But because of him, when Alain offered me regular shifts, I accepted. I blotted out the hundreds of finicky, complaining, leering, hurried, cheap, rude customers and dwelt on one who had a warm smile.

I thought of this stranger, caressed the thought of him, for the next several days. As I worked on my novel, immersed in illness and departure, he would emerge in my mind like a whale surfacing with its spray of water and my head would become full of blue sea and bright fish. Until I would force myself to get back to work. "You don't even know his name," I would chide myself.

When I saw him again, my heart skipped and three platters nearly crashed to the ground. He was *so* good-looking! By which I don't just mean the way he looked to me, but the way he *felt* to me. It was as if I were in a distant outpost of a body, a border big toe, say, and Tito's arrival was the sudden, nearly incredible fulfilment of a promise from the metropolis, the heart, that has been pending so long that by now it's no more than a persistent rumour; namely, that fresh blood is on its way. Just catching sight of him as he came in — with his heavy winter coat, his foot-stamping, his looking around, his red face — I felt invigorated, recharged. Instantly, serving carrion to the snippy, snappy maggots — when I laid food on the tables I saw the eaters as blind, soft-bodied, legless grubs, their form defined by their function, nothing but digestive tracts with one orifice hovering above the table, waiting to ingest, and the other, below, waiting to excrete — serving grub to the grubs was manageable and I displayed a grace under pressure that would have dazzled Hemingway. Without looking at him, because I was nervous, I let him sit at a table, hoping, praying, that he would sit in my area.

He didn't. I felt like shouting to him across the restaurant, "EXCUSE ME, MISTER, BUT YOU CAN'T SIT THERE, NOT IF YOU WANT US TO GET TO KNOW EACH OTHER." But he was only one table out of my area. I said to Danny, "I'll take Crazy Hair, okay? He's one table into your area." She glanced over. "Sure." When he was settled I got close to him, but without looking at him, pretending to be busy with another table; then I turned, looked him straight in the eyes and smiled, said "Hi!" and delivered a menu and a clear glass of water with beads of freshness on it. Then I was off, his "Hi" trailing behind me and a surprised someone else getting my spill-over smile (and I a great tip). I was happy with the world at that moment, with its noise and rush.

"A raw Louisiana again?" I said to him next time by.

"Sure," he replied, and again that smile.

We were for ever Mary-Lou and Luigi to each other now, so I said to Luigi, "Luigi, make that Louisiana extra special, would ya? It's for a friend," and he replied, "Coming up, Mary-Lou, coming up!"

When I had in front of me a Louisiana Super Supreme, I was pleased with myself for remembering a small detail: "Luigi, could you give me a dollop of hot mustard in a paper cup, please?"

"Here you go, Mary-Lou."

"Thanks."

I made sure his Belgian flag was upright. Crazy, I thought to myself, you don't even know the guy. He could be married with kids for the last ten years.

After that, once again, not much. But it was all right. Our greetings and smiles were like busy diplomats on shuttle missions, and what they brought back from negotiations bode well.

It was perhaps four days, what seemed like a long time, before I saw him again. It was mid-afternoon. I had been working for several hours — real work, my novel — and was out for a walk. The sky was a shattering blue, the air in a deep, clear freeze. I had an hour and a half till work — money work, slavery — and I was walking up Rachel Street, heading for Mount Royal for my usual walk up to the belvedere. My mood was upbeat. Perhaps he would come to the restaurant during my shift.

At that very thought, who should turn the corner a block ahead of me but the man himself. We saw each other some distance away. As we got closer, our darting eyes and the half-smiles on our lips acknowledged that we would meet. We stopped.

"Hello," he said.

"Hi."

A pause. What an awkward, delicious moment. But we must talk of something. I thought of the weather. He beat me to it.

"A beautiful day, isn't it?" he said.

"Mmmmm, yes, gorgeous." I looked about. "I'm off on a walk to enjoy it before work."

"Up the mountain?"

"Yes." Should I invite him? Of course I wanted to, but wouldn't it be too forward? He was a stranger, after all. Didn't even know his name. Better if he asked to come along, wouldn't that be great, although not very likely, very bold on his part. But if he did, we could talk and talk and talk all the way up the mountain. I liked his voice. He had an accent, an unusual timbre derived from I don't know what native tongue, though his English was flawless, and he spoke in a measured way. His words didn't come out in a hurried, jumbled pile the way mine did, but one at a time, each with its own dignity and heraldic right, a sort of aural pageant. I registered every word he said, even the vassal words, the *the*s and *and*s. Listening to him, I was aware not only of what he said, but of the language we spoke, as if I were on the outside, hearing English for the first time. His coat wasn't buttoned correctly. All his buttons were one too high. It looked funny. I felt like bringing my hands out and putting things right. Excuse me, mister, your coat looks like a geological fault line. You must be a funny, distracted mister. All of this in a quarter of a second. "I go up to the belvedere everyday. It's my way of psyching myself up for the hell of waitressing."

He was looking towards Mount Royal, but turned to me and laughed when I said the line about waitressing.

"It gets hectic, doesn't it?"

"You wouldn't believe it."

"Well, I'll see you later then. I was thinking of dropping by for a coffee this evening."

"That'd be great." Ouch, too bold.

We began to pull away. It was over. Then:

"What's your name?" he asked.

That's when I found out his was Tito. As I scurried up through Jeanne Mance park towards the mountain, I was practically giddy with pleasure at knowing his name. Tito, Tito, Tito, Tito, Tito. What a funny name. Like Marshal Tito of Yugoslavia, but as a first name. Instantly the country was fascinating to me, propped as it was between Soviet hegemony and Western sprawl. I tried to remember its constituent republics. Tito, Tito, Tito, Tito, Tito. Dubrovnik and Split were supposed to be jewels. I had read a jolly little book by Lawrence Durrell that took place in Zagreb, in diplomatic circles. And I'd heard of a novel called *Bridge on the* — well, some river — by Ivo Andric, which was supposed to be great. Tito, Tito, Tito, Tito, Tito.

But Tito was of Hungarian origin, not Yugoslav. He was a Magyar, he said.

He did come by for coffee. Around seven o'clock. The place was reasonably calm, the customers less hurried than at lunch-time. Plenty of opportunities for capsules of conversation, especially since he sat at the counter, where I had to return all the time to get deserts and to make coffees, teas and hot chocolates. I offered him pecan pie, the best of the pies, and left it off his bill, one of the great, illegal powers of a waitress. We exchanged bits of biography. I kept saying his name; already it was my favourite Hungarian word, the jewel of my tongue. A few times when he said my name I acted like a dog: I nearly dropped whatever I was handling and looked up, as if I had been called.

He was of Hungarian origin, but not from Hungary. He was from the minority that lives in Czechoslovakia, in southwestern Slovakia. He and his mother had come over in 1968, right after the Soviet invasion, when he was fifteen. They had settled in Toronto. (Father not mentioned. I found out later that he stayed behind, was a liberal apparatchik, hoped, fared miserably, died of cancer. Memories, a few letters, a few photos — all that Tito had left of him.) Quick math told me that he was thirty-three, eleven years my elder.

I was the daughter of diplomats so I carried my roots in a suitcase, but the suitcase was originally put together in Quebec, though I didn't feel strongly about that. I had studied philosophy at Ellis University, in Roetown (he nodded his head, knew where it was), and I'd moved to Montreal after that. I — long hesitation, but I wanted to put my best foot forward — I wrote, had had a lengthy short story published in *Best Canadian Short Stories* (I hadn't heard yet about my Norwegian story).

"What's your short story about?" he asked.

"It's about dentures and love."

"Dentures?"

"Yes. You know, artificial teeth."

"Artificial teeth and love?"

"Yes. You'll have to read it. What do you do?"

There was a dreamy, reflective edge to him. I was curious to know how he accounted for his daylight hours. Between the question and the answer came several orders and deliveries.

"I make my living," he said, in his carefully enunciated, slightly metronomic speech, "by being an invisible man."

I looked at him with a puzzled, amused expression. "But I see you now, Tito."

"Thank you!" He smiled and brought out his arms, as if he'd just performed a magic trick.

What a clown, I thought, as I dispensed cappuccinos and odd comestibles.

"I always get up early," he said, when I was behind the counter again. "I don't know why. I must have an early alarm clock in my system. I remember when we got to Canada — it was maybe a month or so after we'd arrived — I went out walking one morning. It must have been around six, six-thirty.

I still couldn't get over the place, how rich it was. There were more things in a Sears store than in all of Bratislava. Anyway, I was walking and I saw this Canadian boy" — but someone at a table was looking my way, trying to catch my eye.

"I'm sorry, I'm bothering you," he said when I got back to him.

"Don't be silly, Tito. Not at all. Keep going."

"This boy was doing something very strange. I followed him. I wanted to know what he was doing, but I didn't want to ask. You know how there are tales of immigrants who come to America with twenty dollars in their pockets. Well, my mother and I had more than that, but together we had maybe twenty words of English in our heads. In Bratislava I spoke Hungarian at home and Slovak at school, and the only foreign languages I was taught there were Russian and later, because my father worked for the Party, German. But finally I came up to this boy and I managed to ask him what he was doing. He looked at me funny and said what he was plainly doing: delivering newspapers. They didn't have that in Czechoslovakia. I said to myself, "I can do that. You don't need English to deliver newspapers." The boy gave me a phone number and I had my uncle István call. I got a paper route. I began delivering the *Toronto Star*. That was my first job as an invisible man."

I had to do this, that and the other.

"Yes, continue."

"My uncle István drove a taxi. When I turned eighteen I started driving shifts after school. I wasn't supposed to, legally, but I was a careful driver. My English was pretty good by then. Driving a taxi was my second job as an invisible man."

When Tito left that evening, I still didn't know what his present invisibility was. He told me taxi stories, about times when fares spoke to him and he slipped into existence. They were people who entered his taxi as they might a confessional. A man who tried to account for his troubles with his wife. A boy who was on his way to the dentist and was terrified and talkative at the prospect. A middle-aged man whose sense of failure with his job, his family, his life, became shatteringly clear to him the moment he was in Tito's taxi and who sobbed for the whole ride, his face in his hands. An old woman who said to Tito, "You're so young," with a mixture of envy and haughtiness, and who, when he asked her what life was about, replied, "Life? Life is about getting food from the supermarket." But such people were few and far between. Mostly, very little was said and Tito was but a ghost in a machine, *egy szellem egy gépben* in Hungarian, with eyes that occasionally glanced at his fares through the rearview mirror, wondering what they were like, they and their lives.

In the following weeks of that cold, blessed winter, I got to know Tito. He started coming to the restaurant nearly every day, sometimes to eat, sometimes for coffee, usually in the mid-afternoon when things were calm. We had no hesitation in talking to each other any more. Don't sit there, I would tell him, sit here.

"I drove István's taxi for a few years. When I finished high school I went to the University of Toronto. I did a B.A. in Hungarian studies. It was a small department. In fact, it fit in the front of my taxi beside me, Professor Arpád Ferenczi. I liked him. He used to come to our place for supper."

It occurred to me that I didn't know boo about Hungary. A few newspaper facts, Bartók, Kodály, Liszt — that was about it; and that Hungarian was a weird language, related to no other in the area, only to Finnish. I looked it up in the encyclopedia: Hungarian is in the Ugric branch of the Finno-Ugric subfamily of the Uralic languages. The only other languages in the Ugric branch are Ostyak and Vogul, both spoken exclusively in the Ob valley of north-western Siberia. The article on Hungary was a list of names and events that were as familiar to me as Ostyak and Vogul.

"A Bachelor's degree in Hungarian studies is not very useful in Canada so after that I settled down to reading in the taxi."

Now that I knew him, I thought of him all the time. When I remembered him, in other words, when I thought of him anew as I was working on my novel or waiting tables or grocery shopping or taking a bath, it amazed me that I should have forgotten him even momentarily — and it could only be momentarily, for the simple idea of him, the word "Tito", would trigger in me a pulse of happiness, a rippling wave that flooded my system. I went about in a day-dreamy haze in which nothing upset me, not a rude customer at the restaurant, not a stalled queue at the bank, not an impatient librarian, not a transit strike, not dropping and shattering a jar of pickles at the supermarket, nothing. A line-up of shivering prostitutes along an ugly street made me think of the sensuality of human contact. An unshaven beggar wrapped in a blanket with plastic bags for winter boots reminded me of the lightness of being. A staggering drunk was Bacchus in all his glory. In everything I saw happiness or impending happiness. It was the natural, immanent state of the world. Outright tragedy — my neighbour's death, the old Polish woman, who slipped and broke her hip and died in her bathroom an estimated three days later; a seven-year-old girl's death in Saskatchewan after losing herself while taking a shortcut back home despite the determined, frantic efforts to find her by elements of the Canadian army and hundreds of volunteers, who would not give up until a bog produced her decomposing body; pictures of an African famine, personified by a skeletal, sexless child in its mother's weak arms, both as desiccated as the landscape around them; an airplane crash, something which should have seared me — puzzled me, and then faded from my mind. Only in my novel did I acknowledge pain and misery, precisely contained. For being in such a bright mood, stable and confident, I worked on it all the better.

"One day I saw an accident," Tito told me. "Nobody hurt, only material damage. A truck hit another. It was a mail truck. Bags of letters spilled onto the street. It was a windy day. Suddenly I was driving through a tornado of letters. I didn't stop — I had a fare. Hours later it rained. I turned my windshield wipers on. What should appear in front of me, caught in the wiper, but a letter. I looked at it as it swung to and fro. The handwritten address began to blur because of the rain. I stopped the car and picked off the letter. I dried it on the air vents. You could still read the address, but barely. I carefully wrote it over. Then I stopped by a post office and explained what happened. The man at the counter took the letter and tossed it into a letter bin. For the next few days I thought about that letter, about the strange route it had taken to its destination. Shortly after that, I enquired about jobs at the post office."

"You work at the post office."

"Yes."

"You're a mailman."

"A letter carrier. Yes. My third job as an invisible man."

"Do you like it?"

"Oh yes. Less so sometimes in winter, but I like being outside and it's very quiet in the early morning. And usually I'm finished by two in the afternoon."

Tito had a broad build and a peculiar way of walking, with a tilt forward, always battling an imaginary head wind, and he moved with a firm tread, as if with each footstep he were Columbus claiming new territory. He had a large, blunt nose, genetically unkempt hair, eyes of a bright rich brown, clear skin that had no great talent for beards or moustaches, perfect white teeth; and a spirit that animated these features so that his face exuded vital intelligence, an alertness that was warm, engaged, alive. Yet he was reserved, my Tito. He was not one for company. That is one trait that I'm not sure I can convey in words, his way of being that so little suited being with others. It was not that he was socially clumsy. Not at all. But his careful way of conversing did not lend itself to the machine-gun rat-tat-tat of a group interacting. It wasn't only his way of speaking; it was his very personality, his aura, a grace that demanded individual meeting. Even his gestures seemed to be only for you. My Tito was a one-seat theatre (and my one-voter constituency). Only among Hungarians did he approach gregariousness.

"Have you heard of this play that's on tomorrow night, called *Handlet*?"

"You mean *Hamlet*? By the famous Hungarian playwright Witgom Szakespori?"

"Yes, by the famous Hungarian playwright Witgom Szakespori, but adapted. It's a puppet show. It sounded interesting. Would you like to go?"

"Yes."

If I had to choose a single word to describe my time with Tito, it would be that: *yes*.

The night of *Handlet*, of our first date, I discovered the delight and agony of dressing for a man.

As we walked along the snowy streets we kept bumping into each other. If scientists had been monitoring us with thermographic equipment, each touch would have registered as a bright, multicoloured flash, a flare of intense energy.

Handlet was wonderful: *Hamlet* adapted by two British puppeteers who used their four hands to play everybody and everything on a stage the size of a television. When Ophelia went to drown herself, a hand dressed in a gown dove off stage with a little scream and we heard a *ker-ploof* that brought to mind an elephant tripping into a pool. The audience rocked with laughter. Yet at other moments it was deadly serious and we were silent and rapt; the puppeteers had extraordinarily expressive voices. Handlet, micro-dwarf prince of Danemark, was as moving as any Hamlet I've seen. Yorick was thimble-skulled, yet no one laughed.

A heavy snowfall had blanketed the city that day. The snow was still falling, but softly, without a wisp of wind. Big fat clusters of snowflakes crashed into our faces or dented the carpet of snow. We walked along a street that hadn't been cleared yet. The snow came up to our knees, but it was light; it glittered as we easily kicked our way through it. Except for our voices, all sound was muffled. I was aware of a growing excitement within me. The snow was not snow to me, but gold dust. And the street lights were not street lights, but tiaras of diamonds twinkling in the night. And every other colour was not just a colour but a precious gem. Tito suggested we go for a coffee. More gems. Love is a form of childhood in the way we become capable again of being wholly enthralled, able to believe so much so easily so intensely. Tito and I spent hours talking over cups of hot chocolate. And after that, we walked on. When we finally reached my place, late, late into the night, we lingered outside. We would wait; we both felt that. We exchanged phone numbers and addresses. We floated away from each other. "Bye, Tito. See you tomorrow." It has only happened to me twice in my life: I could hardly see him for the fish in my eyes. A density of angelfish, clownfish, goldfish, tigerfish, starfish, a suspension of seaweed, a gentle cavalcade of sea-horses.

I closed the door to my apartment and leaned against it. "Today I have found someone to love. Today I have found someone to love. Today I have found someone to love." The prospect it opened was infinite. It was not a promise, not a hope, not a delusion. It was a simple, defining certainty.

I have never wavered in that certainty. Don't talk to me of the wearying effect of habit, of waking up one morning with a cold heart for the man in your bed. This never happened to me. I was with Tito for roughly three years. Once, afterwards, I counted the days and it came out to 1001, whereupon I changed my unit of measure from days to nights, and then, since days were as important as nights, to both, so that the sum was 2002 days and nights. But early mornings were special too, and afternoons after he'd finished work, so it went up to 4004 days and nights and early mornings and afternoons. I applied myself to refining the units and increasing the sum total of something that is indivisible and never-ending, that has never stopped or decreased since the night I leaned my head against the door to my apartment and repeated to myself, "Today I have found someone to love."

"Why did you move to Montreal?"

"My mother. She remarried and he lived in Montreal. Zoltán Radnoti, a retired electrical contractor. He's very nice, you'll see. I was coming here regularly to see her. I liked the city, its European feel. But it was crazy. After years of studying and reading English I was finally fluent, and then I decide to move to Quebec and it's 1980, the year of the referendum, and it seemed every Anglophone was leaving the province. I sometimes feel I've spent my life taking language courses."

Tito's French was better than functional. He could deal with any letter-carrier situation, he could get by in restaurants and stores and he didn't miss too much in French French movies that weren't subtitled. But rapid-fire Quebec French lost him. If he handled Hungarian like his bare hands, English like worn-in leather gloves, Slovak like mitts, German and Russian like knives and forks, then French he handled like chopsticks.

The first time was at my place. He unbuttoned my shirt. He proceeded with gravity and delicacy, first pulling my shirt out from my pants and then dealing with the buttons north to south, with a gentle east-west spreading as each one was pushed through its buttonhole. I felt a stillness, as if I were in a perfect balance, my every sense poised. My bra, my socks, my pants, my underwear came off in a similar way. Every touch, every little kiss, every breath against my skin was felt twice: once at the point of contact and then the barest reverberation, a tickle in my vulva. Such a sweet deliquescence it is. I reached his chest in a somewhat rougher way. We got to my bed. He went down on me. It felt so powerful it was nearly unbearable. I pulled him up, turned him over and kneeled over him, slowly enclosing him within me, as far as it would go, to the very centre of me, where I didn't want him to leave, ever, even when he came and muttered something in Hungarian. We fell asleep. The light was the clear white light of an overcast winter day.

I didn't give a thought, yet again, to fertility. My period had ended some days earlier. Tito apologized for not having mentioned protection, but I just waved a hand, with a raised-eyebrow expression that said, It happens elsewhere, not here. Yet his semen was spermful, potent, bearer of consequence. But I was lucky that time — and time and again when I went on the pill and took it at irregular hours, sometimes later, sometimes earlier, even missing a day sometimes and having to take two. Never was there a result other than the usual ache and twist of my uterus deciding that there wasn't going to be a baby after all and the wallpaper could go.

It's a luck I bitterly regret now. Even then I sometimes felt a baffling ambivalence. After the shock and the anguish, after the harrowing day of thinking, "This is it. You're going to have a baby. You've thrown your life away, girl," the blood would come like a manumission and I would breathe a deep sigh of relief. "I'm saved." But there would be an afterglow of sadness. Yet again you've stalled fertility, would whisper a part of my mind. Yet again you've not fully engaged life. What if you dared, what if you dared ... ? But I was always lucky, as I've said. When my luck ran out, it was too late.

Over the next weeks and months, we spent time exploring each other's territories. His neighbourhood, my neighbourhood. His friends, my friends. His bed, my bed.

I spent countless hours in the company of the Hungarian language. I met the former Mrs. Imilac, Mrs.

"Megérkeztünk. Ime lássad: ez a Kékszakállú vára. Nem tündököl, mint atyádé. Judit, jössz-e még utánam?"

"Megyek, megyek, Kékszakállú."

"Megállsz Judit? Mennél vissza?"

"Nem. A szoknyám akadt

Radnoti at present, Judit to me quickly. Tito's mother took me in as her own daughter. She was a warm and considerate woman, quick to smile, very much her son's mother. She had a single broad streak of grey that went through her hair, a perfect complement to her naturally elegant way. Her English was idiosyncratic, her French non-existent — she had always moved within the Hungarian community, even after nearly twenty years in Canada. When she spoke with her son, I listened to their voices. Since I couldn't understand a word they said, it was their emotions I heard. Their manner was easygoing, attentive, respectful. They seemed never to interrupt each other. Clearly, mother trusted son and son trusted mother. Mr. Radnoti — "Please! Call me Zoltán. You make me sound like old man. I'm only sixty-four" —

csak fel. Felakadt szép selyem szoknyám."

"Nyitva van még fent az ajtó."

"Ez a Kékszakállú vára. Nincsen ablak? Nincsen erkély?"

"Nincsen."

"Hiába is süt kint a nap?"

"Hiába."

"Hideg marad? Sötét marad?"

"Hideg, sötét."

"Milyen sötét a te várad. Vizes a fal. Kékszakállú, milyen víz hull a kezemre? Sír a várad!"

"Ugye, Judit, jobb volna most volegényed kastélyában: fehér falon fut a rózsa, cserépteton táncol a nap."

"Ne bánts, ne bánts, Kékszakállú. Nem kell rózsa, nem kell napfény. Nem kell. Milyen sötét a te várad. Szegény, szegény Kékszakállú."

"Miért jöttél hozzám, Judit?"

"Nedves falát felszárítom,

was indeed very nice. He was a funny, unpretentious man who had a talent for making his wife laugh, which plainly gave him great satisfaction.

As for the other Hungarians I met, they were of all ages and stations. The younger the generation, the better their French and English, naturally, but whenever I met them in a group it was *de rigueur* that Magyar be spoken. I remembered in my own case how it was inconceivable that I should have addressed my parents in English. Our relationship was a French-speaking relationship. To communicate in any other tongue would have denatured it. And so with these Hungarian Canadians. Tito worried that I was bored silly on these occasions, but I assured him that I wasn't, and indeed I wasn't. Sitting in a room full of Hungarians was a trip to the Near Abroad, a motion-

ajakammal szárítom fel.
Hideg kövét melegítem, a
testemmel melegítem. Ugye
szabad, Kékszakállú. Nem
lesz sötét a te várad, megny-
itjuk a falat ketten. Szél
bejárjon, nap besüssön.
Tündököljön a te várad."

"Nem tündököl az én
váram."

"Gyere vezess
Kékszakállú, mindenhová
vezess engem. Nagy csukott
ajtókat látok, hét fekete
csukott ajtót. Miért vannak
az ajtók csukva?"

"Hogy ne lásson bele
senki."

"Nyisd ki, nyisd ki! Min-
den ajtó legyen nyitva. Szél
bejárjon, nap besüssön."

"Emlékezz rá, milyen hír
jár."

"Gyere nyissuk valem
gyere."

"Aldott a te kezed, Judit."
"Jaj!"
"Mit látsz? Mit látsz?"
"Láncok, kések, szöges
karók, izzó nyársak. . . ."
"Ez a kínzókamra, Judit."

less form of travel. For Magyar is spectacularly
incomprehensible. It tricks
you with the familiarity of
the Roman alphabet and the
dress and deportment of its
speakers, but then it erupts
— and you might as well be
in China. Not a single mor-
pheme will trouble your
comprehension. The first
time I heard Tito speak his
mother tongue, with ease
and delight, my draw
jopped, as I put it to him
later. A new Tito seemed to
arise before my eyes. With a
changed mien, with a different register in his voice, with
expressions and gestures I
hadn't seen before. I wasn't
sure I knew this Tito. I had
to tap him on the shoulder
and say, "Tito, is that you?"
He laughed. "Yes, of course
it is." He was Tito again,
and I had another visa stamp
in my passport. Even after
three years I could renew my
sense of wonder at his fluid
gibberish.

"Szörnyu a te kínzókamrád, Kékszakállú. Szörnyu, szörnyu."

"Félsz-e?"

"A te várad fala véres. A te várad vérzik."

"Félsz-e?"

"Nem, nem félek. Nézd, derül már. Ugye derül? Nézd ezt a fényt. Látod? Szép fénypatak."

"Piros patak, véres patak."

"Minden ajtót ki kell nyitni. Szél bejárjon, nap besüssön, minden ajtót ki kell nyitni."

"Nem tudod ni van mögöttük."

"Minden ajtót ki kell nyitni. Minden ajtót."

"Judit, mért akarod?"

"Mert szeretlek."

"Vigyázz, vigyázz miránk, Judit."

"Szépen, halkan fogom nyitni. Szépen, halkan. Add ide a többi kulcsot."

"Nem tudod, mit rejt az ajtó."

"Idejöttem, mert

When I didn't want to travel, when I tuned out, then Magyar became a seashore, a soothing background noise amidst which my day-dreams could float. Anyway, whether flying for free on Malev or sitting by the seashore, I was never alone for long. One Hungarian or another invariably interrupted my reverie with words that I understood. The older ones took to me greatly. I remember Imre, a Methuselah not five feet tall, with eyes deeply set amidst whorls of wrinkles, who delighted in Tito's Indo-European girlfriend. He would perch himself next to me, feet swinging from his seat, settle his happy eyes on my Indo-European tits and chat me up in English. After a while, by unintended imitation, my English would become as broken as his. I think he was second only to Tito in loving me.

szeretlek. Itt vagyok, a tied
vagyok. Most már vezess
mindenhová. Most már nyiss
ki minden ajtót."

"Judit, Judit, hus és édes,
nyitott sebbol vér ha ömlik."

"Nyisd ki a hetedik ajtót.
Jaj, igaz hír, suttogó hír!"

"Judit!"

"Kékszakállú, nem kell,
nem kell."

"Tied a legdrágább
kincsem."

"Jaj, jaj, Kékszakállú vedd
le."

"Szép vagy, szép vagy,
százszor szép vagy. Te voltál a
legszebb asszony. Es mindig
is éjjel lesz már ... éjjel ...
éjjel...."

We can stay as long as
you want, I would always
tell Tito. Let's not leave
because of me.

And so it would go on,
this Magyar — spoken,
shouted, laughed,
whispered.

Right from the start, we spent all our nights together. It went
without question. A night without him was a night in a cold
bed. Even our sleeping bodies did not brook distance. We
would fall asleep in our own little spheres of space —
Morpheus seems to be a timorous hunter who only preys
upon solitary quarry — but I don't think we ever made it
through a whole night without one of us reaching out. Invariably we would wake up in the morning with at least one
point of contact, a leg, a hand or an arm, me wrapped in him
or pressed against his back. As if our skins were gossips who

were keenly intent on pursuing their chatter in the still of night.

Whoever was closer to that point where somnolence becomes uncontrollable would make the effort of saying "Goodnight" and reach out for a kiss, which the other, only slightly more alert, would echo. Only after those two words and that kiss did we let ourselves dip into sleep. They officially signalled the end of our day.

He lived in Park Extension, farther north, so when we did something downtown we tended to sleep at my place. On weekends or on quiet nights we stayed at his. His apartment was larger and better set up than mine.

I had a schedule in my life now, time imperatives that I had to contend with. There was Slave-Work Time, Novel-Work Time, Miscellaneous-Things Time and Tito Time. I had to juggle to fit them all into my day. I adapted myself to Tito's innate early clock. He had to be at the depot to sort his day's mail at six in the morning. Most weekdays I awoke with him at five. It sounds painful, but it's a matter of habit. I am thankful for all the sunrises I witnessed. And it made for blessed naps together in the mid-afternoon. I usually spent the morning working on my novel, worked the lunch-hour shift at the restaurant, met Tito at two or two-thirty for our nap and spent the evening either working on my novel again or doing something with Tito, depending on how we felt. Breakfast and evening shifts varied the schedule. We usually went to bed a little before ten.

Paradoxically, the more pressed I was for time, the less I thought about it, unlike most resources. As a result my time with Tito seemed to go by in an instant. And I have difficulty remembering the order of things. In my memory the past and present tenses do not measure out temporal sequence, but emotional weight. What I cannot forget repeats itself in the present tense.

FILM LOOP NUMBER 67: I slowly rise to consciousness, sensing that on the seashore someone's beckoning me from my deep blue floating. I surface unwillingly and crack open an eye. Sure enough, Tito and his two wide-open eyes are inches away. He removes two protective strands of brunette seaweed from my face and tosses them onto the pillow. "Are you awake?" he announces. I categorically refuse to answer and my oyster of an eye snaps shut. I go back to work on the pearldom of sleep. I know it's Saturday and we don't have to get up.

I'm on my side, facing him. The sheet rises — he's looking at me. I feel an exploratory finger climbing the slope of my thigh, reaching the summit of my hip, sliding down to the saddleback of my waist, then moving up along the ridge of my ribs until the predictable fall to my breast, where four more fingers join in on the fun. Then the solitary finger ventures south, lingering over my stomach and plunging into my belly button before moving down to scratch my hairs gently. Bitch of a nipple betrays me and starts to get hard. "It *is* one o'clock in the afternoon, you realize," says Tito. "What?" I moan, falling for it, and I make the colossal effort of turning over and peering at the alarm clock. I sink back into the pillow. "It's six-thirty in the morning. You turned the clock upside-down." "Oh, sorry," he says. I turn onto my back. He moves closer, fitting himself to me. "Big sandstorm last night," he says. He gently rubs the corners of my eyes, removing the grit. His hand, this time a band of merry fingers, goes softly traipsing over my body again. I feel with my hand and seize his erection. I sigh. "Et tu, Brute?" He laughs. I look at him through weary, bleary, love-shot eyes, and I stretch. He buries his face in my neck and kisses me voraciously. He brings his mouth to my ear. In an explosive whisper, all wind and hot breath, he makes me an indecent proposition. I laugh and nod. His head disappears under the sheets.

Thus is the night banished. Thus does the sun rise.

FILM LOOP NUMBER 15: We're on a walk up the mountain. It's a radiant spring day. A man appears on the path with a dog on a leash. It's a big, grunting bulldog, complete with stubby crooked front legs, no neck, a flat face and a dreadful underbite. I erupt into giggles and make a beeline for it. The creature's bulging eyes go into orbits of delight as I bend down and play with its multiple folds of skin. The owner benignly assents to the attentions I pay his pet; he must be used to it. The dog's enormous chest is balanced by such a puny rear that I'm surprised he doesn't keel forward, back legs frantically beating the air, as I pat him on the head.

As we walk away, Tito says, "What a monstrosity. I can't believe you liked it."

I look at him and laugh.

"What?" he asks.

"Well, I was thinking about dicks."

"I don't follow."

"You see," I manage to say, still laughing, "the penis, it's so graceless, wouldn't you agree? When it's cold and shrivelled up, it looks like W. H. Auden in his old age; when it's hot, it flops and dangles about in a ridiculous way; when it's excited, it looks so pained and earnest you'd think it was going to burst into tears. And the scrotum! To think that something so vital to the survival of the species, fully responsible for 50 per cent of the ingredients — though none of the work — should hang freely from the body in a tiny, defenceless bag of skin. One whack, one bite, one paw-scratch — and it's just at the right level, too, for your average animal, a dog, a lion, a sabre-toothed tiger — and that's it, end of story. Don't you think it should get better protection? Behind some bone, for example, like us? What could be better than our nicely tapered entrance? It's discreet and stylish, everything is cleverly and compactly encased in the body, with nothing hanging out within easy reach of a closing subway door, there's a neat triangle of hair above it, like a road sign, should you lose your way — it's perfect. The penis is just such a lousy design. It's pre-Scandinavian. Pre-Bauhaus, even.

"But at the same time I'm thinking dicks are so pathetic and deficient, there's something endearing about them. You can't help but feel tenderness for them. You see what I mean? So I'm thinking all that when" — I'm starting to laugh again — "when this dog appears and that was it, it was perfect. A walking dick. With its masses of foreskin."

I'm bent over laughing. Tito has his mock offended look.

FILM LOOP NUMBER 193: Joe tells me in a letter that he and Egon are HIV-positive. They're "all right", he says. I don't know if he means it emotionally or medically. I drench the front of Tito's shirt with tears.

FILM LOOP NUMBER 125: My Christmas present.

FILM LOOP NUMBER 242: Hot day's cycling in the country. In the shade of a tree, in solitude, Tito cups my breasts under my T-shirt and finds them as cool as yoghurts, as he puts it. "What's it like having breasts?" he asks.

"It's like having two small warm companions," I reply.

FILM LOOP NUMBER 1: "I can't imagine sleeping with a man." We've just seen a movie at a repertoire cinema. It's not in the movie — it's a couple in front of us. As the lights are dimming, a young man turns and kisses his boyfriend on the mouth. It's quick and quiet but passionate, with heads that move and eyes that are closed. Just as he turns back into his seat, his eyes and mine meet. He is happy. He is in love. Tito says it without judgement.

"Really?" I say, smiling. "You can't imagine fucking a man? Sucking him? You can't imagine kissing a man?"

"No. I don't think I've had a homosexual thought in my life."

I laugh and take hold of his arm. We walk away.

FILM LOOP NUMBER 186: We make a day-trip to Ottawa in Tito's lawnmower Lada for our first visit to the new National Gallery. It's a beautiful museum, both the building and the collections. We have a wonderful day.

FILM LOOP NUMBER 54: "What do you mean, you don't like hot mustard?"

"I'm just not that crazy about it."

"I thought you loved hot mustard."

"No, I don't."

"Why do you keep eating it?"

"Because you keep buying it."

"But Danny said you loved hot mustard."

"How would she know?"

"Are you telling me you don't like hot mustard?"

"I am."

FILM LOOP NUMBER 118: Yet again the man has buttoned up his coat wrong. Sometimes I do wonder where he has his head. I come up to him and undo the buttons and do them up right. "There you go."

He looks at me, the beginning of a smile on his lips. "You treat me sometimes as if I were ten years old."

"Ten? You flatter yourself. Seven is more like it."

There are countless such film loops in the archives of my memory. They break me into pieces inside.

We moved in together our first summer, the summer of 1986. On July first, to be exact, that fateful date in the majority of Montreal residential leases, the day when most love affairs and roommateships officially start or end and the whole city seems to be on the move. I vacated my squalid hole that I had liked so much and moved into Tito's place in colourful, undeveloped, vaguely disreputable Park Extension, a neighbourhood which I came to love, where the neighbours were friendly and talked to each other from balconies, where Greeks, Indians, Sri Lankans, Italians, Africans, West Indians and, let us not forget them, a few Hungarians, rubbed shoulders with other Canadians and struggled without pretence towards respectability.

I kept a room in my old apartment building as an office. I wanted a space separate from home where I could work, where I could do nothing but work. The building was not far from both the restaurant and Tito's route, so it was a convenient place to meet Tito and to work before and after my waitressing shifts.

Leo, the caretaker cum accident-prone taxi driver, showed me a studio he always had difficulty renting. It had been vacant for a year and a half. It was a box with a window that gave onto the fire exit — a cage to live in, but just the right place to let my imagination run free. It was a floor up from my old apartment, but at the other end of the building. The kitchen was more concept than reality and there was no fridge, but there was a gas stove and the bathroom had a small bathtub. I bargained the rent down to 125 dollars a month and Tito and I repainted the place with paint that the landlord paid for. I chose not to install a phone, for perfect peace, and I heated the place with the gas oven rather than with the more expensive electrical floorboard heater. It was the cheapest office space next to working on a park bench. And it was a room of my own, which I entered, after the symbolic effort of a small journey, for the sole purpose of writing.

At first, out of a purist work ethic, I decided not to have my futon in the room, but making love on my desk was uncomfortable, besides messing up my papers, and a floor is an impossible place to have a nap. So I relented and it became both my workroom and our nap room.

In winter I would often turn the oven up to full blast, for there is nothing less conducive to creativity than cold temperatures. We repainted the walls and ceiling a shimmering golden yellow. However bitterly cold it was outside, my office always felt like the inside of the sun.

I finished my novel. It was a bad novel. It didn't work. I sent it off anyway, to a small and therefore select, not "commercial", publishing house, hoping that they would see genius where I saw none. I never got a reply. I tried another publishing house, equally small. Within five weeks I got my novel back with a letter thanking me for letting them read it, which they had done "with pleasure", but their fiction list was full for the next two years. The thick elastic band that held my manuscript together still covered the same line of text as when I had mailed it, and the tiny scrap of pink paper I had put between pages 20 and 21, like a rose petal added to a love letter, was still there.

I let go of it progressively, at first promising myself that I would return to it; then that I would salvage parts and incorporate them into my next novel; next that I would tear off pieces and turn them into short stories. Finally I told myself that it belonged in the proverbial bottom of a drawer.

Tito cautiously pried into my novel, like a goldfish peering over the edge into the deep, where I was doing shark's work. I didn't tell him what it was about while I was working on it, and when it was finished I wouldn't let him have it. I was afraid that, once he had read it, I would have no more secrets; I would be painfully transparent to him; worse still, what was revealed would turn out to be mediocre and he wouldn't love me any more. I let him read it eventually, and he said all the right things: that indeed it wasn't so excellent as my dentures story or my Norwegian story, though parts were; that the idea was bold and brilliant; that I was young, twenty-three, which didn't mean immature, he quickly added, but simply that I was in the infancy of my art — what writers started so young? Rimbaud, Mailer and a few others, yes, but they dimmed quickly or completely; that this novel wasn't my only idea, I was now free to start something new; and that of course he still loved me, what a question.

I burst into tears once in his arms, a few times on my own. Then it was over.

As in any relationship, there were moments of withdrawal, of a slight pulling away. But it was in the normal course of things. It did not indicate doubt or fatigue. It was like the painter who steps back from her painting to see it as a whole and then moves close again to continue work.

Sometimes I would get to bed tired and empty and glad not to be touched. Tito would be quiet, maybe even asleep, our good-nights said. I would soak up the solitude around

me. When I had had enough, when I was bloated with solitude, I would sometimes move down and gently take hold of
Tito's warm and dormant penis. It would grow slightly
swollen while his face remained impassive and his breathing
deep and easy. I would fall asleep holding onto it, as if it
were a paintbrush and I were working on a detail between
his legs.

My Christmas present came in a box with holes in it. The box
grunted. A puppy bulldog. Spotted brown and white, and
hideous in its beauty. I shrieked. "I got it from a breeder in
Sherbrooke," said Tito. "The ugliest one in the litter, I assure
you. Uglier than this and you're in the realm of science fiction." The alien hopped towards me, grunting like a mezzo-
soprano pig. I couldn't stop smiling. Its name came to me
right away. "Fig Leaf. We'll call him Fig Leaf."
    "*Fig Leaf?*"
    "Yes, Fig Leaf. Come here, Fig Leaf."
    Fig Leaf piddled on the floor.
    The first time we walked Fig Leaf, a couple stopped by us.
"What an adorable dog!" said the woman. She bent down. So
did I. Fig Leaf went wild. The man looked unimpressed. "It's
in fact quite a nice dog. You'd be surprised how much you get
to like it, especially when it gets bigger," said Tito.
    "Oh, I'm sure," replied the man, politely.
    He was a big hit with the Hungarian community too. An
explosion of gibberish. He even distracted Imre from his usual
focus of attention.
    Fig Leaf was so inarticulate, by which I mean that he
seemed to have so few articulations, that I suspect his skeleton
was composed of a single bone. I worried when he went down

stairs. He rarely went down two legs on one step, two legs on the next, like most dogs. His usual way, on steps that were deep enough, was to set himself parallel to the first step, with a crab's sense of direction, and then hop sideways, a motion which had the slight amplitude and dramatic ease of a suicide jump. Having landed safely on all fours on the step below, he would bounce off to the next one without a moment's delay, suicide-jumping the whole way down. He did it incredibly quickly, even down staircases that curved. He never had an accident, but I was always afraid that he would miscalculate his hop or bounce too self-confidently and that I would see him somersault out of control and fracture his undivided bone structure into three or four pieces.

Unfortunately, his Evel Knievel approach to going down stairs was not matched by his approach to coming up stairs. Fig Leaf didn't come *up* stairs. It was obviously an effort for him, but the universe has stairs in it and you can't always be going down them and that's life. But Tito and I made the mistake, when Fig Leaf was small and cute, of wafting him up in our arms whenever he was confronted by even a single step. This early conditioning took for life, no matter what counter-conditioning we attempted when he was big and cute: verbal encouragement, tender morsels of food just three steps up, threats, you name it. More than once I flew into a rage and shouted, "WELL THEN STAY DOWN THERE AND STARVE, YOU PORKER!" and promised myself that I wouldn't fetch him under any circumstances. Which would set him off on his guerrilla-warfare grunting. It wasn't loud or furious, though it did go on non-stop; it was a single porcine grunt emitted precisely every six seconds — I measured it once — that could be heard everywhere in the apartment, even in the closet. The fainter it was, the more maddening. "We'll have that dog for dinner tonight, with applesauce," I would mutter to myself. And I would apply myself with even deafer determination to what I was doing.

But he would wear me down, like any good guerrilla. I would think of my late Polish neighbour, who also used to wait at the bottom of stairs. And what can you do if you were born without joints? I would peer down the staircase, my anger wavering. There he would be, looking up at me, still and quiet, probably very cold, probably very hungry. Guilt would overcome me. I would go down and pick him up and bring him upstairs. He would eat noisily, for the sole purpose of making me feel worse, I'm sure, and then he would settle at my feet, happy to be reunited with me, as I was with him.

For all his eccentricities about vertical movement, Fig Leaf had none where horizontal movement was concerned. He was a great walker. Montrealers who lived in the Plateau west of St-Denis between Roy and Rachel at the time may recall a letter carrier who stepped out of invisibility by always going around with a bulldog. When a dog had the effrontery to bark at his master, Fig Leaf would burst into an indignant grunting rage worthy of Our Lord of the Flies.

I started work on a new novel. One day I spilled a cup of tea on my thesaurus, my New Roget's Thesaurus of English Words and Phrases, in Dictionary Form, Revised Edition, over six million copies sold — a cheap paperback I had bought at the beginning of my first year at Ellis which was much the worse for wear by the time I doused it with Irish Breakfast. Oh well, I thought, the book was falling apart anyway. An occasion to buy a new one.

A few days later I was standing in a second-hand bookshop looking at two thesauri. One, for seventy-five cents, was the exact edition I had had. The other was a fat hardcover. I flipped through it. It was a different sort of thesaurus, unfamiliar to me. Instead of the words and their synonyms being listed in alphabetical order, as would seem logical, in this thesaurus they were divided into numbered categories, each category ending with a list of numerical cross-references. The categories weren't in alphabetical order either. There was an order of a kind page by page; curiously, for a book of synonyms, it was an antonymous order: Elevation was followed by Depression, Hearing by Deafness, Hope by Hopelessness. But there was no perceptible order on a grander scale, or none that I could grasp at a glance. At the back of the book, taking up over four hundred pages, was an index, clearly the entry point into the maze.

I asked the man who ran the bookshop about this thesaurus. "It's an older edition. The original format. The words are grouped into categories; you look in the index to see which category you want. It's a bit cumbersome to consult but it's more complete."

I bought it, so I can say that the genesis of my novel cost me eight dollars.

I read the introduction to my new old Roget's Thesaurus, in Cumbersome Form, Older Edition, surely not many copies sold. It was the reprinted introduction to the original edition of 1852, written by one Peter Mark Roget in an English cheerful, exquisite and oh so Victorian, with sentences that go on like rivers, at length and with meanders, with commas like sluice-gates, semicolons like dams, and a confidence similar to a river's, secure that it is irrigating a needy world — why, here comes a fisherman on his skiff, there some labourers are tilling a field, isn't the future bright? Roget ends his introduction with the hope that his endeavour will assist in bringing about that greatest good of communication: a universal language — and thence world peace, "a golden age of union and harmony among the several nations and races," as he puts it in his farewell sentence.

Until then I had never given much thought to the thesaurus. It was a reference book frowned upon by some, who swore only by their dictionaries, but which I occasionally found useful. On the whole, a minor tool of the trade, an eager-to-please list of synonyms, that's all. The hope that it would be of help in bringing about world confraternity struck me as quixotic even by the high-octane rosy standards of the day.

I flipped to the biographical note on Peter Mark Roget, to see who this fantastical pedant had been.

He was one of those Victorians with an impossibly full life. Born in 1779, died in 1869. A medical doctor. Founder of a charity clinic in London to which he contributed his services gratis for eighteen years. One of the founders of the University of London, where he was professor of physiology. An eminent lecturer on medical and other subjects. Head of a commission on London's water supply, which denounced the simultaneous use of the Thames as sewer and source of drinking water. Fellow of the Royal Society, of which he was secretary for over twenty years, and of the Medical and Chirurgical Society. Contributor to the Encyclopaedia Britannica, Encyclopaedia Metropolitana, Ree's Cyclopaedia and the Cyclopaedia of Popular Medicine. Co-founder of the Society for the Diffusion of Useful Knowledge. Author of a definitive *On Animal and Vegetable Physiology considered with reference to Natural Theology*, of a two-volume work on phrenology, of articles published here, there, everywhere. Inventor of a special kind of slide-rule. An avid chess-player who published chess problems in *The Illustrated London News* and designed the first pocket chessboard.

And — as if that weren't enough — author of his thesaurus, a word which till then simply meant a treasury or storehouse of knowledge, and therefore included in its purview dictionaries and encyclopedias, but to which Roget securely anchored his name, thus assuring his English-language immortality. He started the task at the ripe age of seventy-one, and he was ninety-one when he died. John Lewis Roget took charge of subsequent editions of his father's thesaurus, as did in time Peter's grandson, Samuel Romilly Roget.

Roget & Family, Do-Gooders Inc.

I put the volume down, chuckling to myself.

A week later, Peter Mark Roget — even his name is bright and untragic — was still in my mind. His Society for the Diffusion of Useful Knowledge reminded me, antonymously, of Kurtz and his scrawled "Exterminate the brutes!"

I returned to the thesaurus and considered it carefully. Though Roget states it clearly in his introduction, it was only then that I was struck by the obvious: that his book was a list of words and phrases grouped not by their spelling, as in a dictionary, but according to the ideas they express. To list by spelling you merely need an alphabet, but to list by meaning you must find the equivalent of an alphabet for ideas — which feat Roget had pulled off. In just over a thousand categories, from (1) Existence to (1042) Religious Buildings, he had mapped out the verbal universe, the totality of concepts expressible by the human mind. No matter what the entity, solid or intangible, Sausage or Sadness, it fitted into one of his categories. Language was a village of a thousand extended families, each family peopled by siblings, true synonyms, and cousins and in-laws of one degree or another.

I was astonished. I suddenly marvelled at this book, previously so lacklustre to me. Roget's accomplishment struck me as equal to God's at Babel, but in reverse. Where *He* had divided and confused, *he* had classified and harmonized. Nor were his efforts confined to one language. In his proposed "Polyglot Lexicon", a multilingual super-thesaurus (with English and French as the first two languages, "the columns of each being placed in parallel juxtaposition"), he wanted to show how each language was not only itself a weave of kith and kin, but a twin, a synonym, of the language next to it. From this twinship of languages could emerge that international tongue which would conduce, he hoped, to the aforementioned world peace.

This boundless, ethnocentric optimism would wreck itself against the shores of the Congo River, against Kurtz's hoarse "The horror! The horror!" Nonetheless, I was taken by his vision. What secular nobility it had!

I imagined Roget in the street observing a couple, turning to a row of houses, glancing into the display window of a bookshop, looking up at the sun and sky, running and looking down at his feet and laughing, greeting his wife and children, settling down to write — all the while, at every moment, thinking, "Synonyms!"

I would write a novel about Peter Mark Roget. It would be called *Thesaurus*, and it would take place on that same boat on the river Thames as *Heart of Darkness* — the cruising yawl *Nellie*. It would be a short novel. An evening in the life of a man of good cheer, convinced of the unity of life.

We travelled. To Ecuador, Peru, and Bolivia. To India and Pakistan. To Egypt. To New York. By plane, by train, by boat, by bus, by car, on foot. For six months, for three months, for one month, for one week. Each time Fig Leaf packed off to Hungarian boarding school.

The stories I could tell! The Inca trail and the slow rise to the epiphany of Machu Picchu. Arduous, heavenly trekking around Nanga Parbat. A dawn walk around the immensity of the Kheops pyramid. Matisse at the MOMA. The cows of India's cities, urban bovines as jaded and streetwise as Big Apple drug peddlers. The giant tortoises of the Galapagos Islands, their shells like the dome of St. Peter's, their haughty faces like those of cardinals'. Life on a train in India. Life on a bus in South America. Life on a felucca on the Nile. Early mornings in Varanasi, in La Paz. The organic rot that is Calcutta, that is the Amazon. The walls of Sacsayhuaman. The fields of stupas of Ladakh. The temple of Karnak. Tito's voice and look when he said to me, "Are you seriously suggesting that I take another language course?" when I mentioned one of the good ways of preparing for Latin America. His Spanish nearly as good as mine by the end of our trip.

And these, but a handful of memories, a quarter-turn in the kaleidoscope, a mere glimpse at inexhaustible riches, like Howard Carter replying to Lord Carnarvon, "Yes, wonderful things."

If I had to remember only one place, treasure only one vision, it would be that room lit up by the single bare lightbulb

hanging from the ceiling or that stretch of awful road with
the dramatic backdrop or that green village fleetingly seen
from the train or that bend of river with the water buffalo
wallowing in it or that tumbledown restaurant with the welcome hot tea — if you asked me for the one destination of
which I could say, "Go there — and you will have travelled,"
if you wanted to know where El Dorado was, I would say it
was that place ubiquitous among travellers: the middle of
nowhere.

I would return there any time. With my veteran blue backpack and with Tito, my fellow eyes, my fellow skin, my fellow
thirst.

We fell into the habit of presenting ourselves as husband
and wife, took on this traditional garb to make things easier
in places where the concepts of girlfriendship and boyfriend-
ship might not go down well. At first it was the strangest
thing for me to refer to Tito as "my husband". It felt so old-
fashioned. I would tell fellow travellers, "He's not actually my
husband," and they would nod. But then it started coming
easily. I liked it that our relationship gave us titles. It felt mature, enduring. After being called "Señora Imilac" over and
over, I even began to play with this, the most reprehensible of
marital practices. I began to see identity in it, an important
part of who I was.

We were dreaming of China next, of travels to the Celestial
Empire.

In early 1989 — January 18, to be precise, on a 7:40 a.m. flight
— Tito left for Banff, Alberta, for a conference. Managers,
clerks, sorters, letter carriers, drivers — a whole vertical slab of
the Canada Post hierarchy from across the country would be

attending, and he was one of the lucky chosen letter carriers. He was going for the mountains rather than for the talking heads. He had never seen the Rockies.

He would be gone a week.

I had a secret, but I didn't say anything. I would wait till his return.

I never saw him again.

I had finished the lunch shift at the restaurant and I had bought groceries. I was standing in front of my office door, fishing for the keys in my coat pocket, two plastic bags full of food at my feet. The year's first big snowstorm had settled and the day was cold, clear and sunshiny (a weather much like that three years before, when Tito and I had first got close, though then it had been night-time and now it was broad daylight, a little before three in the afternoon). I mention the weather only because it reflected my mood: bright. It had nothing to do with where I was standing: at the end of a windowless vomit-green corridor whose only

Tito

baby

light was a dying, flickering
neon. I don't recall what I
was thinking at that
moment. My mind had no
reason yet to be as attentive
as a court stenographer. I
missed Tito already, but   Tito
seven Tito-less days meant   Tito Tito Tito Tito
lots of time for my novel and   Tito Tito Tito
the pleasure of seeing him   Tito
again after missing him. I   Tito
was quite certain I was preg-   baby
nant. I had been sloppy that
month with the pill. I believe
I was trying to assign to acci-
dent what I actually wanted.   baby
I was already three days late,   baby
something unheard of in my
caesium atomic clock cycle. I
had a feeling. With Tito   baby   Tito
away, I could make certain.
The prospect horrified me   baby
and thrilled me — rather like
a wonderful gift that comes
in horrible wrapping-paper. I   baby
walked around with no tam-
pons. If I wasn't pregnant, I
wanted to bleed with a
vengeful inconvenience, in
the street or during my waitressing shift. In a far corner

of my mind, at the very back
of a filing cabinet, there was
an insurance policy signed
Henry Morgentaler. That
Tito and I had not been paying our premiums came out
in jokes and comments
about "little Tito babies".

Tito

Tito baby

"Hi," he said. He was
walking down the corridor
towards me.

"Hi," I replied, pushing
the key into the lock and
unlocking my door.

He was a neighbour. The
man with the walrus
moustache. A three-year
acquaintanceship of nods,
greetings and the occasional
brief exchange. I didn't
even know his name.

"Is this where you live?"
he said.

He was beside me,
looking in.

"No, I just use this place
as an office."

"Can I see?"

"Sure." I suppose it was
presumptuous of him, but I
thought nothing of it. He

was moving, he was idly
curious, he was being
neighbourly — something
like that. Nor did I pick up
on the fact that he waited for
me to go in before entering.
"It's a tiny place," I added.

He looked about.

"Well, I have to work," I
said, after a minute or so. He
didn't move.

"Out you go," I said
lightly, with a sweeping
movement of my hands,
treating him as if he were a
contrary child.

He looked at me.

"Take your clothes off,"
he said, closing the door.

The words didn't register.
I was shocked. Right away I
seemed to go numb.   . . . .

"What?"   . . . .

"I said, take your clothes   . . . .
off. Let's see the goods."   . . . .

There was no warning.   . . . .
Things went from normal to   . . . .
terribly wrong in a fraction   . . . .
of a second. There was   . . . .
nothing I could do about it.   . . . .
I had no time to think, to   . . . .

react, to take measures. No.
I even had my boots off,
had removed them upon
entering.

It was a long assault. It
felt as if it lasted hours. How
otherwise can I account for
so much fear? Can fear be ...... fear ..... fear .....
concentrated? Can it enter .... fear .....
your life like a few drops of
food colouring, a few drops
of red that plop in and dilute
and taint your whole life?
The problem with rape is .... fear .....
that it ruins your life, the .... fear ....
whole rest of your life,
because the fear spreads. .... fear ....
When I think back, he was
there maybe twenty minutes.

He didn't have a knife or
a gun. He didn't need one.
He did nothing more threat-
ening than pull my hair with .... pain ....
all his strength and slap me .... pain ....
and punch me and kick me. .... pain .... pain ....

His fist flew out and hit .... pain
me square on the cheek. I
lurched to the side and
collapsed.

"Get up."
I did so, mechanically.

"Now get your fucking
sweater off."

I started to protest, to
plead, I can't remember my
words exactly. He grabbed . . . . fear pain
me by the throat and   fear pain fear pain fear pain
slammed me against the wall. fear pain fear pain fear pain

"Listen, you bitch, you   fear fear fear fear fear fear
start stripping now or I'll kill fear fear fear fear fear fear
you. Who do you think you   fear fear fear fear fear fear
are?"   fear fear fear fear fear fear

His hand was choking   fear pain fear pain fear pain
me. I had to fight to get each fear pain fear pain fear pain
breath into my lungs. I was   fear pain fear pain fear pain
terrified. I thought I was   fear pain fear pain fear pain
going to die. I croaked, "All fear pain fear pain fear pain
right, all right!"   fear pain fear . . . .

I removed my sweater.

"Take your shirt off."

My hands were trembling . . . . fear . . . . .
so much I had difficulty with
the buttons.

"Now the rest."

I looked at him. He   . . . . fear
moved towards me.   fear fear fear . . . .

"Okay, okay."

I took my T-shirt off.
Then my bra.

He stared. He was
rubbing his crotch.

"Take the rest off."

"Oh, please." I couldn't. I   . . . .
just couldn't. His hand shot   . . . . fear fear
up for my throat again.   fear fear fear fear fear . . . . .

    "All right, all right, I   . . . .
will."   . . . .

    I took my skirt and my   . . . .
thick stockings off.   . . . .

    He came up, grabbed my   . . . . . . fear . . . .
underwear and with a rough   . . . .
yank pulled them down. In   . . . .
doing so, he scratched me   . . . . pain . . . .
with his nails. Two lines of   . . . .
red on my lower belly. The   pain . . . .
first acute pain to register.   . . . . pain . . . .

    I was completely naked. I   . . . .
kept my eyes on the floor.   . . . . fear . . .
My stomach was so twisted   . . . . fear . . . .
up it hurt. I kept thinking, ... pain . . . .
"I'm going to die, I don't   fear fear fear fear fear fear
want to die. I'm going to die,   fear fear fear fear fear fear
I don't want to die. I'm going fear fear fear fear fear fear
to die, I don't want to die."   fear fear fear fear fear . . . .

    He slapped me full in the   . . . . . pain . . . .
face. I didn't understand. I   . . . .
was doing what he wanted.   . . . .
He slapped me again. When   . . . pain . . . .
I brought my hands up to   . . . .
protect myself, he started   . . . .
punching me in the face and   pain pain pain pain pain
in the body. I fell to the   pain pain pain . . . .
ground. He grabbed me by   . . . . fear pain fear

the throat and started
strangling me while banging
my head against the wall. I
couldn't breathe. I thought
I was going to die. But he
stopped.

He stood up and took his
clothes off. I didn't look.
There was the taste of blood
in my mouth. He grabbed
me by my hair and pulled me
to my feet. The pain was
excruciating. He led me to
the futon and threw me
down on it.

"Did that hurt?"

He seemed pleased when
I said yes. He knelt beside me
and took hold of my hair
again. He twisted it hard
around his fist.

"I'll do anything you
want, anything. Just please
don't kill me."

He manhandled my
breasts.

He began to fuck my
mouth with his half-hard
penis. It was unspeakably
disgusting. I tried to put as
much blood and saliva

pain fear pain fear pain fear
pain fear pain fear pain fear
pain fear pain fear pain fear
pain fear pain fear pain fear
pain fear pain fear . . . .
. . . .
. . . .
. . . .
. . . .
. . . . pain   pain
pain   pain   pain   pain   pain
pain   pain   pain   pain   pain
pain   pain   pain   pain   pain
pain   pain   pain   pain   pain
pain   pain . . . .
. . . .
. . . .
. . . . pain . . . .
. . . .
. . . . pain . . . .
. . . .
. . . fear fear fear fear fear
fear fear fear fear fear fear
fear fear fear fear . . . .
. . . . . pain . . . .
. . . .
. . . .
. . . .
. . . .
. . . .

between him and me as I
could. I felt like vomiting.
But better a blow job than
him fucking me. I wanted to
protect my baby, didn't want
the pollution of his dick in
my vagina.

He kept pushing in too
far, making me gag.

I pushed his flabby white
belly away and vomited on
the futon. The heaves were
very painful and I couldn't
breathe.

"That's disgusting," he
said, but laughed. "Ha, ha,
ha, ha, ha," he went.

I caught his eyes. I
instantly looked away.

He moved between my
legs. I made to resist.

He punched me
repeatedly in the face. I must
only survive. Death was the
only loss. I spread my legs.

"You just fucking watch
yourself," he said.

He spat between my legs
twice, for lubricant. But he
barely had it up and just
managed to push the head of

. . . .
. . . .
. . . .
. . . .
. . . . baby . . . .
. . . .
. . . .
. . . .
. . . . pain . . . .
. . . .
. . . . pain . . . .
. . . .
pain pain pain fear fear fear
fear . . . .
. . . .
. . . .
. . . .
. . . .
. . . . fear fear fear . . . . .
. . . .
. . . . baby . . . .
. . . pain fear pain fear pain
fear pain fear pain fear pain
fear pain fear pain fear pain
fear pain fear pain fear . . . .
fear fear fear fear fear fear
fear fear fear . . . .
. . . .
. . . .
. . . .
. . . .

his penis into me. He pumped carefully. He held himself up by his arms and kept his gaze fixed between our legs. Every place his warm skin touched mine, something in me recoiled.

I could hear a roar. The subway? It was my heart. It was unbelievable how hard it was pounding.

His penis fell out. He lifted himself to his knees.

He wasn't saying anything. I wanted to say something, but I couldn't get any words out.

He got up and began pulling me about the room by my hair, dragging me over my desk and crashing me against the walls. Each time I tried to get to my feet, he yanked me off balance. When it hurt so much that I screamed, he kicked me in the face and said, "Don't scream, I said don't scream."

He threw me down on the futon and knelt between my legs. He was hard now.

. . . .
. . . .
. . . .
. . . .
. . . .
. . . .
. . . .
. . . .
. . . .
. . . .
. . . .
. . . . fear
fear fear fear fear fear fear
fear fear fear fear fear fear
fear fear fear fear fear fear
fear fear fear fear fear fear
fear fear fear fear fear fear
fear fear fear fear fear fear
pain pain pain pain pain
pain pain pain pain pain
pain pain pain pain pain
pain pain pain pain pain
pain pain pain pain pain
pain pain pain pain pain
pain pain pain pain pain
pain pain pain pain pain
pain pain pain pain pain
pain pain pain pain pain
pain pain pain . . . .
. . . .

He penetrated me again.   . . . pain pain pain. . . . .
This time he pumped   . . . .
furiously. He had his head   . . . .
up, but he kept his eyes   . . . .
tightly closed. I looked away.   . . . .
After the oral sex, after being   . . . .
pulled around by my hair, ...
this was a relief.   . . . .

    I noticed odd things. As I   . . . .
lay there, going through the   . . . .
butchery, I was bothered by a   . . . .
tickling in my ears. My tears   . . . .
were gathering in them.   . . . .

    I tried to bang on the   . . . .
floor so someone would   . . . .
know that something terrible   . . . . fear pain
was going on. But I suppose   . . . .
no one heard. I suppose I   . . . .
didn't bang very hard, too   . . . .
afraid that he would notice. I   fear . . . .
suppose I merely tapped the   . . . .
floor a little.   . . . .

    He ejaculated inside me   . . . .
and burst out laughing.   . . . . fear . . . .

    He got to his feet and   . . . .
walked about the room. I lay   . . . .
still, absolutely still, not   fear . . . . fear . . . .
looking at him, only keeping   . . . .
him in the corner of my eye.   . . . .
He went to the bathroom.   . . . .
He pissed without flushing   . . . .

and cleaned himself. He
came out wiping himself
with my towel.

    He picked through my
groceries and found the
orange juice and the cookies.
I slowly lifted myself, but
only to my elbows. I kept my
eyes diverted. My nose was
bleeding, drip, drip, drip.

    "Where's your purse?"

    "I don't have one. I just
keep things in my pockets."

    He searched my coat
pockets. He brought out a
fistful of crumpled-up bills
and change, my day's
earnings, about fifty dollars,
and laid it on the floor. He
went through it. He took the
fives right away, but seemed
to want to leave the rest.
Then reconsidered and took
the twos. Then the ones. He
was going to leave the
change, but then picked out
the quarters.

    As he ate my cookies, he
looked at the papers that
were scattered all over the
place. "You a student?"

. . . . fear

pain

"No."

"What's all these papers?"

"I'm writing a book."

"No shit. A writer. What's your book about?"

"It's a novel about a man who's written a new kind of dictionary." He was coming towards me. "It's a d—d—d—dictionary of s—s—s—s—synonyms. It's just a boring story. It won't be a bestseller or anything. I'm not very good at it. I —"

"Well, if you say so your-self, I guess I won't buy it."

He was kneeling next to me. His penis hung limply between his legs. I looked away.

"Oh please don't kill me, please don't kill me. I haven't done anything to you. Please don't kill me. We're neigh-bours. Please don't kill me."

He laughed. "Why would I want to kill you?"

There was a harsh noise from his mouth. He spat in my face.

I can't understand it.

....
....
....
....
....
....
.... fear fear
fear fear fear fear fear fear
fear fear fear fear fear fear
fear fear fear fear fear fear
fear fear fear fear fear fear
fear fear fear fear fear fear
fear fear fear fear fear fear
fear fear fear fear fear fear
fear fear fear fear fear fear
fear fear fear fear fear fear
fear fear fear fear fear fear
fear fear fear fear fear fear
fear fear fear fear fear fear
fear fear fear fear fear fear
fear fear fear fear fear fear
fear fear fear fear fear fear
fear fear fear fear fear fear
fear fear fear fear fear fear
fear fear fear fear fear fear
fear fear fear fear fear fear
fear fear fear fear fear fear
fear fear................
....

After what he had done to me, he could do that, spit in my face.

    He seemed to get bored.

    He dressed. He combed his hair in the mirror, spending time on his part. Then he picked up my two bags of groceries, said, "See you around," and left, closing the door behind him.

    I crawled over to the door, reached up, and locked it.   fear fear fear fear fear fear fear fear fear fear fear

    I lay on the floor. I thought nothing. I just lay there.

    I got up. I could hardly stand. I went to the bathroom. My face didn't look beaten up, it looked as if all the skin had been peeled off. I couldn't recognize myself.

    I moved like an automaton. I wasn't there, I was somewhere else. I rinsed a face, don't know whose. With a clean dish-towel I wiped a body, don't know whose. His sperm stank.

    Suddenly, the fear that he   fear fear fear fear fear

was still around, in the building, gripped me. In the
mirror, eyes widened. My
stomach seized up.

I dressed, wrapped my
face in my scarf and put my
coat on, hood up. I gathered
my novel and stuffed it in my
coat pocket. Strands of my
hair were all over the floor. I
went through the window on
to the fire exit.

The walk seemed endless.
I stumbled several times. I
kept thinking he was following me, but I was too afraid
to turn around and check. I
took a circuitous route
home, running down streets
as soon as I had turned
corners and dodging into
back alleys.

I got home. To a dog who
greeted me with his usual
gruff happiness.

As soon as I took my scarf
off, he fell silent.

I went to the bathroom
and started a bath.

fear fear fear fear fear fear
fear fear fear fear fear fear
fear fear fear fear fear fear
fear fear fear fear fear fear
. . . .
. . . .
. . . .
. . . .
. . . .
. . . .
. . . .
. . . .
. . . .
. . . . fear fear
fear . . . . fear
. . . .
. . . .
. . . . . fear . . . .
. . . .
. . . . fear . . . .
. . . .
. . . .
. . . .
. . . .
. . . .
. . . .
. . . .
. . . .

....
....
....
....
....
....
....
....
....
....
....
....
....
....
....
....
....
....
....
....
....
....
....
....
....
....
....
....
....
....
....
....

. . . .
. . . .
. . . .
. . . .
. . . .
. . . .
. . . .
. . . .
. . . .
. . . .
. . . .
. . . .

I stayed in the bath for
hours. Shivering in the hot
water. Thinking nothing.
Washing obsessively.
    I was covered in bruises.   . . . . pain . . . .
My head ached. My face   . . . . pain . . . .
hurt. My neck was stiff and   pain . . . . pain . . . . .
painful. Every time I   pain . . . .
swallowed, a claw lashed out   . . . . pain . . . . . .
at the back of my throat.
Only blinking didn't hurt. I
couldn't even speak to Fig
Leaf, who sat in a corner of
the bathroom and tried to
start a conversation a few
times. I was so sore and   . . . . pain . . . .
swollen that it hurt to touch;   pain . . . . pain . . . .
not just my vagina — the
whole area. The soap didn't

help, but I had to wash, had   . . . .
to.   . . . .
   I could hardly walk when   . . . . pain . . . . .
I got out. I went to the   . . . .
kitchen to make tea.   . . . .
                                     . . . .
                                     . . . .
                                     . . . .
                                     . . . .
                                     . . . .
                                     . . . .
                                     . . . .
                                     . . . .
                                     . . . .
                                     . . . .
                                     . . . .
                                     . . . .
                                     . . . .
                                     . . . .
                                     . . . .
                                     . . . .
                                     . . . .

   I thought of Fig Leaf. I   . . . .
hadn't let him out. Over my   . . . .
bathrobe I put Tito's. I care-   . . . .
fully looked about before   . . . . fear . . . .
opening the downstairs door.   . . . .
I opened it only wide enough   . . . . fear . . . . . .

to let him squeeze through.
He paused on the landing,
but I shook my head and he
understood that he was
going out on his own. I
closed and locked the door,
and waited.

When he was back in, I
climbed the stairs. At the top
I turned and looked at him
looking up at me. "Come," I
whispered hoarsely. He
climbed the stairs.

. . . .
. . . .
. . . .
. . . .
. . . .
. . . .
. . . .
. . . .
. . . .
. . . .
. . . . pain . . . .
. . . .
. . . .
. . . .
. . . .
. . . .
. . . .
. . . .
. . . .
. . . .
. . . .
. . . .
. . . .
. . . .

The phone rang.
"Tito!" I couldn't

. . . .
. . . .

recognize my voice. . . . .

There was silence, and . . . .
then a hang-up. . . . .

It wasn't Tito. He would . . . .
have spoken. Perhaps a . . . .
wrong number. . . . .

But perhaps it was *him*. fear

I dropped the phone. The . . . .
doors were locked, the . . . .
windows were closed, the . . . .
curtains were drawn — but . . . . fear
Alexander Graham Bell fear fear fear fear fear fear
would let him in. I had a fear fear fear fear fear fear
surge of panic. fear fear . . . .

I ripped the phone off the . . . .
wall. . . . .
. . . .
. . . .
. . . .
. . . .
. . . .
. . . .
. . . .
. . . .
. . . .
. . . .
. . . .
. . . .
. . . .
. . . .
. . . .

. . . .
. . . .
. . . .
. . . .
. . . .
. . . .
. . . .
. . . .
. . . .
. . . .
. . . .
. . . .
. . . .
. . . .

I could still smell the
stink of his sperm. I had another bath and washed again.

I dressed for bed. I put on
a pair of Tito's sweatpants, a
T-shirt and a sweater. I went
to bed with the lights on,
even though darkness had
nothing to do with it.

I had chairs blocking
every locked door. I got up
and checked every window
over and over. I had a knife
next to the bed.

. . . .
. . . .
. . . .
. . . .
. . . .
. . . .
. . . .
. . . . fear . . . . .
. . . . fear . . . .
. . . .
. . . . fear . . . .
. . . . fear
. . . .
. . . .
. . . .

. . . .
. . . .
. . . .
. . . .
. . . .
. . . .
. . . .
. . . .
. . . .
. . . .
. . . .
. . . .

But he comes in through my dreams. I'm standing at the end of a long corridor. He is coming towards me. Not him — his face. It's enormous, takes up the entire corridor, is the fourth wall. I feel the compression of space, of light, of air. His face keeps approaching in a way that never ends. I wake up with a scream and a pounding heart.

. . . . fear fear fear
fear fear fear fear fear fear
fear fear fear fear fear fear
fear fear fear fear fear fear
fear fear fear fear fear fear
fear fear fear fear fear fear
fear fear fear fear fear fear
fear fear fear fear fear fear
fear fear fear fear fear fear
fear fear fear fear fear fear
fear fear fear fear fear fear
fear fear fear . . . .
. . . .
. . . .
. . . .
. . . .
. . . .
. . . .

. . . .
. . . .
. . . .
. . . .

I didn't eat.

. . . .
. . . .
. . . .
. . . .
. . . .
. . . .
. . . .
. . . .
. . . .
. . . .
. . . .

There was a discharge. It
wasn't blood, it was
yellowish. I had saved my
baby. The soreness and
swelling were worse. It hurt
when I urinated.

. . . .
. . . .
. . . .
baby . . . . pain . . . .
pain . . . . pain . . . . pain
. . . .
. . . .
. . . .
. . . .
. . . .
. . . .
. . . .
. . . .
. . . .
. . . .
. . . .

. . . .
. . . .
. . . .
. . . .
. . . .
. . . .
. . . .
. . . .
. . . .
. . . .
. . . .
. . . .
. . . .
. . . .
. . . .
. . . .
. . . .
. . . .
. . . .
. . . .
. . . .
. . . .
. . . .
. . . .
. . . .
. . . .
. . . .

Though Fig Leaf had stopped barking, I hit him anyway. A blow against the

side of his head and neck,
one area really. He toppled
over. He got up and scurried
away. His beautiful, ugly
expression, usually so happy-
go-lucky, was blank. He was
terrified. He disappeared
around the corner, nails skit-
tering against the floor. I
realized that I had forgotten
to feed him for two days.
He had waited this long to
protest.

   After some seconds I
started to cry. I eased myself
to the floor.

Oh! Oh!

Why didn't I fight back? I
have read that it only takes a
few pounds of pressure to de-
tach human ears. Why didn't
I do that? During his pain
and surprise I could have got
round the fourth wall.

Never again to be so open
to attack. Never.

This time it started with a terrible headache. I thought my head would split open from the pain. I wanted to scream, but I just lay there all night, holding my head in my hands, aware of each passing minute. In the morning, the downy blonde hairs between my breasts were darker.

Otherwise I couldn't pinpoint the source of pain. Breasts flattened, vulva closed up and then grew outwards, my every subtle aspect changed — without specific discomfort, only a nausea that made me want to die. I vomited several times. Hair grew with an itch and I scratched my chest and legs till I bled, but that was a self-induced pain. My emerging penis revolted me, but that was another self-induced pain.

I lost my baby, my child, my future. Perhaps this was the source of the nausea. Finding that its normal exit to the world was closing, my baby, in panic, migrated north. It swam around my bowels, it squeezed its way past my stomach, it came to my heart, it slid up my trachea. It came to lodge inside my head. This I know with certainty: the day I am found dead and the necessary autopsy is performed, there will be discovered inside my head, just beside my memory, a pale, unhappy fetus, no longer attached by its umbilical cord to a placenta, long ago consumed, but to my very brain, feeding off its flow of blood, oxygen and words, and it will have lived there all my life, adapting to its environment as we all must, an environment dark, lonely and cramped, removed from the sunlit world by only a smooth curve of bone and skin, but inescapably removed. I cannot say I interact with this baby — I don't even know its sex — but it's there, it's there, high up on the side of my head, on the left, though sometimes I feel it move forward to an area above my frontal lobes.

The hormonal maelstrom inside my body helped my wounds heal quickly, my external wounds.

With my newfound strength, in rage and in hurt, I stupidly destroyed some of poor Tito's plates. Fig Leaf cowered in a corner. I cleaned up in tears.

Sleep was as vivid as wakefulness. Perhaps some of my nightmares were daymares. I slept no more than ten hours that whole week. I ate everything that was left in the fridge, until I was eating stale bread with mayonnaise.

I thought of suicide.

I cut my hair. Though my thoughts were dead and calm, my hand trembled.

To him, I was nothing worth respecting. I was reduced to nothing, my being, my feelings, wilfully disregarded. You can't imagine how slippery and difficult the slope upwards is from such debasement back to self-respect. You continually slip back. You become suspicious not only of others but of yourself, of your body. You live in fear, a fear that never leaves you, never. Never. You are often seized by feelings of panic. Your body becomes something alien, beyond your control; it vomits often, contracts colds all the time. You get migraines. Sleep becomes enemy territory, peopled by your worst fears.

I don't know why they call it rape. To me it was murder. I was killed that day and I've had to drag death around in me ever since, a roaming greyness in my colourful interior; sometimes it's my stomach that's dead, sometimes my head, sometimes my intestines, often my heart.

I left Montreal — left my life — abruptly and untidily. I stuffed my backpack with my novel and clothes (and, without thinking, tampons), and departed. Not a word to the restaurant or to the Hungarian community or to Danny or to anyone else. For my dear Tito, a scrawled note, the hardest words I've ever had to write. There was only an angst-ridden Fig Leaf to see me go. I gave him a last walk, left plenty of food out for him, petted him — but he knew something was wrong. As I was closing the downstairs door he grunted louder than he had ever grunted before and it broke my heart. I dropped the key through the mail slot and it left me with an image: his flat snout visible through the slot, sniffing wildly at my hand, imploring me through his nostrils not to leave. But night-time was coming. It filled me with fear. I had to get out of town before it was dark. And a storm was starting — yet more snow. Fig Leaf had to last only a day. Tito would be back tomorrow. I stumbled towards the bus station.

This thing wasted four years of my life. Four years of vagrancy and confusion. And counting.

Sometimes I would forget. It was most often right after sleep, when I managed to sleep. I would open my eyes and look at the geometrical shapes of sunlight against the wall, and for a few seconds I would be open to the day. Then my emotions would wake up and the book of my memory would open at *that* page, among the thousands of pages, and *it* (and the fear, the anxiety, the nightmares, the sleepless nights, the panic, the depression, the loss, the sadness) would come back and the day would become an ordeal, a trap of five senses and one voice inside my head, a voice that never shut up, only sometimes changed languages.

I took a bus to Toronto and arrived early in the morning, but next thing I remember I was in an eighteen-wheeler heading west. I believe I got the ride somewhere along Lake Superior, along that huge reservoir of tears shaped like a fish arching in the air, a caught marlin. I remember that ride only because of a road sign that has stayed imprinted in my memory. The truck's cab is a large, well-appointed space that looms so high above the highway I feel I'm in a low-flying plane. It's very warm. I feel numb. I'm resting partly against the back of the seat, partly against the door, not looking straight ahead but off at an angle, so I can keep the driver in the edge of my field of vision. He doesn't talk much; last thing he muttered was, "Manitoba soon." He's concentrating on the snowstorm outside, the great sweeping gusts of white numbness that obliterate everything with a raging howl. He has both hands on the steering wheel, as big and round as the globe. I don't see much outside. Then a sign appears out of the blankness: "Lake of the Woods". Away, away into the coldness I go. I'm numb, so numb, God, so numb. Away, away I go. I fall asleep as we roar through Demeter's rage.

Looking at a map one day in a fish and tackle store — I was there because I saw the map from outside and went in to look at it more closely — I was surprised to see how many lakes there were in the Prairies. Hundreds of them strewn across the landscape, many without names and most without any access except by air.

The land so far away from the sea, the air so dry, yet so many lakes.

Later, when I was so dried out that my lips were cracked and my skin was like a dried mud-flat, I saw humidifiers on special in the display window of a pharmacy. They were "ultra-sonic". The word seemed to promise comfort. I bought the jumbo ten-litre model and hurried home to my latest rooming-house. I read the instructions carefully, filled the two containers with water and set the control to maximum. A cool, evanescent mist came forth from the nozzle. I breathed in this properly humid air, filling my lungs with it, moisturizing my parched interior. I imagined that I felt better already, much better. This was the solution to my problems. Three days later, when the machine clicked off for lack of water, I never filled it again. I left it behind though it cost me over a hundred and twenty dollars.

It was the same with every other purchase I made with redemption in mind.

I stayed in the Prairies. Am still here. A roving existential monkey. I bought a battered car and moved from Winnipeg to Banff and back, through every big town and many small ones.

I taught French in night-school. I did janitorial work in commercial buildings. Mostly I washed dishes. I liked being a dishwasher. I didn't usually talk to anyone in the restaurants where I worked, tried to understand my predicament only in reference to soap, hot water and piles of dirty dishes. I liked the transformation from dirty and splattered to clean and squeaky. I liked the steam and the humidity and the infinite quantities of hot water. I was a good dishwasher. Never received a complaint, never produced a greasy spoon.

He left me with herpes B. Every birthday it flares up.

You wouldn't believe the things rape eats up. Your taste buds. Your voice: you're left with a weak, hoarse whisper (while yet your brain agonizes). Your libido, completely, not a twitch, not a twinge of desire. Your imagination: your reality becomes deadened, your dream world a graveyard (except for the nightmares that scream through you). Your ability to sleep, nearly. Your vitality: washing dishes consumes every ounce of mental and physical energy you have.

Imagine this play:

DRAMATIS PERSONAE:

    an OLD WOMAN *with a bag of groceries*

    a GOOD SAMARITAN

    a straw-filled DUMMY *with a painted unhappy face*

SCENE: *a bench along a sidewalk*

    (The Dummy *is sitting on the bench. The* Old Woman *appears, slowly walking along the sidewalk.)*

OLD WOMAN *(nodding her head to the* Dummy): Hello.

DUMMY: *(nothing)*

    (Fifteen or so feet past the bench, the Old Woman *slips. She falls heavily, like an injured dictionary. Her groceries scatter. A grapefruit rolls ... rolls ... rolls ... to between the* Dummy's *feet.)*

OLD WOMAN: Oh! Oh!

    (The Good Samaritan *appears.)*

GOOD SAMARITAN: Oh my God! Are you all right? Can I help you? Are you hurt?

(*The* Good Samaritan *assists the* Old Woman. *Helps her get up. Fetches her groceries from here and there. Except for the unseen grapefruit. The* Dummy *leans forward and stares at the grapefruit. Exit the* Old Woman *holding onto the* Good Samaritan's *arm. A long pause. The* Dummy *places a foot on the grapefruit. Feels its bouncy resistance. The* Dummy *squashes the grapefruit. The squashing sound is heard amplified over a sound system for thirty seconds after the action is over. After a pause, it is heard again. Then again. Exit the* Dummy *stage left, shuffling. From stage right the* Good Samaritan *reappears. Looks about. Sees the squashed grapefruit. Looks to stage left. Exits stage right.*)

GOOD SAMARITAN (*from off stage*): I couldn't find it.

OLD WOMAN (*from off stage, in a tremulous voice*): I guess that young man took it.

CURTAIN

There were moments when I thought I had sunk to the very last stage of psychic disintegration. Sometimes I was so distraught that movement, even simple balance, became a source of anguish. I would have to lie down. There, on occasion, I would try to count to ten, a desperate, random symbol of psychological normality. But try as I might — and I tried, I tried, believe me — I couldn't. I would hear myself whisper One . . . two . . . th-three . . . f-f-four. . . . Perhaps five, but never six. I would forget the next number, or my mind would simply lose its bearings and wander onto something else. It was as if I didn't have a will any more. I would just lie there, conscious yet inanimate, only breathing. I can't communicate the pure agony of those moments except to repeat, *I could not count to ten.*

The old man pulled on his cigar. A point of red glowed in the dark. He got up. "A harrowing tale, Captain Marlow," he said, and walked away.

"Who is that?" asked Marlow, who hadn't noticed the old man.

"It is Dr. Roget," said the Director of Companies. "A good man, Marlow. He has done much good for this Thames of ours. And for many sick, destitute people in town. You've no doubt heard of his Thesaurus?"

"Is he the one?"

"Yes. And he's an excellent chess player, possibly your match."

The chess game on the *Nellie* between the aged Dr. Roget and lean, hard Marlow has barely begun — Marlow's king's knight is in a weak position — when my novel falls silent.

It became a pile of tattered papers alien to my dumb brain. I looked at it, cradled it in my hands, carried it in my pockets, but my mind was incapable of the least creative impulse.

I thought of Tito all the time, of our 8008 precious moments together. I supplemented remembered reality by imagining walks with him, talks, restaurant outings, museum excursions, games, love-making. In the feeble realm of my imagination, everything went on as before, the future was still on.

It's sometimes in small ways that the pain comes. I spread my arms and legs and make angels in the snow. But I stop right away. Spreading my legs makes me miss Tito.

I began to dream of my parents. I saw them, I heard them, exactly as if they were in front of me. I would begin to weep in my sleep and I would awake in tears.

I saw him every day, in the street, in restaurants, on buses, at gas stations. I saw his face on every man. I would turn a street corner and quake with fear at the sight of a stranger, who would look at me, startled, and move away quickly.

There were the nightmares. The exact re-enactments of the whole thing — I am at my office door, he is approaching — with only my screams to break the spell of sleep. Or variations on the theme: he's chasing me, he's behind my locked door but it's a Japanese door made of paper. Or variations on the anguish: I've fallen head first into a barrel full of water, I can't get out, I drown till I wake up. Or I'm in bed, I wake up because red smoke is coming into the room from a window opposite me, I start to choke, I hit the wall beside my bed in an appeal for help, I realize that it's not a wall but the enormous palm of his hand, I choke till I wake up.

I heard my name over the radio once. "Twenty-six-year-old woman. Five foot seven and a half" — the dial was turned in search of music. This was in a corner store. The dial was turned back. "Bilingual. Last seen in" — right to the end of the band, but nothing good found so once again the station with the public service message. "If anyone has seen this woman or has any information on her, could they please contact the RCMP at...."

Only once did I have a nightmare where I directed the violence. Through the dark, limpid air of a street a crossbow arrow travels and strikes him exactly where I aimed it: in the spinal cord. The arrow makes a smacking cracking sound when it hits him. I consider where to send the second arrow. Through his pleading hand and into his begging mouth? Or to burst an eyeball? I will spare his heart, pump of life, symbol of love. Finally my disembodied hands strangle him. I vividly recall the feel of the killing, especially the horror in his face, that glaze of overwhelming fear. He is so afraid that his features begin to melt. I am left strangling a blank head of skin. I awake still strangling him.

Mostly I am too afraid to express my anger, even in my dreamworld. The world is Pandora's box and my eyelids are its lid: every time I blink, evil and horror escape the world and jump in through my eyes.

The simple truth is, I am afraid of men.

I was walking down a street in Regina late at night, a commercial sidestreet deserted of its daytime bustle. I walked quickly. I came upon a man lurching along ahead of me, an Indian so drunk that every step forward was a victory against gravity. He looked like a child learning how to walk. He was in such an advanced state of intoxication that I felt he could do me no harm. His reflexes would be slow, his coordination poor. I felt stronger, tougher. If something were to happen, it would be to him, not to me. I slowed down, fell into step behind him. He turned off. I followed. Curiously, he did not make a sound: not a song, shout or mutter, only laboured breathing. Alongside a brick wall, he stopped and lifted a hand and set it against the wall to steady himself. Then he half leaned, half fell against it, his back to it. I too stopped. I examined his silhouette, some twenty feet away.

"I'd like to kill the whole human race," was what I was thinking. My mouth began to salivate. I had the urge to vomit, which I did. A brief, sudden explosion of whitish vomit. My heart was beating like crazy.

I moved forward. I kicked the Indian's feet from beneath him. He fell to the ground heavily.

"Huh?" he said. He had a fat, round face with thick features. He wore a stupid, uncomprehending expression. I was enraged.

I kicked him again and again. All the while, he said nothing coherent, only a few syllables.

"Oh! Oh!"

I felt invincible. I could have picked this Indian off the ground and thrown him clear across the street.

With one final kick to his head, putting everything into it, I ran off. I nearly wished he had got up to chase me, so that I could run, run, run. But he just lay there.

He said, "You're a young one. Let me suck your cock. Let me give you a good, good suck. Oh, it's a nice one. Let me put that in my mouth...."

I leaned against the tree. My knees were trembling. It was a bitterly cold day yet I remained comfortable within my open coat and undone pants. He was a fat, white-bearded man with a high voice and a wet sucking mouth. He looked like Santa Claus. He was of such girth that he leaned against a tree to ease himself to his knees. I rocked my hips until he broke his seal and said, "Don't move. I'll do the sucking." So I remained still and his head began to bob back and forth. My erection grew in his warm mouth.

After my pleasure climaxed, he said, "Thanks, you've made my day," as he laboured back to his feet. I closed up my clothes and left.

He was the first of a number. For some, the desire was to have me in their mouths. Others I knelt down and took in. I lost myself in this, awoke only when they ejaculated in my mouth and the illusion was broken. Some fucked me, and I tried to feel in the difficult pleasure of sodomy the pleasure I had felt with Tito.

Once, only once, I spent an entire night with a man. He had eyes and a way of walking that were heart-stoppingly evocative of Tito. He directed things, went about his lust with total control, fucking me so hard that I bled, and I managed to forget myself in an ecstatic passivity without terror. Until morning.

I never ate before these encounters, was too nervous, and for a while I resisted going home with anyone. I felt trapped indoors; fear, like a nausea, like an asphixiation, would grip me. A car or a park was a space closed enough for me. I usually went with middle-aged men, figuring that I had a better chance at survival if things went wrong than with a young man.

I remember a gentle, melancholy man who caressed my ass as he sucked me sweetly and vigorously. He was a quiet man in his mid-fifties with salt-and-pepper hair. I met him in a park and he invited me to his home. But I was overtaken by fear and I didn't want to go farther than the front hall, so we fell into the habit — the ten or so times I went to his place — of doing it right there, amidst the winter coats and the boots. After finishing, he would sit back on the floor and say little more than "Thank you," and light up a cigarette, as if we had just made love. I felt he would never hurt me. For the longest time he stayed in my memory as the only person with whom I had a relationship during those hell-times. I felt a sad tenderness for him. It peaked one evening when he gently turned me around and licked my asshole as he masturbated me. When I came against the door, I was in not only a sexual paroxysm, but an emotional one. I felt my entire body was full of tears. The least word, the least motion, would make them spill from my eyes. He smoked without saying a word, considering the space of air in front of him. I carefully brought myself down to the floor and kissed him on the mouth.

These emotions were so difficult! Loneliness, desire, pleasure, bliss — then silence, strangeness, fear, loneliness, with a convulsion as the moment at which illusion would shatter. Each time I was left with nothing, with only the terrible loop in my head, "You are not Tito. You are not Tito. You are not Tito." I thought something must break, that it couldn't go on like this. But nothing broke and it went on.

I had left my car behind and I was walking along a road amidst a sea of wheat-fields. If you've never been, the south of Saskatchewan is so flat the horizon is perceptibly round. Above you, during the day, lords an immense dome of sky so empty it feels like a fullness, with clouds the size of mountains, the sun but a small disk, and a depth of colour that is often chalk blue, oh so chalk blue. At night this reassuring curtain of blue is pulled away and you realize where you really are: at infinity's doorstep. A plain is what a mountain aims to be: the closest you can come to being in outer space while yet having your feet on this planet.

The language of the plain is the wind. It carries sweetness and fragrance, the wealth of the earth. It is a soothsayer, herald of storm and of change of season. And the wind speaks. When you walk in a plain, gusts of words blow through your head, words that have travelled over the surface of the planet. That night the wind whispered words of doom to me.

The sun had set. The horizon was a slowly collapsing explosion of red and deep orange. The wheat-fields no longer matched the sun's radiance, but took on a menacing hue; they looked as if sharks might be swimming in them. Soon the fields vanished into blackness. Had it not been for the stars and the sliver of moon, even the bare outline of the road would have disappeared and I would have been blind.

I lay flat on the gravel beside the road. A car once in a while roared by. Each vehicle was divided in two at the headlights. The larger, front part was pure, blinding white light; the back part was a more humble and compact volume of metal. The roar was divided evenly between the parts. Every car pushed me to the question. I would lift myself off the gravel a few inches and stay suspended, my muscles tense. To be or not to be? I would waver on the edge of life, prey to a mere chemical fluctuation in my brain. I could see how it would go: a sprinter's start . . . a lurch into the illuminated threshold of death . . . a clash of light, metal and flesh . . . mind and memory jostled . . . a little pain . . . and then the pain gone, all gone.

I lay there, car after car, the gravel chilling me and pricking me. Now? This one?

No.

No.

No.

No.

No.

No.

Then I was over the edge. Suddenly all desire to live was gutted.

I sprint-started and I stood trembling, blinded by the light. I closed my eyes. A screech tore through the night. At any moment — now! now! now! now! now! — I was expecting violent relief. But the screech stopped and there was a sickening silence. I heard the sound, so universally familiar, of a car door opening. I opened my eyes. Everything in me was twisted up. There was a car at an angle to the road. A bull of a man was emerging from the other side of the car. His face was flushed and contorted. In the passenger seat was a woman with her hands on the dashboard and wide-open eyes. "ARE YOU CRAZY! I NEARLY HIT YOU!" shouted the man. He was making his way around the car. I was suddenly terrified that he'd do the very thing I wanted — kill me. Though I could hardly control my legs, I began to run. He shouted after me. I kept running.

I heard his car. He was coming after me. I was convinced that he wanted to run me down. I plunged into the wheat-fields.

I stopped only when the dead black silence convinced me that I was alone. In the distance he was still there, in the form of a lit-up car. Was he still shouting? What did he want? What had I done to him?

I stayed in the field all night, acutely aware of every rustle of life. The wind blew above me, over the wheat, like a spirit haunting the sky. I crept back to my car in the early morning, exhausted and overwrought. I will never forget the sound of my car starting up.

I was sitting in a cemetery with my head in my hands.

Sadness was sifting through me, touching every part of me. My feet were sad. My palms were sad. My eyelids were sad.

I heard a female voice come through my ears. It seemed to come from miles away. She was right in front of me.

"Do you like cemeteries too?"

I looked up.

"Oh, I'm sorry," she continued, "you're grieving. I didn't mean to bother you."

"No, no. Not at all. Well, yes. But it's all right." My voice was rough and gruff. I cleared my throat several times. "I *do* like cemeteries."

"So do I. So peaceful and beautiful, and some of the epitaphs are lovely. Did you see that some over there are in French?"

"Yes."

It happened like that. One item of small talk led to another, a little awkwardly at first, then with greater ease as the conversation took on a life of its own. It felt strange to talk. Such an effort. Such a pleasure. She sat down beside me. I told her I was grieving for my twin sister. But she hadn't died here. It was out east. In a car crash.

We walked around the cemetery. I translated some of the French epitaphs for her. Her name was Cathy.

The first time we undressed, I was bashful. She interpreted my impotence as a consequence of mourning. She patiently coaxed my penis to an erection. I was a tepid lesbian. But a deeper satisfaction drew me on. A warmth after a long period of cold. The comfort of my own sex. The absence of fear. Our gentle, peaceable ways.

"You're the saddest guy I ever met," Cathy told me once.

I never told her about Tito or about *him*. We met in the present tense and moved on to the future. How do you explain horror, anyway? And why? Revelation would not thaw the numbness, would only bring on the additional pain of her pain. My soul is like Bluebeard's castle: it has a few locked rooms in it.

She was older than I, thirty-seven to my twenty-nine. She gave no particular thought to her age except with regards to childbearing. She was aware that, if she wanted children, it had to be soon.

Cathy and I travelled to Thailand. It was her choice of country, for the warmth of the sun. Bob and Ben, two Australians who were wearing *The Bob and Ben Fuckorama Tour* T-shirts when we met them, were on hormonal overdrive. The tits, stomachs, asses and legs of female bodies-for-hire spoke a language they wanted to hear.

We saw a Jack the Ripper movie in a bar. The only emotion it inspired in me was terror. I could not help but identify with the female victims who walked the fogbound streets of London unaware of their imminent death. I imagined this would be the reaction of any woman. But the women in the bar just watched the movie, as passive and entertained as the men.

We stayed on a remote island, practically alone. I liked it there. The sun. Wonderful snorkelling. We played card games and did crossword puzzles.

She lay on her side, her eyes closed. I looked at her, at her breasts. I have no breasts, I thought. I lay down. A hand came up from behind me and gently touched my hip; I moved close to her. I could feel her breasts against my back. I moved closer still and her breasts went through me — I had breasts. She liked the name Adam for a boy — she wanted a boy. I fell asleep.

CHAPTER TWO

I AM THIRTY YEARS OLD. I weigh 139 pounds. I am five foot seven and a half inches tall. My hair is brown and curly. My eyes are grey-blue. My blood type is O positive. I am Canadian. I speak English and French.